THE
NEGOTIATOR

Book **Six** in the
Munro Family Series

CHRIS TAYLOR

LCT Productions Pty Ltd
18364 Kamilaroi Highway, Narrabri NSW 2390

ISBN. 978-1-925119-11-4 (Print)

The Negotiator is a work of fiction. Names, characters, places, brands, media and incidents either are the product of the author's imagination or are used fictitiously. Any resemblance to actual persons, living or dead, events, or locales, is entirely coincidental.

Published in the United States of America

When ten-year-old **Andy Warwick** witnesses the murder/suicide of his sister and father, his world is torn apart. Twenty years later, despite his tragic childhood, Andy's a highly respected police negotiator based in North Sydney. He's living a comfortable life, but still suffers from guilt-ridden nightmares from his past and yearns for a family to replace the one he lost.

Sixteen, pregnant and abandoned by those she loved, **Cally Savage** has learned early to fend for herself, but raising a son on her own hasn't come without a price. It's a decade after Jack's birth, but she's struggling to make ends meet, despite taking on a second job as a cleaner at the North Sydney Police Station. On top of her financial woes, her house has recently been burgled and she's terrified the perpetrator might return...

In desperation Cally turns to the hot looking detective at the station and seeks Andy's permission to place a "roommate wanted" advertisement on the noticeboard in the squad room. Attracted to Cally's innocent beauty and intrigued by the vulnerability in her eyes, Andy offers to move in with her. The more he gets to know her, the more he wants to be part of her life. But first, he has to break through the barriers she's erected around her heart.

Just when things appear to be on track, the man who believed for more than ten years that his child had been aborted, discovers Cally's deceit. Enraged, he vows not to give up until he's found his son and punished the woman who lied to him...

THE MUNRO FAMILY SERIES

THE PROFILER
(Book One—Clayton and Ellie)

THE INVESTIGATOR
(Book Two—Riley and Kate)

THE PREDATOR
(Book Three—Brandon and Alex)

THE BETRAYAL
(Book Four—Declan and Chloe)

THE DECEPTION
(Book Five—Will and Savannah)

THE NEGOTIATOR
(Book Six—Andy and Cally)

THE CHRISTMAS VIGIL
(A Munro Family Series Novella)

THE RANSOM
(Book Seven—Lane and Zara)

THE DEFENDANT
(Book Eight—Chase and Josie)

THE SHOOTING
(Book Nine—Tom and Lily)

THE MAKER
(Book Ten—Bryce and Chanel)

DEDICATION

This book is dedicated to all of the Police Negotiators
who daily put their lives on the line for others
and as always, to my sexy, real life hero, my husband, Linden.

ACKNOWLEDGEMENTS

As usual, no book comes into being without a lot of help and support by my friends and family. A world of thanks must go to my friend and fellow author Angela Bissell, critique partner extraordinaire, and a girl who loves the Munro family as much as I do.

To Pat Thomas, the best editor in the world. I love working with you. You turn my humble offerings into something truly amazing. I couldn't do it without you. To Detective Superintendent Michael Kilfoyle, thank you for lending my story credibility. Any mistakes are wholly my own.

To Alisha of damonza.com, thank you for yet another fantastic cover. To my sister, Nicole Guihot, thank you for your excellent editorial comments and suggestions. Nic, I hope you like the final result.

To Amy Atwell and her dedicated staff at Author EMS who are so much more than book formatters. Amy, once again, thank you for your magic.

To the fantastic writer organizations such as Romance Writers of Australia, Romance Writers of America and Romance Writers of New Zealand for all the help, support and encouragement they offer new and aspiring writers, including me.

To my readers, thank you for your support and love for the Munro family. Your encouragement and enjoyment make this journey all worthwhile.

And lastly, to my friends and family, especially my husband and children. Thank you for putting up with late dinners and even later conversations as I've emerged day after day from the sometimes scary but always enthralling world I've created on my computer.

Prologue

Stewart Brady strode down the sidewalk of Watervale's busier-than-usual main street, his long steps eating the pavement. He barely had enough time to grab a sandwich and a coffee from the deli around the corner before he was due back in court. The trial was only two days in and promised to be more than tiresome.

It was obvious the Crown Prosecutor had it in for him. The man seemed to be going out of his way to antagonize him: all those snide remarks; all those digs at his character. How dare the asshole insinuate Stewart was nothing more than a spoiled brat who'd only managed to stay out of jail this long because he had a daddy who stepped in and bought his son's way out of his problems, including the jam he was in today.

So what if his father had offered the mouthy little prick a few Gs? Cold hard cash had always worked to quiet things down in the past. If it had been up to Stewart, he wouldn't have offered the asshole anything. He was the one who'd started it. It was only when he'd made that fucking comment about the size of Stewart's biceps, that he'd been forced to belt him with the barbell.

It was a little unfortunate Stewart's aim was spot on: The barbell had connected with the side of the little prick's head and he'd been put in a coma for a week. The cops felt obligated to lay charges against Stewart and here he was today, enduring yet another headache.

Pushing aside the annoying thoughts, he came to a halt beside the newspaper stand and nodded a silent greeting to the proprietor.

"What can I get for you, Mr Brady?" the man asked, lowering his gaze respectfully.

"*The Sydney Morning Herald,*" Stewart growled and waited impatiently for the man to hand it over. Tossing over a few coins, he snatched the newspaper out of the man's hands and tucked it under his arm. A glance at his watch told him he'd have to hurry if he wanted to make it back in time.

Rounding the corner, he sighed in relief when he spied the short queue at the deli. The bailiff was an asshole and would probably become alarmed if he arrived late. There was no sense breaching his bail unnecessarily.

A woman with a pram and a man dressed in jogging sweats were the only ones in line. Within moments, the woman reached across the counter and collected her coffee. She nodded her thanks and moved aside, juggling her change along with the baby.

The jogger stepped forward and placed his order: a whole wheat ham, tomato and bean sprouts sandwich, no butter, and a bottle of mineral water. Stewart couldn't believe anyone would eat that kind of crap. Not bothering to hide his smirk, he flicked open the newspaper and scanned the headlines. A little lower, the picture of a woman and a child standing outside a house snagged his attention. The story mentioned something about another burglary. There'd been a spate of them in one of Sydney's better parts of town.

He stared at the woman in surprise. His heart thudded hard and his mouth went dry. *It was her.* He was sure of it. Even from the black-and-white newspaper photo, it was obvious she'd blossomed from the pretty teenager he'd known a lifetime ago into a woman who could steal his breath.

Despite the irritations of the morning, a surge of desire hardened his cock. The feeling was both familiar and distant. It had been a long time since he'd fucked her. *Way too long.*

His gaze slid to the boy who stood beside her. The child's eyes were wide and solemn in his pale, heart-shaped face. A lock of messy blond hair had fallen across his forehead. The boy stared at the camera as if mesmerized.

Shock ricocheted through Stewart. All at once, he found it difficult to breathe. The boy's features were as familiar as his own. The hair was much lighter, but there was no doubt about it. The resemblance was so strong it was like looking into a mirror and seeing himself as a boy.

His face burned with anger. She'd told him she'd had an abortion. He'd even driven her to the clinic. For ten fucking years, he'd believed she'd gone through with it.

Rage erupted inside him, flooding his veins in a fiery river of fury and disbelief. His hands clenched into fists.

She'd lied to him.

The fucking bitch had lied to him. He had a son.

A son.

CHAPTER 1

Detective Senior Sergeant Andy Warwick gazed at his reflection in the bathroom mirror and made a silent vow: *I'll tell her tonight.*

Smoothing his hair back with a hand that wasn't quite steady, he brushed his teeth, taking care not to splash his pristine white dinner shirt. He used the mirror to adjust his bow tie and then picked up his jacket and shrugged it on. He'd bought the Armani suit three weeks before his lottery win and it had set him back almost a month's wages, but his best friend and fellow New South Wales Police Officer, Will Rutledge, had managed to convince him every man needed at least one decent suit.

His condominium was another luxury, but it had been purchased after the win. Three-bedroom units in the popular Sydney suburb of Bondi didn't come cheap. In fact, no property in Bondi did, particularly those with a view of the water. The condominium had cost him a fair chunk of his winnings, but apart from splashing out on a top-of-the-line Audi A9, he'd been careful to invest what was left. After the poverty that had permeated his childhood, he'd been determined to have something behind him, something to call his own.

He grimaced. Despite his flourishing career as a police negotiator and his recent lottery win, life hadn't always been so good. He remembered his childhood years spent living in cheap government housing, never knowing whether there would be enough money for his mother to put food on the table. And that wasn't the worst of it...

He strode back into his bedroom, determined to thrust the unhappy memories aside. From near the double glazed sliding glass doors that led out onto a balcony, he took a moment to contemplate the lights that spilled out of the shopfronts that lined the promenade along Bondi Beach. The dark shadows of a dozen or so hulking ocean liners smudged the horizon where it met the Pacific Ocean.

It was a view he never tired of. His girlfriend, Nikki Simons, loved it too, and commentated on it every time she was there. She'd been dropping hints for the past few months about how much she'd like to move in with him, but he'd managed to sidestep the question whenever she brought it up.

He wasn't stupid. Taking their relationship to the next level would inevitably lead to a quest to share his innermost secrets and she wouldn't give up until she'd achieved her goal. He'd come a long way from the nightmare of his childhood, but he wasn't prepared to open the vault—even for Nikki. Now, he was more than grateful he'd resisted the pressure. She was demanding more and more of his time.

In all of his twenty-eight years, he'd never been in love. He wondered if he was even capable of such a depth of feeling. A renewed wave of nervousness surged through him. By the end of the night, he'd be single again and he wasn't entirely certain how Nikki would take it. He'd worked beside her for months and had always admired her professionalism, but this was personal. He wished he felt differently, felt more connected to her, but the truth was, he didn't.

Of course, he still believed in love. Something deep inside him yearned to know what it felt like. He saw Will and Savannah, the way they looked at each other—the special spark they had—and was saddened he didn't have that, or anything like it, with Nikki.

He'd made his mind up a couple of weeks ago to end it, but somehow, he hadn't found the right time and working together made it tough to deal with. Now that he'd transferred to the North Sydney Police Station, it would be easier to make a clean break. He'd let her enjoy the annual Emergency Services Ball and then he'd tell her. He'd take her home afterwards and let her down as gently as he could.

It was nearly seven. Time to call for a cab if he wanted to arrive at the Hilton on time. He'd felt a little under the weather when the last ball was held, so he hadn't been there on the night Will had officially been introduced to his wife, Savannah. Tonight, Savannah would be sharing their table.

Andy grimaced at the irony of the situation. A little over twelve months earlier, his best friend had fallen in love and was now looking forward to fatherhood. Andy and Nikki had been dating almost as long, and after the ball they would go their separate ways.

He hoped she was aware his feelings had cooled. After all, they hadn't had sex for a fortnight. Surely, she'd read something into that? Weren't women good at picking up signals?

With a sigh, he picked up the phone and dialed a cab. Far be it for him to try and determine what went on in a woman's mind. He hoped she'd take their breakup calmly and without tears. He was a sucker for tears. They did him in every time.

Ten minutes later, the taxi's horn sounded from the street below. He collected his cell phone and entry ticket off the hall table and slid them into his pocket. With a last fortifying breath, he closed the door behind him and made his way down the concrete steps and into the balmy evening.

———————

"You're awfully quiet tonight, Andy," Savannah Rutledge murmured less than thirty seconds after Nikki stood up from their table and excused herself to go to the bathroom. The four-course dinner was finally over and the end of the night was drawing closer. Will had left for the bar.

Andy gave Savannah a tight smile and tried not to squirm under the concerned regard of his best friend's wife. Since Will's marriage, Andy had gotten to know Savannah pretty well. Both Will and Savannah were fond of Nikki, and Andy was afraid they'd be disappointed when he told them he was ending it.

Savannah continued to watch him expectantly. He sighed and decided to come clean. After all, the first phone call he'd make after talking to Nikki would be to Will. Glancing in the direction of the restrooms, he leaned in closer and pitched his voice low. "I'm breaking it off with Nikki."

Her eyes widened in surprise. "Oh, Andy, I'm so pleased."

He frowned in confusion. "But, I-I thought you liked Nikki."

She shrugged and looked down at her hands where they lay across her protruding belly. "It's just... She seems to like you as much for your car, your clothes and your beachside condo as she does for you. Does she know about your lottery win?"

He grimaced. "Yeah, she found out about it from one of the guys at work."

Savannah nodded, her lips compressed. "She's a nice girl, Andy, but I guess... Will and I want more for you than that." She looked at him. Her face was tinged with embarrassment, but her eyes flashed with determination.

Andy looked away, uncomfortable with her regard, despite the fact that she was on his side. He didn't want to discuss it; all he wanted was to get it over with. He swallowed a sigh and wished he'd told Will, instead of Will's wife. His mate would have accepted his decision with barely a comment. It's what guys did.

To his relief, Nikki's return saved him from further conversation. He jumped up as soon as she reached them. "Let's dance," he murmured close to her ear and studiously ignored the narrow-eyed look Savannah shot his way. No doubt she thought he'd be better to keep his distance, rather than encourage Nikki's feelings by showing her too much attention.

"Oh, Andy, I'd love to." Nikki's hand caressed the expensive cloth of his jacket and her eyes gleamed. "Are you wearing Armani?" Her smile widened. "You *are*. No wonder you look so hot tonight."

He remembered Savannah's comment and frowned. He'd been aware of Nikki's interest in his financial status, but he'd never before noticed how obvious she was about how he spent his money. Irritation shot through him and it was all he could do not to break it off with her, there and then.

But, he couldn't do that. Not in front of everyone. Not when she'd gone to so much trouble with her dress and her shoes and her hair. He'd asked the taxi to stop by her place on the way in and she'd told him all about her lengthy preparations for the evening.

Swallowing a sigh, he turned away from their table. Taking Nikki's hand, he pulled her toward the dance floor. He hated to prolong the impression they were a couple, but he sure as hell wasn't going to break up with her in a room full of people. He wasn't a complete jerk.

He held her at a respectable distance and tensed when she moved in closer, flattening herself against him. When she rested her cheek against the lapel of his jacket, he had no choice but to hold her close. At last, the song ended and he had an excuse to move away. Knowing he couldn't endure another minute of enforced intimacy, he drew her off the dance floor and leaned down so she could hear him.

"Are you ready to go?"

She looked up in surprise and then smiled, a knowing gleam in her eyes. "I'll go and collect my bag. I left it under the table."

Andy suppressed a groan, aware of the conclusion she'd drawn. With nothing to be done about it, he ushered her through the press of bodies and threaded their way back to their table.

Will returned with fresh drinks. He frowned when he saw them. "What are you two doing back so soon? You're usually the regular John Travolta out there, Andy. What's going on, mate?"

Andy forced a smile. "Not tonight. In fact, Nikki and I are going to call it a night."

"But it's not even midnight," Will protested.

Savannah poked him discreetly in the side with her elbow.

Andy was grateful for her intervention. As he waited for Nikki to retrieve her evening bag, he tried to stem his impatience, now just wanting to get it over with.

"I'll catch up with you later," he muttered. "Goodnight."

"Is everything all right, Andy? You've barely said a word all night." Nikki reached for his hand. The taxi was headed toward her house in Newtown, a few miles west of the city.

"Just tired, I guess," he muttered as he disentangled his fingers.

"Really? Is that all?" Her eyes sought his in the dimness.

He kept his gaze fixed on the back of the driver's head and swallowed a sigh. It seemed, despite his best efforts, he was destined to break up with her in public. "You're a great girl, Nikki."

She tensed and inched away from him. "Why can I hear a "but" coming?"

"I'm going to be honest with you, Nikki. I think we both deserve that." He took a deep breath. "You're a special girl, but I'm not the guy for you. There are things about me you don't know, things from my childhood that aren't...good. I need some time on my own to work through them."

He hated the taste of the lie on his lips, but if it meant leaving her feeling better about herself and the breakup, he was willing to do that. Besides, it wasn't entirely untrue. There were plenty of nights when he'd wake in a lather of sweat, the sheets twisted tightly around his waist, the sound of gunfire echoing in his head.

He closed his eyes briefly against the surge of memories

and then looked back at Nikki. Her bottom lip quivered. The cab passed beneath a streetlight and he caught the shimmer of tears. His heart sank. This was exactly the scene he'd hoped to avoid.

"I wish you'd give me the chance to help you—"

"No." His voice was firm. "I'm sorry. It's not you; it's me." Wincing inwardly at the lame line, he added gently, "It's something I have to work through on my own. Please understand."

The tears disappeared. "I've given you twelve months of my life, Andy. This is the way you repay me?"

He had no words that would soften the blow, so he chose to remain silent. She was entitled to her anger. It wasn't her fault that he was damaged.

After a moment, she huffed and turned to stare out the window, her jaw set. He felt badly about hurting her, but he'd made the right decision. He was twenty-eight. She looked like thirty-something had already knocked on her door. At their age, dating took on a whole different perspective. It was no longer a casual way to pass the time. People their age were looking for life partners.

The taxi slowed and came to a stop at the curb outside Nikki's house. The three-story terrace was dark except for a soft yellow glow from the light on the front porch. Releasing his seatbelt, Andy leaned forward and asked the driver to wait. The air seemed heavy with suspense and all of a sudden, he couldn't think of a single thing to say.

Nikki clutched her black evening bag to her chest and studied him with sad eyes that were still tinged with anger. He bit his lip and hugged her clumsily, depressed that a twelve-month relationship had come to this—a brief, awkward embrace that felt like they were strangers.

He was the first to pull away. "I'll call you."

She sniffed, close to tears. They both knew he was lying.

"You're going to make some lucky woman a wonderful husband one day."

"You too, Nikki. A-a wonderful wife, I mean," he stammered and cursed beneath his breath. Heat flooded his face.

She gave him tight smile and turned away. Fumbling with the door handle, she climbed out of the taxi and hurried up the short flight of steps to her front door. She didn't look back.

Andy slumped against the seat, relieved that it was over.

The driver pulled away from the curb and flicked Andy a glance through the rearview mirror. "Where to?"

"Campbell Parade, Bondi."

They traveled along the near-empty backstreets in silence. It was going on for midnight. A deep weariness invaded Andy's bones. Switching his attention to the road in front of them, he caught the driver's curious gaze.

"Girl trouble?"

Andy kept his gaze fixed on the back of the man's gray, closely cropped hair and remained silent. He so didn't need this conversation.

"They're worth it in the end."

A streetlight gave him a sideways view of the driver's grizzled face and white-stubbled chin. Knowing to continue to ignore the man would be rude, he sighed. "I take it you're speaking from experience?"

"Forty years this November." The gravelly voice was laced with pride. "Four kids, ten grandkids and a wife I still look forward to coming home to."

"Congratulations."

The driver made eye contact again. "I couldn't help overhearing the conversation with your lady friend. You've been together twelve months?"

Andy leaned back in his seat in an effort to get more comfortable, not knowing why he suddenly felt the urge to talk after all. He guessed it had something to do with the anonymity of the situation. Whatever it was, his tongue abruptly appeared to be free.

"Yeah."

"You've been going out with that lady for that long and you're only now working out she's not right for you? What's wrong with you, lad?"

Andy frowned and tried not to take offense. "What do you mean, what's wrong with me?"

The driver sighed dramatically. He took his hands off the wheel and threw them up in the air, shaking his head at the same time.

"Listen, lad. Working out whether you're with the right one or not should never take you twelve months. You've obviously been with lots of wrong ones if you haven't worked that out." The man chuckled. His shoulders shook with mirth.

Spying Andy's sober face in the mirror, his laughter gradually subsided. "When you meet the right one, lad, you know the minute you set eyes on her. I don't know why, but that's the way it is. Simple as that."

Andy remained silent, trying to process the words of wisdom offered by the old man in front of him.

Could it really be that simple? If that were true, how come so many people got it wrong? The divorce rate climbed higher every year and men and women had been getting together since Adam and Eve. Surely, knowing when you met the "right one" couldn't be that easy?

"I can see from the look on your face that you don't believe me," the driver said, offering him a wry grin.

Andy shrugged, not knowing what to say. The man was entitled to his opinion. Besides, he had at least thirty years on Andy. It would be disrespectful to argue.

"Whereabouts on Campbell Parade?" The driver's query interrupted his thoughts.

Turning his attention to the window, Andy recognized the familiar buildings and shopfronts that lined Bondi Beach. As they came over the rise, the dark mass of the Pacific Ocean spread out before them. The ships he'd spied earlier were now indistinct shadows silhouetted against the slightly lighter dimness of the sky, illumined by a round, golden moon.

"Take a right onto Campbell Parade. I'm about halfway up the hill."

The traffic was heavier in Bondi, even though the hour was late. Popular with locals and tourists alike, the streets were still alive with crowds, despite the fact it was a weeknight. The cab turned into Campbell Parade and began the climb.

"Next one on the right." Andy reached into his jacket pocket and pulled out his wallet. As the taxi came to a stop outside his building, he leaned forward and handed the driver a fifty-dollar bill. "Thanks for the ride, mate. You have a good night."

Andy opened the door and climbed out. The driver called out behind him. "Hey, don't forget your change."

Andy leaned in through the man's open window. "Keep it."

The driver shrugged. "Suit yourself."

"Thanks...for the ride." Smiling, Andy stepped back and watched the taxi drive away. For some inexplicable reason, he suddenly felt as light as the balmy summer air around him. Recognizing the unfamiliar feeling as hope, he drew in a deep breath and let the warmth of it seep into his veins.

He pulled his house keys from the pocket of his suit pants and let himself into his condominium complex.

CHAPTER 2

S*he was being followed.* She was sure of it… Well, pretty sure. Cally Savage took another peek in her rearview mirror. Earlier in the week, as she'd reversed out of her driveway, she'd had a weird feeling she was being watched. Coupled with the recent break-in at her house, she was as jittery as a criminal awaiting sentencing. A fresh bout of fear and nervousness surged through her.

The dark-blue sedan traveling two cars behind hers looked exactly like the one she'd noticed a few days ago parked across the street from the house she shared with her son, Jack. Hot afternoon sun blazed through the windscreen of her old Toyota, making it almost impossible to see the road in front of her, but her view from behind was crystal clear.

Not being a car person, she couldn't tell exactly what make it was, but it was an average-sized sedan. She caught a glimpse of the familiar, silver-colored badge on the hood of the car as it changed lanes and pulled in behind another vehicle. *Some kind of Toyota.*

"Damn." She was too late to note the license plate. Jack leaned forward from the back seat.

"What's the matter, Mom?"

She forced a smile and glanced at him over her shoulder. "Nothing, darling. I…ah, I just remembered I left the third grade reading journals at school. I meant to bring them home with me to mark tonight." The lie fell quickly from her lips and she breathed a quiet sigh of relief when he seemed to accept her explanation without further comment and settled back against his seat. Returning her gaze to the mirror, she scoured the mass of cars around her, hoping to spot the blue Toyota again.

"What's that noise?"

Cally frowned and forced herself to pay attention. She suddenly realized the car was steering funny and there was an awful noise coming from right beneath her feet. Lifting her foot off the accelerator, she carefully maneuvered her way over to the shoulder of the road and brought the car to a halt.

"Stay here, okay, Jack? This is a very busy road and I need to know where you are."

He rolled his eyes, but nodded in agreement. Opening the door, she stepped out onto the hot asphalt and turned to check her vehicle. She stared in dismay at the flat tire.

Shit. She mentally went through her options and groaned. A flat tire was the last thing she needed. She felt a headache coming on behind her eyes. Jack poked his head out of the open back window.

"What's the matter, Mom?"

"Only a flat tire, sweetheart. Nothing major." She forced a smile.

He grinned. "Cool! Wait 'til I tell the boys at school."

She smiled, glad one of them at least would get some pleasure from this. All she could think about was how she was going to find the money to repair it.

Jack looked down at the now wholly deflated tire. "Are you going to change it?"

She laughed without humor. "Oh, honey, I wish I could. I wouldn't have a clue how to go about changing it."

He frowned and she hurried to reassure him. "No need to worry. Lucky for us, we have roadside assistance. I'm going to call and see if they can come and get us back on the road."

"But, we haven't got a phone."

Cally winced and pulled open his door. "That may be so,

my lad, but I happen to know there's a phone booth right up the road. Come on, we're going to have to walk."

With a groan, he slid across the seat and climbed out. She collected her handbag from the floor of her car and slung it over her shoulder. Pulling the keys out of the ignition, she locked the car and began to walk with him in the direction of the booth.

Ten minutes later, sweat beaded across her forehead and upper lip. Her blouse was stuck to her skin and Jack complained with every other step. As they reached the phone booth, she opened her handbag and riffled through the cards in her wallet until she found the one she was looking for. She sent up a silent prayer of gratitude that she'd renewed her roadside assistance membership.

It had fallen due a couple of months earlier and she'd spent a few restless nights tossing up whether or not she could afford it. She was glad now she'd erred on the side of caution. Her little Corolla was nearly twenty years old and, sadly, had seen better days. And of course, there was the other factor: There was no one she could call if she was in distress.

As the heavy Friday afternoon traffic roared by them, she found some change in her purse and dialed the number that was listed on the back of the membership card. With her ear pressed tightly against the phone, she waited on hold for what seemed like forever.

A friendly voice finally answered. After taking her details, the operator advised her it could be a while before someone got there. Cally swallowed a sigh and did her best to remain positive.

"When you say it could be a while, how long are you talking, exactly?"

"I can't really say. We've had a higher-than-normal number of calls this afternoon. We'll get someone there as soon as we can."

Dismay surged through her. She pinched the bridge of her nose between her fingers to alleviate the persistent ache that now intensified.

"Okay, well I'd really appreciate your help as soon as possible. It must be at least a hundred degrees out here."

"Of course, Ms Savage. Is there anything else I can help you with today?"

Cally gritted her teeth. "No, there's nothing else."

Hanging up the receiver, she rested her forehead on the slightly cooler metal of the phone booth and closed her eyes on a heavy sigh.

"What's happening, Mom? Are they going to come and fix it? When are they going to get here?"

Forcing her eyes open, she lifted her head and looked down at her son. Impatience clouded his features. His thick blond hair, woefully in need of a haircut, partially obscured his deep brown eyes.

His father's eyes.

Her heart clenched every time she noticed them. The shape, the color, even some of the expressions she'd catch in them reminded her of Stewart. Jack had inherited her cheerful personality but the only physical trait he'd inherited from her was his hair color.

Emotionally, he was more like her than she cared to admit. She worried his honest and trusting nature would make him vulnerable to people who would take advantage of him. She knew only too well how easy it was for that to happen—and how dire the consequences could be.

Pushing the gloomy thoughts away, she gave him what she hoped was a reassuring smile. "They'll be here as soon as they can, sweetheart."

He gave her a crooked grin. "I guess I could always do my homework while we wait."

She laughed in surprise. "Really? Since when have you been so keen to do your homework?"

"Nah, just kidding. Besides, it's Friday. We don't get homework on Friday."

Smiling at the cheeky look on his face, she sent up a silent prayer that God would watch over her little boy and keep him safe. He was all she had and he was more precious to her than all the money in the world. Not that a little bit more cash wouldn't be appreciated. Especially in times like this. She had no idea how much it would cost to repair the tire, but nothing to do with cars ever came cheap. The cost of gas alone put a healthy dent in her weekly budget.

With a tight smile, she slung her arm over Jack's shoulder and they made their way back to the car. It was parked where they'd left it. Wiping the perspiration off her forehead and neck, Cally climbed in the front. Jack took his customary seat in the back.

The temperature inside was only marginally cooler than outside, but at least it provided shelter from the broiling sun and the pungent smell of exhaust fumes. Besides, she'd rather be within the safety of the car if the blue Toyota happened to come back past.

"Wind down the windows, honey. It'll cool things down a bit."

Jack leaned forward to do her bidding and she attended to the windows in the front. Her budget hadn't stretched to a car with air conditioning and they were used to driving in the February heat with the windows down—which worked all right when the car was in motion. Now, halted on the side of the road with the heat rising off the asphalt in almost palpable waves, conditions were less than ideal.

"To say the least," she murmured.

"What did you say, Mom?"

"Oh, honey, I was talking to myself. It's pretty hot, isn't it?"

"Yeah. Too bad we haven't got a pool. Jimmy Baker has a pool. Did you know he can swim ten laps of the big pool without stopping?"

"Really? That's pretty good. He must get lots of practice."

"Yeah, he goes to the pool in North Sydney for swimming lessons. Can I get swimming lessons, Mom? It'd be great if I could swim ten laps, too. Then Jimmy and I could have races. That really would be cool, wouldn't it?"

Cally concentrated on holding her smile, hoping her much-too-observant son wouldn't notice the bleakness in her eyes. Even working two jobs, the money she earned barely stretched to cover the weekly commitments. By the time the car payment, the house payment, the phone, electricity and grocery bills were taken care of, there was never very much left over for anything else. For things like haircuts, new tires, cell phones, swimming lessons.

It was so different from the childhood she'd had. There'd been more than enough money for anything she wanted. All she'd had to do was ask. She'd been petted and pampered and loved—probably even spoiled. She'd never known what it was like to do without or to have to leave something on the shelf because she couldn't afford to buy it.

But then she'd fallen pregnant right after her sixteenth birthday and life as she'd known it had ended…

She fought against the familiar pain and squared her shoulders. That was then. She'd managed to make a life for herself and her son. Everything was fine. Everything was great.

She sighed heavily. *Yeah, right.*

"Mom, are you okay?"

Blinking back the memories, Cally peered at Jack through the rearview mirror. The concern clouding his eyes nearly broke her heart. "Of course, honey. I… It's just the heat. I-I'm fine."

"You look so sad."

Swallowing the lump in her throat, she forced a smile. "Sometimes grown-ups feel a little sad, but it's nothing for you to worry about. I guess I'm thinking about the flat tire and how much it's going to cost to repair."

"Do we have enough money to fix it?"

"Honey, you don't have to worry about things like that. That's what Moms are for."

"But—"

"Jack, please don't worry about it. Besides, ever since I started that new cleaning job, we have heaps of extra money," she lied.

His face brightened. "Really? So I can get swimming lessons?"

She bit back a groan of desperation. The smile stretched tight on her face. "Of course. Why not?"

"Cool! You're the best." He grinned at her, his face alight with excitement.

She bit down hard on her lip to stifle the sob that threatened to escape. *She'd find the money somewhere.* She just needed to get a bit more creative with their finances. If she took in someone else to help pay the bills that would be a bonus.

Sighing softly, she turned her face back toward the open window, watching the endless stream of cars pass by them in waves of heat and exhaust fumes. So many cars and not a single roadside-assist vehicle in sight.

"Are we cleaning tonight, Mom?"

"Yes, honey, we are. We'll have an early dinner and then get going. Provided we get the car fixed, that is. Otherwise we might be taking the train."

"I don't mind. The train's pretty cool. Lots of people to look at and I love going through the tunnel."

She smiled: To be ten years old again and see the world through unjaded eyes. For her, innocent pleasures in the simple things had come to an abrupt halt the night she'd told her father his teenaged daughter was having a baby.

"'Scuse me, luv. You been waitin' for roadside assistance?"

A burly head, covered in untidy gray hair, thrust itself through her open car window.

Cally gasped in surprise. Her thoughts scattered like the wind. The mechanic had arrived.

CHAPTER 3

"You got a spare?"

The man who spoke with the rough Australian vernacular, grinned at her. He wore dirty blue overalls with an embroidered name tag that identified him as "Mike". His teeth were yellowed with tobacco stains and he chewed a piece of gum with ferocious concentration.

"In the trunk," she replied, thankful he'd finally arrived, even if he did look like he needed a bath.

He moved away and then yelled out from behind the car, "You might have to flip it open for me, luv."

Cally flushed with embarrassment and fumbled around the side of her seat for the lever, grateful he couldn't see her. She heard him work the spare tire and jack out of the trunk, snapping his gum in time with his movements.

"You might have to get out of the car, if you don't mind. I gotta get the jack under there and even though there's not much of you, it'll be easier to jack it up with you outside it."

"Of course. I'm sorry." She opened the door and stepped onto the hot asphalt. "What about my son? Is it okay if he stays in there?"

Mike poked his head through the open back window and gave Jack a toothy smile. "G'day, mate. I'm Mike. What's your name?"

Jack grinned back at him, completely unperturbed by the man's filthy appearance. "I'm Jack. Do you think I can get out, Mike? It's getting pretty hot in here."

"No worries, mate. But get out on the far side, over there, won't you? Too much traffic on this side. And better stay close to your mom, okay?"

"Sure, Mike. Thanks." Jack pushed open the door and stepped out onto the shoulder of the road. Cally came around to stand with him, feeling vulnerable and exposed. It was difficult to admit how much the recurring appearance of the blue Toyota rattled her—not to mention the blow to her hard-fought independence having to rely on the filthy, but friendly mechanic to change her tire.

First thing she would do when she got a spare minute or two was to read her car manual. She'd be damned if she'd sit back helplessly a second time.

"The tire's in pretty bad shaped, luv. I can take it with me, if you like. Save you havin' to get rid of it."

She stepped forward in alarm. "Oh, that's all right. I'm not going to get rid of it. I'll need to have it repaired."

Mike chuckled, shaking his head in amusement. "You're not gonna be able to repair that one. The wall of the tire's been shredded. It's rat shit, I'm afraid."

"But... Are you sure?" She frowned, knowing the cost of a new one would completely blow her budget.

"Yep, and you really should put a new one on the other side, too. It's not safe to have one good one and one old one runnin' together. The tire around the front passenger's side's gonna go too, before long."

Desperation seeped into her bones. All at once, she was overwhelmed by the continuing struggle to keep things afloat. As if things weren't already stretched to the limit, now she'd have to find the money for two tires.

Aware that Mike was still looking at her, Cally forced a smile. Checking to make sure Jack was sitting well away from the road, she walked up to the mechanic until she was close enough to speak to him without having to yell over the noise of the traffic.

"How bad do you really think it is?" She pointed to the tire on the passenger side.

"Well, it's fairly well worn. The spare I've just put on is in pretty good nick, but we don't recommend havin' tires with different wear on them bein' run together."

"Why not?" she asked, wondering how serious the issue was and whether it could be delayed until she'd managed to save a little more money.

"Well, it can affect your steerin' a bit. Your car will try and pull in the direction of the worn tire." He shrugged. "It's just not somethin' I'd recommend."

"So it's not a matter of life or death or anything?" she persisted. "I mean, it's not going to cause an accident, is it?"

"Well, that's a question I can't rightly answer." He scratched his stubbled chin with a grease-stained finger. "Who knows what could happen if you took your attention from the road for a few seconds and your car started veerin' off into another lane. If you're travelin' beside a big semi or somethin' you could find yourself right underneath it."

She tried to suppress a shudder. She'd just have to make sure she concentrated for every second she was in the car and take her chances with the tire until her finances improved.

As Mike replaced the jack in her trunk and hoisted the ruined tire onto the back of his truck, she walked over to Jack and helped him up.

He grinned at her and pushed his sweat-dampened hair out of his eyes. "Are we going?"

"Yes, honey. We're going."

Jack called out as he climbed back into the car. "See you later, Mike!"

Mike gave him a cheerful wave. "See you, Jack."

Cally came up to where Mike stood outside his service truck. She gave him a weak smile. "Thanks for all your help. I really appreciate it."

"No, worries, luv. You take care now and make sure you get yourself a couple of new tires as soon as you can."

She didn't reply, but gave him a small wave of thanks and headed back to her car. She couldn't bring herself to confess to him she'd be happy to buy a couple of new tires—if only she could afford them.

Sighing heavily, she turned to check that Jack's seatbelt was secure before she switched on the ignition and headed back into the afternoon traffic.

———————

"Come on, honey, we're going to have to get a move on. I need to be down at the police station in half an hour. We lost a fair bit of time waiting on the side of the road, and I don't want to be late on my third night."

"Okay, Mom." Jack finished the last piece of sausage on his plate. Picking up the glass of milk near his elbow, he drained it in a few quick swallows before setting it back down on the table with a triumphant sigh.

"Thanks for dinner." He smiled over at her where she stood at the kitchen sink loading the dishwasher.

"That's fine, honey. Now hurry up and have a quick shower and change into some clean clothes. It'll be time for bed when we get back."

He began to undo the buttons on his school shirt. "Can I take my *Zac Power* books with me?"

"Of course. It's been taking me a couple of hours to clean the building, so it'd be a good idea for you to bring something to amuse yourself."

"Maybe I could help you?" A hopeful look filled his face.

"You probably could and I appreciate your offer, but just let me get settled in for a bit first. This is only the end of my first week and I need to get a feel for it, all right?"

"Sure." He turned away and tossed his dirty clothes in the direction of the laundry.

"Hey, what's this?" She pointed toward the pile of clothes on the floor, well shy of the washing machine.

He shot her a cheeky grin. "I'm just trying to help you get a feel for it, Mom. Cleaning, I mean."

"Very funny." She bent down to pick up the dirty clothes.

"Well, washing clothes is a cleaning job."

"Jack." Her voice held a warning, even as laughter bubbled up inside her.

"Okay, okay, Mom. I'm sorry."

She came over and put her arms around him. His near-naked body looked longer and thinner than it did when it was concealed beneath his clothes. "You need to put a bit of meat on your bones, my son."

"Yeah, so you keep saying. Maybe it's just who I am." Turning suddenly serious brown eyes upon her, he added quietly, "Maybe my dad was tall and skinny?"

Cally drew in a shocked breath. Apart from the very occasional vague question about his father, he'd never before directly asked her anything about him. She'd always known the issue would have to be dealt with at some stage, but she suddenly felt completely unprepared.

Feeling like a coward, she changed the subject. "Hey, how about that shower?"

His shoulders slumped and he looked away. He mumbled a response and turned and left the room.

Cally's heart clenched. Swiping at the hot tears that pricked her eyes and threatened to spill over, she finished tidying the kitchen. Their small cottage, tucked away behind a row of much larger, grander homes in Chatswood, one of Sydney's leafy northern suburbs, was pretty snug with only two average-sized bedrooms and a sleepout.

It may have been small, but the cottage was surrounded by stately old gardens filled with enormous ancient fig trees which meant their modest backyard was shaded from the heat for most of the day.

As far as she was concerned, it was perfect. She'd loved it from the moment the realtor had unlocked the door and motioned her across the threshold.

"Now, it might seem a little cozy," the man began as he led her through the modest rooms, but she'd barely heard him. The immediate feeling of familiarity had overwhelmed her.

This was it. She was home.

The kitchen was vintage 1950s—old and worn, but the

scrubbed linoleum floor gleamed and the mint-green laminated countertops reminded her of her Aunt Mary's house in Armidale; a house where she'd felt wholly and completely loved. A house where she'd raised her son for the first eight years of his life. A house she would never have left if fate hadn't intervened.

Even now, more than two years later, she could recall, as if it were yesterday, the smell of star jasmine and honeysuckle that had filled the warm spring air the day her aunt had sold the only home Jack had ever known.

Glancing at the clock on the wall of the kitchen, Cally gasped. She was going to be late.

So much for trying to make a good impression. The way things were going, she'd be lucky to get there at all. What, with the flat tire setting them back over an hour and now wasting time reminiscing, her day didn't look like it was going to end well. With no time to shower and change, she headed quickly toward her bedroom, calling out to Jack as she did so.

His tousled head, still wet from the shower, appeared in the doorway of his room. "I'm in here, Mom. Is it time to go? I thought you were going to take a shower?"

"Yes, sweetie, it is and I was, but we don't have enough time now, so I'll go as I am. That's all right, isn't it?"

"Sure, you look fine." His gaze swept briefly over the soft cotton sundress she'd worn to work. "A bit rumpled, maybe," he added with a grin.

"Gee, thanks, buddy." She grinned back at him. "You'd probably look a bit rumpled too if you'd had the day I have. I swear, every boy in the third grade had ants in his pants today. Talk about unable to sit still. I thought I was going to have to get them all to run a few laps around the oval to wear them out."

He rolled his eyes at her. "We've only been back to school a few weeks, Mom. It takes a bit of time to get used to it again."

"Don't I know it," she laughed and pulled a brush quickly through her short, straight bob, thankful her hair was so easy to take care of. Once upon a time, she'd never have taken a pair of scissors to her trademark long hair—the hair her father had been so proud of. But that was a lifetime ago...

Refusing to allow her thoughts to wander again, she picked up her keys and handbag. "Okay, honey, let's go. Grab your books or whatever you want to take with you and I'll meet you at the car. Let's hope we don't have any more mishaps along the way."

CHAPTER 4

Andy Warwick's heart pounded and the blood pulsed in his ears, making it almost impossible to hear. Rivulets of sweat ran down his forehead and into his eyes. Ignoring everything, he remained focused on the man who stood a few feet away from him.

Precariously balanced on what felt like a microscopic window ledge, Andy battled to keep Wayne Tucker from throwing himself to the sidewalk, thirteen floors below. The late afternoon sun beat fiercely against Andy's face. His eyes burned from the salty perspiration. He didn't dare move a muscle. With his gaze fixed on the portly, middle-aged accountant, he tried again.

"Wayne, keep talking to me, mate." To his relief, his voice remained calm and firm, in stark contrast to the turmoil swirling inside him. He prayed for a response—something, anything—to indicate the man was still listening.

Nothing.

He held his breath. The only movement came from a wisp of hot air that lifted Wayne's longish, lank hair. Fear slid insidiously through Andy's veins.

"Why don't you move a bit closer, Wayne? We can talk better that way." He swallowed against the urgency that had crept into his voice.

The man lifted his head and slowly turned it toward him. "What are you still doing here? You know I'm going to do it."

Tucker's pain and anger reverberated between them over the stifling air.

Andy kept his gaze steady. "I'm not going anywhere."

"Go away!"

"Mate, listen to me. I want you to slide your foot over a bit. Move a little closer. It's hot as hell out here. Don't make me yell in this heat."

"I've already *told* you. You're *wasting* your time. Just leave me *alone*."

Andy's stomach tensed at the anger in Wayne's voice. It wasn't a good sign. Taking a deep breath, he willed himself to stay calm. The next few minutes would be crucial. If he had any hope of saving the man, he had to convince him to move close enough to fit a rope around him and clip him to the safety harness strapped to Andy's back.

Filling his lungs again, he forced himself to speak evenly. "I'm not going to do that, Wayne. I'm not going anywhere without you. If you jump, I'm coming with you."

Wayne's gaze narrowed on Andy's face. His voice sharpened with suspicion. "What the hell are you talking about? You're not going to jump. You're full of shit."

"Mate, it's me. Andy. I've been sitting up here talking to you for the last three hours. I'm not bullshitting you. You jump, I jump." The lie fell easily from his lips. He prayed he sounded convincing.

Members of Andy's team, all elite officers of the State Protection Group, stood behind him, tense and watchful from inside the safety of the double glazed glass of the steel-and-concrete North Sydney skyscraper.

Andy waited.

Had he said enough? Had he managed to penetrate the fog of anger and pain that had muddled Wayne's reasoning and turned a completely ordinary man into a potential tragic headline for the six o'clock news?

Not daring to breathe, Andy was almost paralyzed at the thought he might fail. An image of his dead sister flashed through his mind and he bit down hard on his lip. He needed to concentrate. He couldn't fail. With his chest tight, he tried again.

"Tell me, Wayne. How old is your boy, now? Six? Seven? And your daughter, Sophie? She's going on ten, isn't she?" Andy prayed the information he'd been given was correct.

"He's seven. Marcus is seven." The reply was soft and hesitant.

Andy's breath eased out between his tense lips. Conversation was good. It was progress. He had to keep it going.

"Marcus. That's a fine, strong name. I bet he's a good kid. With a name like that, he'd have to be."

A fleeting smile crossed Tucker's face. "Yeah," he whispered. "He's a good kid. So is Soph."

Andy's gut tightened in anticipation. This was it. This was his chance. "Come on, Wayne. Come over here. Come closer, so I can help you back inside. Marcus and Sophie need you."

It seemed to take a lifetime, but eventually Tucker moved. One step. Two. Each one brought him a little closer. Andy almost collapsed with relief. Standing rigid, he waited as the man placed another foot gingerly along the cement ledge and brought himself within arm's distance. His tortured eyes burned into Andy's.

"That's it, Wayne. That's it. Keep going, mate. You're nearly there." With quick efficiency, Andy unhooked the rope at his waist and slid it over Tucker. Within seconds, the man was secured. As if the bravado that had kept him on the roof ledge for the best part of three hours had suddenly evaporated, Wayne slumped hard against him. Andy braced himself against the additional body weight.

Moments later, members of the SPG surged forward. Arms reached out for both of them, dragging them through the open window to safety. The tension drained from Andy's body. He slumped forward onto the carpeted floor, dragging Tucker with him. Similarly affected, the man gulped in great lungsful of air. Tears poured down his cheeks.

Two paramedics who'd been standing by, leaped forward and began assessing Tucker for injuries or other physical health concerns. Andy looked away and did his best to restore his heartbeat to normal. Detective Sergeant Tom Munro strode over, relief flooding his swarthy features. He unhooked the steel link that tied Andy to Wayne.

"Good work, Andy." Tom's voice was low and rough with emotion.

Andy grimaced and nodded his thanks to his work partner and friend. He was beyond words.

He'd done it. He'd saved Tucker.

Three hours later, Andy leaned against his comfortable, ergonomically approved office chair and put his feet up on his cluttered desk, trying hard not to relive his afternoon. Loose papers and pens scattered beneath his heavy police boots, but he was so tired he was beyond caring. His body ached in every place he could think of and even some that he couldn't.

The time he'd spent on the ledge with Tucker had drained him, physically and mentally. He loved the job, but the aftermath always took its toll.

"Are you still here, Andy?" Detective Superintendent Patrick Redding strode into the main squad room where Andy's desk stood amongst a half dozen identical ones, cluttered with unfinished paperwork.

Andy lifted his chin and wearily looked at his boss. "Yeah, I was just finishing up the report on Wayne Tucker."

"Good work on that one today. Tom told me it was touch and go there for a while."

"Thank you, sir." Taking a deep breath, he released it slowly and shook his head. "I thought he was going to jump. I couldn't seem to get through to him. But I kept at it—what else could I do? I don't know what changed, but for some reason he started to listen to me, *really* listen." He shrugged. "I caught a lucky break."

"More than luck, Andy. You're a damned good negotiator." Redding indicated the open file on Andy's desk, and continued, "They're the lucky ones. All of those unstable souls out there like Tucker who had your help when they needed it most... If it weren't for you, there'd be a lot more of them rotting in the ground right now."

"Thank you, sir, I appreciate your vote of confidence." He shrugged self-consciously. "I do my best. It's all I can do." His voice lowered. "It's the ones I might not save who keep me up at night."

Redding frowned. The deep wrinkles lining his forehead became more prominent. "Now, you listen to me, Andy Warwick. You might have only a year's experience behind you, but you're a good police officer and one of the best negotiators I've worked with. It's a shame we didn't have a few more of your ilk working here. Our success rate might be a little higher and that would please all concerned."

He stepped closer and gripped Andy's shoulder. "It's normal for you to get down on yourself when you don't succeed—especially in your position where failure can mean death. But don't ever doubt yourself or your abilities. You're one of our finest, Andy. Don't forget it. Besides," he added, "you haven't lost one yet, so stop stressing about it."

Andy fought back the lump of emotion that lodged in his throat and lifted grateful eyes toward his boss. "Thank you, sir. That means a lot to me."

"I meant every word of it." Redding's voice was gruff. The beard-roughened skin of his cheeks turned pink. Collecting his briefcase from where it sat at his feet, he headed for the exit. "Don't stay too late, will you?" he called over his shoulder. He opened the door and disappeared.

Andy was momentarily distracted by the sound of a vacuum cleaner from one of the other rooms. He glanced at his watch. Nearly eight. The night had folded in around him, unnoticed until now.

The noise moved closer. His pulse rate accelerated. He

took deep breaths and did his best to avoid the impending panic attack. No one had ever told him why the sound of the vacuum cleaner had always annoyed his father. He could remember how his mother would rush from work to collect him and his little sister from school and then race home to get the vacuuming done before his father arrived.

Occasionally, she'd run late and his father arrived home before it was finished. She wouldn't hear him come in over the noise. Moments after his arrival, he'd knock her flying with a heavy fist.

Andy's gut tensed. To his relief, the noise stopped. A few minutes later, the door to the squad room opened.

"Oh, I'm sorry. I didn't realize there was anyone still here. Do you mind if I do some cleaning?"

Andy looked into a pair of the bluest eyes he'd ever seen. His dark memories vanished with a jolt. He tried to process the vision in front of him.

Was he dreaming? He was bone tired after standing for hours in the hot sun with Wayne Tucker—perhaps he was delusional. Surely she couldn't be real? Her skin was too lustrous, her hair too blond, her eyes too luminous for her to be a flesh-and-blood woman.

He must have fallen asleep. It was the only explanation. Grinning ruefully, he leaned back further in his chair and once again made himself comfortable. If this were a dream, he intended to enjoy it for as long as he could.

With his eyes closed, he willed the vision of the woman to reappear. His body stirred. It had been more than a fortnight since he'd slept with Nikki. Now that he'd broken up with her, sex was not in his immediate future.

He'd never been the type to indulge in meaningless sex with girls who were virtual strangers. The few encounters he'd had were within semi-committed relationships, something his best mate, Will, had found impossible to understand—until he'd met his wife, Savannah. Will now marveled at how he'd sustained such meaningless relationships and actually thought they were a good thing.

Lately, he'd even taken to urging Andy to find a nice girl and settle down.

"Uh, excuse me, are you all right?" The soft voice was hesitant.

He opened a single eye and stared at the angel of his dreams. She took a step backwards in surprise and then spoke again.

"I-I'm sorry, but I need to clean in here. Are you all right?"

Both his eyes snapped open. The chair came down hard. His feet hit the floor. She stood before him in a sleeveless summer dress that ended just above her knees. It was the same color as her eyes, with big white flowers splashed all over it. She held a cloth in one hand and a bucket in the other. He suddenly noticed the long green rubber gloves on her hands.

So, she wasn't an angel. She wasn't a figment of his imagination, either. She was the cleaner. And she was talking to him. Again.

"I'm sorry if I've interrupted you, but I really need to get this finished. My son—"

"No, no. Of course, of course," he mumbled. He stood and pushed his seat away from his desk.

"I'll try to be as quick as I can, but I need to wipe down the desktops and..." She stopped. Her gaze skimmed over the desks, most of them completely covered in paperwork, reference books, charge sheets and other paraphernalia. "That is, the ones I can get to, anyway." She gave him a tentative, nervous smile.

"Um, sure... No problem." He realized how stupid he appeared, staring at her as if he'd seen a ghost. With a sharp shake of his head, he started toward the locker room, intending to get his stuff and leave. He'd only taken a few paces when the phone on his desk rang.

Knowing she'd also heard it, he stopped. He turned and sat down in his recently vacated chair then picked up the receiver.

"Andy Warwick."

"Hey, mate, I was beginning to worry about you. I've

been trying you on your cell phone all afternoon and I kept getting your voice mail. What are you up to?"

"Will." He smiled, relieved it wasn't another emergency. Even though he was officially off duty, if extra hands were needed, everyone received the call, no matter what the hour.

"I'm surprised you're still at the office."

"Yeah, I was just finishing a report on a job I caught today."

"I saw it on the news. I thought you might have been involved. How'd it go? They said you stopped the bloke from jumping."

Andy sighed. The memory of the relief and exhilaration he'd felt when Wayne Tucker climbed back through the window flooded through him again. His voice was filled with quiet pride. "Yeah, I did."

He relaxed back in his chair. The cleaning woman had moved to the far side of the room. Lifting potted plants that had seen better days, she wiped away the dirt where it had fallen onto the gray, laminated countertops.

"So what's with your cell?"

"Oh, I um, turned it off and left it in my locker when I was called to the job. I haven't had a chance to get it."

"Yeah, well, I just wanted to see how you were going." A beat passed. "Savannah told me you're going to break it off with Nikki."

Andy sighed wearily. "Yeah. I already did it last night, after the ball."

"Shit, Andy, not after the *ball*? She was having such a good time. Couldn't you have waited a little longer? How did she take it?"

"About as well as you'd expect and for your information, I've been trying to do it for the last fortnight. There just didn't seem a proper time. I mean, is there ever a right time?"

"You're asking the wrong bloke, mate. I never went out with the same girl more than once or twice. Savannah was the first one I even *wanted* to spend more than a night or two with."

"Lucky for you she felt the same way."

"You can say that again. Although, I have to tell you, these pregnancy hormones have me running in circles. I've been putting up with it for eight months. One minute she can't get enough of me and the next she's screaming bloody murder if I get anywhere near her. Then there's the gherkin fetish. I tell you, I'll be pleased when it's over and I can get my wife back again."

"So you've changed your mind about pushing me toward holy matrimony?" Andy smiled into the phone, watching the blond angel from the corner of his eye as she emptied wastepaper baskets that were under the desks. He could tell she was trying to do it quietly because he was on the phone. Her thoughtfulness intrigued him.

"Of course not," Will was saying. "You just haven't found the right one yet. Don't worry; we'll find you someone."

"Just don't go setting me up with one of your exes. Those stick insects you used to go for are so not my style."

Will chuckled. "Okay, okay. I'm only trying to do my duty as your best friend and find you a wife. I know you want one, even if you are being a bit picky."

Andy swiveled his chair so he could follow the woman's progress around the room. She'd moved closer and was now using her cloth to swipe across Tom's desk, one of the tidier of their team.

"You're right. I want a wife. I want kids. I want soccer matches. I want white picket fences. But I don't want that with just anyone. I'm in it for the long haul. I want to be certain she's the one, you know."

"Yeah, I know. I am one wholly converted bachelor who thought there was no such thing as love at first sight."

"Yeah. That's exactly my point. I might not have been raised with much love, but I know what it looks like. I can't say I know what it *feels* like because I honestly don't think I've ever been in love. Not the way you are with Savannah, anyway. But I haven't given up hope. She's out there somewhere."

He recalled the taxi driver's words of wisdom. "A cabbie

told me last night when the right one comes along, I'll know her the instant I meet her." He braced himself for Will's burst of laughter.

To his surprise, his friend remained silent. Will's reply, when it came, was slow and thoughtful.

"You know what, mate? He might be right. When I think about that first night I met Savannah—hell, I thought she was a prostitute. But there was something about her—I couldn't get her out of my head. I reckon I probably did fall in love with her from the moment I saw her." He laughed wryly. "I think your cabbie's right on the money."

"Maybe he is," Andy murmured. He watched with interest while the cleaner bent down to pick up another wastepaper basket. Her dress pulled tight across her shapely butt. His body hardened in response. She turned and moved toward him, oblivious to his lascivious thoughts.

Eager to speak with her again, he brought an abrupt end to his phone conversation and replaced the receiver in its cradle just as she reached his desk.

"You didn't have to hang up." Her vivid eyes darted away from his. Her hands clenched the top of the trash bag. "I would have been quiet, I assure you."

He extended his hand. "Andy Warwick. I don't think we've met."

She shook it firmly and offered him a tentative smile. A pulse beat rapidly in her neck.

"Cally Savage. Nice to meet you. And no, we haven't met. I only started here this week." She smiled again and he noticed how perfect her teeth were and how she was even more beautiful up close.

Blood pounded in his ears and his palms turned sweaty. He felt like a teenager on his first date.

Cally stared at the carpet; a slight frown creased her forehead.

He searched frantically for something clever to say. *She's probably wondering what the hell is wrong with me.*

"So, have you been working here long?" As soon as the words left his mouth he wanted them back. She'd just *told* him it was her first week. Now she really *would* think him a dolt. A wave of heat stole up his neck.

He stood and turned away abruptly, covering his mouth with his hand and pretended to be caught up in a coughing fit.

"Are you okay?" she asked, concern lining her voice.

He forced himself to turn around, certain his face was now crimson. "Um, I just… Yeah, um, I'm fine. Thanks."

She stepped toward him and he instinctively backed away.

"I'm fine, I really am. But thanks, anyway," he repeated.

"Are you sure? "You look a bit…flushed."

The door to the squad room opened, saving him from replying. A young boy walked in.

"Are you nearly finished, Mom?"

Surprise replaced Andy's embarrassment. *Good looking boy.* He watched the lad walk slowly toward them, curiosity illuminating his dark eyes.

Cally also seemed relieved to see her son. "Jack, honey—this is Andy Warwick. A police officer, right?" She turned to face him.

"Negotiator, actually, but close enough." He grinned, relieved to discover his heart had slowed enough for him to think rationally again.

"Cool." Jack nodded approvingly. "What does that mean?"

Andy laughed, appreciating the boy's forthrightness. "It means I try to help people who are very sad by convincing them things are not as bad in their life or in the world as they may think."

Jack came to stand beside him, his face filled with inquisitiveness. "How do you do that?"

"Well, it depends on the situation a little bit, buddy, but I talk to them about things that are important to them and try to get them to remember the good things in their lives."

"Sounds pretty cool. How come you're so tall?" Jack strained to look up at him.

Andy laughed. "I don't know; I just am. My dad was pretty tall, so I guess that's where I get it from."

Jack smiled back at him. "I think my dad was tall, too."

Andy noticed the boy's use of the past tense and flicked a questioning glance toward his mother. Meeting his gaze, she gave him a slight shake of her head, her eyes pleading with him to let it go. He shelved the intriguing information for another time. Besides, he was still so aware of her, he was finding it hard to concentrate.

"Come on, Jack. We'd better leave Sergeant Warwick to get back to his work, and I'd better get on with mine or we'll be here all night. I still have the bathrooms to do."

"Call me Andy, please," he interjected.

Her lips turned up politely. She gave him a slight nod. "Andy it is then." She turned away.

Wanting to prolong their conversation, he cast around for something else to say. "How long does it normally take you to clean?" he blurted.

She stopped and slowly turned back around to face him, her reluctance obvious. "A couple of hours, I guess. We're usually out of here by eight-thirty. We're running a little late tonight." She gave him a tight smile.

It was obvious she wanted to bring their conversation to an end, but he couldn't help himself. "That's quite a late night for a young fellow."

She stiffened. Her eyes flashed with anger. He cursed himself silently for saying something stupid again.

"Jack's fine," she ground out.

"I didn't mean—"

Without giving him a chance to explain, she fired back at him, "I don't know if I look like someone who enjoys cleaning toilets, *Andy*, but I assure you, I don't. Unfortunately, money doesn't grow on trees and I have bills to pay." Twin spots of bright color now stained her cheeks. Her eyes sparked fire.

He was mortified. "I-I'm sorry. I didn't mean to imply—"

"What? That my parenting skills aren't up to scratch? That I'm an unfit mother? That my son should be home in bed, getting a good night's sleep?" She was breathing heavily through her anger.

"No! I only meant—"

"Forget it," she interrupted again, shrugging her shoulders as if it no longer mattered. "You don't know anything about me or my son."

"Maybe we could change that?" He spoke without thinking, desperation overcoming his usual reticence. He offered her an uncertain smile, unwilling to let her walk out spitting fire at him.

Her eyes widened in shock. "You're kidding me? First you insult me and then you ask me out?"

"Well, I didn't actually ask you out, but if that's what you'd like..." He grinned, knowing it was probably going to infuriate her further, but somehow unable to stop himself.

"Oh! You are simply unbelievable! What I'd *like* is to finish here, go home and go to bed. Now, if you're through insulting me, I'd appreciate it if you'd pass me the trash can under your desk so I can empty it and get out of here."

He looked down at the overflowing waste basket. If he refused to heed her request, she'd be forced to come in very close proximity. In fact, if he chose to sit back down, she'd very nearly have to put her hand between his legs if she wanted to retrieve it.

Seeing the tension in her body and noticing, for the first time, the tiny lines of fatigue around her eyes, he relented. It was obvious she'd had a hard day. It was even more obvious she wasn't in the mood for teasing.

He leaned forward and picked up the trash can and went to hand it over to her. Their fingers brushed, eliciting a gasp from both of them. Heat sizzled up his arm. She pulled her fingers away as if she'd been burned.

With her gaze averted, she stumbled away from his desk, reaching out blindly toward her son. "Come on, Jack. Let's go."

She took the boy by the arm and dragged him with her out of the room, leaving Andy looking on, bemused. The overflowing wastepaper basket had been left in his hands, abandoned.

What the hell had all that been about?

Chapter 5

Fingers of morning sunlight filtered through the gauzy white curtains that hung across Cally's bedroom window. She rolled over and squinted at the alarm clock: six forty-two. She groaned. Her eyes were gritty and tired and her body ached after four nights in a row tossing and turning over her dire financial circumstances and her unease that the man who'd broken into her home might return.

She buried her head under the pillow in an effort to block out the arrival of the morning, but her heavy thoughts over the past few days refused to leave her. The problem was simple: She needed to earn more money. The difficulty came in how she was going to achieve it.

While her teaching job paid well, it was only part time. Mondays, Wednesdays and Fridays she taught the third grade and no matter how hard she'd tried to secure teaching employment for the other two days, it hadn't happened. A few months earlier, the Department of Education had offered her a fulltime job in an outer western Sydney suburb, but it was so far away from their home in Chatswood, she'd have to relocate for it to become viable. She needed to be close to Jack's school so she could be there to collect him, or at least be at home when he arrived off the bus. Her only other option was to put him in before and after school care.

She'd looked into the care option when they'd first

moved to Sydney and had quickly discovered the cost was exorbitant. The child care fees would entirely negate the benefit of the extra income a fulltime job would provide. No matter which way she looked at it, she was stuck.

The reality was, if her finances didn't improve, she'd be forced to put her beloved cottage on the market and look for something cheaper. It would definitely mean a move from the northern suburbs and she grimaced at the thought of leaving the comfort and security she'd found in their cottage in Chatswood.

"What to do; what to do?" she muttered under her breath. If only she had someone to talk to about it.

Her thoughts shifted to her best friend from high school, Kate Collins. She was Kate Munro, now. Cally had reconnected with her nearly three years earlier when Kate returned to their hometown of Watervale to search for her missing mother. Cally had been devastated for her friend when Kate eventually called with the news her mother had been found murdered.

The only bright light during the whole sad episode was that Kate had found true love in the form of the investigating police officer. Kate and Riley Munro were now happily married and had added twin girls to their family. It was the kind of happy ending fairytales were made of and Cally couldn't help but wish her life had been so blessed.

The low hum of the television came from the living room. She glanced at the clock again and sighed. It was almost seven. There was no time now for a leisurely phone catch up with her friend. Besides, with the twins not quite two, Kate probably wouldn't appreciate an early morning call.

Throwing off the bedclothes, Cally stood. Though it was Tuesday, one of her days off, she still had to drive Jack to school. It was too bad that what she felt like doing was turning her back on the day and going back to sleep.

In between tossing and turning about her finances, she'd dreamed of a tall, blond stranger with melting chocolate eyes. A feeling of safety and security emanated from him and had drawn her inexorably closer. Just as she'd started to move toward him, the burglar had sped past her in a dark blue car and she'd been forced to jump away or risk being hit.

She'd woken with her heart pounding and the sheets tangled around her legs. The familiar sound of the early morning trains rattling along the steel lines in the distance had brought her slowly back to reality.

It was no surprise that the nightmares had started right after the home invasion. It wouldn't have been so bad if they'd caught the man, but despite front page headlines, countless police hours and a decent shoe impression left in the dirt outside her back door, the perpetrator hadn't been identified. He was still out there and Cally was more than worried he might return. It wasn't any wonder she couldn't get a decent night's sleep.

"Mom, are you awake? I think we're out of Rice Bubbles." Jack's voice drifted to her from the direction of the kitchen.

"You'll have to eat Weet-Bix." She sighed. Her choice of Weet-Bix over Rice Bubbles in last week's grocery shop had been a purely financial decision. She braced herself for a whine or complaint, but there was nothing.

He was such a good boy, most of the time. It certainly hadn't been easy raising him on her own and if she hadn't had Aunt Mary's love and support, she was sure he wouldn't have turned out as normal and grounded as he was.

It worried her that he didn't have any significant male influence in his life. With no father, grandfather or even an uncle in the picture, he rarely came into contact with men. Her aunt hadn't considered it a problem when Cally had raised the subject with her. Jack had been five at the time and had asked Cally if he could play dress-ups in her closet.

"You worry too much about that boy," Aunt Mary had replied. "Things don't always turn out good for kids just because they have a Mom *and* a Dad. Or bad if they only have one."

Cally, of all people, knew how true that was. But recently, her concern for Jack had intruded on her thoughts again, right when she had so many other issues vying to send her stress levels through the roof. With the money problems and her fears about the stalker in a dark-blue Toyota, she didn't need to be weighed down by renewed feelings of guilt that she'd failed her son by not providing him with a positive male role model before he like…left home.

Unbidden, the broad shoulders and long lean body of Andy Warwick filtered into her consciousness. It was much too early to trust him, but at the thought of his George Clooney eyes, heat spread through her limbs, leaving them heavy and limp. It had been a long time since she'd allowed herself any sort of sexual feelings. Ten years ago, she'd had a new baby to take care of and her social life had been nonexistent. That was exactly how she'd wanted it. After her experience with Stewart Brady, she'd vowed to steer clear of men for the rest of her life.

She'd been sixteen when Jack was born and "the rest of her life" hadn't quite felt like the lengthy period of time she now knew (and hoped) it would be. At the ripe old age of twenty-six, she had a little more perspective on life and what she wanted from it, and if she were truly honest with herself, she'd admit over the last few years, she'd been lonely for male company.

When Jack was younger, it had been impossible for her to contemplate devoting time to her own life. Later, when her aunt's health had deteriorated, she'd spent every available spare moment at home by her aunt's side. But on days like today, when she had a little time to herself, the needs she'd denied for over a decade were less easily suppressed. She didn't know if she'd ever have the courage to act on them—things hadn't turned out so well the last time she'd given in to her feelings—but they were there, just the same.

Not that she'd ever regretted keeping Jack—he was the only good to come from the entire awful episode—but the pain and heartbreak and countless nights crying herself to sleep over the cold abandonment by everyone she thought loved her had taken some getting over.

Irritated with the direction of her thoughts, she pulled her nightgown over her head and tossed it onto her bed, intent on dressing for the day. She had more important things to worry about than her sex life—or lack thereof.

Catching sight of her body in the full length mirror affixed to the back of her door, she turned side-on and sucked in her stomach, pleased to see it was still almost-flat and her breasts were high and full, despite her advancing years. She grinned. Twenty-six wasn't old—but it wasn't exactly young, either.

"Mom, do you need to use the bathroom? I want to brush my teeth."

She jumped guiltily at the sound of Jack's voice on the other side of the door, suddenly feeling like she'd been caught doing something wrong. Hastily pulling underwear from her drawer, she called back to him. "That's fine, sweetheart. You go ahead. I'll be out in a minute."

Selecting a worn pair of denim cut-off shorts, she teamed them with a faded yellow T-shirt that had seen more washes than she cared to remember. Like everything else, her wardrobe had been sadly neglected as she'd struggled to make ends meet. Every now and then, she wondered whether she'd be better off selling and moving back to Armidale—or even to her hometown of Watervale. With Kate now living there with Riley and their twins, perhaps things would be different?

As quickly as the thought entered her head, she banished it. Straightening her spine, she firmed up her resolve. No, she wasn't going back. There were too many memories. The country towns held some of the best memories of her life, but they also held the worst. Besides, her father still lived in Watervale and she'd be damned before she'd risk running into him again.

With a grimace, Cally forced the melancholy aside. She didn't have the luxury to waste time on memories. If she didn't hurry, Jack would be late for school. With a small wistful sigh, she opened her bedroom door and headed toward the kitchen.

———

Cally turned onto the Pacific Highway, her thoughts still on Jack. He'd given her a cheery wave on his way into the schoolyard and she'd breathed a quiet sigh of relief that, despite her concerns, he appeared to be like any other normal, well-adjusted ten-year-old.

Spying her driveway up ahead, she eased off the accelerator and flicked on her indicator to make the turn. Beyond, she saw a dark blue sedan parked a few yards from her driveway. Fingers of fear clutched at her belly. She picked up speed and took the turn faster than was safe. A minute later, she skidded to a halt outside her house.

Scrabbling with the seatbelt, she leaped out of the car and tore across the yard. Her breath came fast. She reached the house and fumbled with her keys. At last, the lock turned and she slammed the back door closed behind her and slid the deadbolt home.

She made her way to the front of the house with the blood still thundering in her ears. Taking a deep breath, she pulled the heavy damask curtain aside a couple of inches so she could peek out the window.

The view afforded her a glimpse of the main road, about fifty yards away. Twisting to the left, she peered through the shrubbery and made out the car parked at the curb. It was the same as the one that had been following her. The figure of a man sat behind the wheel.

Her stomach dropped. Panic threatened. She had to call the police. Dropping the curtain back in place, she strode across the living room to the telephone and picked up the hand piece. She dialed the number on the card the detective had given her after attending the scene of the break-in. To her relief, he answered on the second ring.

"Detective Black, I'm so glad you answered." Cally drew in a breath in an effort to still her racing heart then quickly explained the reason for her call.

"I see," the detective replied. "And you've seen this car how many times before?"

"Um...at least twice parked in my street and I'm almost sure I saw it following me home on Friday."

"Almost sure?"

Cally bit her lip. She could hear the skepticism in the officer's voice. *What could she tell him?*

"It was definitely the same color and I think it was the same make. A Toyota."

"Did you get a license plate?"

"No, I'm sorry. I-I didn't get close enough. The road was busy. It was really only a few moments..."

Her excuses were met with silence. The detective eventually broke it.

"Is the vehicle you think you saw on Friday still parked outside your house?"

"Yes. At least, it was a few moments ago. I-I'll go and check. She crossed the room and eased back the curtain and saw it. Her pulse leaped. Dropping the curtain and stepping back, she spoke quickly into the phone. "It's still there."

"Okay, no problem. We'll send a car around. Everyone is out at the moment, but as soon as I can I'll have an officer swing by. Try not to worry. I'm sure it's not the man who broke into your home. He discovered there was nothing much of value the first time and he'd hardly be keeping watch in plain sight outside your house. But, we'll check it out. I promise you."

After thanking the detective, Cally ended the call. Her heart was still racing, but frustration and anger slowly replaced the fear.

Was she being ridiculous? Jumping to wild conclusions? The detective was right. If the burglar planned to return, it would be more likely in the dead of night, like the first time, not during the day when he could be seen. She couldn't even be certain it was the same car.

She shook her head with annoyance. It wasn't the man who'd invaded her home. It wasn't a stalker. It was probably someone who lived nearby or, more than likely, this whole I'm-being-stalked feeling was a product of her overactive imagination. It wasn't like there were men lining up to frighten her. Apart from the teachers at Jack's school and some of the parents of her third grade class, she didn't know anyone in Sydney.

In every movie she'd ever seen with the stalker theme, it turned out to be someone the victim knew. Like a crazed ex-husband, or something.

Her pulse hitched. Thoughts of Stewart Brady crowded her head, but she immediately dismissed them. It was ridiculous to think he would stalk her, after all these years. She hadn't seen him since that awful day outside the abortion clinic. He hadn't tried to contact her. As far as he knew, there was no reason to.

Irritation surged through her. She'd never been the nervous and edgy type and over the years, she'd only become tougher and more resilient. She didn't know what it was about this car that made her feel threatened. She ought to march straight up the driveway and confront the man and demand to know who he was and why he was following her.

If it was someone who happened to be innocently pulled over on the side of the road, she could live with that embarrassment. *If it wasn't...*

What if it *was* someone she knew or someone with sinister intentions? What would she do then? Her screams would never be heard over the constant roar of the traffic, and knowing her luck, no one would even notice if she were suddenly bundled up into the Toyota and spirited away.

It could be hours before anyone would realize she was missing. There was no guarantee what time Detective Black's officers would drive by and she couldn't be sure they'd even check on her if they discovered the blue car she'd complained about had moved on.

Jack would be the only person in the whole world who would be concerned when she didn't show up outside the school gates at three o'clock, and even then, he wouldn't panic right away.

Eventually the police would be called and someone

might make the connection with her earlier phone call—or maybe not. Jack would probably be taken to one of his friends' houses in the short term. She didn't know how he would cope if she wasn't there to say goodnight.

What if they *never* found her? What if Jack was put into a foster home, never to know the love of his mother again?

"Oh, for goodness sake! Would you stop already?" She shook her head in irritation, unable to believe how far she'd let her imagination run out of control. She was being ridiculous. From the time she'd been abandoned by those who loved her, she'd vowed never to allow anyone control over her life again. She was fiercely proud of the life she'd made for herself and her son and was even more proud that she'd done it largely on her own.

The terrifying moments after discovering an intruder had been in the house had left her more than a little jittery, particularly when the perpetrator was still at large, but as the detective had assured her, it was unlikely the man would make a second attempt in broad daylight.

What she needed was to get the license plate. That way, if she saw the car again, she'd be certain it was the same one; she'd have something concrete to take to the police. Decision made, she took a fortifying breath and squared her shoulders.

"Okay, let's get this sorted out, once and for all."

Not wanting her new-found courage to desert her, she quickly slid the deadbolt open and stepped through the back doorway. Striding up the dirt driveway, she caught glimpses of the car through the branches of the huge fig trees that grew on either side.

Her cottage had originally been built as a caretaker's residence for the main house which still stood about forty yards from her front door. Although the larger house was almost completely hidden by the veritable jungle of fig trees, ivy and all manner of other plants and shrubbery, when she'd first moved in she'd taken comfort from the fact there was another home not too far away.

As it turned out, the owners of the main house lived in

Singapore and were very rarely in residence. She could count on one hand the number of times she'd seen lights shining from its windows, yet according to the police, they were one of the few houses in her street that hadn't been burgled.

"So much for neighbors," she mumbled.

She continued along the driveway, past the silent mansion that stood in front of her cottage. The closer she came to the Pacific Highway, the harder her heart thumped. It was one thing to be brave in the safety of her home, when the strange vehicle was fifty yards away, but now, when she was so close she could almost read the license plate, her courage faltered.

Slowing her pace, she forced her feet forward until she was able to make out the figures. Too late, she realized she'd come out without a pen and a piece of paper and she gritted her teeth in frustration. Swallowing a groan, she did her best to commit the plate to memory.

"CHT 157, CHT 157, cat, hat, tat 157," she repeated, hoping she wouldn't forget it by the time she returned home. She was less than thirty feet away from the rear of the vehicle and could clearly make out the man's form in the driver's seat. His dark hair was cut short and she spied the collar of a white business shirt. A fair portion of his head was above the headrest.

The window was wound down and the man's arm rested on the door. His hand tapped to a beat she couldn't hear and she saw ear buds in his ears. His shirt sleeves were rolled up, exposing his arms. They were covered in a light scattering of dark hair.

The familiar silver Toyota badge on the back of the car boosted her confidence. At least she was right about the make of it. Gazing across the trunk, she caught the words "Camry" on the left hand side, right above the brake light.

With adrenaline still coursing through her veins, she ducked behind a sprawling jacaranda tree and debated about whether to confront him. It was the easiest way to get it sorted out, and hadn't that been her plan? She shouldn't have to rely on the police or waste time wishing there was a man in her life to do it for her. She was Cally Savage. If she wanted something done, she darn well did it herself. It had been that way for a decade.

Taking a deep breath, she thrust back her shoulders and moved out from behind the tree. With narrow-eyed purpose, she strode toward the vehicle.

The car's ignition turned over. She gaped in surprise and pulled up short. With a squeal of tires, the dark blue sedan pulled away from the curb and disappeared into the throng of traffic.

Cally blinked and her shoulders slumped, deflated. In a daze, she returned to the house. After hurriedly taking down the license plate number, she sank down onto one of the pine chairs at the kitchen table and let her pulse rate return to normal.

Her sleepless nights, coupled with her concerns about Jack, and now another curious appearance of the blue Toyota, overwhelmed her. All at once, she wanted to lay her head down on the table and have a good cry. It was times like this she really missed her friend Kate. They'd been as close as sisters when they were younger.

With a surge of determination, Cally pushed back her chair and strode to the phone. She dialed Kate's number from memory and smiled with relief when it was answered on the first ring.

"Hi, stranger. You must have been standing right by the phone."

"Cally! What a surprise! I thought you were Riley. Daisy's sick with the flu and I need to take her to the doctor. I'm waiting for Riley to call me and confirm he's on his way home. He's going to look after Rosie for me while I'm out. She hasn't caught it yet, thank goodness and I'm trying to keep her quarantined. The bugs that are going around at the moment... I can only imagine how many of them are floating around the doctor's waiting room."

Cally felt a stab of envy. *How good would it feel to have someone to love like Kate loved Riley; someone to rely on for little things that were so important?* She closed her eyes briefly and shook off her melancholy. It was only the culmination of so many stressful events that had her so out of sorts.

"Poor Daisy. I hope she's feeling better soon."

"I'm sure as soon as we get some antibiotics, she'll be as good as new. How have you been?"

Cally bit her lip. A few moments earlier, she'd been desperate to unload on her friend, but Kate had her own worries.

"I'm fine," she answered. "Busy at work, but otherwise good."

"How's Jack?"

She forced a laugh. "Growing faster by the day."

"What's the matter, Cally?"

Cally sighed. She'd never been able to put much past Kate. "I-I guess I just wanted to say hello. I-I've been feeling a little overwhelmed lately—what, with the break-in and stuff."

"Did they find out who did it?"

"No and it's beginning to freak me out. I-I keep seeing this car parked on the main road outside my house. Last week, I thought I saw it following me." Her breathing hitched. "I'm probably imagining it, but I can't help it. I-I'm scared."

Kate's voice filled with understanding. "Of course you're scared. Who wouldn't be? I'd be beside myself if my home was burgled and I lived alone with a young child. And I'm sure you're not imagining it. You've never been someone to exaggerate. Have you called the police?"

"Yes, they're looking into it."

Kate's sigh spoke volumes and Cally suppressed a grin. As the wife of a police officer, her friend knew better than most the demands on their time.

"How's the new job working out?" Kate asked.

Relieved to switch her focus, Cally smiled. "Well, I've finished the first week and they haven't fired me, so I guess that's a good start—and the extra income's a help."

"I wish you'd let me help you with that. I've told you how

well the gallery's going. I can spare the money, Cally."

Cally shook her head. "We've already been over this, Kate. I love you dearly for your kind offer, but I can't accept your money, even if it is a loan. At the moment I'm worried I… I might not be able to pay it back."

"It's only you who's determined to label it a loan, Cally. I'd be more than happy to give it to you."

"Yes, Kate and I'm grateful, but I need to do this on my own. It's important to me."

Kate groaned. "You and your damn independence."

"At least you aren't calling me proud and stubborn like the last time." Cally smiled at the thought of their last conversation.

"Well, it's not that I don't think it!"

"You've always been such a good friend. I really appreciate you being here for me."

"Anytime. It's not like you wouldn't do the same for me."

"You're right."

"How about advertising for a roommate? They could help share expenses and you'd have another adult in the house."

Cally had considered that before and now pondered the idea again. It quickly gained merit. "I think that might relieve the pressure, Kate. A roommate might be just what I need. "

"You could put up a notice at the police station. Who better to protect you then someone sworn to do just that? I could even ask Riley to put the word out amongst his colleagues, if you like."

"Kate, you're a genius! I've been so caught up with everything, I haven't seen the obvious. A police officer would be perfect! I'm cleaning again tomorrow night. I'll see if I can put up a notice then."

"The sooner the better," Kate agreed.

Sudden tears burned behind Cally's eyes. "Th-thank you," she stammered.

"Like I said; anytime," Kate replied, her voice thick with emotion. "And let me know if you need help from Riley. He'll be more than happy to assist you."

Cally cleared her throat. "Thank you, I will. Say hi to him for me and I hope Daisy's feeling better soon."

"Thanks. Let me know how it goes. And give Jack my love."

A few moments later, Cally ended the call. Her thoughts returned to Kate's suggestion, and hope and excitement sparked in her belly. A roommate would go a long way to solving her problems and a police officer would be even better. How much safer could she get than having a policeman in residence? Of course, she'd still proceed with caution. She wasn't stupid. Not everyone in a uniform could be trusted.

Fleeting images of smiling brown eyes and unruly blond hair flashed through her mind. The negotiator's ruggedly handsome face intruded on her thoughts. Andy's impressive physical presence had captured her attention the minute she walked into the squad room, but it was the warmth and humor that shone in his eyes and the way he'd taken the time to answer Jack's questions that had intrigued her. Not to mention the approving glances and the sexy grins he'd given her every now and then.

She frowned when she remembered his remark about Jack. *Had he meant to imply she was neglecting her son's needs, or had she overreacted?* Being a single mother, she was used to going on the defensive when she considered herself under attack. Had she misread his intention? He certainly appeared genuine when he'd apologized.

With a small sigh, she wandered into the kitchen and pulled a coffee cup out of the cupboard. She'd put up a notice the first opportunity she got and hope someone would take her up on it. Andy's smiling face blossomed once again in her mind and her heart skipped a beat. *Would he be interested?* Butterflies churned in her stomach at the thought of what might be the perfect solution.

CHAPTER 6

Stewart Brady listened to the Crown Prosecutor drone on about the victim's injuries and sighed aloud with impatience, not even bothering to hide his smirk. He wished the asshole had been smarter, and hadn't made that quip about the size of Stewart's biceps. If he'd had the brains to keep his mouth shut, Stewart would never have taken the barbell to him. The stupid prick had deserved it, fair and square.

The way the prosecutor would have it, Stewart had savagely beaten the victim to within an inch of his life and without any provocation. It was bullshit, that's what it was and he'd about had enough. Anger surged through him, made even worse by the knowledge he wasn't in a position to leave.

He glanced toward the two corrections officers who flanked him on either side of the dock. The tall, beefy pair would be hard to escape. Besides, who was he kidding? He'd never survive on the run. He'd lived all his life on his father's bank accounts. He'd never given thought to stashing any of it away. *Was it too late?*

With a sigh, he let the fleeting thoughts slide and reached into the pocket of his suit jacket. He pulled out the crumpled page of the newspaper he'd torn off the front cover, now dated more than a month ago. Smoothing out the folds, he stared at the woman and child.

Renewed anger surged through him. *He still couldn't*

believe she lied to him. She'd gone into the clinic. He'd watched her go inside from where he sat in the car and he'd waited more than an hour. He'd passed the time texting his mates and updating his Facebook status to single. When she'd finally exited the building, he'd taken her home. Before she stepped out of the car, he'd told her they were over.

Okay, so he hadn't actually asked her if she'd done it, but she'd been in there so long, it hadn't occurred to him that she hadn't gone through with it. He clenched his fists and was infuriated all over again that she hadn't said anything to him. So what if he hadn't wanted the kid at the time? It didn't give her the right to have it and keep it from him for *ten fucking years.*

Jack Savage, the newspaper said. She hadn't even given the boy Stewart's fucking name. Jack *Brady,* that's who he was. Jack Brady, his son.

He thought of his wife, Tiffany and his other son, Luke and then remembered them as he'd last seen them: Cold and gray and lifeless on matching stainless steel tables. He'd been asked to identify them at the morgue. A stab of familiar pain went through him at the memory. He couldn't believe they'd gone.

Okay, he may have told Tiff they were getting a divorce, but it didn't mean he wanted her dead. It may have made things a little easier, but he'd have paid her whatever she wanted if it meant his son hadn't died in the same accident...

He gritted his teeth and forced back the moan of pure anguish. *Lukie, poor little Lukie.* He'd always hated the dark. Now it surrounded him. It wasn't fucking right and it sure as hell wasn't fair.

Just like his discovery of the other bitch's deceit.

Renewed fury gushed through his veins. He had to find Cally Savage. She'd stolen his son. A son who was still breathing. A little older, but a son who could replace the one he'd lost. Steel determination surged through him. He'd find both of them and when he did, he'd make her pay. Of that, he had no doubt.

Nikki Simons stared at the white satin and lace wedding dress that mocked her from the rail inside her closet. The dress was all she'd ever dreamed of: perfect in its utter simplicity, with tiny, hand-sewn pearls. It had cost her most of two pay packets. She'd owned it for more than a month. She'd been so certain Andy would propose to her; that it was only a matter of time.

They'd been together for twelve months. Long enough to decide they were right for each other. They had so much in common and usually managed to have fun. Okay, so perhaps the sex hadn't been spectacular, but she'd done all she could. It wasn't her fault Andy wasn't into threesomes or that he didn't want to share.

She ought to be flattered he wanted her for himself and she had been, most of the time. Every now and then, she'd caught herself wishing he was different, more exciting, more willing to live it on the edge.

Still, at thirty-five she couldn't afford to be so picky. She was desperate to have children and her biological clock was winding down. He would have been perfect father material, despite her boredom with him in the bedroom. She'd seen the way he interacted with the children of their work colleagues. She'd seen the yearning on his face. On top of that, he was wealthy, too. *What more could she want?*

He'd never shared his childhood with her, but she'd sensed it hadn't been great. He'd said as much the night he'd broken up with her. She was still annoyed he wouldn't let her in. Twelve months of her life she'd given him and it had all been for naught. She was back where she started, single, old and afraid.

She didn't want to end up alone, dependent upon alcohol and friends to get her through the day. She had a good job and a shapely figure many female workmates envied. She was a good catch, dammit. It was a shame Andy Warwick hadn't seen it that way.

Recalling how he'd dumped her, in the back of a taxi, no less, her anger bubbled to the surface. She reached for the bottle of rum that stood on her nightstand and tilted it toward her throat. A mouthful, two and it was empty. She tossed it to the carpet in disgust. It only seemed like moments ago when she'd opened it. Her gaze returned to the wedding dress and fury and disappointment overwhelmed her.

She staggered to the chest of drawers that stood on the other side of her bedroom and wrenched open the top drawer. Her fingers glanced over a hairbrush, a compact, two lipsticks... She thrust them all aside. With her fingers working more frantically now, she at last gave a triumphant yelp. Taking an unsteady step backwards, she brandished a pair of large scissors in the air.

Turning on her heel, she stumbled to the closet and took hold of the wedding dress in her fist. With wild stabs, she attacked it, tearing and shredding the cloth. Moments later, the fog of rage cleared and she stared at the remains of the dress. It hung in tatters, destroyed beyond repair.

The scissors fell from her hand and she slowly dropped to the floor. Sobs tore through her in agonizing waves. She gasped and curled her legs up to her chest and rocked against the pain. *This was all because of Andy.* It was his fault she was in such a bad way. He should have tried harder to love her. He should never have tossed her aside. They were meant to be together. She had to make him see...

CHAPTER 7

Detective Superintendent Patrick Redding strode out of his office, his face grim. "He's back up there again, Andy."

"Excuse me?" Andy frowned and looked up from the pile of paperwork on his desk.

"Wayne Tucker, your jumper from last week. He's back up there," Redding replied.

"You're kidding?"

"I'm afraid not. I just took a call from the psychiatric unit of Royal North Shore Hospital. They discovered him missing about an hour ago. No one knows how he got out—or at least, no one's saying—but he's back up on a window ledge. This time it's the ninth floor of the Nurses' residence, about four hundred yards from the bed he'd been keeping warm in the psych unit."

Andy sucked in a breath. Adrenaline surged through him. He pushed his chair away from his desk and stood. Quickly and efficiently, he emptied his pockets of his wallet, cell phone and keys and prepared for what was to come. "Who's at the scene?"

"A couple of cars from St Leonards, a couple more from Artarmon. The State Protection Group's on its way. They want you to lead the team, seeing as Tucker knows you and you managed to talk him down last time."

"Yeah." Andy channeled his thoughts to the task ahead. He knew from other negotiators that a second attempt almost always spelled trouble. He strode toward the locker rooms. "Who's riding with me?"

"Craig Winters, Sandy Ashcroft and Hugh Power are already on their way. Tom Munro's waiting for you downstairs."

A little of the mounting pressure inside Andy subsided. Despite the fact he was only in his late thirties, Tom Munro was a veteran and had been the primary negotiator in more than a hundred high-risk situations. He'd won more than he'd lost and Andy was glad to have him by his side.

During his time at the North Sydney Police Station, Andy had come to know Tom and his family. His wife, Lily, was a primary school teacher and was as sweet and gracious as Andy fondly remembered his own primary school teachers were. Their two children, Cassie and Joe were cute, well-mannered teenagers. The Munro clan was the epitome of a wholesome Aussie family and Andy couldn't help the stab of longing that went through him whenever he thought of them.

He pushed the thoughts aside. Now wasn't the time to wish things were different. A man's life was at stake and Andy was responsible for saving him. Depositing his phone and other personal items on the shelf, he stripped down to his underwear and pulled on the navy SPG overalls he kept in his locker.

One of the first things he'd learned in his training was how to ensure there was nothing on his person that could distract the jumper and possibly cause a disastrous ending. A flash of sunlight on a watch face or the sudden ringing of a cell phone could mean the difference between life and death. It was an understatement to say the people he dealt with were not exactly stable.

Threading his gun belt through the loops on his overalls, he checked that his sidearm was primed and loaded. Not that he'd be using it at the scene. It was standard operating procedure to hand in his gun to the supervisor at the scene. It was the intention of the negotiator to build a rapport with the subject and gain their trust. A sidearm, in full view of the subject, tended to jeopardize those kinds of efforts.

Banging the metal door of his locker shut, he made his way out to the squad room. Giving Redding a somber wave, he headed downstairs to meet Tom.

Andy saw the mob of people gathered around the front of the Nurses' residence and grimaced. He counted half a dozen uniforms doing their best to keep the crowd at bay, but the officers seemed to be losing the battle as curious onlookers pushed closer and closer, seeking a better view of the scene unfolding above them.

He didn't know what it was about events like this that turned ordinary people into macabre spectators, where they seemed to get some sort of almost sick excitement by watching the unfolding drama. It never failed to stir his anger. A man's life was in danger. It wasn't a scene from a trashy Hollywood movie. It was real. One wrong move, one wrong word and it could all be over.

"Andy, over here." Tom beckoned him toward a uniformed officer. Stepping over the blue-and-white police tape that had been used to cordon off the area, he walked to where Tom and the other three negotiators had halted at the front of the building.

"Andy, this is Senior Sergeant Harry Matthews. He's stationed at St Leonards. Harry was the first on the scene."

The sergeant's gray hair, weathered face and calm air of experience immediately gave Andy confidence. He stuck out his hand in greeting. "Pleased to meet you."

"Likewise. I understand you managed to keep our man from jumping last week. I'm glad you're here."

Andy ducked his head in embarrassment. "Thanks." Clearing his throat, he turned to the business at hand. "What can you tell me, Sergeant?"

"Harry. Call me Harry, please."

Andy acknowledged the request with a nod. "How long's he been up there?"

"About half an hour or so, I think. The hospital staff noticed he was missing when he didn't show up in the breakfast room. They searched the ward for a while and when they couldn't find him, they called security." He grimaced. "Someone spotted him up here."

Tom pursed his lips. "Has anyone been up there to talk to him?"

"Not as far as I know. Certainly not since I arrived. I wanted to wait for you guys."

Andy shielded his gaze from the sun and looked toward the ninth floor. "You did the right thing. It was hard enough to talk him down last time. I'm glad you didn't send a novice up there." He turned back to Harry. "Does anyone know what set him off this morning?"

"Nothing that anyone's saying, but I read in the hospital notes he took a phone call last night from his wife."

"You've seen the notes?" Tom asked.

"Yeah, for last night, anyway. I asked security to get me a copy. I have them right here, if you want to take a look." Reaching into his back pocket, he pulled out a couple of sheets of paper and unfolded them.

Andy indicated the hospital notes. "Anything else in there we need to know?"

"Probably not. The only thing of interest was the call from the wife. The rest is just the usual medical jargon. He had an uneventful day and a pretty quiet night, apparently."

Andy grimaced. "Apparently." He turned back to face the building. "Do we know the layout inside? Which room he's near?"

"According to the switchboard operator who mans the phones for the residents, there are elevators that stop at each floor. After exiting the elevator, you enter the floor via a set of doors that lead into a common room situated in the center of the building. The rooms branch off from there, down separate corridors that run the length of the building."

Andy nodded, frowning in concentration. With another

brisk nod, he encompassed Tom, Craig, Sandy and Hugh in his gaze. "Okay, I'm going up."

"We'll be right behind you."

Andy made his way into the building and over to the bank of elevators. He thought of the man perched precariously on a window ledge nine floors above him. The familiar rush of adrenaline flooded through him. His stomach tightened with nerves and he sent a silent prayer heavenward that he'd be able to make Wayne Tucker see that his life was still worth living.

The elevator chimed as it reached the ninth floor and Andy waited for the doors to slide open. He stepped into the deserted foyer and noticed a couple of young officers guarding the doors that provided entry to the floor. When they spotted him, they visibly relaxed, almost as if their jobs were done now that he'd arrived. He wished he had as much confidence in himself and his abilities as the young officers apparently did.

One of them stepped forward and greeted him. His badge identified him as Constable Reynolds.

"Boy, are we glad to see you, Detective Senior Sergeant Warwick."

"Has anyone else been up here?"

The second officer shook his head vigorously. "No, sir, there's been no one. Ever since Senior Sergeant Matthews ordered us up here, we've made sure no one's entered this floor."

"Good job, boys." Andy compressed his lips and looked around. "Where is he?"

Reynolds swallowed and pointed an unsteady finger in the direction of the closed doors. Behind it, was the common room.

"He... He's through there."

Andy made his way quietly through the doorway and into the common room, battling feelings of déjà vu. The room was empty—eerily so for seven-thirty in the morning. It should have been a hub of activity as nurses came home from night duty and others came in for breakfast.

The room was sparsely furnished with a single worn sofa in a dull olive color and an old television set. A small kitchenette was off to his left, containing a hotplate, fridge and a microwave—everything people with no time or inclination to cook extravagant meals required. He knew the scene too well.

Moving further into the room, he spied the dark shape of Wayne Tucker outside the open window and his body stilled. A faint breeze drifted in, cooling the sweat which had formed on his lip—a combination of the already-warm February morning and the usual rush of nerves he experienced at the beginning of any negotiation. It was funny how most of those nerves disappeared as soon as he made contact. He didn't know why, but he was grateful they did, because it allowed him to concentrate all his energy on talking to the people who needed his help. And right now, Wayne Tucker needed some serious help.

The accountant stood on the very edge of the window ledge, no more than two feet in width. There was nothing to hang on to, save the rough brick wall of the building. The slightest movement of his body could unbalance him and send him falling to his death.

Andy forced air through his lungs in an effort to slow his pulse. With methodical precision, he pulled on the safety harness. Out of the corner of his eye, he saw Tom come into the room, keeping low, out of sight of the window.

In silence, he handed his partner the end of the rope that was attached to his safety harness and waited for him to secure it around a concrete pillar not far away. With a deep breath, Andy moved closer to the window and called softly to the man on the ledge.

"Wayne, can you hear me? It's Andy. Remember, from last Friday?"

He held his breath and willed the man to answer. Very occasionally, a negotiator was unable to get any dialogue started and the whole sad episode was over before it began. The odds of succeeding rose dramatically if a conversation commenced. He continued to pray silently while he waited for the man to speak.

"Don't come any closer!" Wayne Tucker's voice trembled.

"It's okay, mate. Take it easy. I'm not going to come any closer. I'm going to stand right here. Is that all right?"

The man nodded hesitantly. Hope bloomed in Andy's chest. At least Tucker was responding to questions. It was a good start.

"What are you doing out here, Wayne? I thought we sorted this out last week?"

"I should have done it then and got it over with. What good did another few days make? It hasn't changed anything. I've still lost everything."

"What about your wife, Wayne? Cheryl, isn't it? She'll be devastated if you jump."

Wayne turned slightly and his foot moved precariously close to the edge. He wobbled and Andy's heart stopped. Blood thundered in his ears, momentarily blocking out sound. Tucker regained his balance and Andy released his breath.

His relief was short lived. Tucker turned toward him, anger and pain ravaging his face.

"Cheryl! Huh! She won't give a damn! She rang last night to tell me she's leaving and she's taking the kids with her."

Andy's heart sank and all of a sudden, his nerves were back. Many a time he'd been able to convince a jumper to give it up by emphasizing the loss and pain their families would experience if they were no longer around. That option had just been totaled, at least where his wife was concerned.

He floundered for something to say and called on everything he'd learned. Pressure built behind his eyes and sweat rolled down his forehead. He spied Tom out of the corner of his eye, holding up a piece of paper with the word "kids" on it. Slowly and carefully, Andy stepped closer to the window and spoke once again.

"I'm really sorry to hear that, Wayne, but you still have

your kids. Marcus and Sophie, isn't it? They're as much yours as they are hers. Do you really want them to grow up and not know you or anything about you? If you're not around, the only person left to tell them about you is Cheryl. Is that what you want?"

Wayne took an unsteady step toward him, his face purpling with rage. He stabbed a trembling finger in Andy's direction.

"What I *want*," he ground out, his eyes wild and unfocused, "is for you to shut the fuck up. *Do you understand?*"

Andy forced himself to remain calm. With steel-like control, he kept his face impassive and waited Wayne out. A few minutes later, the anger drained out of Tucker and his body went slack. He wobbled on the narrow ledge.

Bending low, in one quick movement, Andy vaulted over the window frame and stood on the ledge next to Tucker. The broken man hunched over as if in pain, seemingly unaware of Andy's proximity. With his head bowed low, Tucker crouched on the narrow strip of concrete that was all that remained between him and certain death.

For long moments, they remained immobile. The heat from the eastern sun swelled. Andy's arm inched upwards to wipe the sweat out of his eyes and he was relieved when Tucker didn't notice. A high-pitched keening started from the man crouched close beside him, sending shivers down Andy's spine.

Gradually, the noise diminished to a sad whimper and Andy tried once again to engage Tucker in conversation.

"Tell me about Marcus and Sophie, Wayne. I bet they love playing football with you, right? I loved playing football with my dad when I was a kid." Andy forced the lie past his lips.

Tucker looked up at him and then lowered his gaze. "Yeah, they like to play football. Marcus has a really good boot on him, for a kid of his age. He was the top goal scorer last season. Sophie's more into netball, but she comes to the park with us every now and then."

Andy nodded encouragingly, feeling more and more relieved. "It sounds like Marcus might be good enough to play for Australia one day. You want to be around for that, don't you, Wayne? How cool would it be to know you're the father of one of those players?"

For a long moment, he didn't think Tucker was going to answer. Slowly, inexorably, the man lifted his head again and stared at him. Tucker's eyes were red and snot ran from his nose, but it was the bleak look of utter despair in his eyes that made Andy turn cold.

"Marcus won't want anyone to know about me, once he finds out what I've done. I've lost everything; the house, the car...the lot. I wanted to give them a better life. Instead, it's all gone. I've been stupid, so, so stupid and now Cheryl left and she's taken the kids." Wayne's voice broke, hoarse with pain and desolation.

Andy's heart pounded. With a sudden sense of urgency, he reached out a hand toward the broken man, urging him to take hold of it. Tucker eyed Andy's outstretched hand in silence. Andy could almost hear the war of words going on inside the man's head.

Take it, take it, take it... The words reverberated in Andy's head, above the thudding of his heart.

Tucker sighed heavily, a sigh of surrender. Andy half-relaxed against the wall and prepared to pull the man to safety.

"What the fuck. I'm out of here." With that, Wayne Tucker threw himself off the ledge.

Andy screamed Tucker's name, throwing himself reflexively toward the man. Losing his footing, he swung off the ledge, free falling until the rope hooked to his safety harness pulled him up short.

Tucker's body hit the concrete below and landed with a sickening thud. Pain sheared through Andy until he could barely breathe. Screams from the onlookers added to the madness. Grappling with the rope, he was hauled back onto the narrow ledge by his men. He pulled himself back through the window and collapsed onto the floor of the common room.

He'd failed… In Wayne Tucker's hour of need, he'd failed.

With his head in his hands, Andy let out a howl of pain. His failure and the shock of watching a man jump to his death sent white-hot shards of agony through his body. In some small, saner part of his mind, he knew it had been Tucker's decision, but right now, he was the one responsible for the man who lay dead and broken on the pavement.

Unable to stop himself, he replayed their conversation over and over before the final, fateful moment.

Where had he lost him? What had he done wrong?

"Stop it, Andy. Stop it right now." Tom's voice was sure and firm.

Andy's eyes were on fire. There was a dull roaring in his ears. He raised his head and stared up at Tom, who had hunkered down beside him.

"I know what you're doing. I've been there, too. Let it go, mate. Let it go. It wasn't your fault. Let it go."

Anger and despair coursed through him and he turned on his partner and yelled. "Of course it was my fucking fault! I was the one out there with him. I was the one responsible for getting him down. And now he's dead. *Dead!* Did you hear me? How is that not my fault?"

Tom's gaze remained steady on his. "Andy, don't do this. I know how hard it is to accept—believe me, I know even better than you, but it's not your fault."

"But—"

"Listen to me!" Tom shouted, his face only inches away. "You know I know what I'm talking about. You're not the only negotiator to lose one." He sucked in a breath and made an obvious attempt to reign in his emotions. Andy stared hard at the floor.

"You're not the first one of us to lose one, Andy," he repeated, his voice now lower and more controlled. "And unfortunately, you won't be the last. These people are unstable and just plain sick, but they *need* you, Andy. They need you to care about helping them. They need you to believe that what you do matters…because it does. It always does. *Every. Single. Time.*"

Andy wanted to block his ears, to shut out Tom's words of wisdom, but Tom was only trying to help him and deep down inside, he appreciated his partner's efforts.

"Every time you go into a negotiation, Andy, it matters. Sometimes we fail, but most times we win and those are the times we have to focus on. Not on those we lose, but on the ones we help save."

Andy dragged his gaze up to Tom's who shook his head sadly. "Wayne Tucker didn't want to be saved, Andy. It's as simple as that. You saved his life a few days ago, but he didn't value it like you did. He gave up, Andy. *He* gave up. You did all you could."

"But it wasn't enough." Andy's voice was raw with emotion. He shook his head slowly back and forth. "It wasn't *enough*."

With a sigh, Tom stood and held out his hand and Andy reluctantly came to his feet. He leaned awkwardly on the other man for support. His body was numb, his limbs were leaden and his feet just plain wouldn't move.

"It's okay, mate. Let's rest here awhile."

Forcing deep breaths into his lungs, Andy concentrated on holding onto the air for as long as he could. What Tom said was true, but right here, right now, the truth of his words didn't seem to make much difference. The heavy burden of failure weighed him down. His thoughts turned to Tucker's wife and children and a renewed shard of pain seared through him. There were no winners here.

It took a long time for Andy's heart rate to return to normal. He turned to Tom and offered him a sad smile. "Thanks, mate. I owe you one."

"No, Andy, you don't. It'll happen to me again one day and I know I can rely on you to be there for me." Tom stared hard at him. "It doesn't matter how many times it happens, it always feels the same. It's human nature to remember our failures. It's as if the successes have never happened. I know mate, I've been there." He turned to include Craig and Sandy and Hugh. "We all have."

Tom gripped him tightly by the arms. "I'm not going to tell

you not to think about it, because that's plain impossible and the first time you lose someone is always the hardest, but try to remember the successes, too."

Andy barely inclined his head. Tom's gaze burned into his, fierce with emotion. "All I ask, Andy, is that every now and then, you remember the ones you've saved."

———

Back at the station, showered and changed and feeling slightly more in control, Andy glanced at his watch for what seemed like the hundredth time. It was nearly seven. The squad room was deserted. He should have been gone long ago. The report on Wayne Tucker sat half completed on the screen in front of him.

She was late.

The sound of a vacuum cleaner starting in the adjoining room brought with it a surge of anticipation. This time, the noise didn't bring forth bad memories. With the Tucker catastrophe fresh in his mind, he hadn't thought about the beautiful cleaner all day, but now that night had claimed the sky and the passing hours had dulled a little of the memories of his day, his nerves were fairly jumping.

The last time he'd seen her, he'd left the station feeling out of sorts. It had upset him that he'd offended her. He'd spent more than one restless night since dreaming about vivid blue eyes and long tanned legs and a mouth that had been made to be kissed. Each time, he'd awoken feeling tense and dissatisfied.

The outer door to the squad room opened and the noise of the vacuum cleaner got louder. His heart picked up its pace. In an effort to appear casual, he hurriedly leaned back in his chair and put his boots up on his desk. Sensing a presence behind him, he swiveled in his seat and braced himself for the dramatic impact of her eyes.

The heavy figure and drawn face of a woman well past her prime stood before him. His boots hit the floor with a soft thud and his mouth fell open. The woman's coarse black hair was short and frizzy. A huge shapeless dress draped her rather large body. Her sharp black eyes narrowed on him with suspicion.

"Somethin' the matter?"

Her voice was a full octave lower than most of the men in his squad. He closed his gaping mouth and tried and failed to form words.

"Whatcha lookin' at? I got work to do."

"Um, I was just wondering… What happened to Cally?" The woman gave him a blank look. He tried again. "Cally Savage, the girl who was here on Friday?"

"Fridee? That's not my day. I do Tuesdees and Thursdees. Dunno who works Fridees. Used to be Maureen Smith did Mondees, Wednesdees and Fridees, but her arthritis is playin' up again. I dunno who they got workin' for 'em now."

He absorbed this information slowly, disappointment flooding through him. *Today was Tuesday.* He'd had the last two days off. He'd missed her yesterday. Now he had to wait another twenty-four hours to see her again.

It was a shitty end to what had turned out to be a wholly shitty day.

CHAPTER 8

"Come *on*, Jack, we're going to be late for school."

Cally sighed in frustration and picked up her car keys and handbag while she waited for her son to finish brushing his teeth. She'd spent another long night tossing and turning and was tired and irritable. Her precarious financial position, coupled with her stress over the home invasion and her disquiet about the possible stalker meant that sleep continued to elude her.

The fact the car had sped off just as she'd drawn near appeared sinister. Then again, maybe it was merely a coincidence that when she'd finally built up the courage to approach him, the man had chosen that same moment to leave. She couldn't quite explain away the speed of his departure, and the questions had chased themselves around in her mind for the best part of the night until, by morning, she no longer knew what to think.

She sighed again. The thought of having a roommate was more and more appealing. It would go a long way toward allaying her fears. Then there was the money issue. She could no longer deny she was in dire straits. A roommate would contribute to the cost of the utilities and the rent she could charge would go somewhere toward keeping her head above water.

"Mom, I'm ready." Jack materialized in front of her. "*Mom, I said I'm ready!*"

Cally blinked her eyes rapidly and her thoughts scattered

like dandelion seeds in the breeze. "Okay, okay. I'm coming. Go and get into the car."

Hurrying into the bathroom to make a final check on her appearance, she smoothed down the short skirt of her floral summer dress and leaned in close to examine the dark circles under her eyes. She smudged on a little concealer, rinsed her hands and strode back toward the kitchen, sending a wistful look at her bed as she passed by.

She had at least six hours of teaching twenty-four third graders and then another couple of hours of cleaning before she'd be anywhere close to returning to its inviting comfort. Swallowing a sigh, she lifted her head and squared her shoulders. Pulling the door closed behind her, she made sure the deadlock caught before making her way across the back yard to her car.

———

Andy saved the document he had open on his screen and shut down his computer. He still had reports to complete, but right now he couldn't concentrate on anything but the clock. It was nearly six-thirty. Night was closing in and apart from the officers on night shift, the station was almost deserted. The administration staff had left an hour ago and the phones had fallen mostly silent.

Redding was still in his office and every now and then, Andy caught the low murmur of his voice on the phone. Tom was also rostered on with him for the night and had stopped by Andy's desk earlier to ask him how he was getting on. They both knew he wasn't being entirely honest when he assured Tom he was fine.

Tom invited him over for dinner later in the week and Andy thanked him and agreed to think about it, appreciating his friend's thoughtfulness.

In an effort to forestall memories of yesterday's tragedy, Andy had spent most of the last night encouraging lurid fantasies of Cally. Although it had helped to keep him from dwelling on thoughts of Wayne Tucker, he'd woken feeling tense and irritable and with a hard-on he hadn't been able to fully assuage. Now his heart pounded in anticipation that he might soon get to see her again.

He couldn't remember ever feeling so excited about a woman. He'd never been the type to go out trolling for girls. There had only been a handful of women in his life over the years and those few had been special to him, even Nikki.

It was just that none of them had been *the one*. Never before had his heart thumped so hard it felt like it was going to bounce right out of his chest merely at the thought of seeing the woman. Never before had he felt so disappointed when she hadn't appeared. Last night, he'd been gutted when he'd realized it was Cally's night off.

At the time, he'd convinced himself his reaction had been part of the aftershock of his tragic afternoon with Tucker, but in the early hours of the morning, he'd started to give credence to the cabbie's words from nearly a week ago.

Maybe there was such a thing as love at first sight? Will hadn't scoffed at the idea. That, in itself, was something. Not that Andy was even thinking along the lines of love. Hell, he barely knew the woman. But, despite the emotional upheaval he'd experienced over the loss of Tucker, he couldn't deny his mind kept returning to Cally, again and again. It had been almost forty-eight hours ago to the minute since he'd seen her, he thought, glancing at his watch again. She should be walking through the door right about...now.

As if on cue, the door opened and Jack bounced into the squad room. Andy's heart jumped at the sight of him and his mouth went dry. The boy's arrival meant his mother was surely close by.

Jack looked around the room. He spied Andy at his desk and his eyes lit up in recognition. A warm feeling spread through Andy at the pleasure on the boy's face.

"Andy, you're here!" Jack rushed over to him, his face breaking into a grin.

"Hey, Jack. Good to see you again. What've you been up to, buddy?"

"Nothing much. Just the usual; school and stuff."

"School's pretty important, you know. What grade are you in?"

"Four."

"Wow, grade four. That must mean you're about...ten?"

"Good guess. I turned ten on January eighth."

"I'm on August eighth. How's that for coincidence? We're nearly twins." He ruffled Jack's tousled, blond hair.

The boy grinned, appearing to enjoy the attention. Andy reached for another chair. "Here, take a seat."

"Thanks." Jack grinned again and Andy's heart took another blow. His thoughts glanced off Wayne Tucker and his children who would never see their father again. He forced the darkness away and concentrated on the carefree boy beside him.

Such innocence, as if nothing bad had ever happened to him.

He could only imagine how *he'd* appeared to adults at the same age. By then he'd learned the hard way it was safer to be seen and not heard...

He forced those memories aside and glanced toward the door of the squad room, but it remained stubbornly closed. *What if she hadn't come?* He quickly squelched the irrational though and made sure his voice remained casual. "Where's your mom?"

Jack nodded toward a second door which led off the squad room. Two interview rooms were on the left and three offices were on the right that eventually led to a utility room at the far end of the corridor.

"She's back there, cleaning the offices."

Just like that, Andy's nerves resurfaced. His pulse picked up speed and he swallowed convulsively.

"Are you okay, Andy? You look a bit strange."

Andy knew his smile was strained. For a young kid, the boy was way too observant. Not good when you were trying to appear cool, calm and unaffected.

How could a woman he'd only just met evoke such a strong reaction? He was more nervous now than he was right before he engaged in a negotiation. That *definitely* made no sense.

Before he could examine that thought any closer, the door leading to the interview rooms opened and Cally walked in lugging a vacuum cleaner behind her. She caught sight of him across the room and her eyes widened in surprise.

"Oh, hi. I-I didn't realize you were here." A charming blush suffused her cheeks. "Um, I can come back later—"

"*No!*" Andy checked himself and modified his tone. "I mean, please, go ahead." She walked toward the plug on the far side of the room. He couldn't take his eyes off her.

She wore a faded orange T-shirt and a pair of white cotton shorts. His gaze skimmed over shapely hips and a pert bottom. She looked as inviting as the beach outside his condominium window on a hot summer day. Even more of a blessing was that she'd distracted him from memories usually dredged up by the sound of the vacuum cleaner. For that alone, he could love her forever.

Cally felt his gaze all the way across the room and it made her even more nervous. She fumbled with the plug of the power cord and tried a second time to fit it into the socket. Her hand shook, making her fingers clumsy. It seemed to take forever to get the thing connected. She breathed a sigh of relief when the metal prongs finally slipped into the holes.

Keeping her back to him, she switched on the vacuum cleaner with her foot, thankful for the noise which would save her from having to converse any further with the hunky police officer who'd filled her restless dreams.

Despite the chaotic emotions he stirred up inside her, finding him at the station was somewhat of a relief. Earlier that day, she'd drawn up a poster requesting a roommate. The principal had agreed to let her pin one on the staff noticeboard at her school and she was hoping to ask Andy if she could do the same at the station.

She lifted her gaze and glanced in his direction and was disappointed to find his chair was empty. She looked around the room, but he wasn't there. He'd disappeared and so had Jack.

She frowned a little, not sure if she was comfortable with her son being alone with Andy. He appeared honest and genuine, but she barely knew him. Her instinctive reaction was to trust him, but she'd been wrong on that score before. She only had to think of Stewart Brady to be reminded of that.

Then she caught the sound of Jack's excited chatter over the dull thrum of the vacuum cleaner and gave a stern shake of her head. Of course Andy hadn't done anything untoward to her son. She had to learn not be quite so mistrustful. Not everyone set out to lie and deceive.

The two of them appeared in the doorway of the squad room and headed toward Andy's desk. Her son trotted by Andy's side, his animated face tilted backwards as he spoke. Andy leaned down so he could hear Jack over the noise. Her heart tightened at the tender scene. With their thick mops of unruly, blond hair, they looked enough alike it could be assumed they were father and son. Cally switched off the vacuum cleaner and moved closer. In the deafening silence her nerves returned full force.

"Hi." Andy grinned at her, looking sexier than a man had a right to look, dressed in his work clothes.

His navy-blue police shirt was rolled up at the sleeves and was teamed with a pair of khaki drill pants. The shirt exposed the muscular shape of his forearms and a nice expanse of tanned skin that was covered in a sprinkling of golden hair. Becoming aware that she was staring, she blushed and took a few steps backwards. She came up hard against another desk.

"Ouch!" Her cheap, synthetic sandals slipped on the

carpet. Losing her balance, she landed on the floor, colliding heavily with a corner of the metal desk on her way down. Papers, books and pens scattered beneath her.

Gingerly rubbing her hip, she cursed the bargain-basement footwear. She should have worn the sensible lace-up shoes like she'd intended. It was only that the weather was so hot and her vanity had gotten the better of her. She'd opted for the cute, but oh-so-impractical sandals, a decision she now sorely regretted.

Warm fingers encircled her bare upper arm and helped her upright herself. She stared into Andy's eyes and her pulse beat madly in her neck. Mesmerized, she couldn't look away.

"Are you okay, Cally?" Her name sounded almost like an endearment on his lips. His eyes were full of concern.

He was holding her way too close. She stumbled backward, throwing a quick glance over her shoulder to ensure there were no other obstacles in her way.

"I'm fine; I'm fine." Embarrassment flared hotly across her cheeks. Averting her face, she lurched in the direction of the vacuum cleaner, hoping to take solace in its noise.

"Mom, are you sure you're all right?"

Jack's voice reached her just as she was about to flick the switch. She was forced to halt her retreat and face him—which also meant facing Andy.

She gave her son a reassuring smile. "I'm fine, Jack, honestly. I'm so embarrassed I'd be happy if the floor opened up and swallowed me, but yes, sweetheart, I'm otherwise unharmed."

She risked a glance at Andy and reluctantly returned the grin that lit up his face. *So what if she'd just humiliated herself in front of the most gorgeous man she'd ever come across? She'd get over it.* In about a hundred years.

His eyes sparkled with humor. "Why don't you take a break and sit down for a few minutes?"

Knowing the bruise now forming on her hip was probably no worse than the dent to her pride, she sighed in defeat and accepted the chair he held out for her. He folded his long body into his seat and pulled his chair close. *Very close.* Butterflies jumped in her stomach.

His gaze remained steady on hers. "It's good to see you again."

Cally swallowed her nerves. *Please, God. Please don't turn me into a blithering idiot.* It's absolutely not right the first guy I have even the remotest interest in makes me so tongue-tied I'm almost mute. Whatever will he think of me?

"Um, thank you. It-It's nice to see you again, too." She bit her lip and inwardly grimaced at the banality of her reply.

"How have you been?" he asked, not seeming to notice her discomfort.

She nodded. "Good. Busy. I've been at work today and now I'm cleaning and—"

"What else do you do?" His eyes were alight with curiosity.

"I'm...I'm a primary school teacher. That's my day job." She lifted her chin, awaiting his reaction.

"A school teacher?" His expression reflected his surprise.

"Yes, a school teacher. I've only managed to get three days a week at Jack's school. It's hard, because I'm kind of limited to finding work within a short distance of where we live. With Jack not being old enough to be left at home on his own..."

"You've taken on a cleaning job to supplement your income."

"Yes. So far, it's worked out pretty well. Jack comes with me and does his homework or reads a book and I clean. There are other jobs out there, but they're usually either too far from home or not the kind of job where I can take Jack with me. I've looked into jobs I could do on the days I'm not at school, but I haven't been able to find anything that will let me start at nine and finish by two-thirty."

She saw his curious expression and added, "I have to be at the school by three to collect Jack."

He nodded. "Which means having to leave by two-thirty."

She sighed. "You see my problem."

"Yes, I do. I guess it must be a problem for lots of parents. I've never given it any thought."

She shrugged. "If you don't have kids, there's no reason for you to think about it." She paused. "Do you have kids?"

"Nope, just me."

"What about family—parents, brothers and sisters?"

He hesitated and a shadow passed across his face. "Nope, just me."

Sensing he didn't want to elaborate, she changed the subject. "So, what is it exactly that you do here?"

"Well, I'm a detective, but like I told Jack, I'm also a negotiator. I'm part of a team that provides a negotiation service in high risk and critical situations, say for example, someone who's threatening suicide. We also resolve siege and hostage situations, conduct high-risk searches—things like that. That's when the SPG are sent in."

She frowned. "The SPG?"

"The State Protection Group. It's made up of specialist tactical, negotiation, intelligence and command support services. The selection of the team depends upon the actual situation."

She was filled with respect for the man who sat before her. Compared to what he did for a living, her daily grind was a walk in the park. She couldn't even imagine a typical day in his life. "It must be incredibly stressful for you."

"Yeah." His voice held a wealth of feeling. "It can be that."

"How do you deal with it?"

He shrugged, his face expressionless.

"It must be difficult when things don't go right?"

His face closed. "Yep."

Tactfully, she changed the subject again. "Um... I was wondering if I could put up a poster on your staff noticeboard? Even with the second job, funds have been a little tight and I've decided to look for a roommate."

Andy's eyebrows rose, but he nodded. "Of course. It's in the tea room. I'll show you, if you like."

"That's okay, I know where it is."

"Then I'll help you put it up. It's no trouble." He unfolded himself from the chair and stood. Cally tilted her head back to look up at him.

"Jack's right," she grinned. "You *are* tall."

Andy shrugged and looked away, as if embarrassed. He strode to the other side of the squad room. Cally turned to follow him.

"Mom, I'm going to stay out here," said Jack, pulling a library book out of his bag.

"That's fine, Jack. I won't be long."

By the time she made it to the tea room, Andy was already inside. It was a small room outfitted with a counter and a sink, overhead cupboards, a table and a scattering of mismatched chairs.

"The noticeboard is right over there," he said, pointing it out.

She looked in the direction he'd indicated. A noticeboard brimming with various brochures and notices hung on a wall.

"Do you have your poster with you?"

"Um...yes." She reached into the pocket of her shorts and pulled out the folded piece of paper. Smoothing it out on the table, she moved toward the noticeboard.

"I'll pin it up for you," Andy offered.

He reached for the poster and his fingers brushed hers. Again, her breath hitched from the contact and her belly somersaulted.

Get a grip on yourself, she admonished silently. He was only a man and after her experience with Stewart, she'd vowed never to get close to one again, no matter how tempting.

She took a deep breath and willed away her jitteriness, watching while Andy moved a handful of the other notices out of the way until her poster hung in a prominent position.

"There, now it's sure to be seen," he said, turning to her with a triumphant grin.

Despite her best intentions, Cally's heart fluttered again. She tried to stem her response to him, but she might as well have been trying to hold back a tsunami. Heat flooded her cheeks and once again, she was tongue-tied.

"Are you looking for anyone in particular? Female? Male?"

She nodded and did her best to regain the power of speech. "I-I think I would prefer to have a man around—" She broke off, suddenly aware of how that sounded. Andy eyed her with interest.

"W-what I mean is, J-Jack would love some male company. He hasn't...um..."

"I take it his father's not on the scene?"

She shook her head, wondering a little frantically how they'd come to this point. She had no intention of sharing her family history with a man who was little more than a stranger, no matter how good-looking and how interested he appeared. He turned away and she was relieved when he dropped the topic.

"I-I guess I'd better keep going. I still have a few more rooms to clean, including the squad room. It's going to be late getting home as it is." She moved toward the door. Andy turned to watch her leave.

"Thanks for helping me with the poster and...and for hanging it up and...everything," she stammered. "I really appreciate it."

He stared back at her, his expression thoughtful. "No problem. I was happy to help. Besides, I'm curious, why you'd seek an officer to share your house? I assume that's who you're targeting, seeing as how you've put it up on our noticeboard."

Cally bit her tongue. She didn't really want to get into the details of it with him, but still, perhaps he could pass on her needs to his workmates? It might save even more embarrassing questions later.

"I...um..." Her shoulders slumped. "It's complicated."

He spread his arms wide. "Hey, I'm a police negotiator. I can do complicated."

She kept her gaze fixed on the polished brass buttons of his navy-blue police shirt. "Well, um..." She took a deep breath. "It's kind of a long story."

He leaned back against the countertop and crossed his arms. "I can do long stories."

"I'm not sure where to start."

"How about at the beginning?"

She sighed and stepped forward and took a seat at the table. "The thing is, like I told you, I need the money. I'm working two jobs and it still isn't enough. The bills are piling up and if something doesn't happen soon, I'm going to be forced to sell my house." She paused and took another breath. "The other reason is, I-I think I'm being followed." She peeked at him from beneath her lashes and anxiously awaited his reaction.

A frown marred the smooth, tanned skin of his forehead. "Have you spoken to the police?"

Relief coursed through her. At least he hadn't burst out laughing. From the look on his face, he appeared to be giving her statement credence.

"Of course." She looked away and then bravely met his gaze again. "I-I haven't told you everything."

Andy raised an eyebrow, his expression blank. "There's more?"

"Yes. A little over a month ago, my house was broken into."

"Were you harmed?" His voice reflected his concern.

"No, no. Jack and I were both asleep at the time. We didn't even know it had happened until we woke and discovered the front door open and a few household items missing."

"Did they arrest anyone?"

Cally shook her head. "There were footprints in the dirt along the driveway heading into and out of my property. From the size of the shoe, they determined it was a single male offender. The police are still looking for him."

"What did he steal?"

"Not much, to tell you the truth. We don't have anything of any real value. Even the TV is not worth stealing."

"Tell me about the person you think is following you."

"It began last week. I noticed a blue car parked on the side of the main road not far from where I turn into my driveway. I live on a tiny block situated behind a very large house and my cottage is barely visible from the road. In fact, if you didn't know it was there, you could easily drive right past it."

She shrugged and continued. "The sight of the car didn't alarm me at the time. It's just that I noticed it. It's a very busy highway and it was unusual to see a car parked there. I hadn't given it any more thought until a few days later, driving home with Jack after school. The same blue car was traveling a couple of cars behind me."

"How do you know it was the same one?"

She sighed. "I don't, but it was definitely the same color and the same make. It was a Toyota."

At his querying look, she added, "I saw the silver Toyota badge on the front. I drive a Toyota too, so I know what it looks like."

"Okay, so you saw a blue Toyota which was similar to a car you'd seen parked near your house a couple days earlier. There must be thousands of blue Toyotas in this city. Why would that make you think you were being followed?"

"It's just that it *felt* odd. First, I notice a blue Toyota parked near my driveway where cars don't usually park and then a couple days later, I'm almost certain I see it behind me in traffic. Then yesterday, I saw it again. Parked in the same place, a few yards from my driveway. Something about it doesn't feel right."

"I can understand you feeling jittery, but your stalker theory seems a little thin. Do you think it could be a delayed reaction to the burglary?"

Cally groaned in frustration. "You don't believe me. This is exactly why I was reluctant to tell you."

He pushed away from the counter and came toward her. "I never said I didn't believe you, sweetheart, but what you've told me so far doesn't amount to stalking."

She refused to acknowledge the warmth that spread through her at his use of the endearment. "Would you please let me finish?"

"Okay, okay." He threw his arms up in surrender and returned to lean against the counter. Cally stood and began to pace.

"Yesterday, when I saw the car again, I decided to go and speak to whoever was in the vehicle."

He frowned at her. "You told me you thought this guy's been stalking you and yet you decide to approach him? Alone? Not a smart thing to do. What if he'd been a real sicko and he'd snatched you or something? No one would've known what happened to you."

Cally flushed because she'd considered the same thing. "Well, as you can see, I escaped unscathed. Besides, I phoned the detective investigating the home invasion and told him about it before I left the house. He agreed to send someone over. They at least had some idea what was happening there. Not that my act of bravery got me very far. As soon as I got close, it sped off. I saw a man behind the wheel, though. A man with short dark hair."

"Did you get the plate number?"

"Yes."

"That's a start. At least you have something to go on if you see him close to your property again. Did you give the plate number to the police?"

"No. I'm not sure if they did a drive by, but he was long gone, if they did. I didn't hear from the detective. I guess he thought the problem was resolved."

"I can run a check on it, if you like. I have access to the same database."

She frowned. "Isn't that illegal? He hasn't actually done anything yet."

"Yes, it's kind of illegal without just cause, but do you want to know who owns the car, or not?"

"I don't want you to get into any trouble. I've seen the news reports on police officers illegally accessing information. It's taken very seriously. I couldn't have that on my conscience."

Andy shrugged. "Suit yourself, but don't say I didn't offer." He paused and then spoke again. "So, correct me if I'm wrong—you want a man to help provide for you financially and in his spare time, scare off the boogie man, but only by legal means?" His eyes widened innocently. "Did I miss anything?"

"Yes, as a matter of fact, you have." She lifted her chin defiantly. "I'm also concerned about my son. Jack needs a male influence in his life. I've thought about approaching his soccer coach, but the season doesn't start for another three months. A male roommate would provide a kind of kinship Jack might identify with. He's getting older. It's important to provide him with good male role models. I've been reading some books about it..."

Andy cocked up an eyebrow. A grin threatened. "Really?"

Cally's defenses went up. Anger began to simmer. "Don't laugh at me. These books make a lot of sense. And what would you know about raising boys, anyway?"

When he didn't answer, she plowed on. "It's just that..." She paused, suddenly uncertain how much she wanted him to know. Briefly, her thoughts warred in her head before she decided to be completely upfront with him. "It's just that Jack's never had a male figure in his life. I think it's time he did."

"What about his father?" Andy asked, just as she knew he would.

CHAPTER 9

Taking a deep breath, Cally released it slowly and tried to ease the nervous tension that had her heart beating so rapidly. She felt the weight of it like a tangible, living thing in her chest. Something about Andy inspired trust and invited confidences. *She wanted to tell him.* Besides, it would be a relief to have someone else to talk to about it. Ever since the death of her aunt, there'd been no one but Kate to confide in and she'd only been back in the country for two years, after living overseas for a decade.

"Jack was born nine months after my sixteenth birthday," she began, crossing her arms over her chest and staring down at the floor. "Jack's father—the boy I thought was as madly in love with me as I was with him—told me to get an abortion. He told me he was too young to be a father. He wouldn't even consider keeping it. He forced me to make an appointment with a clinic, but I didn't want to go ahead with an abortion."

The awful memories assailed her. When she spoke again, her voice was harsh with emotion. "I was too scared to tell him... I didn't want to risk his anger. I wasn't sure what he'd do. I was scared he might hurt me."

Andy's face darkened on a frown and his lips tightened, but he refrained from commenting. Cally drew in a ragged breath. "From the moment I told him I was pregnant, he changed—and not in a good way. We'd never had so much as an argument before and yet, after that it seemed it was all we ever did. One afternoon, he put his fist through the wall of his bedroom."

She sighed at the memory of that terrible moment when she'd been sure he was going to use his fists on her and forced herself to finish. "So, I did what any other pregnant teenager would do: I went home and told my parents."

The pain of that meeting felt as fresh and raw as if it were yesterday. She trembled as she remembered.

"It was after dinner. Dad had retired to his study to go through some half yearly school reports. He was the principal of the local high school in Watervale," she explained.

"I was nearly eight weeks along. Mom and I had always gotten along all right, but I had been Daddy's little girl. I didn't think there was anything I could do to anger him." Her trembling became more violent.

In an instant, Andy was beside her, putting his arms around her and drawing her close against the solid wall of his chest. His heart beat steadily beneath her ear, reassuring her with its strength. Gradually, she calmed.

Pulling back slightly, she looked up at him. "I'm sorry. I thought I'd buried my feelings about it a long time ago. I guess some things are too hard to forget."

"Cally, if you don't want to talk about it—"

"No, I'm fine. I-I want to. I think I'd rather you know, if that's okay?"

"Of course it is. I just thought—"

"I *want* to tell you."

He nodded. She pulled out of his arms and moved across the room. Leaning her back against the sink, she folded her arms protectively across her stomach and continued in a quiet voice.

"My parents had tried unsuccessfully for many years to have children and when I finally came along, I was loved and cherished like the long-awaited child I was. There was nothing they wouldn't do for me."

"So, what happened when you told them?"

Her smile was mirthless. "They threw me out."

Andy reeled back in shock. No way had he seen that coming. After all, she was a well-educated, professional, young mother who appeared to be doing the best she could to raise her son. She was having some money troubles, and he knew all about that. But he'd never have guessed she'd been abandoned at a young age by those who were meant to take care of her.

Christ, she'd been little more than a baby herself. A surge of anger tightened his throat. He thought of the men who'd deserted her. Their abandonment was so foreign, he could barely believe it.

It was obvious she wasn't lying. Her guileless blue eyes shone with openness and honesty—and a few tears. His job required him to read people well and as far as Cally Savage went, he was sure she didn't have a deceptive bone in her body.

"What did you do? You managed to finish your education and go to university. That couldn't have been easy with a young baby?"

"You're right. It wasn't easy." She gave him a small smile. "But I didn't do it on my own. I had the love and support of my aunt. After my parents threw me out, I moved in with her."

"She looked after Jack while you went to school?"

"Yes. I was halfway through year ten when I fell pregnant. After Jack's birth, I went back to finish my Higher School Certificate through my local TAFE college. Later, with my aunt's encouragement, I applied for university in Armidale, where I lived."

"What about Jack's father? How did he react when he realized he had a son?"

Color exploded across her cheeks. She looked away. "I never told him," she murmured.

Andy frowned. "You never told him you had the baby?"

Cally shook her head, her gaze now fiercely defiant. "No, I never told him I had the baby. He hadn't wanted Jack from the outset. *I* was the one who wanted to keep him. Jack's *my* son. End of story."

"But—"

She stared at him hard. "End of story." Turning on her heel, she left the room and went to check on her boy.

———

Andy stared after Cally, his thoughts in chaos. A few moments later, he heard the vacuum cleaner start up.

He couldn't deny her story intrigued him. The vulnerability in her eyes as she'd recounted her past had tugged at his heartstrings and his primeval urge to protect had raced to the fore. It had been all he could do to stop himself from holding her close and promising her he'd never let anything bad happen to her again.

In fact, he *had* held her close. The memory of her in his arms crowded his thoughts. Even those few, fleeting moments were branded on his mind. The feel of her soft warmth; the smell of her hair: Everything about her drew him.

His gaze glanced off the poster he'd pinned so recently to the noticeboard. From the moment he hung it there, he'd wanted to take it down. He couldn't imagine how he'd feel knowing one of his male colleagues was sharing her house. Okay, she was looking for a roommate, not a life partner, but he couldn't help but feel a twinge of jealousy at the thought of someone else being the man in her household.

A germ of an idea took hold. *He* could move in with her... He immediately frowned at the wayward thought and did his best to dismiss the idea. He wasn't looking to relocate. He had a perfectly nice condo overlooking the beach. His commute was a little longer than he cared for, but the view and the proximity to the ocean more than made up for it. Besides, he didn't even know where she lived. For all he knew, she lived in the boondocks.

Curious, he stepped closer to the poster and focused on the details:

Wanted: roommate to share three-bedroom house in Chatswood. $300 per week, excluding utilities. References required. Please phone 993266250.

Okay, so she lived in Chatswood. It was on the opposite side of the harbor from where he lived and nowhere near the beach. Still, it was closer to work and would cut down significantly on his commute. And he could afford it.

What the hell was he doing? Was he seriously considering taking her up on her ad? Was he mad? He didn't even know her. More likely than not, neither would the person who she eventually accepted into her home.

What if she was taken in by some crazed maniac who disguised himself as normal? What if someone like that moved in with her and murdered her and her son in the dark of night?

It wouldn't be the first time. People thought they'd recognize evil when it came knocking on their door, but Andy knew better than most that sometimes the most normal-looking people housed unimaginable evil.

Could he bear to have that on his conscience if something happened? It wasn't like he was responsible for them, yet he felt a strong urge to protect. And no matter how hard he tried, he couldn't deny Cally's vulnerability tugged hard at something deep inside him; he couldn't shake the feeling Cally and Jack were his.

He made an impatient sound in the back of his throat. The fact that he yearned for a family of his own didn't mean he had to latch onto the first possibility that came by. It was ridiculous to think like that. He spun on his heel and left the tea room.

Tom was at his desk on the far side of the room, a phone pressed to his ear. Andy looked around for Jack, but couldn't see him. Cally was also on the far side of the room, not far from Tom. She held a dusting cloth in hand. She glanced up when he entered, but quickly averted her gaze.

Andy's gut somersaulted. He clenched his jaw and gritted

his teeth, his mind still a whirl of confusion. Throwing himself down in his chair, he tugged his keyboard toward him and did his best to block out her distracting presence, determined to finish the last of his reports.

After re-reading for the third time the last line he'd entered on the report in front of him, he cursed under his breath. *How hard could this be?* He'd never had a problem concentrating before. In fact, he prided himself on being able to get on with the job, no matter the distractions.

Yet here he was, reading and re-reading the same sentence over and over and still not having a clue what it said. Any attempt to complete the reports with her in the room was an exercise in futility. Accepting the obvious, he sighed and gave up.

His gaze was immediately drawn to her. She'd finished the dusting and now lugged the vacuum cleaner behind her. He watched while her faded T-shirt inched a little higher on one side. The movement exposed a glimpse of tanned belly to his appreciative gaze. She bent forward to pick up a wad of paper off the floor and her breasts filled the opening of the V-neck of her shirt. Blood flooded to his groin.

The mere thought of another man enjoying such liberties sent a heated denial rushing through his veins. Without conscious thought, he pushed away from his desk and strode toward her, his long legs eating up the distance.

She looked up in surprise. Her eyes widened further when he reached out and took her by arm in an effort to hold her attention.

"I'll do it."

She frowned and flicked off the vacuum cleaner. "Do what?"

"I'll move in with you."

"You...you want to move in with me?"

"Yes, why not? You said you'd prefer a male roommate. It got me thinking... Why not me? I earn enough to cover the rent, I don't mind kids and I'm big and strong enough to scare off the boogie man." He shrugged and shot her a disarming smile. "What more do you need?"

———————

Cally stared at him and did her best to get her pulse rate back under control. *When he smiled at her...* Oh, goodness, it was enough to weaken her knees. She didn't have a clue if he was joking or not. Why would he want to share a house with a woman he barely knew...?

Then again, it was normal for someone who answered an ad not to know the person who placed it. Was this really any different? In fact, it was probably even better because this gave her an opportunity to make a few enquires, to check into his background, if necessary. She wasn't about to let just anyone have access to her home or her son.

She recalled the telephone conversation she'd overheard the night they'd first met and frowned again. He'd told the caller he wanted a wife and family and she had no reason to believe he lied. *Had she inadvertently offered him the opportunity he'd been looking for?* Were she and Jack going to be the family he apparently wanted? The thought was too weird for her liking. She pulled away from him and put some distance between them.

He looked honest and forthright and normal. He looked *nice.* She'd even struggled to keep her libido in check, especially when he smiled. But what if it was all a farce? A ploy to get what he wanted? What if there was something sinister behind the easy grin and the gorgeous eyes?

She shivered and rubbed at the gooseflesh that suddenly popped out on her arms. She hadn't survived a decade as a single parent without honing her protective instincts. *Something didn't feel right.*

He stared at her and a shadow passed over his face. It was almost as if he sensed her withdrawal. He took a step toward her and her adrenaline kicked in. She tensed, poised to flee.

"What is it, Cally? What's the matter? You look like you've been sentenced to death and you've just caught sight of the executioner." He offered her a grin, but it was strained around the edges.

"I'-I'm sorry," she stammered. "It's just that it seems a little odd—you wanting to move in with us. I mean, I assume you already live somewhere, right? If you were looking to move out, why didn't you say anything earlier?"

Andy drew in a breath and she could see he was struggling with what he wanted to say. Her suspicions escalated. Was he even now fishing around for a suitable excuse? A reason he thought she would swallow?

"The truth is," he started, a flush spreading up from his neck, "I like you and I like Jack, too. I have a place in Bondi, but I want to help you out. And your place is closer to work. You told me how desperate you are to offset a little of your financial burden. Desperate people make desperate decisions. I don't want you saying yes to just anybody, without giving them proper consideration."

Anger kindled in her belly. *Did he think she wouldn't be checking him out?* She narrowed her eyes at his arrogance. "Oh, and you're the perfect candidate, is that what you're saying? That you're so kind and honest and flawless, I wouldn't need to look into your credentials. In fact, I should be throwing myself at your feet, in gratitude for your beneficence. Is that what you're trying to tell me?"

He was shaking his head at her even before she'd finished. The amusement had long since vanished from his face.

"You know what? Forget it. Choose whoever you like. Pick some random stranger who sees your ad and thinks it's just what he needs. You never know, you might get lucky. Then again, tell that to the countless women who have disappeared without a trace. Statistics show the perpetrator was likely someone they knew. Do you want to risk your safety like that? Do you want to risk Jack's?"

His barb hit its mark and she flinched and dropped her gaze. The stony expression in his eyes stayed with her and gave her pause. *Perhaps he was just trying to help?* Perhaps he did care about them? But how could he? He barely knew them. Unless he was just exactly what she thought when she met him—a really nice guy?

Her shoulders slumped on a sigh and she shook her head in confusion. *Had she let her imagination run away with her, yet again? Was that all this was about?* A by-product of the tension she'd been gripped by ever since she realized her home—her inner sanctum—had been breached?

Was Andy's offer as simple as he'd suggested? Had it really originated from his need to look out for her, to ensure she and Jack were safe?

She looked up. He caught her gaze and held it. For long moments, she stared at him, at his beautiful chocolate eyes. He was a police officer, a man who had sworn to serve and protect. She wasn't naïve enough to assume all men in uniform could be trusted, but it didn't mean none of them could. In fact, if she'd been asked, she'd have said she considered most policemen honest. It was only a very few who gave all the others a bad name, like in any profession, including hers.

"I can understand your need to be cautious," Andy continued, the anger now gone from his voice, "and I'm more than glad to see it. It reassures me that you might not be so quick to invite a stranger in, regardless of how badly you need the money." He paused and ran a hand through his hair, setting it all askew.

"The truth is, I live on my own and like I told you before, I have no family. No wife, no girlfriend, no kids. It would be nice to come home to a house well lit, knowing there's someone I can talk to." He shrugged. "You need a roommate; I'd like some company. It seems like we're perfect for one another."

A tiny grin tilted up the corners of his mouth. Cally couldn't help but respond. She smiled and silently cursed the blush that stole up her neck. *Maybe it was as simple as he'd said? Maybe he was just lonely?* She knew exactly how it felt. She wouldn't mind some company, too.

Of course, he wouldn't be sharing *every* aspect of their lives. He'd be a roommate and nothing else—someone to help with expenses, be around for casual conversation and just kind of *be there*. She'd make it clear their relationship would be strictly platonic and that he was free to see other women. After all, she could hardly expect him to be celibate...

She recalled the way her body had reacted to his touch and suppressed a shiver of desire. She couldn't deny he was an incredibly attractive man who made her so nervous she could hardly string a single sentence together when he stood too close. But surely that didn't mean she couldn't spend time with him as a *friend?* Despite the pounding heart and dry mouth she experienced in his company, she was almost certain she could enjoy a meal with him or an occasional evening in without expiring from the jitters. After all, that's what roommates did, didn't they? Not that she'd ever had one. She'd only lived with relatives.

She wondered if Andy would be happy with the arrangement. He wasn't exactly getting a wife and children, but she'd offer companionship and once she'd satisfied herself he wasn't a man with an unhealthy interest in her son, she'd be more than happy for him to spend time with Jack.

But, he'd said he wanted a wife. That implied far more than mere companionship. Her mind veered away from images of Andy in her bedroom...and her fists clenched by her side. What happened to her as a teenager had damaged her beyond repair. She was broken deep down inside and couldn't imagine entrusting her life or her heart to anyone ever again.

Andy hadn't even said anything to her about wanting a wife. It was likely he didn't realize she'd overheard him. If it truly was that important to him, surely he wouldn't offer to move in with them?

She thought about what might happen if he did move in and then started dating someone else. What would happen to Jack if he and Andy had bonded and he moved out? Perhaps this wasn't such a good idea...

"I take it from your silence, that you're not totally against my offer?" he grinned again.

Cally's stomach did a somersault and she bit her lip to stem the butterflies. "Yes...um... No. I mean, yes, I'm not totally against your offer, but I have to think of Jack. I'm his mother. I'm all he has. It's important I make the right decision."

"Of course, I understand. What would you like to know?"

She drew in a deep breath and tried to gauge his sincerity. "You'll answer any question I ask?"

His eyebrows raised and a suggestive gleam came into his eyes. She blushed and looked away.

"Of course," he smiled. "Ask whatever you like. I don't have anything to hide."

A shadow passed across his face, but was gone so quickly she decided she must have imagined it. "Okay, I want to know why you don't have any family."

The expression on his face froze. Her breathing hitched and her heart skipped a beat. *Oh, God. Something wasn't right.*

He took a long time to answer. When he did, his eyes were so dark and bleak, she wasn't sure she wanted to hear what he had to say.

"My family died when I was young. My father, my mother and my sister. I was placed in a foster home where I lived until I was old enough to join the police force."

She gasped, shocked beyond belief. It was the last thing she'd expected him to say. "Th-they died together? Like, in an accident?"

"My father and little sister were killed together. My mother died a few years later."

"Oh, my goodness! You poor thing! And here I thought I'd had it tough. How old were you when it happened?"

Andy drew in a deep breath and eased it out between taut lips. He looked at her, his expression still bleak. "I know I said I'd answer your questions, but if you don't mind, I'd rather not talk about my family anymore. It was a terrible time. Sometimes, it feels like it happened yesterday..."

Cally hastened to reassure him. "Of course, I understand. I'm sorry I brought it up."

He shrugged. "You weren't to know."

"You're right, but I know what it feels like to lose your family and mine *chose* to abandon me. I can't imagine what you went through and now..." She shook her head, amazed at what he'd achieved. "Look at what you've become? Look what you've made of your life? Your family would be so, so proud." Her voice broke on the last words and she turned her back on him, not wanting to see how much his story had affected her.

And she had wondered if he might be a pedophile! She couldn't believe she'd been so far off the mark. She was only grateful she hadn't said anything. She'd have just about died from the humiliation. He was lonely for a family, just like he'd said. Surely, after what she'd heard, she could find it in her heart to share hers? And if it didn't work out and he moved on, she'd deal with the fallout if and when it happened.

His hand closed gently around her shoulder and he turned her slowly around to face him.

"Please, don't get upset, Cally. I didn't tell you to upset you. You asked and I answered. That was the deal, right?"

His soft smile nearly undid her. "Yes, you're right. Next time, I won't bother. You're good and kind and strong. All the things I thought you were. It would be an honor to have you share my house. That is, if you still want to?"

"Of course. I wouldn't have offered if I hadn't meant it. I'll have to sort out a few things with the place I have at Bondi, but it shouldn't be too much of a problem." He made his way back to his desk and sat down in his chair. She followed him more slowly and thought about her terms. Heat immediately flooded her face. Knowing it was best to simply get it over with, she opened her mouth and let the words fall out in a rush. "There's just one thing I need to make clear."

"Go on."

"The other night, I-I overheard you talking on the phone."

A shrug. "Okay."

She took another breath. "The thing is, you said you wanted a wife. A-and kids. I-I just wanted to make it perfectly clear this will be a platonic relationship, nothing more. I mean, I'm not... We're not..." Heat spread across her cheeks, turning them to fire. "If you want to bring a woman home, then I guess that's okay, but I'd like you to be discreet about it. Jack doesn't need to be exposed to...you know." She ducked her head unable to bear looking at him a moment longer.

What sounded suspiciously like laughter reached out for her. She glanced up and met his gaze. His eyes glinted with humor.

"Okay, so let's go back to the part where you thought you heard I was looking for a wife?"

Embarrassment once again savaged her cheeks. She grimaced. "I'm sorry, I obviously got that totally wrong and it just goes to show, you should never listen in on other people's conversations. But, I wasn't really listening in. I was just—"

"Whoa! Would you be quiet for a minute?" Andy shook his head in disbelief.

Pressing her lips together, she scrunched her eyes closed and willed away the fresh wave of heat that spread across her face.

What was it about this guy that made her blush like a teenager?

"If you let me get a word in edgewise, I'll tell you what you thought you overheard."

Cally eased open her eyes. Andy took a deep breath and continued.

"I was talking to my best mate, Will Rutledge. I'd had a fairly difficult day at work and he'd called to see how I was. You *did* overhear me say I wanted a wife and kids, but I think you missed the part when I said I didn't want just *anybody* and I'm not in the habit of bringing women home."

He pinned her with his gaze and Cally tried hard not to squirm. She'd *so* misread the whole situation. The thought of making an abrupt exit and salvaging what little pride she had left was uppermost in her mind. She stepped away from him.

"Oh God, I'm so embarrassed. I'm sorry. Let's just pretend this never happened. I'll collect my son and walk out the door and if by some unfortunate stroke of luck we happen to run into each other again, I hope you'll forget all about this conversation." Finishing in a rush, she spun on her heel.

Andy's fingers closed around her arm, tugging her back toward him before she could take another step. She yelped in surprise. To her horror, her cheap sandals lost traction again and she toppled into his lap with a mortified gasp. His arms immediately came around her.

"Oh, oh, I'm so *sorry!*" She scrambled to get out of his hold.

Could this night get any worse? Her eyes burned with the effort of holding back tears.

Andy's arms tightened. "It's okay. Please, don't run away. I'm kind of comfortable and I still haven't finished my story."

All of a sudden, she realized her squirming brought her directly into contact with his groin. She froze. Embarrassment scorched her cheeks. Forcing her gaze upwards, she caught the glint of laughter in his eyes.

"Please let me go." Her voice was quiet and deadly. "I think you've had enough fun at my expense."

His gaze sobered instantly and he released her. "Cally, I'm sorry. I'm not making fun of you. I like you. And I'd really like to move in with you, as a friend, and help you out in your hour of need. Okay?"

She nodded, and relieved to move on she reached out for the first thing that popped into her mind. "Do you need to give notice where you're living?"

"No, the place belongs to... It doesn't matter. There won't be any need to give notice. I'll be able to duck over there every now and then and make sure that everything's all right. There's really nothing stopping me from moving in with you right away."

Cally debated his words in silence. Mistaking her hesitation, Andy frowned.

"Is that okay? I thought it was what you wanted?"

She stared up at him and nodded slowly. "It is. I-I just

thought it might be harder than that to sort out. You wouldn't believe the number of sleepless nights I've had trying to work out a solution. It-it just seems to have worked out too easily."

Andy shrugged and smiled. "Sometimes we get lucky."

Relief surged through her and she smiled back. "You're right. Sometimes we do. It's about time a little luck came my way."

"So, when would you like me to move in?"

Cally glanced behind him to make sure Jack hadn't returned. She was pretty sure he'd be fine about the arrangement, but he'd never had a man living in a house with them before and she wanted to talk to him about it first. She certainly didn't want to thrust the information upon him as Andy unpacked his bags.

Jack had been the only male in their household since the day he was brought home from the hospital. She wanted to give him a little time to adjust to the fact things were about to change. From the way he and Andy seemed to be getting on, she didn't really have any concerns that he'd object, but he was her son and she wasn't going to trample all over his feelings.

"I need to talk to Jack, first. I'm sure he'll be okay, but, you know..." She shrugged, hoping Andy would understand.

He bent his head closer. The spicy scent of expensive cologne tickled her nose. Holding her gaze, he smiled.

"Of course, I understand. Jack's at an age where he knows what it's like to be the man of the family. I want you to know I'm not going to do anything to upset him in that regard."

She smiled gratefully. "I do know. That's one of the reasons I've agreed to let you move in."

His eyebrow rose an inch. "So, what are the other reasons?"

She blushed and looked away. "Let's just say it feels right." She purposely kept her reply vague, unwilling to closely analyze why she acted as she had and said what she'd said. She knew the logical, practical reasons why, but that didn't really explain why she'd asked a perfect stranger to move in with them.

And yet, she had.

Besides, what she'd told him wasn't that far off the mark. It *did* feel right. *He* felt right. He felt safe. Right now, that was enough.

"Mom? Andy? Are you in here?" Jack's voice called out from the hall.

"Yes, honey," she replied and moved off Andy's lap. She didn't want him to see them in such an intimate position and jumping to the wrong conclusion.

"There you are." Jack's eyes were softly accusing. "I've been looking for you *everywhere*. I even looked in the evidence room."

Her smile placated him. "I was just finishing up in here. Get your things together. We'll be leaving in a few minutes."

Jack sighed, but dragged himself back out through the doorway. Andy studied her while she lugged the vacuum cleaner to the storage closet.

"How many nights do you work here?"

"Three. Monday, Wednesday and Friday."

"No wonder you look tired."

Cally tried not to take offense at his comment. After all, she *was* tired. With sleep mostly passing her by the last few nights, she was more than looking forward to the end of the week. She sighed and glanced up at him.

"About you moving in...um... Are you working Friday night?"

He nodded.

"Good, that'll give me time to talk to Jack and make sure he's all right with this. "I'm sure he'll be perfectly fine; don't worry," she reassured him. "I wouldn't have even considered it if I thought he wouldn't be."

"So, how big is my room? Do I have a closet? I'd like to know if my stuff will fit."

She ducked her head in embarrassment. "Well, I wouldn't exactly call it a room, despite what the poster says. It's more like a sleepout. There's a sofa bed and a table and a cupboard and there's a shed out the back you can use for storage. I'm sure you'll be very comfortable," she added hurriedly, "and it's screened in, so you won't get eaten by mosquitoes."

He smiled and her belly flip-flopped. "That's good to hear. Mosquitoes and I don't get on."

She smiled back at him and opened the door to the storage room. Andy leaned against the wall opposite and folded his arms across his chest. She tried not to notice how the movement caused his biceps to tighten.

"So, if I take on all of these manly duties, remind me again what it is I get in return?"

She squirmed. A hot flush worked its way across her face. When he put it like that, the deal seemed a little one-sided. She met his gaze with reluctance and caught the sparkle of humor in his eyes.

With a self-deprecating smile, she shrugged. "You get the pleasure of my company whenever I'm there and if you like, I'm happy to share meals with you. Cooking for one more won't make much difference."

"Oh, I wouldn't want to put you out." His face was a picture of innocence. "After all, the things you expect me to do are so..." He paused dramatically. "Insignificant. They fairly pale in comparison to clever conversation and a decent, home cooked meal."

Cally choked, trying not to laugh. He was right: It wasn't fair. This golden Adonis was making fun of her and all she wanted to do was laugh right along with him. But she needed to establish her tone as landlord. He was, after all, about to become her tenant. Clearing her throat, she schooled her features into what she hoped was a serious expression.

"Well, I'm not promising you a home-cooked meal *every* night and of course, I said nothing about it being decent."

"Of course." His eyes glinted with mischief. "What about a good-night kiss?"

Instant awareness of his hard male body flooded through her. She was standing much too close. The smell of his cologne mixed with the warm male scent of his body once again teased her nostrils. Her heart pounded with excitement and fear. She wasn't ready. She wasn't—

"I'm sorry, Cally. I didn't mean that. It was a joke." He looked worried.

"It-it's okay. I know you weren't serious. I have utmost faith in your integrity. I'm sure you'll respect my boundaries."

"Of course. I was teasing. Your house, your rules."

"Mom! Are you *coming*?" Jack's plaintive whine traveled up the hall. A moment later, he joined them with his books under his arm. Cally jumped guiltily and glanced down at her watch.

"Oh my goodness, it's nearly nine o'clock! I can't believe it's so late. I have to get Jack home and into bed. It's a school night." She tossed the cleaning cloths into a bucket on the floor of the storage room and shut the door. With a small smile of farewell tossed in Andy's direction, she collected Jack and turned to leave.

"Cally!" He waited for her to stop and turn around. "I'll see you on Friday night, right?"

"Of course. I'll be here. I'll see you then." Her eyes connected with his. Her heart skipped a beat and then pounded against her chest. She dragged her gaze away and drew in a quick breath, then turned and walked toward the door with Jack trailing behind her.

Andy stared after Cally and her son and his shoulders slumped on a sigh. Forty-eight hours suddenly felt like a lifetime away. He couldn't believe how hard and how fast he was falling for her. The insight she'd given him into her early life had further endeared her to him. She'd done it tough, was still doing it tough and yet she'd felt sorry for him.

A stab of guilt went through him at the thought that he hadn't been entirely honest with her. She'd asked about his family and he'd replied the best way he could. If she ever found out the truth of his childhood, she might never come to care for him.

He was already a little in love with her and he'd known her for less than a week. He wanted to hold her, protect her and keep her safe from the blows life sent her way.

He'd done his best to keep his feelings to himself. He didn't want to scare her off by declaring how he felt too soon. Her past experience with men had been anything but positive. Something told him getting her to trust him wouldn't come easy. Then again, anything truly worth having never did.

CHAPTER 10

Cally glanced at her son. "Jack, would you sit down at the kitchen table for a minute? There's something I'd like to talk to you about."

Dinner was over and she'd just finished packing the dishwasher. Jack lay sprawled on the couch in front of the television. Pushing himself upright, he wandered into the kitchen and sat beside her at the worn pine table.

"What is it?"

It was Thursday night and she'd spent most of the night before—and all of that day—deciding how to approach him with the news that Andy was moving in. She thought her son would take it well, but it was such a huge change for him, she couldn't pretend she wasn't nervous about his reaction.

She took his smaller hand in hers. Despite her rigorous sunscreen routine, the summer sun had dyed his skin a dark color, contrasting starkly with the blond of his hair.

"Mom, what's going on? Why are you holding my hand? You're acting weird."

She grinned. *Trust a ten-year-old to tell it like it was.* "I'm sorry if I seem weird, sweetheart. Everything's fine. I want to talk to you about Andy."

Jack frowned. "You mean Andy from the police station?"

"Yes, honey, Andy from the police station."

"What about him?"

"Well, I've been thinking about this for a while."

"Thinking about what?"

Cally breathed deeply. "About getting a roommate. You know, someone to move in and help with the bills and stuff."

"Like you and Aunt Mary?"

She smiled, liking his analogy. "Yes, kind of. Although we were related, so she wasn't strictly a roommate, but you're on the right track. The person would live here, just like we did with Aunt Mary, and they'd pay rent. They'd also share food expenses and other things like the electricity and gas. Sometimes, we might share meals or watch television together. Things like that."

"Why do we need a roommate?"

"Well, the extra money would be a big help."

"What about the cleaning job? I thought you said we had heaps of money now?"

She tried not to grimace. *Darn, his memory.*

"Yes, honey, it's helping, but things are always cropping up, like that flat tire. Having someone to share the household costs would really help." At least with Andy's assistance, she'd meet her monthly commitments and even have a little left over.

"So, how are you going to find one?" Jack's question interrupted her thoughts.

"Sorry, honey?"

He rolled his eyes at her. "I said how are you going to find one?"

"One what?"

"A roommate? Do you put up a notice or something? I could ask my friends at school. Maybe one of their moms might want to move in with us. That'd be cool, wouldn't it?"

She smiled, glad he seemed to be embracing the idea, even if it had gone in a different direction.

"Actually, I already have someone in mind. In fact, I've spoken to him about it and he's keen to give it a go."

"He? You mean another *guy* is moving in here? Who is it?"

"What would you think about Andy?"

His eyes widened in surprise. "Andy? *He's* the one moving in?"

She nodded, holding her breath. "What do you think?"

"You've already asked him, so it doesn't matter what I think." Jack pushed away from the table, his face filled with hurt.

"Jack, that's not true. It does matter what you think. In fact, I told Andy last night I had to talk to you about it before it would be a done deal. I'm not going to do anything you're not happy with."

He looked unconvinced. She tried again. "Honey, we really do need to get someone in to share the expenses, but it doesn't have to be Andy. I only asked him because he's nice and he seems like someone we can trust. He's a policeman, after all."

Jack stayed quiet, his face turned away from her. She waited nervously for him to speak.

"Where would he sleep?" His voice, soft and uncertain clutched at her heart. "It better not be in *my* room."

Cally swallowed a sigh of relief. "Of course I wouldn't give him your room. I told him about the sleepout."

"The sleepout? But it's not even air conditioned. He won't want to sleep out there."

"He didn't seem to mind."

"Did you tell him how hot it is? There's no way *I'd* sleep there!"

A smile tugged at her lips. "Well, now that you mention it, I think I might've forgotten to say anything about that. I guess he'll work it out before too long. The weather's not going to cool down any time soon."

He smiled back at her without malice. "Poor Andy."

"Yeah, poor Andy."

Cally drove to the North Sydney Police Station in heavy Friday evening traffic. Jack was in his customary seat in the back of the Corolla, gazing out of the window into the darkness.

"When's Andy moving in, Mom?"

"I'm not sure, honey. I'll speak to him tonight and see what he wants to do."

"I hope he moves in on the weekend. Then I could help him unpack. I bet he's got some really cool stuff."

"Maybe." Cally smiled, pleased to see how well Jack was adjusting to the idea. She'd meant it when she told him if he wasn't happy, they'd look for someone else, but it was Andy she really wanted.

Not in any sexual sense, of course, rather in the sense she felt drawn to him in a safe, secure kind of way. The fact his movie-star looks made her heart accelerate with nerves didn't mean anything as far as she was concerned. It was only because she was so inexperienced around men—ones that looked like him, especially.

Once the newness of him had worn off and she'd gotten used to him, she was sure her pulse rate would return to normal and he'd become just another person in the house.

That's what she was counting on, anyway.

"Mom, the light's green."

Forcing her attention back to the road, Cally drove forward. A couple more blocks and they'd be there. Her pulse began beating a rapid staccato and all of a sudden, the butterflies were back swarming in her stomach.

Andy checked the clock on the far wall of the squad room for what felt like the hundredth time. It was a standard, government-issue clock with a round, white face and big black numbers that could be seen from any desk on the floor. Right now, it was almost six-thirty.

A surge of excitement and nerves flooded his chest, making it hard to concentrate. He'd thought about Cally all day, while he'd been sorting through stuff at his condo. In anticipation of Jack's consent, he'd made preliminary arrangements with his housekeeper to move in temporarily. She'd been more than happy to oblige.

He'd waited impatiently for the day to end so he could return to the police station and see Cally again. It had been two whole days since he'd spoken to her. He'd never known time to crawl by so slowly.

Tom was also there for another nightshift and had chided him about it not long ago, when he'd noticed Andy's obsession with the clock. Andy had brushed off Tom's friendly jibes with a laugh and a shake of his head, but he'd taken care to use a little more discretion when he'd checked the time a little while after.

This preoccupation with her was scaring him a bit—even more than a bit. The feelings she stirred inside him were terrifying. He'd never before felt so incredibly *connected* to a woman on so many different levels and within such a short period of time. And he hadn't even *kissed* her!

Too bad she didn't feel the same way. But maybe it wasn't him? Maybe it was men in general who made her nervous? After hearing her story, he understood why she had set some boundaries.

The door to the squad room opened. Jack's tousled, blond head appeared in the doorway, followed closely by his mother's. Andy's heart jumped. She was dressed in another knee-length summer dress. This one was white with huge, red hibiscus flowers printed all over it. It was cut moderately low and the soft cotton fabric cupped her breasts. She looked fresh and bright and beautiful—and nothing like a cleaner.

"Hey, Andy!" Jack grinned. "Mom says you're moving in with us. Is that right? Are you?"

Andy's gaze tangled with Cally's. "Well, if it's okay with you and your mom," he said slowly. He watched Cally closely, wanting to gauge her reaction to her son's enthusiasm.

She held his gaze, her eyes as clear as the summer sky. A smile lifted the corners of her mouth. "Of course. Jack and I would love to have you."

She sounded so sincere. Emotion tightened his chest. His heart clenched. *What the hell; he was always up for a challenge.* He'd have plenty of time at his own leisure and on her turf to win her over.

"When are you moving in?" Jack's voice was full of excitement.

Andy focused his attention on the excited boy in front of him. "Well, I'm off this weekend. What if I start moving my things in tomorrow?"

"Cool! That means I'll be able to help you."

Andy looked at Cally. "If that's all right with your mom?"

She gave him another smile. "Of course. If you're sure he's not going to get in your way?"

"I won't get in your way, Andy; I promise!"

The earnestness on the boy's face made Andy's heart catch. He recalled the childhood he'd never had. He couldn't remember ever feeling unafraid like this youngster. Forcing the memories away, he smiled at Jack.

"I'm on duty until six in the morning. I'll go home and grab some shut-eye, throw some gear together and head over to your place sometime after lunch tomorrow. How does that sound?"

Jack spun around to face his mother. "Are we going to be home tomorrow?"

She ruffled his hair. "I think so, sweetheart. Now, how about you go and sit in the lounge down the hall and pull out your *Zac Power* books. I want to speak with Andy for a moment."

"Okay." Jack shot Andy another quick grin and headed toward the door. As soon as he was out of earshot, Cally took a deep breath.

"Jack's really pleased to have you moving in with us—we both are. I-I just wanted to remind you I meant what I said about this being a purely platonic relationship. I need a roommate, that's all." A blush stained her cheeks, but she held his gaze

He smiled and shrugged. "Like I told you, your house, your rules."

"Thank you." She cleared her throat. "Talking about rules, I do have a few of those."

He bit back a grin and gave an exaggerated eye roll. "I would've been disappointed if you didn't."

Her lips twitched. "Okay, first of all, there's no smoking in the house. If you have to, you'll go outside—"

"I don't smoke. What's next?"

"All right, I'm happy to throw a little extra on the stove if I'm cooking dinner, but I'm not going to clean your room or do your laundry or any of those other domestic things. Just because I'm the only woman in the house, doesn't make me the housecleaner."

He replied without hesitation. "No problem. What else?"

"Well, we only have one television. I'm not sure how much TV you watch, but if you want free reign with the remote control, you'll have to bring a TV of your own. There's a spare table in the sleepout where you can set one up."

"What about music?"

"I have an old CD player. The budget hasn't stretched to an iPod, so there's no dock, either."

"No worries, I can bring that with me. Microwave? I'm pretty big on TV dinners."

Her mouth fell open in shock. "TV dinners? How could a man like you survive on TV dinners?"

"What's wrong with TV dinners?"

She shook her head, aghast. "Look at the size of you? A TV dinner isn't enough to even begin to fill a man like you. And with the long hours you work—"

She broke off, as if she suddenly realized she sounded way too concerned. She drew in a breath and then continued. "Not that I care, of course. You eat what you like. There is a microwave and the cottage came with a dishwasher. I'd appreciate it if you cleaned up after yourself, whether it's your breakfast bowl or the plastic TV dinner container. I hate dirty dishes left in the sink."

"Me, too. Who'd have thought we'd have so much in common?"

She narrowed her eyes at him. He held back the grin for as long as he could and then lost the battle. Laughter burst from his lips. Her frown deepened and he did his best to curb his mirth. "I'm sorry," he said. "It was a joke."

She nodded and offered a tiny smile. The effect of it stole his breath. In an effort to distract himself, he latched onto the first thing he thought of.

"Give me your telephone number, in case I need to call you to tell you I'll be late getting home for dinner." He grinned again.

She rolled her eyes at him in exasperation.

"Better still, give me your cell number. That way, I'll be able to reach you whenever I need to." He grabbed a pen and some paper.

"Um...actually... I don't have a cell."

Andy frowned in surprise. "What do you mean, you don't have a cell? Everyone has a cell."

Cally shook her head, avoiding his eyes. "Not me."

"Don't tell me you're one of these people with a problem about them? Worried about the radiation giving you a brain tumor?"

She stared at him defiantly. "No, Andy, I don't have a problem with cell phones. My problem is finding the money to *pay* for it."

Heat rushed to his face and he was flooded with remorse. He reached out to her, but she stepped away and walked toward the door that led to the back offices.

"I'd better get moving. I haven't even started cleaning yet and the time's getting away."

"Cally, come back. I didn't mean to offend you. I'm an idiot. I didn't think. I'm sorry."

She stopped and turned to face him. "Just in case you missed it on the poster, the rent's three hundred a week. You'll also pay a third of the bills—food, telephone and electricity. I think that's fair." Her eyes challenged him to disagree.

"I'll pay half."

"That's not necessary. I've done the sums. If you pay a

third, it'll be enough for us to get by. I don't want to feel obligated to you in any way."

"Don't be ridiculous. I'm offering to pay half. Just take it and be grateful and let's leave it at that, okay?"

"But—" she protested.

"Put the extra money toward something Jack wants, then. If you can't take it for yourself, take it for your son."

Cally sighed in annoyance, her expression clearly irritated. He could almost hear her silent curse. He tried to keep the satisfaction off his face. He knew damn well she wouldn't be able to refuse it now. It's what he'd been counting on. She didn't disappoint.

"Half it is."

They both turned at a loud noise in the corridor. Tom and a couple of other officers appeared in the doorway of the tea room, with looks of varying curiosity and concern on their faces. The noise grew louder and the door to the squad room swung open, spilling Nikki into the room.

Andy frowned in consternation, shocked at Nikki's appearance. Her head swung wildly from side to side, as if she were searching for someone. When her gaze locked on his, she cried out in triumph and staggered across the room toward him.

Andy shot a panicked look in Cally's direction. She stood unmoving not far from him, as if her feet had been glued to the spot. Her eyes were wide and clouded with confusion. Nikki continued to advance upon him and by now he could see her eyes were red and bloodshot.

She came up close beside him and he was grateful when Cally stepped away. He could only imagine what she was thinking, but he didn't have time to explain.

Nikki looked back and forth between them. She smelled of alcohol and her body reeked of revenge. He tried to shepherd her away from his desk, and away from Cally, in particular, but his ex-girlfriend resisted his attempts and pushed back hard against him.

"Don't touch me, you fucked-up jerk!" she spat, inches from his face. "Why didn't you tell me before? You had a few problems to work through, you told me. You needed to do it alone. You never said—"

"Nikki, please, let's not do this here," he begged and tried not to breathe in her fumes. "Let me take you home." He took her by the arm in an attempt to move her toward the door, but she wrenched her arm out of his grasp.

"I'm not going anywhere! I haven't finished with you, yet. Why didn't you tell me about your fucked-up family? I'd have never wasted my time on you, had I known. I can't believe I wanted you to father my child. That kind of sickness is probably hereditary. You're probably as fucked up as he was."

Andy froze, well aware she was referring to his father. *How had she found out?* What had he said? He'd been so careful not to give anything away. He'd been concealing it for nearly twenty years. Unless he could get her out of there before she said anything else, his life would be in ruins. Panic began to set in and he looked around in desperation for a solution.

Out of the corner of his eye, he spied Tom approaching from the tea room. He held out a consoling hand in Nikki's direction and slowly closed the distance.

"Nikki, is it?" Tom asked, his tone low and even. "Why don't you come with me? I'd like to find out what this is about. You're obviously mad at Andy. Don't worry, Andy makes lots of people mad. It's just the way he is."

Andy listened to Tom's banter and hoped Cally couldn't hear what he said. No longer certain where she was in the room, he could only hope she'd left. Tom had gone into action and was saying whatever it took to get Nikki to move away. He was grateful for his partner's intervention, but prayed that if Cally was close and listening, she'd understand.

Having Nikki confront him like this was a nightmare he couldn't have envisaged. She'd been upset when he'd broken it off with her, but he never imagined she'd become so...unhinged. It was frightening how little he'd really known her. They'd been together for over a year and he hadn't had a clue she could be like this.

To his relief, Nikki didn't resist Tom's attempts to lead her away. Within a few moments, she'd left the way she'd come, Tom right there beside her. Andy breathed out a heavy sigh and swung around, looking for Cally. He found her on the far side of the room, her eyes wide, her face pale.

With a curse, he strode toward her, needing to reassure her what had happened wasn't his fault. She stared at him and he cursed again at the shock and fear in her eyes.

"Cally, I'm sorry. I didn't know that was going to happen. I—"

"Who is she?"

He glanced away, knowing he had to come clean. "Nikki Simons. My ex-girlfriend." He watched her assimilate the news and realized it didn't come as a surprise. She'd probably heard every word Nikki had said. He stifled a groan of despair.

Just when he'd been breaking through Cally's defenses, Nikki had to pull a stunt like this. *And what was she trying to prove?* He was hardly going to take her back. And what was that crap about fathering her a child? He hadn't even asked her to share his house, let alone share his life.

He moved closer and lowered his voice. "I'm sorry, Cally. You shouldn't have had to witness that."

"How long were you together?" she asked tonelessly.

"A little over a year. I broke it off with her a week ago." He shrugged a little desperately. "I thought she was okay; I thought she understood. I tried to let her down gently. I tried to take the blame. I told her it was my fault things didn't work out—"

"She seems to have remembered that part," Cally broke in dryly.

Andy shook his head. "Please, Cally. She's drunk and she's upset. She's talking utter nonsense. I don't—"

"Did you want to have a baby with her?"

He frowned in bewilderment. "*No!* Of course not! We hadn't even talked about it! She's crazy! I don't know what she's talking about. Please, you need to believe me. Please."

Cally stared at him in silence. The seconds dragged on forever. It seemed like a lifetime had passed when her face finally relaxed and she nodded.

"I believe you," she whispered and Andy collapsed against the wall in relief. He reached for her hand and squeezed it. "Thank you," he said. "You have no idea how much it means to me."

Cally nodded and then frowned again. "Have you told her you're moving in with me?"

"No, I haven't spoken to her since last Friday night. She works at a station way out in Penrith, where I used to work. I didn't expect to ever see her again."

Cally's eyes widened in shock. "She's a police officer?"

"Yes," Andy replied, his voice grim. "Scary, isn't it?"

It was much later in the night when Tom broached the subject of Nikki with Andy. He'd returned shortly after seeing her out, but had waited a few hours into their shift before making mention of it again. Cally was long gone and for that, Andy was grateful. He couldn't imagine what she'd thought, listening to Nikki's drunken rant and he was glad she hadn't retracted her offer to have him move in with her.

After their earlier excitement, Tom and Andy's evening had been largely uneventful. They'd been rostered on because it was Sydney's annual Gay and Lesbian Mardi Gras festival. The parade wasn't scheduled until the next night, but the city's population had already swelled in anticipation.

The organizers of the event were expecting upwards of three hundred thousand people to watch the parade from the streets, with more than ten thousand of them marching. At the end of the parade, many of the revelers found their way over the Harbour Bridge and arrived in North Sydney, pumped and ready to party. It was then that the trouble could start.

But so far, the extra police presence had been unwarranted. They hadn't received a single call. It would be a different story the night of the parade, but for now, Andy was grateful for the quiet.

"So, what's the story with Nikki?" Tom asked casually, when their colleagues left for a coffee break, leaving them alone in the squad room.

Andy closed his eyes briefly and gathered his thoughts. Providing Tom with an explanation after what he'd done to diffuse the situation was the least that he could do.

"Until last Friday night, she was my girlfriend. We dated for just over a year. She's a copper out at Penrith. I was stationed there before I applied for this transfer."

"I take it she took the breakup pretty hard."

Andy shook his head, still at a loss to reconcile Nikki's behavior with the woman he'd known intimately for more than twelve months.

"See, that's where I'm confused. When I told her it was over, she was a little upset, especially in light of the length of time we'd been together, but I left her outside her building that night with the genuine belief it had gone down really well. I expected her to be disappointed, and she was, but if anyone had asked me, I'd have told them we'd left on good terms."

"Not according to her. She called you every name under the sun while I was escorting her out of the building. I remember thinking you must have really done a line on her, to warrant so much anger."

Andy looked across at Tom in bewilderment, unable to find the words to explain. He'd been shocked with the Nikki he'd seen earlier. In all the time they'd been together, she'd never once exhibited such irrational behavior. Even now, hours later, he was still flummoxed by what had happened.

"What did you say to her?" he asked, knowing if anyone could defuse Nikki's mood, it would be Tom.

"I agreed with everything she said. I told her you didn't deserve her; that a pretty girl like her would be snapped up overnight. I told her not to waste any more time or alcohol bemoaning her failed relationship but to put her energies into finding someone new, someone who appreciated what she had to offer."

"Gee, thanks, mate," Andy replied dryly.

Tom spread his arms wide, his face a picture of innocence. "Hey, everyone knows you never argue with a drunk. What did you want me to do? Besides," he added, "it worked, didn't it? She left you and your lady friend in peace."

Heat crept up Andy's neck and he studiously ignored Tom's curious gaze. Andy was sure no one else had noticed; he'd tried desperately to be discreet. He kept his conversation with Cally to a minimum when the others were around. He had no idea Tom had picked up on his interest. It just went to show he could never be too careful, especially with a cop as observant as Tom Munro around.

Not that he couldn't trust Tom with the information, it was just that he wasn't ready to talk about Cally. It was still early days in their courtship—he hadn't even moved in with her yet.

"It's all right, Andy. I understand. Your secret's safe with me. I just don't want you using her as an excuse not to deal with what happened on Tuesday. Losing your first jumper is always a hard blow to take. Whenever you're ready to talk about what happened with Tucker, I'm here for you, ready to listen. Take my advice and don't bottle it up. Your recovery's always quicker if you deal with it sooner rather than later."

The reminder of Wayne Tucker and the way he'd died flashed in bright Technicolor through Andy's mind. Tom was both right and wrong. Right, in the fact Andy had done his best to forget about it and had almost succeeded at work. It was only in the dark hours of the night when the memory of Tucker's last moments brought out a cold sweat on his brow and caused his heart to pump hard.

But Tom was wrong about Andy's interest in Cally. It had nothing to do with Tucker. He'd been keen on her long before Wayne and his fateful decision, but he couldn't deny the timing of it sucked and he could see why Tom thought they were connected.

"How's Lily?" he asked in a blatant attempt to change the subject.

Tom stared at him hard for a moment longer and then turned away, leaving Andy feeling relieved.

"She's good," Tom responded and leaned back in his chair until he could stack his boots on his desk. "She's decided to do further study. She wants to do her masters. She goes to Sydney University three nights a week. The kids and I fend for ourselves while she's out."

Andy thought of Tom and his kids fighting over who was in charge of the kitchen and he grinned. Though Tom pretended it was a burden, he actually loved to cook. He'd shared his secret with Andy one night when Tom invited him over for dinner. Andy had offered to man the barbeque.

"It'll be all right, mate. I've got everything under control," Tom had told him. "The steaks have been marinating for hours and the eggplant and peppers are ready. I'll throw them on the grill right before I pull the steaks off. They don't need as long as the meat."

Andy had been impressed with Tom's culinary skills and Tom confessed he used cooking as a way to relax, to let the day's stresses go. It was so far removed from his daily grind, Andy could see how it might work. So far, however, he hadn't been inspired to try it out for himself. His quip to Cally about microwave dinners hadn't been said in jest.

"Tell me, Tom. How long have you been married?" The question fell off his lips, surprising him as much as it did Tom.

"Well, let's see. Cassie turned fifteen awhile ago, so I guess we've been married fourteen years." He grinned, unabashed. "What can I say? Lily put up a fight to get to the altar."

Fourteen years. Andy whistled in awe. It sounded like a lifetime. His parents had barely made ten and every single one of those years were a long way from happy.

"How did you know she was the one?" he asked, curious now.

Tom shrugged and smiled at his memories. "I think I just did, you know. We got off to a rocky start but we managed to sort it out. Apart from the daily stresses of life and two young teenagers in the house, I'd say we're closer than ever. It's nice to find that with someone. I couldn't imagine not having Lily to come home to."

Andy compressed his lips against a surge of emotion. His friend's words echoed what the taxi driver had told him.

A surge of longing for someone to love him, and to love...where they could care for one another like Tom and Lily, tightened his chest and his limbs were suddenly leaden. He dragged in a breath and did his best to force his thoughts into safer territory.

Try as he might, images of Cally kept resurfacing. He imagined coming home to her for dinner and sharing his day over a drink; helping Jack with his homework or laughing over a joke. It was what families did together. At least, it was what he imagined families did together. It had never been that way in his family.

With an impatient noise, he pushed the sad memories aside, refusing to spend any more time contemplating them. His childhood was what it was; there was nothing he could do to change it. What he could do was create his own memories; new memories with a family he could call his own. He hoped with quiet determination that it might include Cally and Jack.

Only time would tell.

CHAPTER 11

"Jack, can you answer the phone, please? My hands are covered in flour."

It was only three o'clock, but Cally was already making rissoles in preparation for dinner. Rissoles, peas and mashed potato—Jack's favorite meal. It was their usual fare on Saturday night—cheap and easy.

Jack bounded into the kitchen a few moments later. His face was alight with excitement. "That was Andy. He's on his way over. I gave him our address and told him to look out for the green mailbox. He said he's about twenty minutes away."

Her heart leaped into her throat. She was acting like a girl waiting for her first date. It was ridiculous how she was getting so worked up. A man who looked like Andy would never be single for long.

A sharp stab of longing took her by surprise. She immediately repressed it. He was moving in as a roommate, a friend. That's what she'd wanted. That's what she'd demanded. She wasn't about to get all green-eyed with jealousy because of Nikki, and go and change the rules.

Besides, she'd had enough of good-looking charmers. Her high school infatuation with Stewart had well and truly seen to that. Her life was fine the way it was. Now that the financial pressure had been relieved, she might even save enough money to have a little fun. She could take Jack on a cruise of the harbor. Or a trip to Taronga Zoo.

She glanced at the clock on the wall. She still had nearly half a dozen rissoles to roll in flour. If she hurried, she'd be able to get them coated and ready for grilling and have just enough time to tidy up.

Not that she cared what she looked like, but that didn't mean she wanted him to find her with flour on her hands and a dirty apron tied around her waist.

Fifteen minutes later, she finished with the last of the rissoles and rinsed and dried her hands. She covered the patties with plastic before putting them in the fridge. She'd only just untied the strings of her apron when there was a knock at the front door. Jack leaped off the couch and bolted for the door, flinging it open before she could utter a word. Andy grinned at him from the doorway, his hands loaded with several large bags.

She ran a self-conscious hand through her hair, slipped off the apron and hid her sudden nervousness behind what she hoped was a welcoming smile.

"Hi," she murmured and ducked her head. She hadn't seen him in casual clothes and the combination of the pale blue short-sleeved polo shirt stretched tautly across his broad chest and the knee-length denim shorts had her stomach turning somersaults. Tanned, muscular calves ended at a pair of feet shod in casual, brown leather loafers.

She forced herself forward and held out her hand to relieve him of some of his bags. His heated gaze swept over her from head to toe and lingered on her bare feet. She scrunched up her toes as if that would help. Warmth stole up from her belly and spread slowly across her face.

Get a grip, you silly girl! He's just a man with flaws and frailties, like everyone else. Stop looking at him like he's a god.

Spinning on her heel, she headed back into the kitchen in an attempt to put some distance between them. Andy remained standing in the doorway. With an effort, she cleared her throat and finally found her voice.

"Um, Andy, your room's right through there." She kept her gaze planted on the doorway that led to the sleepout. He walked into the kitchen with Jack closely behind him.

"Jack, can you show Andy to his room, please?" she added.

"Yep, follow me, Andy. It's right through here." Jack's voice was high with excitement. He pushed open the old French doors that led onto the enclosed porch.

She'd furnished it simply with mismatched pieces from local second-hand shops. At one end, a pale green sofa folded out into a double bed. A small wooden table stood next to it. A cupboard that had seen better days and a couple of old leather armchairs framed a low coffee table at the opposite end.

The smell of fresh flowers wafted from the ceramic vase she'd sat on top of the table. She'd picked them from the garden that morning, telling herself she'd have done it for any guest. It was a little welcoming gesture, nothing more.

Earlier, she'd opened the louvered windows along one side of the porch to allow the fresh air to blow in, but now the sun's rays had replaced it, as it made its way westwards across the sky. She hurried forward to close them, hoping to keep the worst of the heat outside.

Glancing up at Andy where he stood right inside the door, she caught the wry look on his face.

"I take it there's no air conditioning?"

She flushed guiltily and looked away. "No, I'm sorry, there isn't. But I have an old upright fan I can set up near the sofa. It should help a bit. And once the sun's gone down, the heat won't be so bad. It's just that this side of the house faces west, so..."

"Yeah, I get the picture." He paused to wipe beads of perspiration off his lip with the back of his hand.

"I bet Mom didn't tell you how hot your room is?" Jack grinned up at him innocently.

Andy pinned her with his gaze. "No, mate, she must have forgotten to mention that."

"Look, Andy, I'm sorry. I should have said something." She met his gaze bravely, bracing herself for his anger. Instead, she found his eyes were sparkling with humor. He set his bags down on the polished wooden floor.

The boards were old, like the rest of the house, and had definitely seen better days, but they were clean and their golden chestnut color still gleamed as they must have in the past.

"I take it this is the bed?" Andy's dry query broke into her thoughts. He indicated the sofa.

"Yes. Like I told you, it's a sofa bed." Stepping forward, she showed him how it worked. "See, you pull off the cushions and then you grab this bar here and you pull it out and then you fold out these legs—and *voila!* You have yourself a bed!"

She turned back to him, smiling. His only response was a raised eyebrow. She couldn't tell whether it was amusement or disgust and she wasn't game enough to find out.

She rushed on. "I'm not sure if you've brought any linen with you, but I have plenty of sheets and pillowcases. You're welcome to borrow them. I don't think you'll need a blanket..." Heat burned her cheeks again.

"No." This time, a smile tugged at his lips. "I don't think I'll need a blanket."

She turned away. Butterflies filled her stomach again, flipping it upside down each time he smiled at her. He touched her lightly on the arm, mistaking her consternation.

"Don't worry about it too much. It's nothing that can't be fixed."

She forced herself back around, even as she tried to ignore the tingle of awareness at his touch.

"Are you sure? Because, I mean, I'd understand if you didn't want—"

"The room's fine. I have a few things outside that will make it a bit more comfortable."

"Of course." She nodded, relieved. "It's your room. Do as you please. After all, you're paying good money to use it."

"I might bring my stuff in now, if you don't mind? I'm going to have to duck down to the shops before they close. I'll dump it all in here and sort it out when I get back."

"Of course. We'll come and help you, if you like."

He flashed her another high-wattage smile. "That'd be great."

———

Andy held the front door open, allowing Cally and Jack to walk ahead of him and out into the yard where he'd parked. At some stage during his nightshift with Tom, Andy had asked to borrow Tom's pickup and trailer.

"What for?" Tom had asked, eyeing him curiously.

Andy tried not to squirm. "I'm moving some stuff to a friend's house."

Tom raised a single eyebrow and stared at him. Andy held his gaze, but it was all he could do not to look away.

"Stuff?"

"Yeah, a bit of furniture and stuff. That's why I need a trailer."

"This wouldn't have anything to do with a certain blond cleaner, would it?"

Heat crept up Andy's neck. He struggled for something to say. He swallowed a sigh in relief when Tom decided to let it go and merely offered him a wink.

"Of course you can borrow them. The boss has me rostered on again tomorrow night, in anticipation of the parade so I won't be doing much more than trying to get some sleep. I'm surprised he didn't ask you to rearrange your days off."

"He did, but I explained to him I'd already made arrangements to...to move this stuff and my friend was expecting me. I think he called in Craig, instead."

"What time do you want them?"

"I'll come straight after work, if that's all right? I'll leave my car at your place. That way, it will be easy to swap them back over when I've finished. It probably won't be until Sunday morning, though. Is that okay?"

Tom nodded. "Yeah. As I said, I've pulled another

nightshift. If I'm home by the time you return them, I'll likely be asleep. Just park them on the street and leave the keys in the mailbox if there's no one around."

Now as he approached Tom's pickup with the trailer still attached and with Cally and Jack walking ahead of him, Andy took a quick mental inventory of the things he'd loaded into it. From the way Cally spoke about her modest lifestyle, he assumed she didn't have a lot in the way of material possessions. Whilst he'd taken pride in furnishing his condo with the latest gadgets and gizmos, he was the first to admit most of them weren't necessary and he'd taken care deciding on the things to bring.

A flat screen television and a DVD player had been wrapped carefully in foam packaging. His iPad and a couple of weeks' worth of clothes had also been included. A collection of DVDs filled another box. One of his favorite things was watching old movies. As a kid, he loved to get immersed in a television show or movie, often dreaming it was his life on the screen. He didn't need a therapist to tell him what that was all about. Now, the thought of curling up on the couch in front of one with Cally held enormous appeal.

A king-sized bed frame and mattress was also roped onto the trailer. He'd remembered Cally saying something about a sofa bed. With his six-foot-three-and-a-half frame, he and a sofa bed were never going to work. The size of his bed was extravagant, but it was the only one he had.

Now he'd seen the room, he intended to head straight to the nearest electrical store and buy an air conditioner. It was summertime. There was no way he was sleeping on a porch where the only cooling was an old upright fan that had yet to materialize.

"What do you have in there, Andy?"

He looked to where Jack pointed and reached in and pulled two items out of the box. "It's a dive mask and snorkel," he explained and showed the boy how to use it.

Jack's eyes went wide. "That's pretty cool, Andy. What do you do with it?"

Andy flashed Cally a look of surprise. She shrugged and dropped her gaze. He realized she was embarrassed her son didn't know what a snorkel was.

He recalled his own childhood and remembered how limiting life could be when money was scarce. His father had never been a good provider. Whilst there had been violence and fear in the bucket loads, food and other material goods had been in short supply. He didn't need a shrink to make the connection between his difficult early life and his need to surround himself with material things and he'd learned to accept that for what it was.

He looked at Jack and his heart clenched at the thought of all the things the young boy hadn't been able to experience simply because of a lack of funds. He vowed to do something to change that.

Leaning down, he ruffled the blond head. "Tell you what, Jack. How about I take you somewhere tomorrow and I'll show you how to use it?"

"Really?" The boy's eyes shone with excitement. He turned to his mother eagerly.

"Can I, Mom? Can I go with Andy?"

As Cally watched her son interact with Andy, emotion welled up inside her and she pressed her lips together in an effort to contain it. Money woes aside, seeing the two of them together, it was clear how much Jack needed the influence of a man in his life. Already, a bond was developing between them.

She recalled the ugly scene the night before between Andy and his ex-girlfriend and wondered again at the accusations she'd thrown at him. He'd told Cally his family had been killed, but he'd never divulged the circumstances. She frowned and wondered if she should investigate it a little further. Her instincts told her she could trust him, but she'd potentially put her safety and the safety of her son at risk by inviting him into her home. She had to be sure her trust wasn't misplaced.

"Hey, if you'd rather he didn't, it's fine with me," Andy murmured, mistaking the cause of her frown.

Cally pushed her sobering thoughts aside and offered him a strained smile. "No, it's not that."

Andy closed the distance between them and lowered his voice. "Then what? For a moment or two, you looked scared."

Cally heaved a sigh. "You urged me to be cautious with this whole roommate thing."

Andy's expression displayed a little uncertainty, as if he wasn't sure where her thoughts were headed. "Yes, I did."

"Of course, I was never going to rush into it without being careful. I was even prepared to have the principal at my school run a working with children check on anyone who answered my ad."

Andy's gaze was steady on hers. "Good for you. Did you run one on me?"

She shook her head. "I didn't think there was a point. You wouldn't be employed by the police service if you had a criminal record."

"You're right. All you have to go on is your gut instinct, but feel free to speak with my friends and colleagues. You've already met some of them. Tom and Craig and Sandy were on duty last night. I saw you speaking with Tom."

She nodded. "Yes, I asked him to pass me the wastepaper basket."

Andy smiled. "See, you already know him. Ask him whatever you like."

Cally sighed. "I want to trust you, Andy, I really do. You've done nothing to make me think you're not the best thing to have happened to both Jack and me, but I can't help thinking of your ex-girlfriend and the things she said." She bit her lip and then blurted the rest of it out. "What did she mean about your family? What haven't you told me?"

Andy's face turned to stone and Cally's spirits sank. *So, there was something.* She should have known he was too good to be true. He stared at his feet for so long, she thought he was going to ignore her, but then, with a look of resignation, he threw a glance toward Jack and muttered, "You're right. We need to talk, but not here. Is there somewhere else we can go?"

————————

It was more than half an hour later, with Jack ensconced in the living room in front of Andy's widescreen television, that he and Cally withdrew to the kitchen. She pulled a pair of French doors closed and effectively sealed them from where Jack watched a movie and then took a seat at the table. She looked as scared as he felt.

He was filled with dread and his stomach churned at the thought of what he was about to reveal and how she might react. He drew in a deep breath and eased it out, knowing he had no choice but to tell her. *If they were ever going to have a chance of making a life together, he needed to come clean.* He positioned himself in a corner of the room and remained standing, his arms folded across his chest.

"My father was a violent man. He was also an alcoholic. Not that he needed it to give him courage. He'd fight whether he was drunk or sober." He risked a glance at Cally, but her face remained impassive.

"We never knew when it would happen. One minute, he'd be having a perfectly normal conversation and the next he'd be pummeling my mother with his fists. I was a child. I never could work out what set him off. It never seemed to be the same thing."

He sucked in a ragged breath and continued, wanting to get it over with. "My mother once told me my father had been raised in a violent household. Apparently, my grandfather ruled with a heavy fist and dictated how things were to happen, right down to the television shows the family watched. If instructions weren't followed to the letter, he became enraged, striking out at anyone and everyone, including his wife and my father."

"I don't think that's any excuse," Cally said quietly, her gaze lowered to the table.

"Neither do I," he said. "I told my mother as much at the time."

"What did she say?"

"She told me it was all that he knew."

"It still sounds like an excuse to me."

"I agree," he said softly.

"Is there more?"

He nodded and dragged in another breath. "My father hated the sound of the vacuum cleaner. The noise used to set him off. I never found out why. My mother learned the hard way to make sure the vacuuming was well and truly finished before he came home."

He shrugged sadly. "Most of the time, she managed it, but every now and then, my father would come home early." He closed his eyes and fought off the memories. "I remember hiding under the covers, trying hard not to listen to him beating her, hoping my baby sister, Gracie, couldn't hear."

"Oh, Andy," Cally gasped, her eyes filling with unshed tears.

Ignoring the urge to go to her and lose himself in her embrace, he forged on, determined to get through it.

"My father's drinking got worse and with it, the violence escalated. I was only ten years old, but I could tell he was completely out of control. One night, I heard him yelling at my mother and I climbed out of bed and went into the kitchen. I was determined to stand up to him, to protect her from his anger.

"I found her cowering near the kitchen sink, my father not far away. The noise must have woken Gracie because she was crying piteously from the room that contained her cot. No one else seemed to notice." Remembered fear held Andy in its grip, but he forced himself to continue.

"My father advanced upon my mother, his face blotched

red with anger. I didn't know what had set him off, but from the look of fear and resignation on my mother's face, an ugly scene was imminent. I walked into the kitchen just as my father raised his fist. My mother flinched and brought up her hands to protect her face. I ran toward them and yelled at him to stop."

His breath came faster and his heart thudded. He didn't dare look in Cally's direction.

"He didn't stop, did he, Andy?" she whispered.

"No," he gasped, "he didn't."

"What happened, Andy?"

"I was frozen with fear. I'd never felt so terrified. But, I knew I had to do something. I was sure if I didn't, he'd kill her. I shouted at him again, but my words were lost in the sound of his meaty fist as it connected with her face. Blood poured from her lip.

"Fury sent me surging toward him. I didn't even think. I threw myself on his back and pummeled him with my fists. All the time, I yelled at him to leave her the hell alone.

"My father was a big man. He barely even registered I was there. He threw me off with a sharp flick of his wrist and I flew through the air and slammed into the door of the refrigerator. My teeth went through my lip and I tasted blood."

Hot tears burned behind his eyes, but he denied them release. He had to tell Cally all of it, while he still had the strength and the courage.

"I wanted desperately to get up and offer help to my mother, but I was bleeding and desperately afraid. Instead, I lay there and watched while she endured yet another beating. Gracie was still crying in the other room, her wails had now reached fever pitch. I lay where I'd fallen, tears drying on my cheeks, hating the man I called my father...hating myself even more."

The sob he'd tried so hard to hold back burst inside his chest. Tears ran down his cheeks and he was helpless to stop them. As if in slow motion, he watched Cally push away from the table and come toward him, her own cheeks wet with tears.

Her arms went around his waist. He shuddered and sobbed and held on tight, as if she was a life preserver and he was lost in a stormy sea. It was a long time later that he raised his head and offered her a strained smile.

"Thank you."

She stared up at him, her eyes dark and unfathomable. "For what?"

"For listening; for understanding."

"None of it was your fault, Andy. Surely, you believe that?"

He stared at her and swallowed hard, dread once again weighing his gut down like concrete. "I haven't told you everything."

A shadow passed over her face, but she didn't look away. Instead, she nodded as if in acceptance and said, "Tell me."

He squeezed his eyes shut and sucked in some air. The memory of that awful day had never faded. Nearly two decades later, he could still recall every detail, despite how hard he'd tried to forget it.

When he opened his eyes again, Cally was watching him, her eyes full of warmth and concern. He couldn't remember the last time a woman cared about how he was faring. Even Nikki had encouraged him to remain independent in all of the ways it counted. Taking courage from the knowledge Cally was different, he stumbled through a recount of what had happened that fateful day.

"Dad came for us at school," he started, his voice hoarse with emotion. "It was lunchtime and he'd come to the office to pick us up early. The teachers found Gracie on the kindergarten playground. They told her Dad was waiting in the office to take her home. I was in the bathroom. When the teachers came looking for me, they couldn't find me. I found out later they returned to the office and told Dad they were still looking, but he decided not to wait." Andy's voice broke. Once again, Cally moved close and tightened her arms around his waist.

The feel of her pressed against him brought him a comfort

he'd never known and he shuddered. Images of his sunny, smiling sister with her white-blond curls and tiny baby teeth filled his head.

"Catch me, Andy! Catch me!" He could still hear her high-pitched voice as she jumped off the trampoline, completely fearless in the knowledge that her older brother waited for her below. He'd never let her fall.

But he did.

"I let her fall, Cally. I let her fall." Pain tore through him, but he couldn't give in to it yet. It was going to get worse before it got better.

"What happened, Andy?" She asked the question with so much reluctance in her voice, Andy could tell she was scared of what he was going to say. He wished he could find the words to warn her, but it was all he could do to finish.

"Dad took Gracie home. I didn't know at the time, but Mom had told him the night before she was leaving and she was taking Gracie and me with her. He phoned Mom at work and told her if she even mentioned leaving him again, she'd have the blood of her kids on her hands. He told her he already had Gracie and if she didn't come home quietly and forget all about her stupid notion of leaving, she'd never see their daughter alive again."

Cally's face paled and her eyes went wide with shock. It was almost as if she could tell what was coming. "W-what did your mom do?"

"First, she phoned the school. She didn't know if Dad was bluffing. He played with her head like that, sometimes. The school confirmed he'd taken Gracie, but that I was still on the grounds. Mom then called the police."

Andy steeled himself for what was coming, knowing he had to see it through. "When the police arrived, Dad was inside the house with a gun. He threatened to shoot Gracie if they tried anything. One of the police negotiators asked Dad to let Gracie go. 'Just open the door and let her come out,' he said. But Dad wasn't having any of it."

"Where were you, Andy?" Cally whispered.

He dropped his arms and stepped slightly away and directed his gaze to the floor. There was no way he could look at her when he told her the final, awful truth. A shudder ran through him, this one heavy with dread.

"When Mom found out I was still at the school, she drove there and collected me. The police were already on their way over to our house and I guess she just wanted me close. When we arrived, the front yard was full of police. I didn't know what was happening, but I was terrified just the same.

"The police asked Mom if she'd talk to Dad and try and get him to hand over the gun or at least, let Gracie go. She agreed to do whatever she could and climbed out of the car. I lay down on the floor of our station wagon and hid beneath a blanket."

His voice cracked. Cally's eyes were full of tears, but he forced himself to go on.

"The stand-off lasted five hours. Dad refused to give up his weapon and Gracie was going nowhere. The negotiators were at a loss. They gathered together to regroup and come up with a new game plan when we heard them: two shots. *Bang. Bang.* Dad had shot Gracie and then turned the gun on himself."

Cally gasped, shock flooding her face. "Oh, my God! Andy! How utterly devastating! How did you ever cope?"

Beyond words, he hauled her in against him as close as was physically possible. Raw sobs of agony were dragged from his throat. He cried for the beautiful little girl whose life had been stolen. He cried for the mother who'd never recovered from her loss. He cried for the young boy he'd been and for the thousands of lonely hours he'd lived ever since.

"*It should have been me!*" he choked, his voice thick with guilt and grief. "If I'd climbed out of the car, maybe I could have stopped him, gotten Gracie out of the way. Who knows? Instead, I hid like a coward, abandoning my little sister to her fate."

"*No!*" Cally's voice was low and guttural and so different from her usual tone, it startled him momentarily.

"Andy. Listen to me! You're wrong. You're dead wrong. It shouldn't have been *either* of you! *He* was the one who was sick. He should have gotten help. *He* was the adult. You were only a little boy!"

She drew in a ragged breath, her chest heaving. "He was ill, Andy. He was very ill. It was all him, Andy. All *him*. Not you. *Never* you," she said fiercely, staring at him hard.

Andy held her gaze and something gave inside him. The pain and the torment and the guilt over not only his family, but over the death of Wayne Tucker, began to ease and were slowly replaced with relief. He lowered his head and kissed her. Her lips were soft and full of wonder and it felt like the most natural thing in the world. It felt like coming home.

Cally's arms crept around Andy's neck and she tentatively kissed him back. His lips were warm and full and desire kindled low in her belly. She pressed herself even closer against him and felt his erection pushing into her belly. Her nipples hardened with the knowledge of how much he wanted her.

Deftly turning her around, he walked her back against the counter, his lips still melded to hers. She reached out a hand to steady herself and her fingers grazed the kettle. Realization that they were in the kitchen, with Jack only a closed door away crashed in upon her and broke the feverish desire that held her in its grip.

"Jack!" she gasped. "What about Jack?"

Andy lifted his head, his eyes dark with need. Confusion slowly replaced it.

"Jack? Oh, Christ. *Jack!* What the hell was I thinking?"

His breath came as fast as hers. He struggled to regain control. Cally turned away and put some distance between them. When her breathing had finally returned to normal, she risked a glance in his direction and found him staring at her, looking as shell shocked as she felt.

Recalling all that he'd gone through, she turned back to face him and offered him a shaky smile. "Are...are you okay?"

He compressed his lips, but nodded. "Yeah, I think so." She stepped toward him and he opened his arms. His heartbeat was strong beneath her ear.

"Thank you for telling me," she whispered, her voice muffled against his shirt. "I know how hard it must have been for you."

His arms tightened around her. "Not as hard as I thought it would be."

She pulled slightly away and looked at him. His eyes were still shadowed with pain. She hesitated, choosing her words with care. "Have you ever talked to someone about what happened? Someone professional, I mean?"

He shrugged. "When I was a child. I was sent to so many therapists, I lost count. None of them really made a difference. Perhaps as an adult it would be different."

"No one would expect you to get through something like that on your own. As it is, it's a real credit to you that you've managed to keep your life on a straight path." She paused. "How did your mother cope?"

He sighed. "Not so good. She had a nervous breakdown right after it happened and was admitted to a psychiatric facility. Three years later, she committed suicide."

"Oh, Andy." She was devastated all over again. He drew her closer, hushing her softly.

"Hey, don't look so sad," he whispered against her hair. "Things turned out all right for me in the end."

CHAPTER 12

A knock, coming from the other side of the closed French doors, followed immediately by Jack asking for a drink, broke the moment. Cally stepped out of Andy's arms, guilt and embarrassment heating her cheeks.

"Of course you can have a drink, honey," she hurriedly called out to her son and slid open the French doors.

"How's the movie going, buddy?" Andy asked.

"It's great. It's only just been released on DVD. Even Jimmy Baker hasn't seen it yet. Do you think I might be able to invite him over? It would be cool if we could watch it together."

Cally smiled, her heart filling with warmth at the sight of his excitement. "I'm sure that would be okay, but not today. Andy still hasn't moved all his things in and it will be dinner time before we know it. How about you invite him over tomorrow?"

"Cool," Jack smiled, and then he frowned. "Hang on, I thought we were going snorkeling tomorrow?"

Cally glanced at Andy, who nodded. "If it's okay with your mom, I'm still keen," he said.

She smiled. "It sounds like fun. Do you mind if I come with you?"

"Of course. I wouldn't expect you to leave Jack alone with me."

Cally blushed and shook her head, knowing he'd gotten the wrong idea. "It's not that I don't trust you. I do. It's just that I'd like to come with you. It's going to be a scorcher again tomorrow. A day at the beach sounds great."

Andy gave her a wide grin. "We could probably throw a picnic together and make a day of it."

She felt the warmth of his smile clear down to her toes and her gaze zeroed in on his lips. The memory of their kiss flooded her mind and her heart kicked into a higher gear. "That sounds good," she managed.

"I might go and bring the rest of my stuff inside. I want to get to the shops before they close."

She frowned. "I'm pretty new at this roommate thing and I know I said I wasn't going to cook for you every night, but I've made some extra rissoles for dinner. You're welcome to share them with us if you like. There's no need to go to the shops."

"Thanks, that sounds nice, but I'm not going food shopping. I'm going to buy a portable cooler."

"Oh!" Her face burned. "Do you really think you need one?"

"Yes, but don't be embarrassed." He shrugged. "I like to sleep in a cold room. I appreciate the offer of a fan, but I don't think that's going to cut it in this heat. Besides," he added, "I bet it's pretty cold out there in the winter, too. These old homes aren't known for their insulation."

She nodded, warmed by the thought Andy might still be living with them come winter. Besides, if he wanted to go to the expense of buying an air conditioner, she wasn't going to argue with him. After all, he was right about the heat—and the cold. When she'd decided to advertise for a roommate, she hadn't thought about the practical considerations of it. In fact, she hadn't given much thought at all to the comfort of the person who would use the room.

It was comfortable and clean and was far enough away from the other two bedrooms that no one would feel they were intruding on each other's space.

Of course, there was only one bathroom, but Andy worked shift work and that meant most of the time, there wouldn't be a rush for both of them to get into the shower at the same time.

She blushed at the thought of running into him in the bathroom in the early hours of the morning—or at any time—and wondered if she was ready to share her house with a man. The only one she'd ever lived with was her father and that didn't count at all.

He glanced over at her and frowned, misinterpreting her silence. "Cally, I didn't mean to offend you. The fact is, it's damned hot. I do my fair share of nightshifts and I'll never get to sleep without it."

"Oh, the air conditioner? That's fine." She waved her hand dismissively. If you're willing to spend your money on one, I'm not going to argue." She paused. "I was thinking about...other things."

"Oh?"

She looked away again. "Um, I'm not sure if I mentioned it, but there's only one bathroom." She shrugged. "It's a small cottage."

He grinned. "No, you must have forgotten to mention that. Along with the fact the sleepout will hit about a hundred degrees in the middle of the day." His face was a picture of innocence. "Is there anything else you've forgotten to *mention* to me? A leaky roof right above my bed? Creaky floorboards? A window that rattles all night?"

Heat flooded Cally's face again, but she caught the glint of laughter in his eyes. "Look, I'm sorry about the air conditioning thing and the fact you don't have your own bathroom. I really did forget about mentioning them." She shrugged. "I guess I've gotten used to living without certain things and it doesn't occur to me to miss them."

"Hey, it's no biggie; don't worry about it." He grinned at her again, obviously trying to put her at ease. "That reminds me, I have something for you."

He dug into the pocket of his shorts and pulled out a cell phone. "Here."

"Cool!' Jack grinned. Cally frowned. "A cell phone? Why are you giving it to me?"

"I bought it for you. You said you didn't have one."

"What I said Andy was that I couldn't *afford* one. And I still can't. I don't want you buying me things you think I should have. I'm—we," she corrected, "are used to living pretty simple lives. We don't need flash gadgets and gizmos from the glossy catalogs that flood my mailbox."

"Cally." His voice remained infuriatingly calm. "I'm not trying to buy you gadgets and gizmos you don't need. Someone broke into your home. You suspect someone's stalking you. Think of the phone as a personal alarm. It goes with you everywhere and it's there if you need to use it in an emergency."

She set her jaw and eyed him in silence.

"Think of Jack. Take it for his sake. You never know when you might need to contact someone in a hurry."

"Yeah, Mom. Take it for me."

She bit her lip, angry that Andy had put her in such a position. Then she thought of the breakdown at the side of the road and uncertainty flooded through her.

"Okay," she agreed with reluctance, "but please don't go buying me anything else. We're supposed to be roommates, nothing more. Roommates don't buy each other expensive gifts. It's just not how it works."

Andy concealed a grin and emotion surged through him. Even when she was upset with him, he was drawn to her. *Easy, mate.* She was a long way from feeling what he did and if he wasn't careful, he'd be the one picking up the pieces of a broken heart.

He'd been hopeful when she didn't run for the hills once she learned about his family, but he already knew she was kind and compassionate. She would probably have reacted that way to anyone who'd shared with her such a tragic tale. It didn't mean she had feelings for him.

But then he thought of their kiss and his spirits lifted. She'd been more than an active participant. With only the tiniest bit of coaxing, she'd turned to fire in his arms. When she remembered Jack was in the other room, and pulled back, it had been all he could do to switch off his feelings and dampen the passion that burned through his veins. He longed to kiss her again.

He thought of the ex-boyfriend who'd treated her so callously and his hands tightened into fists. It was an understatement to say that her experience with men had been less than favorable. He had to take things slowly though; he didn't want to scare her away. Yes, he'd had fallen for her and had fallen hard. The fact he'd only met her a week ago didn't seem to matter. She was the one. He just *knew*. Like what the cabbie said. Andy's biggest hurdle would be convincing her.

The ringing of his cell phone dragged his thoughts back to the present. Recognizing Will's number, he was tempted to ignore it. Just like with Tom, he wanted to get used to his feelings for Cally and see if she felt the same way before he told his friends, but knowing she could hear it ringing, he swallowed a sigh and answered the call.

"What took you so long? I was just about to hang up."

"Hey, Will. What's up?"

"Just calling to say hello. I had to go into the office to sort out some stuff with Dad. With his first grandchild on the way, he's decided to do some estate planning." Will expelled a dramatic sigh and Andy chuckled.

When Will chose his career in law enforcement rather than following his father's successful footsteps into the world of advertising, their relationship had become strained, but time and a greater effort on both of their parts was slowly working to bring them closer; a grandchild would further cement their relationship. Andy was pleased things were working out for his mate. Will had done it tough in the past, too.

"What are you up to?" Will asked. "The weather's so good, I was hoping to take the yacht out this afternoon. Do you fancy a sail? Savannah's refusing to come out with me.

She's complaining it makes her sick and she had more than enough of that in her first trimester to want to repeat it again."

Andy laughed. "Yeah, well if I'd hung over a toilet bowl as often as you told me Savannah did, bringing on another bout would be the last thing I'd want to do, too."

"So, are you up for it?"

Andy glanced at Cally who stood a short distance away. "No, mate. Not this time. I'm busy. I'm moving some stuff into a...um...a friend's house. I'm...uh...I'm house sitting over on the north side."

"Really? Who for? Have I met him?"

"No, no one you know," he replied hastily. "Anyway, I'm kind of in the middle of things here. I have to go."

"Okay. Oh, I almost forgot, Savannah asked me to invite you over for lunch tomorrow."

"Tomorrow? Er...um...Tell Savannah thanks, Will, but I've already made plans."

"Okay. Sure," Will replied, a little uncertainly. "I guess I'll speak to you later."

"Yeah. Thanks for calling, mate," he added, already feeling guilty. He ended the call and averted his gaze from Cally, not sure she was ready to hear the reasons why he'd withheld the truth from Will. He was relieved when she made no mention of the call, instead offering to help him carry the last of his things inside.

Jack skipped along beside her and Andy brought up the rear. Most of the smaller items had been brought in already. Cally nodded toward the bed frame and mattress that still sat in the trailer. "I didn't realize you'd brought your own. I told you there was a sofa bed."

"So you did. I hope you don't mind?"

"No, of course not." Her eyes glinted with rueful laughter. "But you could have said something before I gave you the full demonstration on how to turn a sofa into a bed."

He grinned back at her and then leaped up onto the trailer and maneuvered the mattress to the edge.

"I've never seen a mattress so big," Cally smiled. She

reached up and steadied it while he stepped down to the ground.

"Yeah, it's big, but it's comfortable. Trust me, once you've slept in a king bed, you'll never go back." He flashed her a slow, sexy smile. "You're welcome to try it out."

She turned beet red and stammered out a response. Taking pity on her, he grinned again and added, "When I'm not using it, of course. There'll be plenty of nights I'll be at work. Who knows? Once you get a feel for it, you might never want to give it up."

Cally couldn't drag her gaze from his. Her heart rate spiked. Her breath came fast. She did her best to bring both of them under control.

Get a grip on yourself, Cally Savage. She wasn't a teenager any longer, flinging herself into an affair without care or thought for the consequences. She had Jack to think of now. It wasn't just her heart involved.

If she did something stupid like fall in love with Andy and it all ended badly, Jack would be hurt too. She could tell how much he liked Andy already and the pair of them had only spent a few hours together. She'd do well to remember all of that, the next time she decided to wrap herself in his arms and kiss him like she never wanted to let him go.

"I'll get the door, Andy!" Jack took off at a gallop, ahead of the man who dominated her thoughts. She'd made it clear to him they'd be roommates in the narrowly defined sense of the word. She was sure he'd honor her wishes.

It was her own traitorous reactions she'd have to monitor. The way she kept responding to his nearness, she'd have to make sure she stayed well away from him lest her body betray her. She was pretty sure she could trust Andy, but could she trust herself?

She watched the broad muscles of his back flex under the weight of the mattress and hurried to lend him a hand.

Walking behind him, she admired the way his taut butt filled out the denim of his shorts and admitted she wasn't quite so sure.

"I guess that just about does it." Andy had set up his bed and they finished making it up with fresh linens Andy brought with him. He'd done his best to keep his mind from wandering to the uses the bed could be put to and from the determined look on Cally's face and the way she avoided his gaze, it appeared she was trying to do the same.

It was a little after seven. He'd already purchased a portable, reverse-cycle air conditioner from a nearby electrical store and had plugged it into the wall socket. The cool air it pumped into the room provided immediate relief from the heat. Though the sun was now low in the sky, its lingering warmth could still be felt through the windows and to sleep would be almost impossible without the comfort the cooler provided.

Cally's modest television set, looking almost as old as Jack, now sat on the small wooden table in the corner. Jack had returned to his movie and was sprawled across the sofa, a smile of contentment on his face.

"This TV is so cool, Andy! Even Jimmy Baker hasn't got one this big and he's got *everything*."

Andy grinned back at him. Cally may have thought they were happy without flash gadgets and gizmos, but it was obvious her son was delighted about the sudden entry of improved technology into his life. Watching the movie on the giant screen, Jack looked like he was in heaven.

Andy looked over and caught Cally's eye where she stood off to one side of the living room. She smiled softly back at him, her eyes full of warmth and gratitude. A surge of emotion raced to his loins and his cock hardened with the sudden rush of blood. His head might be telling him to take it easy, but his heart and other parts of his anatomy had other plans. He clenched his fists by his side in an effort to stop himself from closing the distance between them and hauling her into his arms.

As if she sensed his sudden tension, Cally broke eye contact and turned her head away. A faint blush stained her cheeks. A primeval sense of satisfaction flooded through him, knowing she recognized his need. She swallowed uneasily and cleared her throat before darting another glance in his direction. He bit back a grin.

"I-I have dinner ready, if you'd like to join us."

He smiled warmly, hoping to put her at ease. "That sounds great, thanks." Cally smiled back at him and turned toward the kitchen. Andy looked over at Jack.

"You ready for dinner, buddy? Mom said she's good to go."

Jack lifted his head off the arm of the sofa and shot him a grin. "Sure. I'll be there in a minute."

"You'll need to show me where I can sit. I don't want to take someone else's chair."

"You can sit next to me, Andy," Jack leaped off the couch and headed straight for the kitchen table, his eyes still wide with excitement.

"As long as that's all right with your mom?"

Cally was busy at the stove. He waited for her to turn around.

"Of course, Andy. Would you like gravy?"

"Yes thanks, that'd be great." He took a seat next to Jack and noted the trouble she'd gone to in setting the table. He picked up a folded white linen napkin and laid it across his lap.

The table cloth was also linen; its deep blue color reminding him of her eyes. A small vase of blue and white flowers sat in the middle of the table. They immediately brought to mind the ones he'd noticed in his room. A pleasant warmth stole through him at the care she'd taken to prepare for his arrival.

His gaze swept over her. Although she hadn't changed for dinner, her hair had been brushed recently and it now shone golden under the electric light. He remembered the feel of her against him and his fingers itched to run through its softness.

———————

Cally turned and started for the table. She caught sight of Andy staring at her and stumbled. Her gaze darted away from the intensity in his eyes. Her heart, which had been in her throat since he'd kissed her, now beat at a frantic pace; a pulse throbbed in the side of her neck.

They'd worked well together, unloading his things and even later, when they'd made the bed. It had felt so normal, so natural, sharing that every day, mundane chore. She wondered what it would be like to have someone around permanently.

Not that he'd offered to stay long term. He was doing this to help her out "in her hour of need." They were his words and she appreciated his efforts, even if a part of her now longed for things to be different.

He'd also been generous with his money. When the last of his things had been hauled in from the trailer, he'd handed her a check from his wallet. She'd read the amount printed on it and her eyes widened in shock.

"Five thousand dollars? What's this for?"

"It's to cover the rent. I thought I'd pay you in advance."

"Sure, th-that's fine but this check's going to cover you for nearly half a year. Surely, you don't want to pay that far ahead? I mean, you might not even stay that long and what about your place in Bondi?"

"Don't worry about it. I can always duck over every now and then to check on things."

Biting her lip in indecision, she glanced around uncertainly. "I feel like this is all so one-sided; that you're giving way much more than you're getting."

"I asked for this, remember and you're giving me much more than you think. Maybe not in a material sense, but now that you know my history, you can appreciate how highly I might value having someone to come home to, to talk to, even just to share my day." His eyes darkened with emotion. "For so long, I haven't had that."

Heat crept up her neck and spread across her cheeks. The memory of the kiss they'd shared prodded at her conscience. She'd made it clear from the outset they were only going to be roommates and yet she'd gone ahead and kissed him. She'd led him to believe there could be more. She didn't know if the thought pleased or terrified her.

Mistaking her silence, he spoke again. "Cally, if it makes you feel any better, I could look around for someone to rent my place. That way, I'll be able to offset the rent on this one and I won't be out of pocket."

A reluctant smile spread slowly across her face. "Okay, if you're sure it's not going to stretch you too thin. I know what that's like. Believe me, there are a hundred and one things I can put this money toward, starting with a new set of tires."

Decision made, she folded the check in half and put it inside her wallet. Without thinking, she moved closer to him and kissed him lightly on the cheek. She smelled the spicy tang of his cologne and her lips tingled where they met the warmth of his skin.

"Thank you." It was all she could manage while her heart went into overdrive.

And here he was, sitting at her dinner table, looking for all the world like he belonged there. It was far too early to trust her heart to him, yet that was exactly what her body urged her to do. She wanted to give him the family he yearned for, to replace the one that had been so tragically stolen from him. She wanted to remove the haunted look that came into his eyes every time he talked about his parents and his little sister. She wanted to make him smile and laugh and forget about his past. She wanted him to love her and for her to love him back.

But could she trust him not to let her down, not to break her heart as Stewart had? Was it too soon to be feel so strongly about a man she'd only just met? Was she completely mad for even letting herself *think* like this?

She forced her thoughts away from him and set down plates of food. Amongst their murmured thanks, she took her usual seat across from Jack and directed her attention to her meal.

"Can we still go snorkeling tomorrow, Andy?"

"Absolutely, mate. Where do you normally go swimming?"

"We usually go over to Manly. We catch the bus from Chatswood Chase. Mom says it's cheaper than running the car all that way and then we don't have to pay for parking."

Cally choked on a mouthful of rissole, her face blazing. Grabbing a napkin, she coughed heartily into it, turning away from the table to avoid Andy's gaze.

"Your mom's right, Jack. With the cost of gas, it probably is cheaper to take the bus."

"So, are we going to Manly then?" Jack's face was alight with excitement.

"Well..." Andy flicked his gaze to Cally's. "I thought we might go over to Bondi. It's in the eastern suburbs, on the other side of the Harbour Bridge. Have you been to Bondi before?"

"Mom, have I been to Bondi before?"

Cally took her time chewing and swallowing the food in her mouth, buying time. Eventually, she had to speak. She kept her eyes fixed firmly on Jack's face. "Um, no, I don't think so, honey. We usually go to Manly."

"Cool! So, now I not only get a ride across the Harbour Bridge, I also get to go to a beach I've never seen before. Wait until I tell Jimmy about all of this. Maybe he could come with us?"

He looked so hopeful, Cally couldn't help but say, "I guess we could call his mom and see if he's free."

Jack pumped the air with his fist. "Yes!"

Andy laughed. "It sounds like the pressure's on me to show you both a good time. Lucky for me, I've spent a lot of time in Bondi. I know all the best places to go snorkeling and

I might even know where the ice cream shops are."

"Yay!" Jack shouted, grinning madly.

Cally smiled, but nerves jangled in her belly at the thought of spending more time with Andy. Almost alone.

On a beach.

In a bikini.

Her heart pounded. She swallowed. "It sounds great."

CHAPTER 13

"Are we there yet, Andy?"

Cally groaned. It was the fourth or fifth time Jack had asked and if it wasn't Jack, it was Jimmy. After calling Penny Baker and obtaining her permission to allow Jimmy to come with them, they'd swung by his place and collected him. There was much excitement from both boys and many curious glances from Penny shot in Andy's direction. Cally had refused to answer any of the questions she saw burning in Penny's eyes and hurried the boys to the car.

Now, Andy chuckled at her frustration with the boys' impatience. He glanced across to where she sat in the passenger seat of his Audi. He'd returned the trailer and Tom's truck earlier that morning. The Munro household had been quiet and still. Grateful he'd avoided Tom and his questions, he left a note of thanks along with the keys of Tom's truck in the mailbox. He returned to Cally's place in the Audi he'd left outside of Tom's.

He still felt a little guilty over lying to her about subletting. He wouldn't be renting his condo out. He'd only said it to convince her to let him stay. Besides, he didn't want her to wonder how he could afford to pay rent and meet his monthly mortgage payment. In Sydney, only a person of above-average means could afford to pay what was, in effect, double rents.

Even though he was pretty sure Cally wouldn't be swayed

by money—his experience with Nikki made him wary; he couldn't completely discredit the idea. If Cally formed deeper feelings for him, he wanted to know it was for him and not for his bank balance.

"It's a beautiful day," she murmured, gazing out across the harbor.

Andy nodded in silent agreement. His gaze lingered on the soft peaks of her breasts which were clearly outlined beneath her snug, navy-blue T-shirt. White cotton shorts that finished mid-thigh and brown leather sandals completed her ensemble. A long expanse of tanned skin, starting at the point where her shorts ended, was bared to his gaze.

Desire kindled low in his gut and his board shorts grew uncomfortably tight. He'd always been a legs man and Cally's didn't disappoint. Knowing there was nothing he could do about his erection, he swallowed a sigh and dragged his gaze away to concentrate on the road.

Bright sunlight glinted off the deep blue water of the harbor and glittered like white diamonds. The Sunday morning traffic was heavy and their progress was slow. People were making the most of their weekend and the warm summer day. He was as impatient as Jack and Jimmy for the sight and smell of the beach.

"Wow, I can see the Opera House! And look at all those boats over there! Mom, can you see them?"

"Yes, sweetheart, I see them. They're a long way down, aren't they?"

"Yeah, they look like little toys," Jimmy added, his head halfway out the window.

"Don't stick your head out too far, Jimmy," Cally warned. "Your mom would kill me if we brought you back without it."

Jimmy grinned, but obediently sat further back in his seat.

"What are we going to do first, Andy?" Jack asked, his voice pitched high with excitement.

"Can we go straight to the rock pools?" Jimmy pleaded.

Andy glanced at the boys in his rearview mirror and grinned. It felt good to be doing this: A family outing—going to the beach. It was another glimpse of what was missing from his life: *a family.*

He snuck another peek at Cally. Her face was relaxed, her hands folded in her lap. Warmth spread through him. It felt so right, being with this woman, sharing the day with her, with Jack and his friend. He needed to find a way to make her feel this rightness, too.

"What would you like to do, Jack? We have all day. You choose."

"Snorkeling! I want to go snorkeling!"

"Snorkeling it is, then." He turned to Cally. "What about you? What's first on your list today?"

She grinned at him. "I'm going to dive into the ocean and catch some waves. It's so hot already, I can't wait to get wet."

"*Mm,* sounds good to me." His gaze dropped involuntarily to her breasts.

Her cheeks turned pink and he grinned inwardly, more than a little heartened at her response.

He let his hand fall near her leg, his fingers only inches away from her bare thigh and heard her sudden intake of breath. Desire surged through him, hot and immediate. He glanced toward her, pleased to see a pulse beating frantically in the side of her neck. *Was she going to admit how much he turned her on, or was that just part of his fantasy?* Perhaps she was going to give him a piece of her mind?

Instead, she turned her head to face him and flashed him a brilliant smile. It caught him by surprise.

"What's that for?"

"I just wanted to say thanks for...everything. Jack loves having you around and I... I do too."

He stared back at her and his heart hammered against his ribs. "Thank you, Cally." He pitched his voice lower. "I know how hard it's been for you to trust anyone and I appreciate the fact you're starting to trust me. I understand better than most how important it is to be cautious. It's a tough world out there and there are a lot of weirdos you don't want to come into contact with."

He kept his gaze steady on hers, suddenly thankful for the queues of traffic that had brought them almost to a standstill. He wanted her to understand how much he meant what he said.

"I get your reticence and I applaud it. You can never be too careful where Jack's safety is concerned. You're a great mom, Cally. He's a very lucky boy."

Their gazes meshed and hers glittered like the harbor below them.

"Why are you crying?" he whispered.

She shook her head, as if she couldn't find the words to explain it. "Th-they're happy tears," she stammered. "I'm sorry I've been a bit of a control freak," she said. "For a decade, it's just been Jack and I. I'm not used to giving anyone else the power to make a decision, especially one that affects us."

"It's okay, Cally. I understand. Really, I do. I'm a control freak, too. After growing up in such a dysfunctional family and becoming orphaned at the age of thirteen, I learned very quickly to rely on no one but myself. Even now, it's hard for me to ask for help or to lean on someone else. Just ask Will or Tom, or any of the guys I work with."

He smiled and she smiled shakily back at him. The traffic started moving again and he returned his gaze to the road.

"What do you say we forget about the shitty childhood we both had and have a great day at the beach?"

She grinned at him, her tears now gone. "It sounds perfect to me."

The sand was hot and golden beneath her bare feet. Cally sighed in pleasure and found a secluded spot to lay her towel not far from the water's edge. After purchasing a couple more snorkels from the shop along the promenade, Andy had taken Jack and Jimmy further up the beach. She could just make them out as they headed toward the rocks.

With their blond heads and long, tanned bodies, they could easily pass for a father with his two sons.

Tugging off her T-shirt and shorts, she squeezed waterproof sunscreen lotion into her hand and rubbed it over her skin. Moments later, she raced down to the water's edge. She waded in until the water was deep enough for her to dive under the waves, relishing the coolness against her heated skin.

The water was divine. Flipping onto her back, she floated on top of the waves, her eyes closed against the bright sun. She glanced over in the direction Andy and Jack had taken, but they'd disappeared from sight.

After enjoying the water for a little while longer, she headed back to shore. Adjusting her bikini top, she stretched out on her towel. The surf cooled her sufficiently that she was now able to enjoy the warmth of the sun. She closed her eyes and breathed in deeply of the salty air. Within moments, her thoughts turned to Andy: smiling, concerned, laughing, serious.

He was all she'd ever hoped to find in a man and he seemed to be as taken with Jack as her son was with him. *What more could she ask for?* Andy wasn't Stewart. He could never be that callous. Andy was kind and gentle and funny. He couldn't be more different from Stewart if he tried.

But he still had the power to break her heart. Could she handle it if things didn't work out? Was she brave enough to try?

She didn't know the answers to those questions, but all at once, she didn't care. Life was too short to live it in fear and uncertainty and "what ifs." She could almost hear her beloved aunt's voice telling her life was full of risks and if Cally wasn't prepared to risk, then she wasn't prepared to live...

It was time she stood her ground. Just because her last boyfriend had been a complete jerk, didn't mean all men were like that. With the heat from the sun making her drowsy, she laid her head down on her folded arms. It seemed only moments and she was asleep. Her dreams were vivid and full of images of Andy and Stewart and Jack.

First it was Stewart, leaning down to kiss her, his dark hair brushing against her skin as his tongue pressed against her lips.

She opened her mouth and it was Andy she was kissing and Andy's strong brown hand cupping her breast, rubbing her nipple through the satiny fabric of her black bikini top. She moaned. Heat and desire pooled deep inside her. Reaching behind her, she untied the strap of her bikini top and tugged it down, exposing her naked breasts to his hot gaze.

She blushed at her boldness and watched his blond head descend toward the hard nubs of her nipples. His warm tongue stole out and her breathing quickened. His mouth closed over one and suckled. She drew in a sharp breath and arched into him. Running her fingers through his thick hair, she held his head against her breasts.

Then Andy's hair turned black. She gasped. Her fingers were threaded through Stewart's locks and now it was Stewart who was licking and biting at her nipples. She twisted and turned beneath him and tried to get away.

From far off in the distance, she heard Jack calling out to her. Guilt and panic seized her. She struggled harder under Stewart's weight, trying desperately to cover herself before her son discovered them.

Wrenching away from the dream, she came awake with a start. Her heart hammered. She sucked in great gulps of air and shook her head to clear it of the dream's residue.

"Mom! Mom! You won't believe what we saw! It was so cool! You have to try it!"

The words slowly penetrated the fogginess of her brain. Jack and Jimmy ran toward her. Andy trailed a short distance behind. Her hand went instinctively to her bikini top and she breathed a sigh of relief when she found the scrap of black fabric still firmly in its place.

Giving them a weak smile, she shaded her eyes against

the sun and looked up at them. "How'd you do, boys?"

Jack's eyes shone with an excitement that was reflected in Jimmy's.

"It was so cool, Mom! Andy took us to the rock pools. He showed us how to use the snorkels and we saw some really cool things under the water."

"I saw some tiny silver fish, Ms Savage and some weird-looking plants and a heap of white and black things that were moving on the bottom—I don't even know what they were."

"Andy told me not to touch anything, and I didn't, did I Andy?" Jack added. "Are you proud of me, Mom?" His smile couldn't get any wider.

Cally stood and put her arms around him, smiling at the happiness on his sun-kissed face. "Of course I'm proud of you, darling. And I'm glad you did as Andy said. You shouldn't ever touch things you see under the ocean. Sometimes they can be harmful and even if they're not, you can damage them if you touch them. They're living, breathing organisms and you want to make sure they're still there for the next person to enjoy."

Jack nodded enthusiastically. "Yeah, that's what Andy said. It's all about being *en-vi-ro-mentally* responsible. Right, Andy?"

Andy was in trouble. One look at Cally in her black bikini and his body had reacted. His cock was rock hard and his breath came short. The scraps of fabric she wore did little to conceal the full roundness of her breasts and the pert, golden globes of her buttocks.

Part of her tan line was visible at the top of one of her thighs where her bikini brief had ridden up when she stood. He was only glad he'd chosen to wear loose board shorts, rather than the tighter, more revealing speedo briefs he sometimes did. He tried desperately to think of anything that would distract his attention from her near-naked perfection.

It wasn't as if she didn't know he was attracted to her—they'd shared a steamy kiss, after all. But they were far from alone and the last thing he wanted was to embarrass her. Realizing the boys were waiting for his response, he took another calming breath and forced his lips into a smile. "Right, Jack."

Cally shot him a curious look, no doubt reacting to his strained tone, but she was either too polite or too naïve to notice his predicament. He turned away on the pretext of looking out at the ocean. "Who wants to catch some waves?"

"Me!" Jack squealed and streaked off toward the water.

"Me, too!" Jimmy hurtled off after his friend.

Andy risked a glance at Cally. "Coming in?"

She looked at the water and then back at him. "Last one in's a rotten egg," she called and ran into the foaming waves.

"So, what would you like for lunch?" Andy addressed the question to the three people who sat around the table with him at his favorite café on the promenade.

"I can't decide," Jack complained good naturedly. "What are you having, Jimmy?"

"I'm having fish and chips," Jimmy announced. "With tomato sauce."

"Fish and chips it is."

"Don't forget the tomato sauce!" Jimmy reminded him.

Andy smiled. "I promise I won't forget the tomato sauce." He turned to Cally. "How about you? What would you like? I can highly recommend the garlic scallops with grilled asparagus wrapped in prosciutto. The scotch fillet is good, too. Then there is the—"

"I take it you've eaten here before?" She smiled.

"Maybe once or twice," he grinned.

"I think I'll try the scallops. They sound too good to bypass."

"You won't be disappointed, I'll guarantee it. Now, have you decided yet, Jack?"

Jack frowned down at the menu in his hands. "I think I'll have what Jimmy's having." He set the menu aside. "And I'll have a caramel milkshake, thanks."

"I'll have a vanilla one. Thank you, Mr Warwick," Jimmy added.

Andy signaled to a waitress who promptly took their order. He added a beer to his list of requests and Cally asked for a soda. As soon as the meals arrived, the boys dived into their food, ravenous. He winked at Cally, who lowered her gaze. He still wasn't sure she was aware of his hard-on, but ever since the moment on the beach, she'd avoided his gaze and her cheeks had remained pink.

After lunch, they went for a walk along the promenade, admiring the view of the ocean in all of its summer glory. When they passed an ice cream shop, both Jack and Jimmy begged them to stop.

"What do you think, Cally? Do they deserve to have an ice cream?"

She looked at the boys and the desperation on their faces and laughed. "I think so. They both ate their lunch. I'm surprised they have any room for ice cream, but I guess everyone leaves room for that."

"Yes!" Jimmy shouted.

"Thanks, Mom," said Jack.

"How about you?" Andy asked. Have you saved room for ice cream?"

Cally giggled and the girlish sound of it tugged at his heart.

"Of course," she smiled. "I *always* leave room for ice cream."

With ice creams in hand, they strolled along the paved promenade that bordered the beach wall. Young people zipped past them on skateboards and bikes. Others had chosen to jog. Even more people walked—like they did—

enjoying the afternoon. The boys were a little way ahead of them, engrossed in their ice creams and each other.

"Whereabouts is your place in Bondi, Andy?" Cally asked after a few moments of companionable silence.

Andy tensed and then forced himself to relax. The more he got to know her, the surer he was that she'd never be swayed by money. She didn't seem to have a clue about his wealth, despite the one hundred and fifty thousand dollar Audi he'd parked in her driveway. Then again, she might not know what it was worth.

He should just come right out and tell her, but he didn't want to complicate things. She was only just beginning to trust him, to open her heart to him. It was obvious she was interested in him, despite the boundaries she'd initially put in place. She'd kissed him with as much passion as he kissed her. If Jack hadn't been in the next room… Who knew where that kiss might have led?

Did he want to risk her fledgling feelings by talking about something as crass as money? He knew how important it was to her. It was the main reason she'd asked him to move in. It had been important to Nikki, too albeit in a more selfish way.

In fact, money was important to most people. He couldn't deny its importance to him. But he didn't want it to be the reason Cally fell in love with him—*if* she fell in love with him.

Could he really be that lucky? Or was it only wishful thinking? After his entirely shitty week, he could do with a little luck. Was it possible she could learn to love him, despite his flaws and failings or was he conjuring up happily-ever-after scenarios that had little basis in reality? And what would happen when she found out he was rich? Would a seven-figure bank balance change the way she felt about him? Would it make her want him more, or would she be angry he kept it from her?

He'd never been good at reading a woman's mind—hell, he didn't know *any* man who was good at that. In his experience, they always reacted the opposite way you thought they would. He'd long ago given up trying to work them out.

What he did know was that he wanted her to love him for himself. If she was going to eventually fall in love with him, he wanted her to fall in love with Andy Warwick, the police officer, negotiator and all-round good guy.

Slowing to a halt, he lifted his gaze to hers and finally answered her question. "My place is a little ways up the hill from here." Purposefully vague, yet not being dishonest, he hoped her curiosity would be satisfied. He should have known he wouldn't get away with it that easily.

"Really? So it's not too far away?"

It was obvious she was angling for information, but he refused to take the bait. "No, not too far." He took a bite of ice cream, filling his mouth and then took his time swallowing it.

"Maybe you could take us there?"

He froze and then forced his lips into a smile. "Maybe. Right now, it's getting late though. We should probably head back."

Calling out to Jack and Jimmy, Cally watched Andy take another bite of his ice cream and frowned. Something wasn't right. That was the second time in as many minutes Andy had deflected questions about his house. Surely he had one? After all, he'd been living somewhere before he'd moved in with her and why would he tell her he lived in Bondi if he didn't? There was no reason to make up something like that.

Unless he didn't want her to know where he *really* lived? Property in Bondi didn't come cheap. She knew that first hand after spending hours scrolling through real estate websites at the local library before she'd moved from Armidale.

Was it possible he'd lied about where he lived to *impress*

her? But what about the five-thousand dollars he'd presented to her? He had to have surplus money to hand over a check like that. She snuck another peek at him as he stared out in silence at the ocean. Had she misread him? Had she gotten another man she liked totally wrong—*again*?

He'd seemed so straight forward, so totally without artifice. At least, that's what she'd thought before he moved in. *What if she was wrong? What if it was all a farce?* What if he'd created this well-to-do persona just to impress her? Did she appear so hung up on money that he thought he had no choice? How shallow did he think she was?

Her frown deepened. Was she jumping to wild conclusions? After all, just because he'd been vague about where he lived didn't necessarily mean his place didn't exist near the beach. Did it? Could she have it wrong? Could there be some other reason why he was disinclined to talk about himself? He'd willingly shared some of the most painful secrets of his past. Why not his present?

She sighed. She didn't know what to think. One minute she was having hot and steamy fantasies about him and the next she'd almost convinced herself he was a deceitful egomaniac. But there was one thing she did know: Anything that seemed too good to be true usually was. And a free lunch could end up being the most expensive meal of your life...

A little over an hour and a half later, Jack lay sound asleep, sprawled across the back seat of Andy's car. They were headed back to Cally's cottage after dropping Jimmy home. She couldn't stop her thoughts from circling around and around the ever-increasing number of questions she had about the man who sat next to her. From the corner of her eye, she saw him glance across at her.

"You're awfully quiet, Cally."

She sighed, knowing he was right, but she wasn't ready to confront him with her suspicions. "I'm tired, that's all."

"Big week?"

"You could say that."

"What's on tomorrow?"

Her gaze rested on his strong, tanned hands that looked so sure and confident on the steering wheel. "I've got school from eight-thirty until three and then a couple of hours cleaning at the station. How about you?"

"I'm on nightshift. I start at six."

"So you'll be arriving at work not long before I do." A wry smile turned up her lips.

"I guess."

"At least we don't have to fight over the shower."

"Not tomorrow, anyway."

She blushed. Despite her misgivings, images of him naked and steamy in the shower immediately crowded her mind. She had to stop thinking of him like that: like he was the most desirable man in the world; like she couldn't wait to put her hands on him, her lips, her tongue...

Suppressing a groan of frustration, she turned away and peered out the window. The day was nearly over and the late afternoon traffic had dwindled. Before long, Andy turned off the Pacific Highway and swung the car into her tree-lined driveway. He brought the car to a halt and she turned to him, offering him a smile.

"Thanks for today, Andy. It was great and I know the boys enjoyed themselves, Jack especially. I appreciate all you did for him today. It's a day he's not going to forget."

His gaze moved over her face and then lingered on her lips. He was close enough to kiss her. She wondered what he would do if she leaned over and pressed her mouth against his. The thought sent a shiver of anticipation running through her.

As if reading her mind, he moved closer and took her face in his hands. He stared at her for long moments, as if waiting for her to object, before lowering his mouth. His lips touched hers so lightly that afterwards she wasn't even sure whether he'd actually kissed her. She pulled back slightly and looked up at him.

His eyes were liquid chocolate, molten with desire. Of its own volition, her hand came up to rest on his cheek. It was all the invitation he needed.

Pulling her hard against him, his lips met hers again. This time, there was no holding back. Andy kissed her with a passion that left them both breathless. The warm pressure from his mouth sent shards of desire shooting through her body. His tongue found hers and tangled in a timeless dance of parry and thrust. His hands moved from her head to fondle her breasts, covered only by the soft black bikini top.

Her nipples hardened beneath the fabric. She strained against him, trying to get closer, groaning in frustration when the gearstick kept getting in the way. His hand stole down to caress her bare thigh and slowly eased higher. She moaned against his lips.

He growled low in his throat and his hand moved higher. He stroked her through the cotton of her shorts. Need throbbed in her core. A moment later, he slipped his fingers under the waistband of her shorts and then her bikini bottom until his fingers tangled in her soft curls. One finger, then two slid teasingly across her wet slit.

She groaned and flung her head sideways against the leather headrest. She was on fire, burning with need. With her eyes almost closed, she caught sight of Jack's sleeping form.

Reality crashed into her. She gasped and pulled back, pushing Andy's hand away.

"Andy, please. Stop. We can't. What about Jack?" She dragged deep breaths into her lungs and tried to regain control.

With his face taut from the effort, Andy visibly fought to regain control. His breath was ragged. His jaw was clenched.

"Cally, I'm sorry. I don't know what the hell I was thinking. I shouldn't have... It's just that, you're so damned beautiful and I-I thought a kiss would be enough." He shrugged, seemingly at a loss for words. His eyes burned with emotion.

She looked up at him, feeling just as confused and uncertain. "I'm sorry, too," she whispered. "I shouldn't have led you on like that. I don't know what got into me. I just..." She blushed and looked down at her hands. Jack stirred on the back seat, blinking sleepily. He sat up. They jumped back from each other as if they'd been burned.

Andy opened his door and climbed out. He pulled the beach bag and their hats out of the trunk and walked around to her side to assist her from the car. Opening the rear door, she leaned in and helped her son from the car.

"Come on honey, we're home. Let's go inside."

Well-hidden behind the dark shadows of the overgrown bushes that crowded Cally's driveway, Stewart Brady stared at her and the man she was making out with in the front seat of a top-of-the-line Audi. The years had been kind to her. She barely looked a day older. Her hair was now short, but it still glinted gold in the late afternoon sunlight. When she turned her face to meet the mouth of the man in the driver's seat, her tanned skin looked almost luminous.

The anger that had been simmering beneath the surface ever since he discovered her treachery, now threatened to boil over. He'd wanted to search for her the very instant he'd read the newspaper article more than a month ago, but the inconvenience of his criminal trial had taken precedence. There was no point in further antagonizing the law. With a bit of luck, his father would see to it that the matter disappeared, but until then, he had to pretend justice would prevail.

It was a stroke of luck that the judge had taken ill. The trial had been adjourned for a week. In the meantime, he was free on bail. Within hours, he'd convinced his father to lend him a set of wheels and he headed south to Sydney.

It had taken him longer than he'd thought to find her. He'd committed every word of the newspaper story to memory, including the street and suburb the article had mentioned, but the Pacific Highway ran for miles and he'd spent the better part of a day walking up and down the busy road searching for the house that looked like the one in the picture.

It had been late in the afternoon when he finally spied the concealed driveway. He'd barely had time to take in the old-but-tidy cottage and the battered Toyota parked beside it before the swish Audi swung into the driveway. He'd darted into the bushes and took refuge there while he studied the new arrivals.

When he recognized Cally in the passenger seat, he'd nearly stepped forward and revealed himself, but a glance at the size of the man beside her had given him pause. Even from behind the steering wheel, it was obvious the man was no lightweight.

Stewart took a swig from the hip flask he kept in his shirt pocket and relished the burn of the alcohol down his throat. The couple in the car a few feet away continued to make out. Even from his hideout, he heard the sounds of their passion.

His cock stirred. It had been too long since he'd had a woman. Ever since he'd been slapped with the assault charge, even the sluts around Watervale had steered clear of him and it wasn't like Tiffany had put out too often. As soon as the wedding ring slid on her finger, sex had become a scarce commodity. If it hadn't been for his son, Luke, he'd have divorced the bitch years ago.

He winced at the thought of his son, now rotting in the Watervale Cemetery. Life was totally fucked up. There was no doubt about it. But then, just when he thought he couldn't take another kick to the guts, it surprised him; and that made him realize life was still worth living. He'd been beyond stunned when he'd stumbled across the discovery of Cally's son—*his* son—alive and well in Sydney. It had given him the impetus he'd needed to reclaim his life. It was too bad he'd had the unfortunate run-in with the prick at the gym. Being the defendant in a well publicized criminal trial, even when released on conditional bail, had a way of restricting his movements.

His thoughts returned to his son. *Jack Savage.* It was a good strong name, a name he might even have chosen himself, if he'd been given the opportunity. Of course, he'd change the boy's surname to Brady as soon as he could. There was no way his son wasn't going to bear his name.

The murmur of voices coming from the Audi snagged his attention. He returned his attention to the vehicle and noticed the figure of a child in the back seat. He froze. Blood gushed through his veins, the sound almost drowning out the voices.

A small blond head leaned toward the couple in the front seat. Stewart gasped. *It was him.* His son. He knew it.

Everything inside him urged him to rush forward and claim the boy then and there, but years of knowing when to be cautious held him back. He'd arrived in Sydney unarmed.

The driver looked like someone who could handle himself. While Stewart was confident in his ability to throw a punch, he never took on a fight he wasn't certain he could win.

It would be foolhardy to reveal himself too early. Cally could take fright and disappear. Who knew how long it could take to find them again if he lost the element of surprise?

Taking a deep breath, he forced the air way down into his lungs and calmed the racing of his heart. Now wasn't the time, but it would come. As sure as night followed day, his time would come.

CHAPTER 14

Cally pulled a sheet over Jack and leaned down to press a kiss against his cheek. His eyelids fluttered, but he remained asleep. With a soft sigh, she left the bedroom, pulling the door closed behind her. Andy was sprawled on the couch.

"How is he?" he asked.

Heat crept over her cheeks. Memories of their kiss were still fresh, no matter how hard she tried to push them to the far recesses of her mind. She averted her gaze. Nerves jangled in her belly, but she cleared her throat and forced herself to answer.

"He's fine. I think he was asleep again before his head hit the pillow."

"Come here, Cally." The words were uttered softly, but there was no escaping the intensity of feeling in the dark eyes that captured hers.

Jittery as a virgin, she walked slowly toward him. Her heart hammered so loudly, she was sure he could hear it and her palms were suddenly damp with perspiration. Perching herself on the very edge of the couch, as far away from him as possible, she drew in a deep breath.

"I'm not going to bite." He grinned and patted the spot next to him.

She moved about half an inch closer. Humor tugged at his lips. Their eyes meshed again and she could no longer drag hers away. She watched in fascination as the laughter faded and was replaced by hot, molten desire.

"What are you afraid of, Cally?" he whispered, his voice husky.

She shrugged wordlessly.

His voice pitched lower. "Do you even know?"

Again, she shrugged, unable to form the words.

"Do you know what I think?"

She tore her gaze away, not at all sure she wanted to hear what he had to say.

"Look at me, Cally," he commanded softly.

Her gaze met his again and her heartbeat doubled its pace. She waited for him to speak.

"I think you're afraid to trust your heart. You've been wrong in the past and you don't know if you can risk being wrong again. Am I right?"

She screwed her eyes shut. "Maybe." Her voice was a ragged whisper. All at once, her fears overwhelmed her and her breath came out in a rush. He was there in an instant, sliding across the old leather couch to take her into his arms.

At first, the tears fell slowly, but when he pulled her into his lap and cradled her head against his chest, it was like a dam had suddenly broken. She sobbed against the soft cotton of his T-shirt. She couldn't even remember the last time she'd been held tenderly by a man. In fact, she didn't think she'd ever been held that way.

"*Shh,*" he whispered, his lips moving against her hair.

She tried to bring a halt to them, but the shuddering sobs continued. His shirt was wet beneath her cheek and still, the tears kept falling.

"It's okay. Let it all out, sweetheart. I bet you haven't cried properly since it happened."

She shook her head and murmured her disagreement. Her words were muffled against his shirt. Gently tilting her chin up, his gaze met hers.

"I'm sorry? I didn't catch that. Were you trying to tell me something?" His eyes were now soft and teasing.

She offered him a shaky grin. Relief flooded his face. She

swiped at her eyes. "I said, you're wrong. I can't remember how many nights I cried myself to sleep during those first few months."

Snuggling back against his chest, she whispered hoarsely. "I was only a teenager, pregnant and abandoned by everyone I thought loved me. I was so scared—for me and for the baby. I didn't know what was going to happen."

Andy's arms tightened about her. She drew in a shaky breath and continued. "And then Aunt Mary saved me. She must have heard me crying, night after night, but she never said anything. Instead, she came to me one evening just after dinner and told me how glad she was that I'd come to stay with her."

Cally turned her tear-stained face up to his. "As if it had been my choice. As if there was no scandal. As if it was perfectly normal for me to arrive on her doorstep, pregnant and unloved, and move into her life." Her voice cracked.

"She told me she understood how scared I was feeling and how she was there to help me in any way she could. She told me to think about my unborn baby and to try, for just a little time each day, to feed him a bit of happiness."

'Babies feel your emotions, Cally,' she told me. 'You don't want your baby to be swimming in your sadness. I know it feels like you're never going to be happy again, but you will, dear girl, trust me. And until you actually feel like smiling again, you need to force yourself to think at least one happy thought a day.'

"She knew exactly what to say to me, Andy. She knew if I only thought about myself and the mess my life was in, I wouldn't have made the effort to come to terms with the position I found myself in. She knew by bringing Jack into it, I'd find the strength from somewhere to drag myself out of the depths of the blackness and head toward the light, at least for a little while each day."

He murmured against the softness of her hair. "She loved you."

"Yes." She sighed heavily. "She did."

"So what happened? How did you and Jack end up in Sydney?"

They were still on the couch, but Andy had maneuvered them backwards until they lay stretched out with Cally tight against his side. She breathed in his spicy, sun-kissed scent and took comfort from the reassuring feel of his heart beating solidly beneath her cheek.

"My aunt got Alzheimer's."

His arms tightened around her. "Oh, how awful. For all of you."

"Yes. It was. At first, we barely noticed anything different, but it's an insidious disease. When it took a hold of her, it didn't let go." She shuddered.

His voice was quiet. "She needed specialists' care."

"Yes. The house was sold to cover the costs. Jack and I moved into a little apartment on the outskirts of town. It was only a bed-sit, really. A tiny bedroom, a bathroom and one room for everything else. It was cheap though, which was all that mattered."

"How long were you there?"

Sadness filled her. "My aunt died about six months after she went into the nursing home. I guess it was a blessing in a lot of ways. Toward the end, most days she didn't even know who we were."

"What brought you to Sydney? It's a long way from Armidale."

Her smile turned wistful. "I don't know exactly. I'd had enough of small country towns and I was looking for something different. For once in my life, I wanted to be able to walk down the street without anyone recognizing me. I might have moved to the next town, but the rumors followed me."

She sighed. "My father was well known amongst the university community that made up so much of the population of Armidale. Jack was eight then, but there were still plenty of pitying looks and whispers behind covered mouths as people recalled who I was—the girl who'd brought such shame to her family, the daughter of the upstanding principal of Watervale High."

Twisting her head, she looked up at him. "I wanted anonymity. What better place to find it than the biggest city in Australia?"

Andy grinned down at her. "You have that right. I couldn't even tell you the names of the people who live in my condominium block. How's that for anonymity?"

Cally smiled back at him. "Exactly. But you know, sometimes it's nice to meet a familiar face. I guess I do miss that a little bit."

"How often do you go back?"

She bit her lip. Her voice dropped to a whisper. "We haven't been back to Armidale since my aunt died. I've never been back to Watervale."

His arms tightened around her again and his lips pressed against her hair. "Thank you for telling me."

They lay in silence, listening to the sounds of the old house as it settled in for the night. Her eyes were sore and heavy. A day at the beach, topped with her emotional outburst had left her drained and exhausted. The comforting feel of Andy's warm chest and the strong, steady beat of his heart made her feel safe and secure. Her eyes drifted closed.

———————————

Cally's breathing deepened. Andy moved slightly, trying to find a more comfortable position. Protectiveness surged through him. It hadn't been easy for her to relive memories that brought her so much pain—just as it hadn't been for him. He couldn't help but admire her courage.

She'd been abandoned by everyone she'd loved—her jerk of a boyfriend, her callous parents. Even her beloved aunt had abandoned her in death. And yet, she'd risen above it, proving she was a fighter. She'd finished her schooling and had gone to college. She'd secured a job in her profession. She'd raised a son almost on her own and had forged a life for them both.

Lately, times had been a little tough, but she hadn't given up. She'd found a second job and when that hadn't resolved their problems, she'd come up with another solution.

He couldn't help feeling grateful that it had been him she'd come to that night, asking for permission to hang up her notice. That small stroke of luck meant he now found himself in this moment—lying on a couch in the dark with the woman of his dreams in his arms.

He smiled softly at the irony of him growing up in Tamworth with Cally living only an hour away and couldn't help but wonder what might have happened if their paths had crossed earlier.

Despite the numerous government-funded therapists he'd endured as a child during the long, uncertain years after the shootings, the wounds he carried from that awful time were still bone deep. The dark moments when he blamed himself for what had happened and questioned whether he deserved to find happiness would catch him off guard when he least expected it and he would see once again his little sister—beautiful, innocent Grace—who hadn't been given such a chance.

After telling Cally about his past, the pain didn't hurt quite so much, but it was still there, just like the pain he felt each time he thought of Wayne Tucker. He squeezed his eyes shut against the rush of memories of what had occurred earlier in the week.

Tom and the other negotiators had assured him it was normal; that the self-blame of losing a man you were responsible for never went away. Over time, it lessened, but it was best if he accepted it would always be a part of his life.

It was what made his job matter. It spurred him on to try again, to try and eradicate the pain of failure, with the sweet relief of success. Tom had urged Andy yet again to focus on his successes. It was the only way to survive.

Andy hoped Tom knew what he was talking about. He couldn't bear to think about giving up his job. From the time he was ten, he'd wanted to be a negotiator; he wanted to prove they could win. Time and time again, he had. And then Wayne Tucker had happened...

Andy sighed heavily and resettled himself on the couch in an effort to get comfortable. Cally's face was peaceful in sleep. Even though his arm had gone numb beneath her, he was loathe to wake her. Resigning himself to lying there a little longer, he closed his eyes and also sought the succor of sleep.

Chapter 15

ndy's cell phone rang, waking him from a deep sleep. It had been way past late when he woke on the couch with Cally still asleep in his arms. He'd carefully carried her to her bedroom, knowing she'd be more comfortable there. For long moments, he'd stared down at her sleeping form, praying for the day he could join her. Now, he reached for his phone on the nightstand and glanced at the caller ID.

It was Will.

"Hey, mate. A bit early to be calling, isn't it?"

"Yes, sorry, but I couldn't wait to tell you. Savannah went into labor early this morning. I'm a father! I have a son!"

A pang of envy went through Andy, even as he smiled at the excitement and awe in Will's voice. "Congratulations, that's great news," he said and meant it. "I assume everything went well?"

"Aside from the fact he arrived a couple of weeks early, everything's fine. Savannah's resting and Cole's screaming the hospital down. For such a little fellow, he has a darn fine set of lungs."

Andy's heart clenched. "You named him after your brother."

Will's voice was rough with emotion. "Yeah. Cole Dylan, after my brother and Savannah's."

Andy recalled the heartaches Savannah and Will faced a

little over a year earlier when each of them lost their only sibling in tragic circumstances.

"He sounds perfect," Andy said, his voice thick.

"He *is* perfect," Will replied quietly. "He looks just like his mother."

Cally pulled the back door closed quietly behind her and double-checked the lock before walking with Jack toward their car. She hadn't seen Andy that morning and could only assume he was still asleep. Thrusting aside the surge of disappointment, she focused on the check she had in her handbag and reminded herself to look in the phone book after work and find a tire dealer. She hadn't seen a whisker of the blue Camry since Andy moved in, but driving around without a spare still made her nervous.

Climbing in, she reached over the back to unlock Jack's door. The remote control on her car keys died a long time ago and she didn't have the money to replace it. She was lucky her early model Toyota could be opened manually, otherwise she'd have to get it fixed. Just another occasion when the money didn't stretch as far as it needed to.

But that could all change now with the check Andy had given her. It would certainly come in handy for the many things they needed and had gone a long time without. She still couldn't believe he'd paid so much rent in advance. He was either a good saver or police work paid more than she'd assumed.

A third possibility occurred to her and she frowned. He could have borrowed the money off a friend, like he'd borrowed the truck and trailer. He could be trying to impress her with his wealth when all along, he was as broke as she was.

That would explain his reluctance to show them his condominium. If he did live in Bondi, which she was now beginning to seriously doubt, it was probably in some awful dump at the bottom of someone else's basement. She'd been warned about places like that by one of the realtor's she'd contacted when she'd been in the rental market herself.

Usually dark and dank and smelling of mildew, they were not the sort of place you'd be proud to call home. *Was that why he'd been so reluctant to show them?* Was he ashamed of where he lived?

She didn't know and at the moment, she didn't care. The money he'd given her would go a long way to easing the pressure of her financial situation. It would be more than enough to cover her outstanding bills and even allow her to get a little ahead on her home loan.

It was what she'd wanted. *So why wasn't she jumping with joy?*

Cally sighed. Was he stooping to subterfuge to win her approval? She hated to think he thought her so shallow that she'd judge him on the size of his bank balance. She, of all people, knew what it was like to find herself short. That usually had nothing whatsoever to do with the kind of person she was.

"Mom, can we go now?"

With an impatient sound in the back of her throat, Cally turned the key in the ignition and reversed out of the driveway, but it wasn't long before her thoughts returned to Andy. This time, they were far more erotic. She remembered how it felt to have her breasts crushed against his chest, with shivery warmth spreading from her belly to her breasts, hardening her nipples. She'd never been so aware of her own body...or so aware of a man's.

She recalled making out in the car and the feel of Andy's hand molding her breast. She blushed when she thought of her wantonness. Considering her only experience with a man had been with Stewart, she hardly recognized the woman she'd become in Andy's arms. She could no longer deny she wanted her roommate. With a passion.

She'd thought keeping her distance would be easy, even when the thought of having him near made her heart pound. She hadn't counted on how quickly she'd fall under his spell.

She smiled softly. For the first time in a long, long time, happiness warmed her from the inside out. Money or no money, heartache or not, she no longer cared. For Andy, she was willing to risk it.

Nikki tipped the rum bottle to her lips and greedily drank the last of it. Tossing it to the floor, she let the slow burn of alcohol do its magic.Her head thumped. She felt like shit. She'd felt like shit for a week. No—more than a week. He'd dumped her on a Friday.

It was early Monday evening and she could barely get off the floor. A pile of vomit pooled on the carpet nearby and she could only presume it was hers. She lived alone. It didn't take much figuring to work out where it came from.

Images of Andy whirled through her head, speeding up like a rollercoaster on the downhill run. Seconds later, the dull glow of anger that had burned inside her for over a week ignited into fury.

He'd dumped her, and for what? Time to sort out his problems, time he needed on his own. She laughed mirthlessly at the memory, knowing it was a load of shit. She'd gone online and had tracked down some stories in a paper that had been written about a tragic incident in his hometown.

She'd been shocked to discover Bob Warwick was a loser and a drunk and that Andy's family had been dirt poor. It was so far removed from the suave man-about-town she'd dated, she'd initially doubted the reports. But the more she investigated, the more truth she uncovered, right down to the final, shocking tragedy.

There had been a picture of Andy and his mother in the paper. It was easy to see the resemblance. The blond hair, the solemn eyes—there was no mistaking it was him. She'd thought the shootings were the end of it—as if they hadn't been bad enough. But then she discovered the later article, detailing his mother's suicide.

According to the newspaper report, she'd cleverly managed to save up her meds until one night, she took them all. Quietly and without any disturbance Marion Warwick drifted out of this world and left her only surviving child alone, to battle out his life in foster homes until he reached his age of majority.

For some, it might have elicited sympathy, but for Nikki, it only triggered her disgust. How could he have dated her for more than twelve months and not have the guts to tell her about his past? Mental illness could be hereditary and while domestic violence wasn't, the stats supported the claim that a person who was abused often became an abuser.

She'd intended to spend her life with this man; would have jumped at the chance if he'd offered. She shuddered now at her lucky escape and wondered how she could make him pay for all that she'd suffered—or more precisely, would have suffered.

Dragging herself to her feet, she stumbled to the liquor cabinet and pulled down her last bottle of rum. Unscrewing the lid, she took a healthy gulp and tried to come up with a plan.

A little while later, she had it.

With a smile, she thought through the details. She'd make an anonymous phone call to his station and make sure he was rostered on. Then she'd set up a mock-suicide nearby, knowing he'd get the call. She'd make him think she was going to do it and watch him beg and plead for her life. Of course, in the end, she'd let him save her and then she'd tell him the truth: She'd only been fucking with his head. It was no more than he deserved.

————————

Andy dumped his wallet and keys in his locker and made

his way through to the squad room. It was a little after six. His twelve-hour nightshift was about to start. He passed Tom in the corridor and nodded a friendly greeting.

"How's it going, Andy? How did your moving go?"

"Yeah, it went well, thanks Tom. And thanks again for the use of your truck and trailer."

"Anytime, mate. I was happy to help. I'm glad to hear it worked out."

Andy nodded and smiled and then grinned wide. "Yeah, it's going to work out. I think it really is."

"So, you're ready to tell me about her. That's progress, no doubt about it. I'm happy for you, mate. I really am. It's about time I saw a smile on your face."

"Yeah, lately, it's been a tough gig. But I'm coming out the other side and a lot of it has to do with you. I want to thank you for listening and for encouraging me to keep going. After losing Wayne Tucker, I wanted nothing more to do with the job and you managed to change my mind. I owe you one, Tom. I won't forget it."

Color crept up Tom's neck and he averted his face, but from the grateful smile that played around his mouth, Andy could tell he was pleased. He had every right to be. He'd done a good job of convincing Andy he had a lot more to offer the team. There were plenty of other lost souls who would rely on his skills to save them. They were the ones he had to keep in his sights, not the ones who chose to end it.

On his way back to his desk, Andy glanced up at the clock. Six-twenty. His gut tightened in anticipation. Cally was due in ten minutes.

He hadn't spoken to her all day and was way past eager to see her. The house had been lonely without her and time and again, his thoughts had strayed to their moments in the car and later, on the couch. He wanted to hold her again, to press kisses all over her skin, but his shift had only just started. It would be hours before he'd be home.

Home. That's how he'd started to think about it. Home was with Cally and Jack. They belonged together, he was certain of it. He only had to convince her.

The squad room door opened. He swiveled around in his seat and caught sight of her. His heart jumped. Jack trailed in behind her.

Cally spotted Andy as soon as she walked through the door. He was in his usual position at his overcrowded desk and she couldn't help the thrill of excitement that raced through her at the sight of him.

He was dressed in the same work clothes she'd seen him in before, but now she knew what he felt like beneath his clothes, she found herself blushing furiously.

"Hi, Andy!" Jack went straight up to him.

Cally was grateful for the few moments it gave her to compose herself.

"How was school, buddy?" He ruffled Jack's hair.

"Pretty good. It was my turn for news and I told everyone about you and the huge TV and about going to Bondi with Jimmy and snorkeling and stuff." Jack grinned up at him. "Everyone thought it was so cool!"

Andy smiled. His gaze flicked up to hers. "Hey." His voice was soft, questioning.

She blushed again under the impact of his heated gaze. "Hey."

"How was school?"

"It was okay." She paused. "I missed you this morning."

"Yeah, sorry, I didn't set an alarm. I was on nightshift, so I didn't bother. I spent all day wishing I had."

"So did I," she whispered, and when she leaned in close his groin flooded with hot desire.

Before he could respond to her admission, Tom strode up and halted near Andy's desk, his expression grim. "I've just taken a call from emergency services. There's a woman on the Harbour Bridge. Christ knows how she climbed up there, but she's threatening to throw herself off."

Andy's heart pounded and adrenaline surged through his

veins. He glanced at Cally and she nodded, understanding in her eyes. He squeezed her hand briefly in acknowledgement and headed straight for his locker. The mental preparation required for a negotiation had already begun.

"Do we have a name?" Andy asked, as soon as he and Tom and the other negotiators had arrived at the scene. They'd been met by a couple of general duty officers, who'd been sent on ahead to secure the stronghold. Already, a crowd had gathered, all straining to catch a glimpse of the woman who stood high above them on a girder that formed part of the Harbour Bridge.

"Yeah," a young constable identified by his badge as "Williams" replied. "I'm afraid she's one of our own. "It's Senior Sergeant Nicole Simons. She's currently stationed at Penrith."

Andy reeled back in shock and shook his head. "Nikki Simons—are you sure?"

"I think so, sir. One of the other officers recognized her. They went through the Academy together."

Tom stared hard at Andy, concern etched into his brow. "Is this the same Nikki I met the other night? The one I escorted outside?"

"Yeah, I think so." He squinted up to where the figure of a woman could be seen high above them. "It looks like her."

"Leave this one to me. I'm not sure you should even be here."

"She keeps asking for Andy Warwick," Williams interrupted. "Which one of you is he?"

Andy's stomach plummeted. "It's me," he offered quietly. "I'm Andy Warwick."

Tom grabbed hold of his arm and pulled Andy away from the others. "No, Andy. You can't do this. I don't give a fuck who she's asking for. You're way too close to the source.

Think about Nikki. How can you give it your best? Your judgment will be clouded by your relationship. You need to leave this one to me."

"But, she's asking for me. I can't just ignore her. She'll know I'm here. She probably planned to do it on my turf."

"That might be so, but it doesn't change anything. We need to get her down. That's the only thing that matters and today you're not the best one for the job."

Andy stared at Tom a moment longer and then nodded. Tom was right. Apart from the fact Tom was far more experienced, he didn't have a history with their jumper. There was nothing to interfere with his concentration and that could mean life or death.

"Okay, she's all yours. Do what has to be done. I'll be down here if you need me. Give me a sign and I'll come up."

Tom sighed with relief. "Will do, Andy, and thanks. I appreciate you seeing sense about this. I can only imagine what you're feeling. Ex-girlfriend or not, no one wants to see someone they know in this kind of situation."

"You're right. It sucks." He looked Tom squarely in the face. "Do what you do best. Bring her back down for me. No one deserves to die like that."

Nikki watched the officer negotiate his way up the cement and steel pylons until he reached the spot where she stood. She was balanced on a beam of steel which was a little more than three feet wide. Plenty of room, really, which was a good thing. After all, she only intended to scare him. She didn't intend to die.

As the man got closer, she realized it wasn't Andy but she recognized him just the same. It was the cute one who'd escorted her from Andy's building when she'd dropped by there last week to pay him a visit. Tom, he'd said his name was. When she asked him, he told her he was married. *Too bad.* There was something about his smile and the way he made her feel that made her wish he were single...

"Hey, Nikki," he called to her and she was pleased that he remembered her name. The rum she'd consumed was blurring her vision and for a while, there seemed to be two of him. *Two Tom Munroes; that would be nice.* Perhaps only one of them was married? She giggled at the thought and blinked her eyes in an effort to bring him into better focus.

"What are you doing up here, Nikki? You're scaring us all to death. This is no place for you to be. Come on, reach for my hand and I'll help you down."

"Where's Andy?" she asked truculently, knowing he must be nearby. She'd called his station earlier. Someone had confirmed he was there.

"He's waiting for you down on the ground. If you hurry, you'll catch him. He wants to talk to you, Nikki. He misses you."

"Bullshit, he doesn't miss me and if he does, that's just too bad. Now that I know what I do about him, I wouldn't take him back if you paid me. He deserves to die lonely and sad, just like his mother."

Tom heard what she said and swallowed a gasp. He knew about Andy's family and the tragedy of their past. He couldn't believe anyone could be so callous as to talk about it the way Nikki was. With an effort, he set his anger aside and concentrated on getting the inebriated woman down. She swayed alarmingly on the girder and his throat constricted in panic.

"Whoa, Nikki. Hold on a minute. That girder you're standing on is not wide. If you're not careful, you'll over balance and fall and I know that's not what you want."

Nikki smiled. "You're right. I'm not going to kill myself. I'm just having some fun. It's just a little fun between me and Andy. It's nothing less than he deserves."

"That might be so," Tom quickly agreed, "but come back down and tell him. There's no point doing it from here. He won't even hear you."

Nikki seemed to consider his words and Tom held his breath and waited. Finally, she nodded once and relented.

"You're right. I should be telling the fucker to his face, just like I did last time. Here..." She took a step toward Tom. "Help me out."

A gust of wind caught her jacket and she wobbled precariously on the girder. She struggled to get her balance and Tom's heart stopped.

"Nikki, take my hand," he shouted and tried to stem his panic. He edged closer to her, until he could almost touch her fingers. She took another step and her hand brushed his, but once again, the wind gusted and she over balanced.

With a cry of terror, she rocked back and forth on her feet, teetering on the ledge. A second later, she hurtled over the side. Tom bit back a scream and stared in horror as she hit the dark water with a splash and disappeared from his sight.

"Somebody get the lights over here! She's fallen in the water," Tom shouted, his voice hoarse.

The crowd erupted with screams and gasps, adding to the melee. There was a scramble of movement far below him and floodlights were suddenly switched on. They scanned the water, but in his heart, he knew it was too late. She'd fallen nearly three hundred feet. Nobody could survive that kind of fall. With his heart and limbs weighed down with dread, he made his way slowly to the ground...

———————

Andy's heart and mind were still heavy with shock when he drove Tom back to their station. He wanted to remind his partner about all of the things Tom had said to him after the death of Wayne Tucker, but somehow, the words wouldn't come and he knew Tom wasn't ready to hear them. Tom was a veteran negotiator. He knew better than any of them how it worked.

Andy turned into the street that housed the station and spied Cally's Toyota in the car park. *She was still here.* He quietly eased out a sigh of relief. His head was in a turmoil. He had no idea what to say to Tom, but to have Cally here, to hold her close... He couldn't wait to get inside.

Of course, the moment he took her in his arms, his cover would be blown. Everyone in the squad room would know he had a thing for the cleaner. But he didn't care. He needed to hold her, to reassure himself she was safe. He brought the squad car to a stop. His body began to tremble with delayed shock. He glanced across at Tom. In the wan street lights, Tom looked as sick as Andy felt.

"Hang in there, Tom. You did the best you could."

Tom stared at him, his expression grim. His face was still deathly pale. Andy sighed inwardly. He'd been there before. Only time would help make it better and right now, the whole tragic incident was fresh in their minds, playing out in all of its vivid Technicolor detail and high-definition sound. Nikki's screams as she'd fallen to her death would stay with him forever.

"We're here, mate. Are you ready to come inside?" He kept his voice pitched low and waited for Tom to respond, not wanting to hurry him.

"She never planned on jumping."

Andy frowned and tried to process what Tom had said. "You mean, Nikki? She didn't mean to jump?"

"She told me she was only trying to scare you; to fuck around with your head. She was ready to come back down. She'd started walking toward me. The wind gusted and knocked her off balance. She fell, Andy. She *fell.*"

Renewed shock ricocheted through him. Disbelief held him immobile. *It had all been a stupid stunt.* She hadn't been crazed with grief; she hadn't been suicidal. She'd done it on purpose—she'd set it all up. Only, she hadn't counted on the wind. She hadn't counted on it going so fucking wrong.

And now she was dead…

He doubled over on a gasp of pain and hit his head on the steering wheel. The sting of the impact across his forehead hardly registered. *Nikki had died trying to gain his attention.* If he hadn't broken up with her, if he'd taken a little more time to ease her into the idea, she might have taken it better.

He'd broken up with her after a ball, for Christ's sake! He'd wined her and dined her—he'd even danced with her—then he'd taken her home and told her it was over.

At the time, he'd thought he was being as kind as he could, but looking back, it was clear he could have handled it better. He could have begun by not returning her phone calls and texts—at least, not right away. He could have slowly, over time, let her come to her own realization that they were over.

But, he hadn't and now she was dead. She was dead because of him.

"It's all my fault," he croaked, raising his head to stare at Tom.

His partner shook his head a little frantically. "Don't be so fucking stupid. It was an accident. You didn't put her up there."

"But I did," he insisted. "She was trying to teach me a lesson. You just told me she wanted to frighten me, to shove our break-up in my face. If we were still together, she'd still be alive."

"If you were still together, you'd have been miserable. Any fool could tell you weren't in love with her. You hadn't even told me about her and you'd been together more than a year. That tells me all I need to know." He shook his head. "I've watched you with the cleaner. Your face lights up whenever she comes into the room."

Tom sighed and rubbed a weary hand across his face. "It wasn't your fault, Andy. People break up all the time. Most of the participants get on with their life. They don't end up in the harbor."

Tom drew in a ragged breath and continued. "Nikki was

obviously unstable. No one goes to a police station drunk or comes up with such a hare-brained scheme in an effort to stick it to their ex. She was a copper. She knew better than most about the dangers of what she was doing. Okay, so she didn't want to jump, but she must have known the risks of falling. She wore no safety harness or other protection. She did nothing to minimize the risk."

"Was she drunk, like last time?" Andy asked quietly.

Tom squeezed his eyes shut and winced. A moment later, he nodded. Andy dropped his head. His breath sawed out between his clenched teeth. "Shit."

"Not drunk enough that she couldn't climb up that steel girder, but she'd had more than her fair share. Her eyes were glazed and she reeked of alcohol. Still, she had enough wits about her to know where she was and what she was doing. She made a mistake, Andy. Let's face it, some people can't be saved."

Andy nodded and did his best to accept Tom's words, trying hard to forget Nikki hadn't wanted to die. He thought of Cally again and suddenly ached to see her, to hold her close, to take succor from her presence.

"Let's go inside," he murmured. "The others will be wondering where we are," he added, referring to the other men from their squad who had also attended the scene. "No sense in alarming them without cause."

Tom heaved a sigh. "You're right. Let's go."

CHAPTER 16

The door to the squad room swung open and Cally looked up from her dusting. She was in the process of wiping the final few desks clean and then she'd be ready to pack up for the night. Jack was in one of the interview rooms, reading a book, as usual. Andy filled the door opening, looking sad and defeated. Tom followed closely behind, his face reflecting a similar outlook.

Despite their grim countenances, her shoulders sagged in relief. They were alive and okay. That's all that mattered. No doubt she'd hear about what had happened on the six o'clock news. For now, it was enough to know that Andy and his partner were safe.

She watched while Andy's gaze roamed the room and then lit upon her. Relief surged through his eyes and the tension in his jaw lessened. She wanted to go to him, to touch him, to reassure herself he was all right, but she was uncertain whether he wanted that, whether he was willing to advertise to his colleagues that they had something going on.

Before she could think about it any harder or formulate a plan, he was standing beside her with his arms outstretched, silently begging her to hold him. Without hesitation, she stepped toward him and wrapped her arms around him. He groaned and buried his head in the crook of her neck, breathing hard. His big body trembled like he was in the grip of malaria and there was nothing she could do but hold him.

She didn't know how long they stood there, but it was awhile before Andy raised his head and looked down at her. His eyes were dark with emotion and anguish was still etched on his face. She reached up with her hand and smoothed it across his cheek, wishing she could smooth away the pain. His large hand covered her smaller one and pressed it against his face and all the while, he held her gaze, as if he never wanted to look away.

The moment was broken when Tom moved close and offered Andy a coffee. With a last look in Cally's direction, Andy stepped backward and accepted the cup with a grateful smile.

"Thanks, Tom."

"I'm sure you'd rather a shot of whisky, but seeing as we're at work, this will have to do."

"You have that right, but the coffee's hot and strong, just how I like it. Thanks, I appreciate it."

Tom nodded and glanced at Cally. She blushed, suddenly feeling awkward and tried to move out of the way. Instead, she tripped over a wastepaper basket and sent trash flying across the carpet.

She caught a glint of amusement in both of the men's eyes and wished she could sink into the floor. On the other hand, amusement was a whole lot better than the sadness and defeat she'd spied in them earlier.

"Cally, come here. I want you to meet Tom."

Andy issued the soft command and Cally had no choice but to obey. After hastily picking the rubbish off the floor, she moved back to Andy's side. Tom had his hand outstretched in greeting and after quickly and a little self-consciously wiping her hands on her clothes, she returned his firm handshake.

"Cally Savage," she murmured, offering him a polite smile.

"Tom Munro. It's nice to meet you. Our only communication seems to be over the trash."

She recalled the last time they'd spoken, when she'd asked him to hand her his wastepaper basket and her smile widened into a grin.

"Where's Jack?" Andy asked, casting his gaze around the squad room. It was still crowded with officers and other personnel who had attended the tragic scene, all of them speaking in subdued tones as the events of the evening were relayed.

"He's down the hall. I was just finishing up in here. It's time for us to go home."

Andy nodded and heaved a sigh. "I wish I could come with you."

She smiled softly and touched his arm. "I wish you could, too."

"Pity it's not going to happen. I have a mountain of paperwork to complete and that's before the media get wind of it. This kind of thing will take forever. People are always looking for someone to blame. We'll have to recall every infinitesimal detail, every glance, every word, every movement. It'll take us the rest of the night." He grimaced and threw a look at Tom.

"You're right," Tom agreed, his voice grim, "and there's nothing we can do about it."

Cally made as if to leave and Andy reached for her. Without warning, he planted a hard kiss on her mouth. The force and swiftness of it left her gasping.

"See you in the morning. Take care driving home," Andy told her, his eyes fierce on hers.

All she could do was nod her agreement before turning and making her way on unsteady feet across the carpet, heading in the direction of the interview rooms.

Tom plunked a mug of fresh coffee down on Andy's desk a couple of hours later and pulled up a chair. "How's it going, mate?"

Andy sighed and pushed aside the paperwork on his desk to make room for Tom's boots. "Yeah, you know."

"Yeah, I do. That's why I'm asking. You need to

concentrate on the good things in life, the things that make you happy. It's the only way to get through the dark times."

Andy blew out his breath on a sigh. "I'm doing my best, Tom, believe me, but right at the moment it's hard to stay focused on the good things. First Tucker, now Nikki." He shook his head and then glanced up at his partner. "Did you call Lily?"

Tom breathed in deeply and eased it out. "Yeah, but she's in class. She won't be home until nine. She was sorry to hear what had happened, but we didn't get a chance to really talk."

"At least she'll be there when you get home in the morning. That must be comforting to know."

"Yeah, it is," Tom agreed. He lapsed into silence, almost as if he was lost in his thoughts. A long moment later, he raised his head and offered Andy a slight smile. "You seem to be rather taken with the cute cleaner. I'm pleased to see she feels the same way. Don't waste time second guessing, Andy. If it's the real deal, just go for it. Life's too short to muck around."

Andy ducked his head in embarrassment. Now that he'd had time to compose himself, he was a little abashed when he realized what he'd done in full view of the team. But even now, knowing he was going to cop flak from the boys, given another chance, he wouldn't do anything differently.

He'd fallen in love with Cally and he wanted the whole world to know. She was everything he'd ever wanted. She made his heart smile. She was *the one*. And as the cabbie suggested, he'd known it the minute he set eyes on her. His attention snagged on a part of Tom's speech and he replayed the words back in his mind: 'I'm pleased to see she feels the same way.'

Could Tom have spoken the truth? Had he seen something in Cally's eyes, something in her behavior that indicated she cared?

Andy's heart surged with hope and anticipation. He sure hoped so because from now on in, he was going to devote all his energy to convincing her she was his.

———————

It was getting close to eleven and Andy was tired. The emotional stresses of the earlier part of his shift were finally catching up with him. With the death of Tucker and now Nikki, it had been an awful time and it had all taken place in just over a week.

But what was time, anyway? He'd known Cally for only eleven days and yet he felt like he'd known her forever. He'd shared with her his shameful past and she'd still looked at him with love. Well, maybe not love, but she definitely exhibited concern and the tears in her eyes when he'd told her the tragic truth about his family had revealed she cared. *Even Tom thought she was taken with him…*

The thought brought a smile to his lips and he glanced at the clock on the wall of the squad room and sighed. He still had another seven hours to go before he could turn his car for home. Home to Cally. Home to Jack.

Frowning slightly, he remembered he hadn't asked her if she'd seen any more of the blue Toyota and whether it was still concerning her. He reached for his phone and then paused. It was late…but she'd told him she was a night owl. Besides, he wanted to hear her voice.

Coming to a decision, he picked up his phone and keyed in the number of her cell. The call went straight to message bank. He grimaced. It was either switched off or the battery was dead. Neither scenario was comforting. Scrolling back through his contacts, he found her home number and pressed the button to call. His heart beat in anticipation. This time, she answered.

"Hello?"

He cleared his throat of the emotion that threatened to choke him. The sound of her voice again, after such a tumultuous evening, was suddenly more than he could take.

"Hello?" she repeated, this time more cautiously.

He swallowed and cursed silently under his breath,

forgetting for a moment she didn't have call display. It wasn't his intention to frighten her. "Cally, it's Andy," he said hurriedly.

"Andy! How are you? Is everything all right?" She sounded surprised, as if she hadn't expected to hear from him. He could understand her reaction. He'd never called her from work before.

"I'm fine." He closed his eyes and relaxed back into his chair. "Just tired. I've had about enough of the day, but I still have more than half of my shift to go. I thought I'd call you and kill some time; take my mind off things."

"Of course, I'm glad you did. I've been thinking about you all night."

His gut tightened in immediate response and blood flowed to his groin. He grimaced at his body's uncontrollable reaction and determinably pushed the erotic thoughts aside. He was sure she was referring to the incident with Nikki, not about having wild fantasies about him.

"How are you doing? How is Tom?" she asked quietly.

"I'm okay. Tom's good, too. He's been doing this a lot longer than I have. Tom was the one up there tonight and yet he was offering *me* comfort. He's a remarkable bloke, Tom Munro. I'm proud to serve beside him." His throat tightened on a surge of emotion and he swallowed hard.

"I'm glad you're both doing okay." She hesitated. "I was worried about you."

Warmth spread through him at the concern in her voice. It had been years since anyone had worried about him. It felt good. It felt like something he wanted to get used to.

"Thanks, I appreciate your concern. It's nice to know you care."

A silence fell between them. Andy waited for her to break it. When the moments dragged on, he forced his tone lighter and steered the conversation away to safer territory. "What's wrong with your cell? It went straight to voice mail."

"Oh, it's probably flat. I forgot to put it on the charger."

He groaned. "Cally, you know it doesn't work if the battery's flat. I bought it for you to use in an emergency.

What happens if you're out on the road somewhere and need to call?"

"You're right. I'll put it on the charger right now."

"Good," he said, feeling slightly reassured and then he remembered what triggered his call. "Have you seen anything more of the Camry?"

"No, I haven't." She sounded relieved. "Maybe I was wrong about him."

"Let's hope so." The thought of someone hanging around her house, hidden among the dense foliage and vines she called a garden, made him nervous. "Just make sure you call the police if you see him again. You have the plate number. They can run that through their system and at least identify the owner of the car. If he turns up near your house again, they'll certainly have just cause."

"Yes, I will. I appreciate your concern. Thanks, Andy."

Her voice was pitched low, intimate in tone—probably in deference to the late hour. No doubt Jack was asleep and she didn't want to wake him. He glanced around the squad room for his colleagues. The crowd of extra officers, called in over the emergency, had long since dispersed. It was back to the usual trio of officers: tonight the nightshift crew was made up of him, Tom and Craig Winters. He could see Tom at his desk on the far side of the room with a phone up to his ear. Winters was nowhere to be seen. He was probably in the tea room, or on break.

Andy relaxed into his chair and tried to picture Cally at home, talking to him at that moment. He wondered if she'd showered in preparation for bed. What was she wearing? Was she in her pajamas? A nightdress? Something soft and slinky?

Images of her at the beach suddenly crowded his mind. The skimpy bikini, the sun-kissed skin, the golden hair... His body stirred. "So, what are you wearing?" he murmured without thinking.

She was silent and he didn't think she was going to answer. But then, he heard her say very softly, "I'm in my pajamas."

He sucked in his breath. "What kind of pajamas?"

"Oh, you know, pajamas."

"Are they soft and satiny?"

"*Mm*, not really, more like practical and cottony."

He laughed. "Practical and cottony still sounds good to me. What color are they?"

"A long time ago, they were white, but an errant red sock in the laundry turned them a pale shade of pink."

His voice dropped lower and his heart picked up its pace. "Are you in bed?"

"I am now. I had to go into the living room to answer the phone. That's where the phone dock is."

"Ah, I see. Where's Jack?"

"He's asleep in his room."

He lowered his voice to a seductive whisper. "Are you lying down?"

"Yes."

His heart immediately began to pound a rapid staccato in his chest. He'd never had phone sex with anyone before—he hadn't ever wanted to. But with Cally, it was different.

"Too bad you're not here," she whispered.

A surge of desire shot straight to his groin. His cock hardened. He squirmed on the chair and suddenly came back to reality. He was at work, surrounded by his colleagues.

Okay, so Tom was still engrossed in his phone conversation and Craig had yet to appear, but he now had a hard-on that he had no way of assuaging.

What the hell was he thinking? He'd only wanted to get an update on the stalker and okay, to hear her voice. He'd had no intention of getting himself so turned on he was going to be uncomfortable for the rest of his shift.

"Are you still in your uniform?" Cally's whispered question drew him out of his reverie. When her words registered on his brain, his heart skipped a beat.

"Yes," he murmured.

"I've always had a thing about men in uniform."

"Really?" He couldn't prevent the smile that tugged up the corners of his mouth. "I never knew."

Cally laughed softly. "I'll let you in on a secret. Neither did I, until I met you."

He chuckled. "Well, I'm glad you've developed that kind of...interest. I'm happy to wear it as often as you like."

"Even to bed?" she murmured, her voice husky with emotion.

Another surge of desire rushed to his cock. He groaned. "What are you doing to me, woman? I'm at work. It's not like I can..."

"Can what?"

He groaned again and then decided two could play at this game. "Actually, I prefer to sleep naked."

She gasped and his grin widened. His voice dipped lower. "Didn't I mention that before? I don't sleep in pajamas. In fact, I don't even own any."

"I see." She cleared her voice. "Perhaps you should have mentioned it earlier."

"Would it have made any difference if I had?"

"Well, you might not have needed to bring your own bed. It might have saved you that trouble."

Andy growled low in his throat at her forwardness. "I like the way you taste," he murmured. "And the way you smell. I wish I could be there right now so I could lick you all over."

He heard her sharp intake of breath and a rustle of clothing. "What are you doing, Cally?"

"Nothing, but I feel..."

Her voice fell away. He gripped the phone harder. "How do you feel, Cally?"

"Like...like I need you to touch me."

Her admission rocked him. Unable to stand it a moment longer, he checked once again that his colleagues weren't around and then dragged his chair closer to his desk until his lap was hidden underneath it. Sliding down the zipper on his pants, he took hold of his cock and slid his hand up and down his engorged shaft.

He groaned softly into the phone. "I want to suck your

nipples until they're hard, as hard as my cock. I want to reach down with my fingers and slip into your warmth. I can feel how wet you are, Cally. Tell me how much you want me."

"Oh, Andy, yes!" she moaned. "Touch me. Please."

Her little gasps of pleasure tickled his ear. "Can you feel me touching you, Cally? Can you feel my fingers on your clit? Can you feel me deep inside you?"

Her breathing became labored. His hand worked faster up and down the length of his shaft. "That's it," he whispered. "Come for me, sweetheart. I want to hear you come."

As if his words pushed her over the edge, she cried out. Listening to her on the other end of the phone, his hand pumped faster until the first pulses of his climax overtook him.

When hot jets of fluid spurted into his hand, he groaned with relief. Slowly, the intense feelings subsided. He reached for the tissues.

"How are you feeling, sweetheart?" he murmured into the phone.

"I feel...good."

"That makes two of us." His heart swelled with tenderness.

"I've never done that before, Andy." Her voice was soft and hesitant. "I hope you don't think that I'm..." She broke off.

"I've never done that before, either, Cally," he whispered back, feeling the wonder of it all over again.

"Really?" He heard the surprise in her voice.

"Yes, really."

"How come?"

"I'm not sure," he said honestly. "I don't think I've ever wanted to do it with anyone else before."

"I'm glad." She was quiet and then added. "I wish you were here."

"Me, too."

Chapter 17

Cally tugged the vacuum cleaner across the floor of the kitchen, picking up toast crumbs from breakfast. After she dropped Jack at school she'd come straight home. Tuesday was not a teaching day, or a cleaning day at the station, which meant it was cleaning day at the cottage.

Sighing, she pushed each chair into place at the table and moved into the living room. Her mind kept circling back to what happened during her telephone conversation with Andy the night before. Heat crept up her neck and spread across her cheeks. She still couldn't believe she'd had phone sex with him. She'd never done anything like that before. She'd never even *thought* about doing anything like that before.

And yet with Andy, it had seemed natural. She'd shocked herself with not only the way she'd spoken to him, but the fact she'd climaxed while he listened on the other end of the phone. Never in her wildest dreams had she thought she was capable of such brazenness or such pleasure.

Not that he'd seemed to mind. A grin tugged at the corners of her mouth. In fact, he'd seemed more than happy with her performance. She remembered his groans of relief as he climaxed and with the memory, renewed desire stirred deep inside her. For too long, she'd denied herself any sexual pleasure and the feelings and passion he'd awakened within her set her pulse racing.

He was due home very shortly and she was beyond nervous about facing him. It was one thing to do phone sex, but having to look the person in the eye the next morning…

Was she being silly? This was the twenty-first century. Women were allowed to have orgasms, with or without a partner. Andy wouldn't think anything of it and she shouldn't either.

With the reminder that he'd be arriving soon, she pulled the vacuum cleaner quickly along behind her and headed through the French doors which led to the sleepout. She spied Andy's bed and came up short. Memories of their intimacy over the phone sent heat flooding into her cheeks. How would it feel to press against his hard body on a bed that had more surface area than her Toyota?

The king-sized bed took almost the entire width of the room. He'd managed to squeeze a small table between the side of the bed and the wall. A clock radio with red illuminated numbers sat below the flowers she'd placed there almost a week earlier. She hadn't been inside his room since and they now drooped, their petals turning brown.

Flicking off the vacuum with her foot, she leaned the wand up against the wall and walked toward the bed to remove the dead flowers. She picked up the vase and a small black-and-white photograph fell face down onto the table. She frowned. It must have been between the vase and the wall.

Suppressing a surge of guilt, she picked up the photograph and turned it over, telling herself that if it was something truly private, Andy wouldn't have displayed it. The picture was of a woman and a little girl. The child had curly, blond hair and looked about three or four. She clung to the hem of her mother's dress. They were both smiling at the camera. It was a happy scene and Cally found herself smiling back at them.

It must be his mother and little sister. There was certainly a close resemblance. Remembering their tragic ending, she sighed and sat down on the side of his bed. She caught a whiff of his familiar cologne and her heart clenched with longing. She was falling for him and falling for him fast. It didn't seem to matter she'd only known him less than a fortnight. Her heart didn't care a fig for time factors.

There was something strange about his reluctance to show her his condominium, but the more she got to know him, the more she was sure there was a good explanation. He was simply too forthright, too honest, too darn *nice* to have any evil intent. If she was being naïve, then so be it. Everyone had to trust someone, sometime.

Carefully, she replaced the photo behind the vase then finished the vacuuming as quickly as she could. She wanted the room clean for Andy. No doubt he was tired and would be looking to sleep. She didn't want to disturb him with undue noise.

Finished at last, she returned it to the storage closet and took a quick shower, dabbing on a light floral scent. The house smelled fresh and lemony. The bright morning sun poured through the open windows. It was another perfect summer day. All that was missing was Andy.

———

Andy swung the Audi into Cally's driveway and cut the engine. It had been an eventful night and he was glad it was over. He was drained, physically and emotionally and he couldn't wait to hit the shower and then crawl into bed.

He spied Cally's Toyota parked in its usual spot and his heart rate picked up its pace. It was Tuesday morning. Jack should be in school. He remembered the previous night's phone call and his cock stirred with interest. All of a sudden, he didn't feel quite so exhausted.

With a renewed burst of energy, he climbed out of his car and jogged up the front steps, calling out to Cally as he went. She met him in the entryway and gave him an unsteady smile and then quickly looked away; a blush stained her cheeks. He knew exactly how she was feeling. He felt a little uncertain, too.

Breaking the awkward silence, he stepped closer and planted a quick kiss on her nose before moving swiftly away. "Mm, you smell nice," he murmured. "And I don't." He looked down at his crumpled uniform. "I'm going to head to the shower."

Ignoring the confused expression on her face, he turned away from her, knowing she'd been expecting more. After what they'd shared the night before, he couldn't blame her for wondering what the hell had just happened. He didn't know, either. What he did know was that he wanted her—hot and hard and fast. The phone sex was just the beginning. All it had done was whet his appetite. He had to put some distance between them so that he could get his libido under control. He had to take things slowly: coax her, convince her she wanted him as much as he wanted her. And then he'd let the magic take over.

That's how it had worked in his fantasies, anyway. He could only hope the reality of it would exceed his expectations. But right now, he was off to the shower, preferably one that was icy cold.

Cally's belly churned with confusion and nerves. A moment earlier, Andy had disappeared down the hall with a towel slung over his shoulder. He'd kissed her and then had left her, almost as if he needed to get away. She didn't know what to make of it.

She might have been brazen over the phone, but now, face to face, it was a different matter. Should she make reference to what they'd shared, or ignore it? She'd never been in this position before. She didn't have a clue how to proceed. She could always ask Kate. Her friend would know what to do... Cally would call her when Andy returned to his room.

With her mind made up, she turned to go back into the kitchen and abruptly came up short. Andy had finished in the shower and now leaned against the doorframe in the hall. He was naked except for the bath towel draped casually around his hips.

Heat burned her face and spread across her stomach before moving much lower. A surge of desire swept through her and her nipples hardened involuntarily beneath her light summer dress. All of a sudden, she remembered how it felt when she'd climaxed to the sound of Andy's deep, husky voice.

Her gaze wandered over him. His broad chest was the color of copper and contrasted with the sun-bleached blond of his hair. Wet from the shower, it looked like he'd finger combed it, making it look even sexier than usual. His cheeks were freshly shaven and she caught a whiff of his tantalizing cologne.

Her gaze moved to his slightly parted lips and she remembered the feel of them pressed against hers. Her gaze dropped lower, moved across his broad chest and then lower still. She followed the thin path of dark hair that trailed down his belly and finally stopped at the bulge behind his towel. Her heart thudded with excitement.

"See anything you like?"

Her gaze flew up to his. Heat flooded her face. When his gaze slid over her, her body burned with fire.

"I-I'm sorry." Her cheeks burned. "I-I...I'll just—"

"Why don't you come over here and say hello to me properly? It's been way too long since I've seen you."

The dark depths of his eyes were mesmerizing.

"It's good to be home," he added softly.

Her heart skipped a beat and then galloped away. Her feet inched forward until she stood less than a foot from him. His arm snaked out and hauled her up against his chest and she gasped.

She tilted her head back and stared up into his eyes, the blood thumping loudly in her ears. Her world narrowed to his beloved face and all of a sudden, there was no one else, but Andy.

Slowly, slowly, his head descended and his lips grazed

gently across hers. She stood on tiptoe and pressed herself against him, holding onto his shoulders for support. As if a match ignited between them, their passion burst into flame. Andy's kiss turned deeper and more frantic and she matched him just the same.

When at last they pulled apart, they were breathing hard. Andy's eyes glittered with heat and desire and Cally was sure she looked just as needy. Her body throbbed, her lips ached, her breasts were heavy with desire.

"I want to make love to you, Cally," Andy whispered hoarsely and waited for her response.

She dragged in another breath and tried hard to calm her racing heart. Knowing there would be no turning back if she made the next move, she swallowed against the lump of nerves which had lodged itself in her throat.

She lifted her hand and cupped his cheek and then stood on tiptoe again. She pressed her lips against his and whispered, "I want to make love to you, too."

Andy growled low in his throat and then bent and swung her up in his arms. With his long strides eating up the distance, it seemed mere seconds before he leaned down and deposited her gently on his bed.

"Oops, the towel's come loose," he murmured in her ear.

She blushed and then reached over and ran her hand down the muscular length of his naked thigh. "I don't think we need the towel."

His eyes widened in surprise and he shot her a lascivious grin. A second later, he joined her on the bed. On his hands and knees, he straddled her, with an arm either side of her head. As if in slow motion, he lowered his head. Her mouth parted on a soft sigh. This time, his kiss was as light as butterfly wings and she reveled in its tenderness. He kissed her over and over again, each more passionate than the one before, until both of them were once again breathless.

Reaching up, she put her arms around his neck and pulled him close against her. The solid hardness of his erection pressed against her belly through her clothes. He sucked in his breath at the contact and she couldn't help the thrill of satisfaction that surged through her. Emboldened, she reached down and touched him.

"You have way too many clothes on, woman," he muttered, his voice husky with need.

Turning her on her side, he found the zipper of her dress and slid it down as far as it would go. Pushing the thin straps off her shoulders, he touched her skin with fingers that trembled.

"You're so beautiful, Cally." He bent to fasten his mouth over her breast, laving it with his tongue through the fabric of her bra. She moaned in frustration, wanting desperately to feel his tongue on her heated flesh. Reaching around behind, she unfastened the clasp of her bra. She pulled it away and her breasts sprang free.

His eyes glittered with desire. He bent his head, intent on one of her nipples and she held her breath, anticipating the feel of his lips against her heated skin. His hot wet mouth sucked on the sensitive nub. She gasped. Desire coiled tight within her, pulsing with warmth and need.

It had been a long time since she'd been with a man, but she couldn't remember ever feeling so aware of her body. Sex with Stewart had always been fast and furious and laced with massive doses of guilt. She'd never achieved a climax.

Nothing could compare to the feelings Andy stirred up inside her. Just when she thought she couldn't take any more, he turned his attention to her other breast. Plunging her fingers into his hair, she held his head. His teeth grazed her nipple. Her clit throbbed with need. She squirmed against him.

"Easy, sweetheart, easy," he murmured, levering his body away from her. "We have all day."

His lips returned to hers. When his tongue sought entrance, she opened her mouth and let him taste her. His tongue swept inside and he moaned. "*Mm*, you taste so good. You always taste so good."

He pushed her dress further down her hips. She lay back against the pillows and lifted her bottom so he could pull it down over her legs, along with her panties. Once both articles of clothing had been tossed onto the floor, his eyes feasted on her lying there, naked before him.

He leaned over her and pressed a soft kiss to her lips. His eyes were almost black with desire. His bare chest scraped lightly against her breasts. She drew in a sharp breath and reached up impatiently to pull him down hard against her.

Her breasts were crushed against the solid wall of his chest. She arched her back, needing to get even closer. The throbbing heat in her center had become almost unbearable. She ached deep in her core.

As if aware of her need, Andy shifted his weight. Leaning on his elbows, he pressed kisses over her stomach and then kept moving lower. Cally's breath caught when his tongue poked into her belly button, swirling and tasting her skin. A moment later, his mouth nuzzled her femininity. Despite the aching in her core, she tensed and pressed her legs together.

"Andy, please!" she gasped. Reaching down, she tried to pull his head away. Undeterred, his tongue pressed against her slit.

"Please what?" His voice was a low murmur as his tongue continued to work its magic.

Cally's face flamed. Turning her head away from him, she tried again. "Please don't do that."

"Do what?" He swirled his tongue lightly over her clit. "That?" He lifted his head briefly to watch her reaction. "Or this?"

His tongue plunged inside her and she gasped again. Never before had she been caressed so intimately and she fought against the sensations as she tried to regain some sense of propriety.

"Andy, stop! I don't think you should—"

"What? Kiss you like this?" He opened his mouth over the lips of her womanhood and sucked them gently into his mouth.

"Don't be embarrassed, Cally. You're so beautiful. I want

to taste every inch of you. There's nothing to be embarrassed about. Please, let me."

His humble request eased her discomfort. Little by little, she let go of her instinctive inhibitions and allowed herself to experience the incredible sensations he created deep inside her.

As if sensing her acquiescence, he deepened the movements of his tongue. Once again, desire began to build inside her. The rhythmic stroking continued. Her fingers clutched at his hair, but this time in supplication as she silently begged him to put an end to her torment.

Her hips moved against him. In response, he increased the pressure of his tongue, licking and laving and swirling around her clit until she didn't think she could stand it another minute.

"That's it, sweetheart; that's it. Come for me, babe, come for me."

Andy's murmured encouragement brought to mind the night before and was all she needed to push her over the edge. Waves of pleasure washed over her. Holding his head tightly in her hands, she cried out in release. Long moments later, as the last pulse of her orgasm receded, she opened her eyes and looked up at him. He leaned over her on his elbows, a look of pure male satisfaction on his face.

"Aren't you glad you let me?"

Heat flooded her face. It was one thing to *do* it, but to *talk* about it afterwards? Could she really cope with that?

"Look at me, Cally," he commanded softly. He waited until she lifted her reluctant gaze to his. "Don't be embarrassed by what we do together. I love you. I love every part of you and I want to show you how much." With tender fingers, he brushed a strand of hair off her forehead. "All the things I do to you are just a way of expressing my love. I hope you can understand that?"

Her heart beat wildly at his declaration. She held his gaze, reading the honesty and sincerity in his eyes. Taking a deep breath, she kept her eyes locked on his. "I love you too, Andy."

His eyes widened with surprise and his face lit up with happiness. "Show me," he grinned.

Though boneless after her orgasm, she pulled herself up slowly from where she lay beneath him. Emboldened by the desire glittering in the depths of his dark eyes, she pushed him gently until he was lying on his back, stretched out before her in all his naked glory. His thick cock sprang up from his groin, surrounded by pubic hair. Her eyes widened in disbelief. Her only experience in that department had been with Stewart and she hadn't realized until that moment how unimpressively endowed he'd been—either that, or Andy was exceptionally big.

His well-muscled chest was smooth and tanned and hairless. Leaning over him, she brushed the tips of her breasts over his chest and watched in awe as his nipples puckered. Pressing her breasts more fully against his skin, she heard the quick intake of Andy's breath. Noticing the strained look on his face, she grinned. "You were the one who told me to show you."

His voice was hoarse. "Did I happen to tell you how wicked you are?"

"*Mm*, not today." She gave him a cheeky grin.

He growled. "As I was saying—"

She silenced him by flicking her tongue over the hard nub of his nipple, first one then the other. He gasped and his hands clamped over her bare thighs where they straddled his hips, holding her still. The hard evidence of his desire pressed into the softness of her womanhood, still slick from her orgasm. She leaned over again to kiss him.

"You are a witch," he murmured. "An enchantress sent to drive me out of my mind."

She reveled in his praise and it made her even braver. Wriggling off his hips, she slowly slid down the hard length of his long muscular legs until her mouth hovered over his impressive erection.

He opened his eyes and stared down at her where she was poised above his hardness.

"Cally, you're driving me insane. Please, touch me. Please."

His raw need filled her with molten desire. He empowered her and the feeling gave her courage. She fit her hand around the solid, hard length of him. He groaned and she bent forward and hesitantly placed her mouth over the tip of his cock. Remembering how he'd swirled his tongue around her clit, she imitated his moves around the engorged head and then slid her tongue lower. He moaned again and her confidence soared.

With his shaft now slick, she moved her hand up and down, squeezing and releasing in a rhythmic motion. A few moments later, his hand stole down and covered hers, stilling its movement.

"No more," he said hoarsely. "I'm not ready to let this be over." Drawing her up gently, he pressed her against him, taking her mouth once again with his lips and as their tongues entwined, renewed stirrings of desire warmed her.

With a swift movement, he flipped her onto her back. He stared down at her, his face hard with need. "God, you're so beautiful. I have to be inside you."

Reaching across her, he fumbled for his wallet and pulled out a condom. Quickly sheathing his erection, he returned to his position between her legs. The tip of his cock pressed against her moist warmth. With a nudge of his thigh, she opened her legs wider and tried not to tense. This was Andy, not Stewart. Andy wouldn't hurt her. Andy loved her.

Slowly, he eased inside her, inch by inch. His arms strained from the effort and his jaw clenched. Her muscles stretched to accommodate his unfamiliar proportions. She gasped.

His eyes immediately filled with concern. "Are you okay? I'm not hurting you, am I?"

"No," she breathed. "You're just so... It feels so different, like you're filling every part of me." She blushed and looked away.

Andy groaned. "God, woman you're killing me." He pushed a little harder and all of a sudden, the whole, hard length of him was buried deep inside her.

She gasped again and concentrated on the feeling of her inner walls enfolding him, his hardness filling her. Slowly, he moved against her until the desire he'd ignited earlier pulsed back to life. Reaching up, she grabbed hold of his shoulders and dragged him down to her so her breasts were pressed tightly against his chest. He continued to thrust inside her slowly, rhythmically. Delicious pressure began to build again until she was close to another orgasm.

As if sensing it, his movements picked up speed and his thrusts became longer and harder. She brought her legs up and tightened them around his hips, drawing him in even closer. As the first waves of her climax washed over her, her eyes flew wide open. She watched as Andy's face, which had been tense with concentration, relaxed suddenly as he too shuddered and reached his fulfillment.

It was much later when Cally stretched and opened her eyes. Andy lay quietly beside her, watching her. He smiled, his eyes full of love.

"Tell me again how much you love me," she whispered, still overjoyed by the feeling.

He gathered her close and squeezed her tight. "You're the first and only woman I've ever loved. You're it. End of story. I want to spend the rest of my life with you."

Her mouth fell open in disbelief. She stared at him, confusion warring with hope. "What are you saying? That you want to move in here for good? As in, you want to move into my life and my bed, and live happily ever after?"

He grinned. "Well, now that I've installed an air conditioner, you could always move into *my* bed."

Happiness burst inside her. If Aunt Mary had been alive, she'd be smiling a mile wide. She would wink at Cally and tell her what a good-looking stud she'd managed to capture.

Andy smiled back at her. "So, what do you say?"

She frowned. "What do I say?"

"Yeah, what do you say? Will you do me the honor of becoming my wife?"

Her smile couldn't get any wider. Although she'd be happy to have him in her life on any terms, deep down inside, she was a traditionalist at heart. She believed in marriage and everything that came with it and she couldn't wait to become Andy's wife.

"Yes! Oh Andy—yes!" Throwing her arms around him, she hugged him tight but then spying his frown, pulled back slightly. "What's the matter? Not having second thoughts already, are you?"

He smiled. "Not on your life. I was just thinking about Jack and how he'll take our news."

She thought about her son and how well he'd adjusted to Andy and reached for his hand. "I think he's going to be over the moon," she whispered.

His lips met hers in a soft kiss that was full of love and contentment. When he pulled away at last, her breath came fast. His gaze swept over her naked form, pausing with great deliberation on the rosy tips of her nipples.

"What time does school get out?"

Cally giggled. "Three o'clock."

"Three o'clock," he muttered and dipped his head to her breast. His warm tongue snuck out and drew one of her nipples deep into his mouth. "Whatever will we do until then?"

"What do you have in here to eat? I'm starving," Andy grinned as he continued opening and closing kitchen cupboards.

Fresh from another shower, Cally tightened the cord at the waist of her white terry bathrobe and padded barefoot across the linoleum floor. She reached for the box of Weet-Bix and pushed it toward him with a dry look. "There's milk in the fridge."

"Weet-Bix? That's all you're offering me for brunch? Haven't you noticed I'm a growing boy? And after all the calories I burned off earlier this morning..."

She shrugged with studied nonchalance. "Take it or leave it."

He came over to where she stood and stopped right in front of her. "You're a hard woman. After all I did for you today."

Images of their marathon morning of lovemaking filled her head. She blushed and averted her eyes. Cupping her face in his hands, he lifted her chin until she was looking at him. His thumb stroked her cheek, his eyes warm and loving. Gently, he pushed a strand of wet hair out of her eyes before bending his head to place a soft kiss on her lips.

"How was the shower?" he murmured and pulled her against him.

She looked up at him and smiled. "It was good. Thanks for letting me go first."

He grinned cheekily. "After everything we've been through, it was the least I could do."

"Oh, you're impossible!" She brought her hands to her face in an effort to stem the heat. "Do we really have to *talk* about it? Why can't we just...you know...*do* it?"

Andy burst out laughing and her face flamed hotter. Ducking her head, she tried to wriggle out of his arms, but he was having none of that.

"I thought you knew? Guys like *talking* about it almost as much as they like *doing* it." Laughter glinted in his eyes. He shrugged. "It's what we do."

Crossing her arms over her chest, Cally did her best not to smile. "Well it's not what *I'm* comfortable doing."

"Maybe we could work on that," he murmured. He bent his head and tickled her ear with his tongue. "*Mm,* you taste so fresh and clean. I think I might have to take you back to bed and get you all dirty again."

He nibbled on her neck. She tried to ignore the shivers of desire that coursed through her. He loosened the tie of her bathrobe and a warm hand stole inside to squeeze her naked breast. A long finger flicked over her nipple. It immediately hardened under his attention.

She sighed in surrender and relaxed in his arms, relishing the feelings he was quickly stirring up deep inside her. After their previous sessions, she was surprised either of them could conjure up the energy for another bout of lovemaking, but it seemed she wasn't the only one who couldn't get enough.

"I think there might be bread in the cupboard. You might be able to make some toast," she murmured as he worked his way across the top of her breasts, taking little nibbling bites of her skin between his teeth.

"*Mm*, what was that?" His lips closed over one of her nipples and drew it into his mouth.

She gasped. Desire shot through and settled in her core. "I...I said there was... There was toast. You said...ah... You said you were...hungry."

"*Mm*, I'm hungry all right." He lifted his head and held her eyes, his meaning clear as his gaze dropped to her breasts, watching them as they rose and fell with her erratic breathing. "In fact, I'd nearly say I'm *famished*."

In one swift movement, he lifted her and sat her on the kitchen counter. She sucked in her breath. Her heart thudded in anticipation.

Spreading her robe wide, Andy feasted his eyes on her nakedness. "You're so beautiful. I can't believe you're mine."

Warmth spread through her. She leaned forward and placed her hands on his hips, drawing him forward between her legs. He was naked but for cotton boxer shorts and his erection jutted defiantly against its soft fabric.

His arousal only served to fan the flames of her desire and she wriggled her bottom to the very edge of the counter so she could press herself against his hardness.

Andy bit back a groan, marveling at the woman before

him. He could hardly believe she was the shy, almost virginal girl he'd made love to earlier that morning. Even after their third bout of lovemaking, she'd still blushed when he'd whispered words of love and passion in her ear.

But now, it was almost as if she'd decided to set her inhibitions aside and embrace whatever physical pleasures came her way. Her enthusiasm was an intoxicating aphrodisiac and his arousal became almost painful in its intensity.

Bending his head, he suckled one of her breasts, tugging on the erect nipple with his teeth. She moved against him, pressing closer, throwing her head back in abandonment. Moving his mouth to her other breast, he brought his hand around behind her bottom and pressed her even more tightly against his throbbing cock. He burned to bury himself in her wetness.

"Don't move," he growled, his voice hoarse with passion. Striding into his bedroom, he shucked off his boxers and sheathed himself with a condom. Seconds later, he returned to Cally's side. He grasped her hips and lifted her until she was once again at the very edge of the counter.

It was just the right height, he thought in dazed satisfaction as he maneuvered himself between her open legs. With just the tip of his cock pressing against her warmth, he watched the desire build on her face. She squirmed against him.

"Andy, please…"

He smiled, enjoying the sweet torture. "Please what, Cally?"

She squirmed harder, trying to raise her hips so she could take more of him inside her. Her eyes were stormy pools of need.

"Please don't stop."

Moving his cock inside her another inch, he held tight to his control. Leaning down toward her, he skimmed his mouth over hers, tasting, sipping from her lips.

"Do you want me?" His tongue found the sensitive part behind her ear that he'd discovered earlier in the day. She gasped.

"Yes!"

"Yes what, Cally?" He pushed his cock in a little further.

"Yes, I want you! Please, Andy. I want all of you—now!"

The urgency in her voice and the tight, warm wetness surrounding him was more than he could take. Holding her hips tightly, he thrust hard into her. They both gasped from the impact.

Their eyes met and held. Her snug, moist heat surrounded him, sheathing him like a glove. His cock swelled inside her. If he didn't slow things down, it would be all over in the next few minutes.

Pulling her legs around his hips, he lifted her bottom and held her still. Slowly, slowly he withdrew. She whimpered and clung to his shoulders, holding him close.

"*Shh.*" His eyes burned into hers. "You turn me on so much, I'm going to come if we don't slow things down. I want to make sure you come first."

She whimpered again and closed her eyes. He inched inside her again. Leaning forward, he flicked her hard nipples with his tongue—alternating from one to the other. His cock continued to slide in and out of her in long, slow thrusts.

Her legs tightened around him and her nails dug into his arms. Her breath came out in little pants. He increased the pressure and speed of his movements, watching her through eyes that were heavy with desire. Her face stilled and her body tensed. She gasped. Seconds later, waves of orgasm gripped her.

He gave her a few moments to catch her breath, his cock still rock-hard inside her. As she opened her eyes, she offered him a shaky smile, a pale blush staining her cheeks.

"Now, it's your turn," she whispered.

Tightening his hold on her hips, he thrust hard into her, once, twice. The third time he stiffened and closed his eyes and poured himself into her. Gathering her close, he stood there with his cock still inside her, savoring the final pulses.

Long moments later, he bent and kissed her lightly on the lips and then winked. "Wanna take another shower?"

Chapter 18

Cally swiped at the perspiration on her brow and shifted to her other foot. It was nearly three o'clock. Any moment, the bell would go and Jack would be released from another day of school. It was Thursday and she'd enjoyed another precious day off with Andy. He was still on nightshift and they'd spent the morning together. The memories of it brought a smile to her face. After an early lunch, he'd reluctantly left her to return to his bed and rest before his night ahead.

Not wanting to rush things with Jack, they'd agreed to keep up the pretense of friends and sleep in separate rooms until Jack had a chance to get used to Andy being there. Gradually, they hoped to bring him around to the idea that she and Andy might get married. Until then, all they had were the stolen moments in the hours when they were both at home and Jack was in school.

She spotted him loping toward her, a smile on his face. The smile widened when he saw her. A moment later, he gave her an enthusiastic hug.

"How was your day, honey?" Cally slung her arm around his shoulders and strolled back to the car.

"Pretty good. I beat Thomas West in handball at lunch time. That was *sick*."

"How did your spelling test go?"

Jack rolled his eyes. "No, Mom. That's tomorrow."

"Oh, right." She squeezed his shoulder. "So, I'm a day early."

"Is Andy still on nightshift?"

"Yes, honey. He'll be at work tonight."

Jack's face fell. "Darn, I don't like it when he's doing nightshift. I hardly get to see him. He's asleep when I get home from school and then he's barely awake and he's gone. I'm usually at school again when he gets home."

"I know, honey and I understand. But that's just the way it is. At least he won't be on nightshift forever and he'll be off on the weekend."

"Really? Do you think he might take me snorkeling again? Jimmy could come, too."

Cally smiled softly. "Maybe, you'll have to ask him."

"I will. Is he asleep right now? I want to ask him as soon as we get home."

"He was when I left to collect you and it would be better not to wake him. It's important he get some rest. He has to work all night when he leaves home."

They reached her old Toyota and she unlocked her door. "Hop in, sweetheart and don't forget to put your seatbelt on."

Jack rolled his eyes. "Yes, Mom."

Climbing into the car, her lips tugged upwards. He hated it when he thought she was treating him like a child. He wouldn't take kindly to the reminder that he *was* still child. With a soft sigh, she pulled out into the traffic and joined the queue of parents leaving after doing the school pickup. Glancing into the rearview mirror, her heart leaped into her throat. The blue Camry was right behind her.

A band of fear clutched at her belly. She glanced at the mirror again and read the license plate. *CHT 157.* It was the same one. It had been more than a week since she'd last seen it. She'd almost convinced herself her imagination had gotten the better of her. *Why had it shown up now?*

"Are you all right, Mom?"

She plastered a smile on her face. "Of course, sweetheart. Why do you ask?"

"You're mumbling under your breath."

She rubbed the back of her neck with one hand in an

effort to ease the tension and kept the forced smile in place. "I'm fine, honey."

"Oh, I almost forgot," Jack cried out in excitement. "I met someone today who said he was a relative of mine. You didn't tell me we had relatives living in Sydney." His voice was almost accusatory.

Knowing there were no such relatives, dread seized Cally's belly in a stranglehold. Her pulse took off like a bullet and she took a deep breath in an effort to remain calm. "Sorry, honey. I didn't hear you over the traffic," she lied, hoping to buy more time. "What did you say?"

He sighed exaggeratedly. "A man called me over to the fence at school. I think he said he was your uncle." Jack frowned. "Or maybe he said he *knew* your uncle?"

Tentacles of fear wrapped icy fingers around her heart. She forced another breath in her lungs. *Something was all wrong about this: She didn't have any uncles.*

"My uncle? Really? What did this man look like?"

He shrugged. "I don't know. He was pretty tall, but not as tall as Andy."

"What color hair did he have? Was it short or long? Did you notice the color of his eyes?" She tried not to sound like an interrogator.

"His hair was short and black, I think. He was wearing a hat, so I didn't get to see too much of it. And sunglasses. He was wearing sunglasses, too."

She digested that information. It sounded like the man she'd spied in the blue Camry. "What else did he say?"

"Not much, although it was a little weird when he started asking me about my dad. I thought if he was my uncle, he'd already know I don't have a dad."

Dread weighed cold and heavy in her chest. Could Stewart be the man in the Camry? It didn't make sense. As far as Stewart knew, she'd aborted their baby a decade ago, like he'd demanded. *But if not Stewart, then who?*

She'd never elaborated on the whereabouts of Jack's father to anyone in Sydney. When work colleagues, or the mother of one of Jack's friends casually posed the question, she deftly side-stepped it and changed the subject. Every now and then, someone would become a little more curious, and she'd end up telling them his father lived in the country—which was true, as far as she knew.

Was it possible Stewart had discovered her secret? Had he tracked her down in Sydney? But, why all the secrecy and subterfuge? She glanced in her rearview mirror and saw the Camry was still right behind her. Straining to get a look at the driver, she made out the dark form of a man. He wore sunglasses and a hat, just as Jack described.

Clearing her throat of nerves, she looked back at her son. "Honey, the man you were talking to in the playground today, did you see him get out of a car?"

"No, Mom."

She tried to ignore the disappointment that surged through her.

"But I saw him drive away in one."

Her brain suddenly registered what Jack said. Whipping her head toward him, she said, "*What* did you say?"

Jack sighed exaggeratedly. "You asked me if I'd seen the man getting *out* of a car. I said no because I didn't. The first time I noticed him was when he called out to me in the playground. I went after a ball that had rolled near the fence. The man in the sunglasses was already there. He called me over."

"I see. And he just started talking to you?"

"Yeah, I guess. But when he asked me about my dad, I felt a bit strange and picked up the ball and headed back. I looked over my shoulder to see if he was still there and that's when I saw him getting *into* his car."

"What kind of car?"

He shrugged. "A blue one. I'm not sure what kind."

"Dark blue or light blue?" Her voice sounded strangled.

"Dark blue, kind of like Jimmy's car, only it was a car like ours, not a big pickup like Jimmy's."

Panic seized her. It was one thing for the man to be parked alongside a busy road near her driveway, or even to follow her through heavy traffic, but to go to her son's school and speak with him?

Her mouth set in a grim line. Fanciful or not, she was going back to the police. This creep, whoever he was, had overstepped the mark. If he thought she would sit back and ignore the fact he'd approached Jack without her permission, he had another think coming. No one interfered with her son. *No one.*

She glanced behind her and flicked on her indicator to change lanes. The Camry was nowhere in sight. Relief surged through her. As much as she wished it were otherwise, her bravado was all a front. The man was getting bolder and the thought made her sick with fear.

Taking the next exit, she turned in the direction of the Chatswood Police Station, which was closest to her home. She hoped the detective who'd dealt with her house burglary would be there. He at least had some background knowledge.

She thought of Andy and suppressed the urge to call him. He'd barely closed his eyes when she left to collect Jack from school. She didn't want to wake him. He had a full night of work ahead of him.

"Where are we going, Mom? This isn't the way home."

Cally closed her eyes briefly and took a deep breath. She needed Jack to tell the police about the man he'd spoken to in the playground. As much as her heart rebelled against the idea of adding extra worries to his young shoulders, it was time to tell him about the stalker.

She bit her lip. "Honey, there's something I need to tell you." She braced herself for his reaction.

––––––––––––––––

Cally opened the door of the police station and was hit with a blast of icy air. She was pleased to see it raised a little color to Jack's pale cheeks. He still looked shocked, as he tried to take in what she'd told him, but she was confident he was resilient enough to cope. At least, she hoped so.

"May I help you?" A male officer whose name badge identified him as Constable Nicholls addressed her from behind the counter. Her stomach sank. He looked barely out of high school.

"Um, yes. I'm Cally Savage. Is Detective Black in?"

"I'll check for you." The officer picked up a phone, pressed a button, and spoke into it. A few moments later, he ended the call. "You're in luck. He'll be with you shortly. Take a seat over there if you like," he added and indicated the row of plastic chairs bolted to one wall.

Cally glanced at the seats and dismissed them. She was too agitated to sit and the constable had said the detective wouldn't be long. A moment later, the tall detective she'd met a little over a month ago when he'd come to interview her over the burglary appeared behind the counter. His green eyes were full of curiosity and his mouth opened in a friendly smile, displaying a perfect set of white teeth.

If Cally hadn't met Andy, she may have even been just the tiniest bit interested in the good looking detective. At their first meeting, she'd been too overwrought at the discovery an unknown man had been inside her home to take much notice of the attributes of the police officer investigating it. Now, with a little more balance in her life, she could appreciate what he had to offer...and remain entirely unmoved.

"Ms Savage, isn't it? What can I do for you?"

"I... You investigated a burglary at my house a little while ago. I spoke to you last week when I believed I was being followed."

"Yes, I remember. We sent a car around, but there was no one there. I take it you haven't seen the offending vehicle since?"

"Yes...no. I mean, I hadn't seen it since I spoke to you and I'd almost convinced myself it must have been a coincidence, but...something else has happened."

The detective nodded. "Okay, would you like to tell me about it?"

Cally bit her lip and glanced down at Jack. He stared up at her, his eyes wide and solemn. *She had to do it.* If she said nothing, something could happen to Jack and she'd never forgive herself. She drew in a deep breath.

"Yes. The man who's been following me has approached my son at his school."

The officer's expression turned serious and he leaned closer to her over the counter. "Why don't you come inside so you can make a proper statement? Is this young man your son?" He nodded in Jack's direction.

"Yes." She remembered Jack had been at school when the detective had come around. She drew her son close against her side. "This is Jack."

"How old are you, Jack?" Detective Black asked.

Jack peeked at him nervously. "I-I'm ten."

Cally tightened her arm around Jack's shoulders, offering him silent reassurance.

The detective gave him a friendly grin. "Do you think you could come in with your mom and tell me what happened at school today?"

Jack nodded cautiously, staying close to her side.

"Good. Now, if you walk over there, I'll come and unlock the door for you." The detective pointed to their left. Cally and Jack walked over and a moment later, the door was opened from the inside by the detective. "Right through here."

He led them through a twisting confusion of corridors and rooms until they arrived at an interview room. It was small and sparsely furnished in a similar fashion to the ones at the station in North Sydney. A cheap, Formica-covered table and four hard, plastic chairs took up most of the space. Cally looked up and saw a small camera positioned high in one corner. There were no windows and all four of the off-white walls were bare.

Icy air from the air conditioning vent made the temperature of the room uncomfortably cool. She shivered as much from the cold as from nerves. Being deep inside the bowels of a police station was intimidating. In silence, they took the seats that were offered.

She supposed that was all part of it. There were probably as many offenders as witnesses brought in here and to have them off-balance in a room like this was more than likely part of the *modus operandi*.

When Detective Black took a seat across from them, her nerves multiplied. She shot a quick glance at Jack seated next to her. Her son's face still held concern, but there was also fascination. She was glad he wasn't as apprehensive as she was. Her fear and discomfort must have shown on her face because the detective suddenly leaned toward her, a friendly smile on his face.

"Relax! I'm just going to ask you some questions about what happened, all right?"

She nodded and took Jack's hand in hers and gave it a squeeze, not sure which one of them she was trying to reassure.

"Okay, are we ready?" he asked, looking from one to the other.

She glanced down at Jack who nodded. Lifting her gaze to the officer, she took a deep breath and said, "Yes, let's get this over with."

"Good, we'll start with you." He indicated Cally and she forced air slowly out of her lungs.

"Tell me again, when did you first notice you were being followed?"

As she began to relate the incidents, the officer continued to take notes. When she got to the part about the license plate number, he paused and looked up at her.

"So, you got the plate number?"

She nodded. "Yes, it's CHT 157."

"That's great. We can run a check on it and see who the car's registered to. It's a good starting point." He wrote down the number and circled it. "When did you see the car again?"

"Last week. Then I saw it again today. It was right behind me as I left Jack's school. In fact, now that I think about it, the car must have been parked somewhere outside the school. It's a really busy time of day and there's always lots of cars pulling up and leaving as parents come to do the afternoon pick-up. It couldn't have pulled in behind me so quickly after I left unless it was already close by."

Turning to Jack, Detective Black gave him a smile. "Okay, buddy, why don't you tell me what happened today?"

Jack glanced up at her, his eyes now wide and uncertain. She smiled down at him reassuringly and squeezed his arm.

"It's all right, honey. You tell the officer exactly what you told me. He needs to know what happened, okay?"

Jack nodded and looked down at his hands.

"Where were you when you first saw the man?" Detective Black asked.

"Me and Jimmy and a couple of the other boys were playing handball near the oval."

The officer nodded encouragingly. "Who's Jimmy?"

"Jimmy Baker. He's my best friend."

"I see. Did anything happen while you were playing?"

"Jimmy missed the ball and it rolled over near the fence. I took off after it."

"And that's where you saw the man?"

"Yes. No. Well, not right away."

"So when did you see him?"

Jack took a deep breath. Cally watched him with concern. It was important for him to tell the police what he knew, but it didn't make it any easier to sit there and listen to him recount something that he was obviously finding difficult.

"I'm not sure if he was there when I first started running toward the fence. I was looking at the ball and I didn't really notice anything else. It was only when he called out to me that I looked up and saw him."

Detective Black scrawled notes on his paper. "What did he say to you? Did he call you by name?"

"Yes. He called me Jack."

Cally gasped in shock. She'd had no idea the man had known her son's name. Now there was no doubt—whoever was behind this was someone who knew them or had taken the time to research. With her heart beating double time, she forced herself to listen as Jack continued.

"When I heard my name, I looked up and saw the man standing outside the fence, right near where the ball had stopped. I remembered the stranger-danger talks we'd had at school last year, so I didn't get too close, but he was on one side of the fence and I was on the other, so I didn't think it would be too bad if I got close enough to hear what he was saying."

"And what did he say to you?" the officer asked, still scribbling notes.

"He asked me how I was and if I liked playing ball. I told him I was okay and I liked ball. He asked me if I played soccer and I said yes, but soccer didn't start until May."

"What else did he say?"

"That's when he asked me about my dad." Jack looked away and then fixed his gaze on his hands, still clenched in his lap.

"What about your dad?"

He shrugged. "I dunno. Just like, if I'd seen him recently and did I know where he was. Stuff like that."

Detective Black shifted his gaze to Cally. "Where's his dad?"

Now it was her turn to look down at her hands. She tried to find the right words. She didn't want to voice her suspicions about Stewart in front of Jack in case they turned out to be false. At the same time, she wanted the officer to take her seriously.

"Um, his father's no longer in the picture. In fact, Jack's never met him."

The detective's eyebrows rose, but he refrained from commenting. Instead, he continued to scribble on the notepad in front of him. Eventually, he raised his head and said, "I'll put out a POI report on the guy as soon as I can. Person of Interest," he added, catching her look of confusion. "The problem is, the sidewalk outside the school is a public thoroughfare. Unless he's a convicted pedophile, there's not much we can do about him being there, or even talking to your son."

He looked up from his notes. "I need to know a bit more about Jack's father. The man who spoke to Jack may have been waiting outside the school for a while now, waiting for an opportunity to talk to him. It could be that he's heard Jack's friends call him and figured out his name or he could know him." The officer's eyes pinned hers. "Who do *you* think it is?"

She dropped her gaze, wringing her hands in consternation. It seemed impossible, and yet it fit: *Stewart had discovered the truth.* She glanced at Jack and then took a deep breath and lifted her gaze. "I think it's Stewart Brady; Jack's father."

Cally tried to sit still as they waited for the detective to return. Shortly after her announcement, he'd left them to run the plate number through the computer. She suddenly wished she hadn't declined his offer of coffee. At least sipping on a coffee would give her something to do. The endless waiting was getting on her nerves.

Jack wasn't faring much better. He squirmed in the chair beside her and she smiled in empathy. *She* was finding it hard to sit still. How much harder was it for a ten-year-old boy? She leaned over and put her arm around him and gave him a hug.

"I'm so proud of you, Jack, for telling the policeman what you knew. I'm sure it wasn't easy, but he needs to know everything if he's going to help us."

Jack looked up at her, his expression solemn. "Do you really think it's my dad who's been following us?"

She nodded. "Yes, honey, I do."

"And his name's Stewart?"

"Yes."

"What makes you think it's him?"

Cally sighed softly. "There are not many people who even know about you, sweetheart. At least, not people who would be following us. My dad—your grandfather—knows of course, but my mother died a couple of years before Aunt Mary and I know my father wouldn't follow us around like that. Besides, the man we saw was fairly young. You told me he had dark hair, just like the man I saw."

She hesitated, but knew it was time to tell him. "Your dad had dark hair."

"Oh. So I don't look like him, then?" Disappointment tinged his voice.

She laughed without humor. "Oh, honey! You look *exactly* like him! The only thing you inherited from me was your hair color." She pulled him close against her.

"So, I *do* look like him, then?"

"Yes, sweetheart, you certainly do."

"Do you think I could get a soda? I'm really thirsty."

Pleased that he seemed to have accepted what she'd shared about his father, Cally brushed the hair out of his eyes and said, "I'll see what I can do. Hopefully, we won't be here much longer. We can stop for one at the shops on the way home."

The door to the room opened and Cally sat up straighter. Detective Black walked in brandishing a computer printout.

"I ran a check on that license plate. The car is registered to Harvey Donaldson."

She shook her head. The name meant nothing.

"He's a private investigator."

"A private investigator? Why would a private investigator be following me? And why would he want to talk to Jack?"

"More likely, someone's hired the PI to find you." He took his seat across from her and trapped her with his gaze. "Tell me about Stewart Brady."

She sighed. She couldn't spill the dirt on her personal life in front of her son. He had no idea about the details concerning his conception and that's the way it was going to stay. She stared at the officer and willed him to understand.

"Jack's thirsty. Is there somewhere he can get a soda? A vending machine, perhaps?"

Detective Black nodded. "Of course, there's one right down the hall. I'll get Janice to take him." He stepped out of the room and a moment later, they were joined by a young constable. She smiled at Jack.

"Hi, buddy. I'm Janice. What's your name?"

"Jack."

"Jack. That's a great name. Lane tells me you want a soda?"

"Yes, please."

"Come with me. I'll take you to where you can find one."

Cally threw the woman a grateful glance and reached for her purse.

"It's okay, we have some in the tea room. Is Fanta all right?"

Cally gave her a smile of thanks. "Fanta will be fine, right Jack?" He nodded enthusiastically.

"Fanta it is. Come on, Jack. Let's go."

When the two of them had departed, Detective Black returned to his seat.

"Thank you for that," Cally murmured.

"No problem. I take it there are things Jack doesn't know?"

Cally grimaced and nodded. "You've hit it spot on." With a deep breath, she recounted the events of her life before Jack.

"Stewart was my boyfriend when I was in high school. We came from the same town, but he was a few years older than me. I met him at a party when he was home on a college break. One thing led to another and I fell pregnant. I'd just turned sixteen."

Black scribbled again in his notebook. "How did Brady take that?"

She sighed, choosing her words with care. "Not good. He demanded I have an abortion. He was only nineteen. He had his whole life ahead of him."

"So did you."

Cally averted her gaze and shrugged with forced nonchalance.

The officer stared at her a moment longer and then asked, "So, what happened? Brady changed his mind about being a father and then decided not to stick around?"

"No, he didn't change his mind." She lifted her chin and stared at him defiantly. "I lied to him. I went with him to the clinic. He waited for me in the car. I sat in the waiting room for more than an hour, crying and wishing things were different. I knew I wasn't going to have an abortion, but I also knew Stewart wasn't willing to be a father."

Her breath came faster. "When I met him in the car park afterwards, neither of us spoke about it. He assumed I'd had the procedure and I never bothered to correct him. Within days, I was sent to live with my aunt in another town. I never saw Stewart again. When Jack was born, he and I stayed with my aunt."

"What about your parents? Why didn't you stay with them?"

A familiar stab of pain sheared through her. With a tight smile, she eyeballed the officer. "Let's just say they thought it would be better if I lived with my aunt."

"They threw you out. Is that what you're trying to tell me?"

Cally gasped at his directness. Coming from a stranger, the callous actions of her parents sounded even worse. Irritation surged through her and all of a sudden she just wanted it over with.

"Look, is this really necessary? I've already told you who I think is behind this. Somehow, Stewart found out about Jack. Now that I know the man following me is a private investigator, at least I can put my mind at ease that he's not some madman escaped from the nearest correctional facility. He's not going to hurt us or break into our home. I assume we can cross that off the list?"

"Looks like it. Harvey Donaldson's a well respected PI. He wouldn't be involved in anything shady. If you ask me, it sounds much like you think. Your ex-boyfriend has hired him to find you. It sounds like he finally wants to meet his son."

Cally's heart slammed against her chest. For ten years, she'd raised Jack on her own. Her mind spun at the thought Stewart might want to become a part of their lives. She lifted her gaze. "What do I do now?"

"Well, you could go and visit Donaldson and see if he's willing to tell you who hired him. I don't know how much luck you'll have, because the type of people who hire these guys depend upon the fact they can remain anonymous. Donaldson's one of the best. I can't see him breaching someone's confidentiality, but I guess you can give it a try."

She grimaced. "What do I have to lose?"

The officer leaned over and tore the top half of the computer printout off and handed it to her.

"Here's the name and address of Donaldson's agency, in case you want to look him up."

She took the piece of paper and folded it in half and thanked him.

"No problem." Detective Black pushed back his chair and stood. "I hope it all works out for you."

The sound of Cally's car pulling up outside his window woke Andy from a deep sleep. Almost immediately, a smile of anticipation stretched his lips wide. It had only been a matter of hours since he'd seen her, but it didn't seem to matter. He couldn't get enough.

He'd managed to scrape together a few hours' sleep and although he was far from feeling refreshed, a few hours was better than nothing. Besides, he wanted to see her. In another hour, he'd be at work.

Throwing off the sheet that covered him, he hurriedly tugged on a pair of shorts. He could hear low conversation in the kitchen. He ran his fingers through his hair in an attempt to straighten it and then pulled open the French doors. Cally and Jack stared at him in surprise and delight. Jack was the first one to speak.

"Andy! You're awake! That's so cool! Mom thought you might still be asleep."

Andy smiled and walked over to Jack and ruffled his thick blond hair. "I was, mate. I heard the car drive in. It woke me up."

Cally frowned. "Oh, no! I'm sorry. I should have parked out on the street."

"Don't be silly," he smiled, his gaze lingering on her face. "I'm glad. It means I get more time to spend with you. Both of you," he added, his gaze encompassing Jack. Besides, I'd rather not have you leaving your car out on the highway. Too dangerous."

She stared at him and pursed her lips. He frowned. "What's the matter?"

Her shoulders slumped and she moved toward the table. Pulling out a chair, she lowered herself into the seat. "I know who's been following me."

His brows flew up in surprise. "What do you mean? So you've seen him again?"

She nodded. "The man in the Camry followed me from Jack's school today."

When Andy opened his mouth to express his shock and outrage, she held up her hand to cut him off.

"That's not the worst of it."

Dread tightened his gut. "You're kidding?"

"He talked to Jack at school."

"*What?*"

"Yes," Jack interjected. "He called me over to the fence and—"

"Jack, please. Let me tell Andy. It's important, honey." She softened the request with a smile and turned back to Andy.

"I was as shocked as you are, but as much as it frightened me to know a stranger had gotten that close to him, it made me more determined than ever to find out who's behind it."

"I hope you went straight to the police?"

"Yes, I went to the station in Chatswood and Jack and I spoke to Detective Lane Black. He was the same officer who dealt with the burglary. He was very nice and very helpful, but because this man was outside the school grounds, there wasn't anything they could do about it." She shrugged. "The sidewalk is a public thoroughfare."

Andy grimaced and shook his head. "That's true. Unless he's a convicted pedophile or something like that and prohibited from hanging around areas where there are young children." He frowned as a thought struck him. "What about the license plate? Didn't you tell me you'd gotten it the last time?"

She nodded again. "Yes. I gave it to the detective and he ran it through the computer." She paused and took a deep breath before continuing. "Apparently, the car is registered to a Harvey Donaldson."

"The private investigator? Why would he be tailing you?"

Cally stared down at the table. A long moment later, she lifted her gaze to his. "I think it has something to do with Stewart Brady."

He looked at her blankly. "Who's Stewart Brady?"

"Jack's father."

"Jack's *father*?" He felt like he was about to explode. "As in the selfish jerk who—" He broke off, suddenly aware of Jack's presence. "You think *he's* the one behind this?" he added a little less forcefully.

She turned to Jack who stood quietly off to one side. "Honey, would you do me a favor and go into the living room? I'm sure you have some homework to do. I need to talk to Andy alone."

A mutinous expression flared briefly in Jack's eyes and his lips tightened, but he obediently did as he was told. After closing the French doors behind him, Cally turned back to Andy.

"Yes, I think Stewart's the one behind this." She shrugged. "It makes sense, doesn't it? Perhaps he's decided he wants to meet his son?"

Andy's gut tightened with fear. Cally's feelings for him

were so new, so fragile. If her ex-boyfriend—and worse, the father of her child—reappeared on the scene, where would that leave Andy? It was utterly and inexcusably selfish, but all at once he hoped with a passion that the man linked to the private investigator wasn't Jack's dad. The asshole didn't deserve a son like Jack. He hadn't wanted the boy in the first place.

Cally stared at him from across the table and concern clouded her eyes. Unable to stay still, he walked across the room and propped himself up against the counter, crossing his arms defensively over his chest. A thick wedge of jealousy lay heavily in his gut.

He had no right to think of Cally and Jack as his, but he couldn't help it. He already did. The woman who sat across from him had been his from the moment he set eyes on her and with her came her son, a boy he'd begun to think wistfully as the son he wished he had.

"Andy? Are you all right?" She pushed away from the table and reached out to touch his arm. "You look so...stern."

He sighed and took her hand in his. Threading his fingers through hers, he squeezed tightly. His gaze burned into hers. "I don't want to lose you, Cally," he said simply.

She smiled back at him and her eyes brimmed with emotion. "You're not going to lose me, Andy. Stewart..." She broke off, obviously struggling to find the words to explain. "He was a long time ago. I was only a girl. A child, really, with stars in my eyes. I was taken in by a smooth-talking charmer."

She looked down at her feet. Andy held his breath and waited for her to continue.

"It was one of the reasons I was so wary of you at first," she admitted. "All I could think about was your movie-star looks and your million-dollar smile and I knew I had to be careful I didn't make the same mistake again. You were so charming and funny and sweet and I was terrified I would leave myself open to the same heartache all over again."

She offered a tentative smile. "But you make it so hard to

resist—and the more time I spend with you, the more I know you are different—you aren't like Stewart at all."

Her eyes found his, dark and tumultuous. "He was a taker. I know that now. In fact, when I think back to those few short weeks we were together, I can see how everything we did was for him. He wanted to go to the movies so we could make out in the back row, and so we did. He wanted to go to the river so we could make out on a picnic rug on the riverbank, and so we did. He wanted to go to a motel so we could have sex, and so we did."

Silence descended. With her free hand, she played with a tassel on the end of her shirt. It seemed a long while later when she added quietly, "I can't remember a single time when he asked what *I* wanted to do. He didn't care about me at all, even when he hurt me. It was all about him. Every single time."

Andy swallowed and cleared his throat. "You're a stronger person for the experience, though. You're the strongest, bravest woman I know." His eyes held hers, hoping she saw the depth of his love. "And you have Jack."

She smiled softly. "Yes, I have Jack. My beautiful, sensitive boy. When I look into the eyes of my son, the pain of abandonment by everyone I loved is almost forgotten."

Hating himself, but knowing he had to say it, he tightened his hold on her hand and looked at her intently. "You have to get to the bottom of this. You have to find out if Brady is involved and if so, what he wants." His gaze burned with intensity. "Stewart Brady doesn't deserve to know his son, but your son deserves to know his father. Jack's the innocent party in all of this. It's only right he gets to choose what happens from here."

She stared back at him. "You're right. Jack deserves to know."

CHAPTER 19

"Whereabouts in Balmain?"

Cally consulted the piece of paper she'd been given by Detective Black and gave Andy the address. She watched while he punched it into the satellite navigation system mounted on the dash of his Audi. It was Saturday and the first opportunity she'd had to pay a visit to the offices of Harvey Donaldson.

A lot of businesses closed for the weekend, and at Andy's earlier suggestion, she'd telephoned ahead to check if the investigator's office was open. She'd listened to a recorded message that advised the office hours were nine to five Monday to Friday and nine to two on Saturdays. Cally quickly arranged for Jack to stay with Jimmy and they had headed out as soon as they dropped him off.

According to the map which flashed up on the screen of the GPS, the private investigator's office was situated in the heart of Balmain's business district. Glancing at the clock mounted on the dashboard, she noticed they had a little under an hour to get there before the office closed.

Andy accelerated through the traffic, switching lanes with practiced ease. The closer they got to the Balmain exit, the more nervous she felt. She stared out the car window at the gloomy industrial buildings they passed, interspersed with an occasional tired and neglected park, empty of children and playground equipment. The February heat shimmered in waves off the asphalt and she was inordinately grateful they were traveling in his car with its climate-controlled, air conditioned comfort.

"How far do we have to go?" Nerves fluttered around inside her stomach.

"Just under twenty minutes, according to the GPS." Andy turned and gave her an encouraging smile.

She clenched her hands together in her lap and tried not to think about what she might discover at the office of Harvey Donaldson. Was Stewart in town or directing the investigator's movements from a distance? Did he really want to get to know Jack, or was there something more sinister behind hiring the PI? Why hadn't he simply called her and asked if they could meet?

She sighed, knowing she didn't have any answers. Those were exactly what she hoped to get out of Harvey Donaldson.

Andy turned into the main street of Balmain and the butterflies doubled in her stomach. She swallowed and licked her parched lips. Andy slowed and began to look for a parking spot. According to the GPS, the investigator's office was at the next intersection.

"There it is." Andy nodded and she looked up and saw the number three hundred and ninety-eight painted in black above a shopfront a few feet from the traffic lights.

Turning down a side street, Andy parked the car and switched off the ignition. Facing her, he held her gaze steadily. "Are you sure you're ready for this? There's no turning back, you know."

She took a deep breath and exhaled shakily. "No, I'm not sure, but it's something I have to do. Whether I like it or not, I've always known there would come a time when I'd have to confront Stewart again." She let out a sigh of resignation. "I guess it was that article in the newspaper."

Andy looked at her quizzically.

Cally went on to explain. "I've been wondering how on earth Stewart could have found out about Jack. Then I remembered. The media came around after the home invasion. We were the fifth house to be burgled in that area in less than a week. Police suspected the robberies were linked. One of the papers took a photo of Jack and me. Stewart must have seen it."

Andy frowned. "He'll be angry you lied. I would be."

Cally's temper ignited, but she tamped it down—it wasn't Andy's fault she was in this predicament. She could never imagine Andy suggesting any pregnant girlfriend have an abortion, no matter what the circumstances.

Her eyes welled with tears. Leaning across the console, she gave him a soft kiss on the mouth. "Thank you."

His eyes held confusion. "What for?"

"For being you. For being here, with me. I don't think I could have come here without you."

"That's bullshit, Cally. You face adversity head on and damn the consequences. I wish even half the blokes I work with had your courage."

Her heart swelled with love. The tears she'd done her best to hold back spilled over. She didn't know what she'd done to deserve someone so wonderful, but she was thanking her lucky stars for whatever it was. "I love you so much."

His face softened. "I love you, too."

———————

"Can I help you?"

The woman with the short, steel-gray hair who sat behind the cheap laminated desk frowned up at them. She held a wrinkled, be-ringed hand over the mouthpiece of the phone she had pressed against her ear.

Cally stepped forward. "I'm Cally Savage and this is Andy Warwick. We're here to see Harvey Donaldson."

"You got an appointment? He don't see no one without an appointment."

"Er, no." She thought fast. "But I did call ahead and um... He told me to meet him here." The lie fell off her lips with a little difficulty, but the woman didn't seem to notice as she began to speak to someone on the other end of the phone.

"Yeah, three-fifty an hour, plus expenses."

Cally watched as the woman listened to the person on the other end of the phone again before responding once more. "Yeah, that's right. Five thousand up front. That's the standard fee. Take it or leave it."

She noticed Andy looking around at the battered and mismatched chairs which sat in the waiting room. A thin coating of dust lay over most of the furniture and the room had a stale, musty smell that seemed to indicate the large windows overlooking the street were rarely opened.

Harvey Donaldson's office was on the floor above a news agent. "HARVEY DONALDSON, PI" was handwritten in small, black letters with an arrow drawn beneath it, pointing toward the stairs. It had taken them a few moments to find the sign tacked near a dingy staircase between the news agent and an empty shop.

The dark, grubby staircase had been the first harbinger of what was to come. Cally was surprised Stewart would hire a man who worked in such filthy surroundings. The Stewart Brady she'd known had always been fastidious about his appearance, sometimes changing his clothes two or three times a day. He'd often meet her after school with a new outfit he'd bought for her and ask her to change into it. At first, pleased he was buying her gifts, she hadn't given any thought to the strangeness of it. It was only as she'd gotten to know him better that she realized how serious he took the whole issue of cleanliness and appearances.

She couldn't imagine him ever setting foot inside these offices and could only surmise he'd never been there. In this day and age of email, cell phones and other various forms of communications, Stewart wouldn't have to have face-to-face contact to get this job done.

She took comfort from the arm Andy put around her shoulders. A few minutes later, the woman behind the desk hung up the phone.

"Mr Donaldson ain't here yet. You'll have to take a seat." She indicated with a nod toward the dusty chairs that lined the wall.

Andy drew Cally in close against his side and eyed the woman disdainfully. "That's okay, we'll stand," he replied. "How long's he going to be?"

She glanced at the watch on her wrist. "Shouldn't be too far away. He's usually here by two. Comes and collects his messages before I leave."

With that, she returned to the untidy pile of paperwork on her desk and started sorting through it, ignoring them.

Shrugging out of Andy's embrace, Cally wandered over to peer through the grubby windows to the street below. Cars ambled past, not in a big hurry like they would be on a week day. She caught a glimpse of the ocean in the distance. Not all of Balmain was as shabby and depressing as the room they were in. The inviting blue water was a world away from the dirty office. She couldn't even imagine what kind of man could work in such squalor.

The door to the room suddenly opened and a man stood in the doorway. With a shock, she recognized him as the driver of the Camry. Before he could demand an explanation for her presence, she stepped forward and held out her hand. "Hi, I'm Cally Savage."

His eyes widened in recognition and his face paled slightly under the bronze of his tan. Harvey Donaldson, in his blindingly white business shirt and charcoal-gray tailored suit pants looked incongruous in the grubby filth of his outer office. His black, lace-up leather shoes were so highly polished she was sure she could see her reflection in them and his dark hair was combed neatly in place. In fact, for a hot Saturday afternoon, he looked obscenely fresh.

He was tall, as she'd suspected and she had to look a long way up to meet his gaze. When she did, he grimaced. "It's nice to meet you. I guess we should go inside."

———

"So, Ms Savage, what can I do for you?"

After showing them to a matching pair of clean, dark

leather wing-backed chairs, Donaldson took a seat behind his desk. He seemed to have recovered from his initial surprise and now smiled at her with practiced ease.

Cally frowned and Andy sat forward in his chair. The investigator's office couldn't have been further removed from the squalor which made up the reception room. The contrast was so great, it was almost disorientating and Cally wondered if that was all part of whatever game he was playing.

The enormous dark walnut desk took up most of the room. Papers and files were stacked in neat piles on top of it. A wide, flat screen computer sat in one corner of the desk and she caught a glimpse of black-and-white photographic images of people on the screen before the investigator switched it off.

A floor-to-ceiling bookshelf lined with books took up an entire wall. A quick scan of their titles revealed they were positioned in alphabetical order. Various original paintings from artists she recognized filled another wall, their positions perfectly aligned. It appeared the PI work paid well.

Andy's face was set in hard lines. "Let's not beat around the bush, Donaldson. You've been following Ms Savage for weeks. Now you've approached her son. You've stepped over the line. We're here for answers."

Ignoring him, the investigator turned his attention back to Cally. His piercing gaze pinned her to the seat. "There's someone who misses you a great deal. He hired me to find you and to report back on how you're doing. He's also very interested in your son. He'd like very much to see you both."

Her heart leaped in her throat and her hands were suddenly damp. Images of Stewart flashed through her mind as he'd been over ten years ago. Laughing, smiling, charming—selfish, egotistical, cowardly.

There was a time, not that long ago, when the news Stewart had come looking for her would have set her heart racing with excitement and anticipation. She couldn't count how many nights she'd dreamed of him finding her and begging her to take him back.

But that was before Andy. Before she knew what real love was. Before she knew that loving someone was as much about giving as it was about receiving. She was no longer the innocent young girl whose head was turned by a good-looking charmer. She'd learned the hard way that life didn't always end up happily ever after. Though it was so much better now...

Her son was the most precious thing to her in the world and a tiny part of her would always be grateful for the contribution Stewart had made to his existence, but she was through with Stewart once and for all. He didn't deserve her. He didn't deserve *them*. He never had.

Glancing across at Andy, she saw the tension in his face. He seemed to have come to the same conclusion—the man who'd hired Donaldson was Stewart Brady. Her heart ached when she saw how his eyes were shadowed with doubt and vulnerability and his hands were fisted in his lap.

Wanting to reassure him, she reached over and took hold of his hand, gently easing his fingers out of their clenched position and entwining her fingers with his. Giving his hand a squeeze, she smiled at him, hoping he could feel her love.

———————

Despite Cally's encouraging smile and the reassuring pressure of her soft hand in his, Andy's gut tightened at the investigator's words. *It had to be Brady.* He was coming after Cally—probably with a view to picking up where he'd left off. Only this time, he had a son. He was going to waltz in and begin playing happy family for however long it suited him this time around.

Andy had no doubt it wouldn't be forever. The Stewart Brady's of the world were always looking for something else. The degree of selfishness required to turn your back on your pregnant, sixteen-year-old girlfriend didn't generally lessen. In fact, that type of inherent self-absorption usually only got worse.

He only hoped Cally would see it for what it was. Brady was a leech. He'd suck her dry of everything good she had to offer and when it suited him to leave her again, he would. Andy understood better than most the Stewarts of the world. His father had been one of them.

Bob Warwick had effectively abandoned his family many years before his death. His drinking and violent outbursts—and later, his addiction to illicit drugs—were all acts of a selfish, self-centered man with no thought or concern for how anyone else was faring.

His father's childhood might have been a train wreck, but that didn't excuse Bob Warwick for perpetuating the same cycle of violence and abuse on his family. After all, despite all the statistics, Andy had managed to pull himself out of the mire of pain and humiliation of his youth and had made something of his life. He simply couldn't imagine ever taking his fists to Cally, or to any woman or child.

As if sensing his thoughts, her fingers tightened in his. His heart tripped over and he returned the pressure, taking comfort from her gesture.

"It's Brady, isn't it?" His eyes were hard on Donaldson's face.

"I'm afraid I can't answer that. I'm sure you appreciate client confidentiality."

The fakeness of Donaldson's perfect smile set Andy's teeth on edge. Anger flared to life. His voice became low and threatening. "Did I forget to mention I'm with the police? Be warned. You go near Cally or her son again and I'll have your license revoked so fast you won't even have time to clear out your office."

Donaldson's smile lost some of its brilliance, but remained firmly in place. "You can't do that. You're bluffing."

He reached into his jacket pocket.

Donaldson tensed.

Andy flashed his badge. "Just watch me."

Andy pushed back his chair and stood. Despite the investigator's impressive height, Andy towered over him, his strength and sheer physical presence dominating the room.

The men eyed each other across the desk. Turning abruptly, Andy helped Cally from her chair and then strode to the door.

"We'll see ourselves out."

"It *has* to be Stewart." Cally stared out the window as Andy drove silently back the way they'd come.

"*Mm*," he replied noncommittally, not ready to get into a discussion about her ex-boyfriend and how she might or might not still have feelings for him. But she was persistent.

"There's no one else who fits the category. 'Someone who misses me a great deal' and who's also interested in Jack? Of course it's Stewart."

He sighed, resigned to the fact that she needed to sort out the thoughts which were no doubt swirling around inside her head, just as they were in his.

"What about your father? Maybe it's him?" he said, more to steer her away from the subject of her ex-boyfriend than to explore any real belief he had that the man involved was anyone but Brady.

He wanted to howl and scream at the injustice of it. She'd agreed to marry him, but that was when there'd been no other men vying for her hand. Now, with the imminent re-emergence of her first love, the father of her child, he couldn't help but wonder if things would be different—if even now she was regretting her hasty agreement to marry him.

After all, as far as she knew, he was just a police officer with a nice car and a big TV. He hadn't wanted her to want him for his material possessions, but if push came to shove in the game to win her heart, he'd pull out all the stops to come out triumphant.

A small voice inside him argued with him about whether he really wanted her if, in the end, she chose him over Brady merely because of his wealth. The thought disquieted him as much now as it had earlier, when he'd decided to keep it secret. But she was *the one*. And if she loved him, too, wouldn't that be enough?

"It wouldn't be my father," she said quietly, interrupting his thoughts. "You don't know him. He's not a man who forgives a wrong and in his mind I wronged him more than anyone. At least, that's how he saw it. He didn't even tell me when Mom died."

Andy choked, shocked out of his reverie. "You're kidding? What sort of a father does that?"

"The same one who was principal of the local school and threw his pregnant teenage daughter out on the street."

He shook his head in disbelief, still amazed any father could react that way. After a few moments, he reached over and took her hand in his and squeezed it hard. "How did you find out she'd died?" he asked quietly.

Cally released a deep, shuddering breath. When she finally spoke, her voice was dull and lifeless. "My aunt told me. I'm not sure how she found out, but after all, they were sisters. I guess she found out through her family."

"When did your mom die?"

"A couple of years before Aunt Mary. Jack was six. She had a massive heart attack. It happened at home. It's funny, she'd never even been sick before. At least, not while I lived there."

"Sometimes these things happen and no one really knows why," he offered, trying to comfort her.

"Yes." She grimaced. "That's what my aunt said."

"Did Jack go to the funeral?"

"*I* didn't go to the funeral."

For the second time in as many minutes, his mouth fell open in shock. "Say, *what?*"

She turned to stare out of the window. He'd almost convinced himself she wasn't going to answer when she turned back to him, her eyes welling with tears.

"My father told me not to go."

He gaped and moved his lips, but words were beyond

him. He shook his head and tried to string a sentence together. "Say that again?"

"My father refused to let me to go," she repeated, her face hardening. "I telephoned him after I found out and he told me I wasn't welcome there."

"You're kidding me? He wouldn't let you go to your own mother's *funeral*? That's incomprehensible. What did your aunt say? Did she go?"

Cally shook her head sadly. "No, she'd been cut off by her family years earlier, my mother among them. As much as she wanted to go, she knew my mother wouldn't have wanted her there and she respected that." She swiped at her eyes. "Not that it didn't upset her. I caught her crying in the garden the evening after we found out."

He let go of her hand and negotiated the exit off the freeway and headed toward Chatswood. "Did your father know you had a son?"

"Yes. Aunt Mary telephoned my parents shortly after Jack was born." Her lip trembled. She struggled on with what he could tell was forced insouciance. "Neither of them came to visit me. Not even once."

His fingers tightened around the steering wheel. In angry silence he cursed Cally's parents who'd hurt her just as much, if not more, than her selfish boyfriend.

"That leaves Brady," he murmured.

Cally's shoulders slumped. "I guess so."

Andy pursed his lips, dread weighing him down. "I think you should meet with him." The words fell out of his mouth.

"*W-what?* What did you say?"

His gaze clashed with hers. He understood her shock. Even he couldn't believe he'd said it, but there was no other way. Brady had to be dealt with. Andy had always believed the best way to deal with a problem was head-on.

"I said, I think you should meet with him."

"You mean with *Stewart?*" Her eyes were wide.

"Yes, with Stewart. It's the only way. Meet him up front, see what he wants and then hopefully, he'll be satisfied and disappear out of your life again."

"But what if he doesn't?"

It was the same question that was killing him, but he wasn't about to admit that. Instead, he shrugged casually. "Then we'll deal with that, if and when it happens. It's not as if he's going to come charging in and whisk you off into the sunset. You're with me now, right?"

He stared ahead, pretending to concentrate on the road in front of him and waited nervously for her answer. It came without hesitation and his heart clenched.

"Of course! It's just that, I'm not sure if I'm ready to…share Jack with Stewart." She glanced across at him. "It's different with you. I mean, you're not his father. You're not someone who might have a legal claim to him. Not like his father would. Do you know what I mean?"

He forced a smile to conceal the stab of hurt. Of course he wasn't Jack's father, but that didn't mean he *couldn't* be—did it? Surely, she'd thought about how things would be after they got married? He wanted to adopt Jack as his own.

He frowned and wondered for the first time whether she'd be unhappy with the idea. He'd assumed she'd be thrilled about it. It never occurred to him she might feel territorial about her son or worse, that she'd be opposed to the idea.

"Andy? What's the matter? Did I say something wrong?"

The uncertainty in her voice clutched at his heart and he exhaled on a loud sigh. He didn't want any misunderstandings between them. If they were going to argue about his role in Jack's life, they might as well deal with that now.

He gave her a sideways look. "You're right. I'm not Jack's father." He pinned her with his gaze and then returned his attention once again to the road. "I'm going to marry you, Cally. You're going to be my wife. So, I was wondering where that leaves Jack? If I'm not going to be a father to him, then what?"

She sputtered, completely taken aback. "Andy…um, I don't know. I guess I haven't… I haven't thought about it. Of course you'll be in Jack's life. He's my son. He and I go together. Love me, love my son."

He nodded, sparing her another glance. "Okay, that all sounds good in theory, but what about when it comes to the hard stuff? What about discipline and deciding whether he's going to the movies with one of his mates or what time he has to be home? Who will decide that stuff, Cally? If I'm going to be the kind of father I want to be to Jack, you're going to have to let me have a say in everything. I'm not only going to be a father to him when it suits you. I can't have you pull the rug out from underneath me if it doesn't."

She stared at him, her eyes widening in surprise. "I-I don't know what to say, Andy. I guess I haven't given any thought to the practical day-to-day stuff. I'm just happy you want to marry me." She offered him a strained smile, but he wasn't buying it.

"You need to think about it, Cally. It's all well and good to be happy about getting married. Hell, I'm thrilled about it. But, we need to talk about Jack. Especially now Brady's back in the picture."

She sighed and her face sobered. "You're right and I'm sorry. It's just that, Jack and I have been a two-man team for so long... It's going to take some getting used to—sharing the responsibility for him with someone else. Even when we lived with Aunt Mary, she never intervened or interfered with the way I raised him."

At the look on Andy's face, she added, "Not that I'm implying you're going to interfere, it's just that..." She shrugged helplessly.

His eyes burned with emotion. "Cally, I'm never going to be happy being a visitor in Jack's life. I accept that he's your son and for the last ten years, you've had total control over him." He glanced across at her again, trying to gauge her reaction. "But I can't and I won't be a part-time dad. It's all or nothing. I need to know I have your support on this."

She was quiet for what seemed like a lifetime. Andy's fingers cramped where they gripped the steering wheel. At last, she spoke.

"You're right, Andy. You're absolutely right. You should have an equal say. And we'll discuss things if we disagree. We'll come to an agreement if we work at it. It will take some getting used to, but you're going to be my husband and probably the only father Jack is ever going to know."

His breath whooshed out in relief. Cally sighed and reached over to take his hand in hers. Giving it a reassuring squeeze, she brought it up to her lips and pressed a soft kiss across his knuckles.

"I love you, Andy and I trust you with my life. Mine *and* Jack's. Together we can make this work."

He looked over at her and smiled. Fierce emotion surged through him and tears pricked the back of his eyes. "Thank you. You don't know how much that means to me. I want to be the best father I can be, but I have to know I have your support before we start, or it'll never work. And you need to know you have my support."

He shook his head. "I've had friends who've taken on step-children and as soon as the going gets tough—and it's usually on a discipline issue—their partner undermines their authority and the whole thing unravels."

She nodded. "I can see how that would cause problems and I don't want that for us. We love each other. We respect each other. I know we can agree or find a middle ground."

"You don't have to say that. In fact, it's unrealistic to think we're always going to agree on what's best for Jack or any other kids we may have. All I'm asking is that we never disagree with each other in *front* of them. We'll work together, anticipate, and consider all sides, in order to present a unified front whenever he's around."

She gazed back at him, her eyes dark with emotion. He swallowed against the lump in his throat.

"I love you, Cally," he added, his voice husky with emotion, "and I love your son. One day, I hope you'll even let him become my son, too."

Her eyes widened in shock. "You want to *adopt* him?"

He nodded. "Of course. You're going to be my wife. I want him to be my son, in every way that's possible."

"What if we have to get Stewart's consent? I'm sure the biological father must get a say in these things?"

He shrugged. "So, we get his consent. Or we go to court. There must be some way to do it. I don't care what it takes or how much it costs, I want him to be ours. I want both of you."

She smiled at him, her eyes full of love. "You make me so happy, Andy Warwick. I don't care what skeletons you're still hiding." Her smile turned cheeky. "Unless of course you have some weird fetish for women's underwear or collecting navel fluff or storing dirty, smelly socks under the bed...for like...*years*." She grinned. "Any of those would be a deal breaker."

Guilt flooded through him, knowing he still hadn't told her about his wealth. His smile was strained. "Nope, can't say I have a problem with any of those."

"What about your personal hygiene...? You don't shower every day? That's it, isn't it?"

"Nope."

Her face turned somber. "It's the toilet seat, isn't it? You just don't know how to put it down when you're finished! I knew it!"

He laughed. "Well, now that you mention it..."

She hit him playfully on the arm.

"Hey!" he yelped in mock protest. "I've been living on my own for years. There's never been any reason to put the toilet seat down."

"Well, if that's all you've been hiding, why all the secrecy?" Her voice was suddenly serious.

He brought the car to a stop outside her garage and killed the engine. Turning to her, his expression sobered. "I have something to tell you."

He reached for her hand, but she pulled it away. This was not going as he hoped. He drew in a deep breath and prayed for the best.

Chapter 20

"I have money, Cally. Lots of it."

"Excuse me?" Her mind reeled in confusion. It was the last thing she expected Andy to say. "What do you mean, you have money?"

He shrugged, seeming almost embarrassed. "It's like I said. I have a lot of money. A few years ago, I won first prize in a substantial lottery. I'm wealthy. *Very* wealthy."

She shook her head, still bewildered. He reached for her hand again, and took another deep breath.

"I own a sizeable share of a multi-million-dollar mining company. I have a penthouse overlooking the beach at Bondi. I have a number of other investment properties around the city. I even own an apartment block in my hometown of Tamworth." He shrugged. "I have money, Cally."

"B-but what about your work? Why would you be working so hard and all those long hours if you didn't have to?"

He shrugged again. "You might find this hard to believe, but work's not always about the money. I love my job. It wouldn't matter if I could finance a third world country on my own, I'd still show up at the station every day."

He caught her gaze and held it, his eyes intense. "My job defines me, Cally. It's who I am. When I'm at work, I feel like I'm contributing to society, aiding in some small way, those who feel help is beyond their reach. What's money, compared to that?"

His lips compressed. "Any psychologist worth their salt would tell you I'm trying to compensate for the fuck-up my father made of his life, and I'd be the first one to agree with them, but it's more than that. Maybe it started out that way, but not anymore. My father was my father, with all his faults and failings. He was what he was. I'm through with him. He no longer has power over me or the way I feel about things and he has nothing to do with the way I live my life now, each day."

He squeezed her hand. "I want to help those who can't help themselves. If I manage to make even one person's life a little easier for even part of a single day, then it's a good day."

When she realized how far off the mark she'd been, she shook her head in disbelief. Her eyes welled up with tears. "Why didn't you tell me this before?"

He grimaced and looked away. "I wanted you to love me for who I am, not for what I could provide. It sounds stupid, but Nikki found my bank balance just as appealing as she found me—perhaps, even more so."

Cally shook her head again. She ought to be offended he'd thought her so shallow, but she knew having experienced the tragedy he had, she could understand his reluctance to be forthright. She reached over and cupped her hands around his face. "What did I ever do to deserve you?"

He leaned over and kissed her, his lips lingering on hers.

"I think the same thing every time I look into your eyes."

Their kiss deepened and Andy's hand stole down to cup her breast through her cotton blouse. Her nipple hardened in response and she arched her back to better fit into his palm.

"You'd better watch out, sweetheart or I might just toss you onto the backseat," he teased before turning his attention to her other breast.

"*Mm.*" She was almost beyond caring what he did as long as he didn't stop the sweet torture.

"What time do we have to go and collect Jack?" he murmured, nuzzling on her ear.

She opened her eyes and grinned at him. "Didn't I tell you? He's having a sleepover."

A single dark-blond eyebrow raised. "A *sleepover*? As in, a sleep-over-*all-night* sleepover?"

Her grin widened. "Is there any other kind?"

"And when do we get to pick him up from this all night sleepover?" His offhand manner belied the keen interest in his eyes.

She shrugged. "Oh, about four o'clock tomorrow afternoon. The boys are going to spend Sunday in the city at the Aquarium."

His eyebrow lifted even higher. "Did you say *four* o'clock tomorrow?"

"Ah huh."

Andy groaned. "In that case, you have way too many clothes on, woman," he growled. "Let's go inside."

Stewart let the branch of the hibiscus bush snap back into place and did his best to keep his anger in check. Cally and her boyfriend had been at it for hours—they'd been fucking like rabbits when he arrived.

He'd slunk down her driveway earlier with the intent of canvassing the area. When he spied the Audi and her battered old Toyota both parked in the drive, he'd taken extra care to conceal himself. It was fortunate there were so many places to hide.

The blinds and curtains throughout the house had been opened to let in the sunshine. It made spying easier and for that he was grateful. He was easily able to locate Cally and her boyfriend in the house. He peered in through the louvered windows and stared at them as they rolled naked in the bedcovers.

He couldn't help but admire Cally's taut, rounded butt and full, pert breasts as she bounced up and down on her lover's cock. A decade had passed since he'd last fucked her, but her body looked much as it had when she was a girl. A little curvier, perhaps, but that only accentuated her appeal. The sight of her lush body sent a surge of blood to his groin and he couldn't resist pulling out his cock and stroking it to full erection.

He watched them fucking with narrowed eyes and stroked and squeezed the engorged flesh in his hand, faster and faster, until he swallowed a cry and spurted hot come up the side of the house. He stared at the thick cock of the stranger as it plunged over and over into Cally's wetness and remembered what it had been like to fuck her—the mother of his son.

Jack.

He'd seen no sign of the boy. He wondered where he was and why Cally wasn't with him. Typical of the slut— leaving the boy in someone else's care while she spent the day fucking. He ought to storm in there right now and demand to know where the boy was.

Rage lit up inside him. His breath came fast. He clenched his fists and took a few steps forward but a voice inside his head urged him to be cautious. He'd come this far. There was no need to blow it now.

Sanity prevailed. He drew in a few deep breaths and forced his heart rate back under control. Slowly, the red haze receded. There would be time enough for action. The boy wasn't even at home.

Patience, that's what he needed. Just a little more patience and the boy would be his.

The man continued to pound into Cally and finally shuddered and then groaned in relief. Rolling off her, he gathered her in his arms and promptly fell asleep. A moment later, Cally also appeared to succumb.

He could do it now. He could kill them both. There were enough sturdy branches around. He could bludgeon them both and make it look like a burglary. After all, she'd already been robbed once. It could be the perfect solution. What better way to take back his son? With Cally's death, the boy would be orphaned. A DNA test would quickly prove

Stewart's claim to be the boy's father. And who had better rights to the boy than the man who sired him?

The phone in his pocket chirped and he cursed the fact he'd forgotten to turn it onto silent mode. He grabbed for it and noticed the call was from his father. With another curse, he turned it off and shoved the phone back into his pocket. He wasn't ready to deal with his father, yet.

He stared through the window at the couple in the bed and saw the man stir. *Had he heard the phone?* Stewart froze and counted long seconds until Cally's lover sighed and went back to sleep.

His shoulders slumped. The moment he'd waited for was lost. He'd revert to his original plan. It was easier, less messy and he'd spent many hours perfecting it. So much could go wrong with a spontaneous plan and he was nothing, if not careful. Retracing his steps, he hiked back up the driveway and came to his car a distance up the road. For now, Cally and her lover were safe...

Chapter 21

Cally came awake slowly, feeling deliciously content. Jack had spent the night at his friend's house and she'd enjoyed a night wrapped up in Andy's arms. Sunlight peeked through the louvered windows letting her know that morning had arrived. She stretched and tried to smother a yawn. It had been late when they'd finally fallen asleep.

"Don't tell me you're still sleepy?" Andy grinned. "You must have had at least three or four hours' rest."

She tossed a cushion at his head and then grinned. "You're awfully cheerful this morning."

"And why wouldn't I? I've spent the night with a beautiful woman who was only too happy to fulfill all of my fantasies. I'm kind of hoping she'll be keen to do it again."

Heat crept up Cally's neck and she looked away, but the smile remained in place. Talking about their intimate moments still made her embarrassed, but she had to admit, she was learning to enjoy it.

"I'm sure that can be arranged," she murmured and watched his eyes go wide. Before she knew what he was up to, he flipped her beneath him and pressed himself against her. He ground his hips into hers and she felt the unmistakable evidence of his desire.

"It's never too early to start," he teased and lowered his mouth.

———————

The sun was high in the sky when Andy opened his eyes for the second time. Cally stirred beside him and slowly woke. She smiled when she saw him.

"Good morning," she murmured.

"Good morning, yourself." He glanced at the clock on his nightstand. "Although, technically, it's almost 'good afternoon.'"

"Really?" She shot a look at the clock. "I can't believe I slept so long."

"You must have been tired."

Cally nodded. "I was. I haven't been sleeping well for the last month or so—since the burglary."

Andy's gut tightened at the reminder, but he nodded in understanding. "I'm glad you're resting a little easier, now. After all, that's one of the reasons you wanted a roommate."

She smiled. "You're right. Little did I know I was getting a roommate with benefits."

He swiped at her backside. "Cheeky girl. Aren't you glad I moved in?"

Her eyes darkened with emotion and he was filled with warmth. "You bet I am."

He bent his head to kiss her, then gently pulled away. "We'd better not start any of that again or you know what will happen. I don't know about you, but I'm starving."

Cally nodded. "Me, too."

"Good. Let's go find something to eat."

An hour later, they were seated at a café in Chatswood Chase, a busy and popular shopping center not far from Cally's house. They'd eaten and were enjoying coffee. Both were relaxed and sated.

"Tell me about your years in foster care," Cally murmured, reaching for his hand.

Her question came from nowhere. He frowned and almost pulled his hand away, but then sighed. If they were going to spend their future together, it was only right that he shared his past—all of it.

"For the first few years, I drifted in and out of foster homes. I was never in any one of them for long. A teenage boy with a chip on his shoulder is hard to place. By the time I was sixteen, I was living on the streets." He said it dispassionately, but the memories were still real. The memory of constant hunger was one he'd never forget.

"How did you cope?"

"I scavenged out of trash cans and begged for food at the back door of local restaurants. There was never much, but it kept me alive."

Cally's expression reflected her dismay. "Where did you sleep?"

He compressed his lips. "Under the railway bridge with other lost souls. The winters were the worst. The temperatures often plummeted below zero." He shook his head. "I look back now and wonder how in hell I survived. I'm alive because of the kindness of Sergeant Harry Walsh and his wife, Allison. They saved my life."

Memories of his years with the couple flooded his mind and his chest tightened. They'd been more a father and mother to him than his own and he'd be forever grateful that the local sergeant had picked him up outside the Caltex gas station one night and offered to buy him a meal.

"What happened?" Cally whispered.

"They took me in and straightened me out. When I was old enough, Harry helped me apply for the police service."

"Are they still in Tamworth?"

"No, they were killed in a car accident about four years ago."

"Oh, Andy!" Cally exclaimed, her eyes welling with tears. He swallowed the lump in his throat and fought off his own wave of emotion.

"I buried them side by side in Tamworth Cemetery. It's what they wanted."

Silence fell between them. A little while later, Andy cleared his throat and squeezed Cally's hand. "I'm not going to lie to you. I've had a rough time of it, but then, so have you. We don't get to choose the life we're given and let's face it, a lot of people do it tough. Sometimes adversity even makes us stronger, more determined and we achieve things we could never have imagined otherwise. Just look at you."

She smiled and brought his hand up to her lips and pressed a kiss against it. "Have I told you lately how much I love you?"

Andy filled his lungs and eased it out, his heart lightening with every second. "Maybe. But I'm happy to hear it again. In fact, I don't think I'll ever get tired of hearing it."

———————

After lunch, they sauntered through the mall, looking at the shops and other things on display. Neither of them were of a mind to purchase anything, and they returned home quickly. Inevitably, they found themselves back in Andy's bed. Sometime later, Cally struggled awake and her eyes gradually focused on the clock on Andy's nightstand.

"Oh, my goodness! Look at the time? I have to go and collect Jack!" Scrambling off the rumpled bed, she hastily went around picking her scattered clothing off the floor. Andy lay with his head propped on his elbow grinning up at her, a satisfied expression on his face.

"So that's it? You ride me like there's no tomorrow and then jump off with barely a good-bye kiss? Talk about wham, bam, thank you ma'am! I thought that was the guy's job?"

She spared him a brief glance and hastily picked up the rest of her clothing. With the pieces gathered in her arms, she sauntered over and leaned down to place a soft kiss on his mouth.

"Thank you, *wham bam*." She grinned cheekily. "Maybe we can do that again sometime."

He grinned back at her. "I live in hope."

"You and me both." She smiled. "But right now, I have to get Jack. Penny will be wondering where I am."

"Speaking of going, I have to be at work in a couple of hours."

Cally looked back at him, surprised. "You're working tonight? I thought you were on a day off?"

"Technically, I am. My shift doesn't start until six. It will be Monday morning when I finish."

She bit her lip and tried to stifle her disappointment. Her gaze rested on his naked chest, already longing for him again. "Well, it's lucky I got to spend the time with you," she teased. "It sounds like you're going to be busy."

"Never too busy for you, sweetheart. Anytime you feel the need, just knock on my door. I'll find the energy from somewhere."

Heat exploded across her face. Andy grinned, unashamed.

She ducked her head. "Okay, I'm really going now." She turned and headed toward the kitchen. She could still hear his chuckle as she walked down the corridor to her room to dress.

Amidst calls of thanks and another round of farewells to Penny Baker and her son, Cally ushered Jack to the car. No sooner had the door closed behind her, than he leaned forward, his face alight with curiosity.

"Where's Andy, Mom? Is he at home?"

Cally checked her rearview mirror before pulling away from the curb. She glanced back at Jack. "He was when I left, honey, but he's working tonight. He might have gone by now. His shift starts shortly."

Jack's face fell in disappointment and Cally couldn't help but feel a pang. Her boy had grown close to Andy and she couldn't be happier. She only hoped Jack's fondness would extend to being pleased when she told him Andy was there to stay.

Nerves jangled in her belly. She wanted to tell Jack about Andy's proposal, but she wasn't quite sure how to do it. It was clear he liked Andy, but that didn't mean he wanted him permanently in his life. It wasn't long ago that Andy had moved in as a roommate. Now, she was about to tell Jack he was there to stay.

"So, how was the sleepover?" The words tumbled out of her mouth and she winced at her cowardice.

"It was great. Jimmy and I got to watch TV until ten last night and this morning, we went to the Aquarium. You should have seen the sharks, Mom! They were absolutely huge. I can't wait to tell Andy all about it."

Emotion tugged at her heartstrings and she cast around once again for a way to broach the subject. "You really enjoy having Andy around, don't you?"

"You bet! He took us to the beach and he showed me and Jimmy how to snorkel. He even bought us ice cream. I can't wait to tell him about the Aquarium."

"I like having Andy around, too."

Through the rearview mirror, she saw Jack staring out the window. His expression didn't change. She was going to have to be a bit more direct.

"You know, Jack, Andy and I really like each other. Over the last few days, we've done a lot of talking and... We've decided we'd both like to spend more time together."

"You and Andy like each other? That's great, Mom. I like Andy, too."

Her heart tightened at his innocence. She grimaced and tried again. "Jack, what do you think about Andy moving in permanently?"

"Permanently? What do you mean, 'permanently'?"

"Oh, you know, like he'd live with us forever."

"Forever? Like never going back to his own place?" His eyes swam with confusion.

"Yes, honey. Like forever." She flicked her eyes back to him. "We *really* like each other, Jack."

"Like you want to kiss him? Is that what you mean?"

Cally started coughing to cover her embarrassment.

Someone had probably written a how-to book about breaking this kind of news to children. She wished she'd taken the time to read one. She could have done with some advice on it right about now. Determined to see it through, she pushed her embarrassment aside and strove for a casual tone.

"Sometimes, when grown-ups *really* like each other, they do kiss. It makes them feel good and lets them show that they care."

"Like when you kiss me?"

"Yes, kind of like that. And grown-ups usually sleep in the same bed."

His brow furrowed. "I saw Jimmy's mom and dad kissing last night. They sleep in the same bed." He turned his head to look at her. "Is that what you and Andy want to do?"

She sighed softly in relief. It looked like he'd finally understood. "Yes, honey, that's what Andy and I would like to do. That's if it's okay with you?"

From the corner of her eye, she saw him shrug. "I guess so. But don't you have to be married to sleep in the same bed as someone else? Jimmy's mom and dad are married."

Her heart skipped a beat. She'd intended to leave the marriage talk for another day, after he'd had time to get used to the idea of her and Andy together, but if he was prepared to talk about it, it would be best to deal with it now.

"Actually, Andy and I have talked about marriage. Would you mind if we got married?" She waited for his reaction, her stomach taut with nerves.

Jack's face turned serious and once again he looked out the window. She held her tongue, wanting to give him time to come to terms with the idea. As she turned into their driveway and brought the car to a halt, he turned back to face her. "If you and Andy get married, does that mean he'll be my dad?"

Her heart melted at the earnestness on his face. "Would you like it if Andy was your dad?"

He nodded hesitantly. "I think so. I've never had a dad,"

he replied quietly. "If Andy became my dad, I'd have someone to bring to school on Father's Day."

Her throat tightened. She fought back tears. On some level, she'd always known he was missing out by not having a father. She'd tried so hard to compensate for the absence of one in his life by loving him with every atom of her being and, until recently, she'd even managed to convince herself that it hadn't mattered.

And here they were.

One of the reasons she'd invited Andy into her home was because of Jack. She couldn't believe how well things had turned out. If she'd known how wonderful it was going to be, she'd have tried taking in a male boarder years ago.

A denial immediately rose up in her throat. It wasn't about having *any* man in their life. It was about Andy.

As images of him bending down to kiss her filled her head, she distractedly brought the car to a stop in front of her garage. His car was gone, of course, and she couldn't help the pang of disappointment that he'd already left for work. It was followed quickly by a slight twinge of irritation at how quickly her emotions had become governed by the presence or absence of a particular male. Knowing she couldn't do anything about her traitorous heart, she gave herself a mental shrug and turned back to face Jack.

"I'm so pleased you're happy about Andy, honey. He makes me really happy, too."

"I can't wait to tell Jimmy and the other boys. They won't be able to tease me anymore about not having a dad."

The pain of his words penetrated her heart at the same time they registered in her mind. She had no idea he'd been tormented about not having a father. He'd never once said anything…

Anger boiled up inside her at the injustice of it. She gritted her teeth and forced an even tone. "Who's been teasing you, sweetheart?"

He shrugged uncomfortably. "I dunno, Mom. Just some of the kids at school. You know how it is." He looked away.

"How long has it been going on?"

He shrugged again and continued to stare out the window. "I dunno. I've always been teased about it."

She thought about what he said and frowned. "You mean, right from *kindergarten*? Is that what you're saying? Even when we were living in *Armidale*?"

"Especially then," Jack mumbled. "The kids in Armidale seemed to know more about my dad than *I* did, especially some of the older ones."

She caught the glint of tears in his eyes and her heart broke. How could she have been oblivious to what he'd been going through for years? Had she been so caught up in her own misery and then later, with her concerns over her aunt, that she'd failed to see what had been happening to him?

Pressing the button to release her seatbelt, she opened the door of the old Toyota and stepped out of the car. Pulling open the back door, she slid across the seat to where he sat and pulled him into her arms.

"I'm so sorry, baby. I'm so sorry," she whispered against his hair. "I had no idea."

Jack's shoulders began to shake and tears ran down his cheeks. He buried his face against her shoulder. He sobbed like his heart was breaking and Cally felt his pain deep inside her. *How could she ever make it up to him?*

She'd done the best she could. Did all she knew how to do. It wasn't about making it up to him, it was about moving forward in a new direction. With Andy at her side.

Her arms tightened around him. Soothing him with mindless murmurs of comfort, she pressed kisses against his hair and prayed the guilt that threatened to overwhelm her wouldn't destroy them.

The ringing of a cell phone startled her. The sound was so foreign, it took her awhile to realize it came from inside her handbag where it lay on the front passenger seat of the car. Andy was the only one who knew the number.

Her heart leaped in excitement and her lips tugged upward in a wry smile. *Yep, she was a goner, for sure.* Her young son was crying his heart out in her arms and yet she still couldn't help the spike in her pulse at the thought of speaking to Andy again.

Knowing she couldn't do anything about answering the call, she listened to it ring out before it stopped, diverted to her voicemail. She found herself hoping he would leave a message and couldn't help the relief that surged through her when the phone beeped to indicate one had been received.

He'd helped set up her voice mailbox the night he'd given it to her and he'd also issued some brief instructions on how to use it. As soon as she had Jack settled, she'd listen to his message and try not to miss him too much.

Jack's sobs had quieted to the occasional sniffle. She lifted his chin until his eyes met hers. "I love you so much, Jack Savage. I'm not sure what you heard about your dad, but the truth is, I loved him then too. Things didn't work out between us, but you know what? It didn't matter because I had you. My beautiful gift from God. My son who I love with all my heart."

She brushed a tousled lock of hair out of his eyes. "I'm sorry you had to hear those hurtful things and I wish you'd told me about them so I could have done something. But none of that changes the way I feel about you, okay?"

He nodded and then hiccupped softly. "I love you too, Mom."

She gave him another fierce hug before releasing him. "Let's get your things inside and maybe we can go down to the corner store and get an ice cream. What do you say?"

Giving her a wobbly smile, he nodded at her. "All right."

Cally wriggled to the edge of the seat and climbed out of the car. Reaching in through the open window, she pulled out her handbag and slung it over her shoulder. She helped Jack with his overnight bag and together they walked up the back stairs and unlocked the door.

Thoughts of Harvey Donaldson and the weekend's events filtered through her mind. Andy was right. She needed to meet with Stewart and get things sorted with him once and for all. She needed closure on that part of her life before she began the next—with Andy. But most of all, Jack needed to meet his father. She realized that so clearly now.

Pushing open the back door, she let Jack walk in ahead of her, watching as he deposited his bag on the kitchen floor before walking down the hall to his room. She'd give him some time alone to gather himself together before letting him know she was going to contact Stewart. She'd call Donaldson's office and leave a message.

She walked into the living room and reached for the telephone before she could change her mind.

CHAPTER 22

"**C**ome *on*, Jack! You're going to be late for school."

Cally walked back into the kitchen. Popping some bread into the toaster, she checked the clock on the wall again. It was Tuesday morning and the last of Andy's latest run of nightshifts. She didn't expect him home before she had to leave for Jack's school drop-off, but she was hoping they could spend some time together after she got back. Even if it was a couple of minutes while he ate breakfast or before he went to bed to get a few hours' sleep.

She'd barely seen him since Sunday. They'd talked briefly on Monday afternoon, before both of them left for work at the station and she'd told him how well Jack had taken the news.

When Jack realized he was home, he almost barreled Andy over in his enthusiasm to greet him.

"Whoa, buddy! Take it easy!" Andy laughed, giving him a hearty hug.

"Andy, Mom told me you're getting married and you're going to be my dad. Is that right?" Hope and doubt warred on his young face. Andy hugged him close again and Cally's heart nearly burst with love.

"That's right, buddy. If you want me to."

Jack pulled back and looked up at him, his face alight with happiness. "Of *course* it's all right! It's the best news *ever*!"

Andy met her gaze above his head. Tears pricked her eyes and she offered him a shaky smile, her throat too choked to speak.

Andy hugged Jack to him tightly once again. "You and me both, little buddy," he whispered.

Afterwards, he'd taken her in his arms and kissed her tenderly, reaching out to lovingly tuck a strand of hair behind her ear. "You're all I've ever wanted, Cally," he breathed. "I thank God every day that I found you."

She kissed him back and her heart swelled with love. "I don't care who you are or how much money you have. You make my life complete."

With Jack only feet away watching TV in the living room, they hadn't been able to do more than kiss, despite their eagerness. Knowing Andy would be at work again that night had made it even harder for them to disengage and step away.

"One more night," Andy had groaned as he put some distance between them. "One more night before I can take you to bed and pleasure you until you beg me to stop." He grinned at her rakishly. "I don't know how you're going to last."

She'd grinned back. "You're right. Now that I know what it's like, I yearn for you every minute of every day. Knowing you're so close, yet so far away, is torture."

He'd smiled. "All good things come to those who wait."

"Not always," she said, remembering the phone sex and wondering if he'd phone her after Jack was in bed. But he'd been busy with calls.

Now it was Tuesday morning and she could hardly keep herself still as she thought of him. She'd gone to the Westfield Mall at Chatswood during her lunch break the day before and had splurged on a beautiful, white chiffon nightdress in honor of their reunion.

The long, sheer nightgown left little to the imagination and she had blushed hotly when she tried it on in the store's dressing room. Satin spaghetti straps kissed her shoulders, revealing her generous cleavage with its plunging neckline.

The fine chiffon was gathered in soft pleats beneath her breasts and then fell in waves of luxury around her legs. She could still remember the seductive feel of the fabric as it swirled around her, touching her skin like a lover's feather-light caress.

In less than an hour, she'd slip it on again and wait for Andy so he could take it off. Glancing at the clock for the third time, she frowned and called out to Jack again.

"Okay, Mom. I'm coming." A disheveled, blond head appeared in the doorway. He took his place at the table, still tucking in his school shirt.

"What have you been doing down there? We've got less than fifteen minutes to get out the door."

Jack shrugged and began spooning Weet-Bix into his mouth. "I dunno. I must have slept in."

She sighed, knowing that any other day, Jack running late wouldn't be quite the drama she was making it out to be. It was just that she was so eager to get home again and get ready for Andy...

"I have to work on a school project, so I'm going to have to stay back after school today."

Cally blinked and focused on what he was saying. "Sorry, darling? What did you say?"

"I said I'm working on a school project with Jimmy this afternoon. We're going to stay back after school and try and finish it. Jimmy said his mom can pick me up and bring me home, if you like?"

She frowned. "How come you haven't said anything about this project until now?"

"I dunno. I guess I only just remembered. It's no big deal, we've been working on it since last week. It's supposed to be finished by Friday."

"What's it about?"

"It's a science project. We're building an electronic device that can take music, a phone, a computer and Foxtel all in the one gadget. It's really cool, Mom. I designed it and Jimmy's doing most of the construction."

"Wow, it sounds very exciting. I wish you'd told me about it earlier."

Jack shrugged. "Yeah, I guess. You've kind of been busy with work and stuff and then with Andy moving in—I forgot all about it until I got to school yesterday."

"Well, I guess it's okay if Mrs Baker is happy to collect you both. I'll give her a call later and let her know it's all right with me. Now," she said as she removed the empty bowl of Weet-Bix and sat two pieces of toast with Vegemite on a plate in front of him, "eat up!"

Cally turned off the Pacific Highway and into her driveway and glanced impatiently at her watch. She barely noticed the warm morning sunlight that filtered through the heavy stand of trees. The traffic had been heavier than usual and it was nearly nine-thirty. She had expected Andy's car to be there, but the driveway was empty. She was torn between feeling disappointed that he wasn't yet home and pleased that she still had time to get ready for him.

Jumping out of the car, she riffled through her handbag, looking for her cell phone to check for any messages. With the noise of the busy, peak-hour traffic, it was possible she hadn't heard it ring. She came up empty-handed and groaned when she remembered she'd left it on the battery charger on the kitchen counter. In her rush to get out the door, she'd forgotten it.

Hurrying up the back steps, she let herself inside. She dropped her handbag on the table and walked into the living room. Her gaze was immediately drawn to the answering machine. The screen was blinking to show a new message. Hurrying over, she pressed the buttons and listened to Andy's voice.

"You won't believe it, sweetheart, but I'm going to be late. We have a situation here and the boss won't let me leave until he knows he's got it covered. I'm really sorry. I was so looking forward to getting naked with you. I'll be home soon, I promise."

Cally replayed the message three times and then sighed. So much for the rush this morning. When she pulled up outside Jack's school, she'd practically pushed her son out of the car, such was her haste to get back. Now she didn't know what time Andy would be home. She hoped they'd still have time alone in the afternoon, before school got out, to become reacquainted.

With that thought in mind, she picked up the electric jug and filled it with water. She might as well have a cup of coffee. She had more than enough time on her hands now.

A knock sounded at the front door. She frowned. Being so far off the main road, she didn't usually get unannounced visitors. Most people didn't even realize there was a cottage buried in the garden, behind the main house.

Walking into the living room, she went to the front door and opened it. Her heart stood still. A second later, she gasped in shock.

"Dad!"

The man who stared at her through the gauzed security screen had aged far beyond his years. The thick black hair that she remembered from her childhood was now snowy white and deep grooves scored his face. He looked travel worn and weary. She would have been hard pressed to recognize him if it hadn't been for his trademark bright blue eyes: *her eyes.*

"Hello, Cally." His voice hadn't changed. She would have known it anywhere. Still rough and gravelly, it was as familiar to her as her own and brought with it a rush of unwanted memories.

"W-what are you doing here?" She clamped her teeth together, trying to control her pulse that began to race the minute she recognized him. She hadn't spoken to him in more than ten years, unless she counted the terse phone call telling her she wasn't welcome at her mother's funeral. She hadn't seen him since he kicked her out. And yet, here he was. Her father. As large as life, on the other side of her screen door.

"Are you going to let me in?" It was more of a demand than a request—like he was still in school-principal mode, even though he surely had retired by now.

Panic welled up inside her, but she refused to give it heed. She was a grown woman. No longer a young and frightened girl. She knew how to take care of herself.

"Why are you here?" she asked again, relieved to hear her voice remained steady.

He gave a nonchalant shrug that looked a little forced, and glanced away. "I'm here to meet my grandson and... I wanted to say sorry."

She stared at him in disbelief. "Don't you think it's a bit late for that? How did you find me?"

He cleared his throat and his reply was as brusque as she was used to. "If you'll just open the door, Cally, I'll explain everything. Harvey Donaldson told me—"

"Harvey *Donaldson*?" Her mind reeled. "You mean to tell me it was *you* who hired him?"

"Of course. Who did you think it was?"

There was a roaring in her ears. She shook her head dazedly, unable to believe she'd gotten it so wrong. She'd been convinced it was Stewart. All along, it had been her father. Then a realization hit her and a pressing weight lifted from her chest: *It wasn't Stewart.* He didn't know about Jack.

"Cally, please, let me in. I'd like to talk to you." His voice lowered. "It's time, don't you think?"

All at once, the anger drained out of her. It *was* time: time to put Stewart Brady behind her; time to make amends with her father, the only parent she had left; time to start a new life with Andy and Jack. Turning the key in the security lock, she opened the door and let him inside.

"You've cut your hair. It suits you, but I always liked it long."

Cally reflexively touched her short, sleek bob and remembered the times when she'd sat at her father's feet. He'd twirl her braids around his fingers. That seemed a lifetime ago. She shook her head to clear it of the memories. "Would you like a cup of coffee? I've just boiled the jug."

He nodded and shrugged off his gray suit jacket and took a seat at the kitchen table, the same one recently vacated by Jack.

"How do you take it?" Sadness seeped into her that she no longer knew even that much about the man she called her father.

"White with one, thanks." He looked around the kitchen. "You have a cozy, little place here."

"Thanks, as soon as I saw it, I fell in love with it. It reminded me of Aunt Mary's house in Armidale."

Her father refrained from commenting and she finished making the coffee in silence. Setting a cup in front of him, she went around to the other side of the table and pulled out a chair.

"Why are you here, Dad? Why now, after all these years? If you're here to try and relieve your guilty conscience, well, I'm afraid you've come to the wrong place."

Unable to sit still, she stood and paced across the kitchen. Memories of the way he'd thrown her out crashed into her. "Apart from tossing me aside like so much unwanted trash when I needed you most, you didn't even have the decency to let me come to my mother's funeral."

She spun on her heel and shot him a withering look. "You turn up on my doorstep with an apology on your lips, as if you expect me to forgive and forget the pain you caused me, just like that." She snapped her fingers sharply to emphasize her point, her breath coming fast.

"I'm not expecting that, Cally." It was his principal's voice, cool, calm and controlled, but his eyes were shadowed with pain. "All the things you've said are true and I've lived to regret my actions and my words." His gaze intensified. "It wasn't your mother's fault. I want you to know that. The fault was solely mine. There were many times when she asked me to let you come home, but I refused to listen. Then she died so suddenly. They said it was a heart attack. I found her lying on the kitchen floor one afternoon when I came home from school."

His voice broke and Cally was starkly reminded of how much he'd lost, too. Her parents had always had a close and loving relationship. It couldn't have been easy on her father to lose his beloved wife way before her time.

He'd loved Cally once like that, too: totally, irrevocably, unconditionally. It was why his reaction to her pregnancy had been so utterly shocking. It had never occurred to her before she became pregnant that he could ever react that way. It wasn't as if a teenage pregnancy was so far beyond what was acceptable in society that it warranted never speaking to her again. At least, that's the way she'd seen it.

She looked at him sadly, determined not to feel guilty. "Because of you, my son doesn't know his grandfather and he was never given the chance to know his grandmother. Aunt Mary, the only person kind enough to love both of us unreservedly and the only relative Jack ever knew, is also dead. Jack's the one who's missed out."

She shook her head. "Please don't tell me how sorry you are. If it weren't for you, none of this would have ever happened!"

To her horror, hot tears welled up in her eyes. She swiped at them furiously. "I could have raised Jack with your love and support—who knows, maybe even Stewart would have been a part of his life. But you made sure that was never going to happen. Once it was all around town that even my *father* couldn't bear the sight of me, a young man like Stewart was never going to hang around."

"Stewart Brady didn't deserve you," her father scoffed. "You might have thought I was happy to have you going out with him, but the truth is, I felt sick with worry every time you went out the door. It was clear he was only looking for someone to dally with during his college break. I was hoping you'd forget about him when he left. I hadn't counted on you sleeping with him and getting pregnant."

"Dad, you say it like it was the worst thing that could have happened to me! I didn't do anything illegal. Life didn't turn out quite as I planned. So what? Having a baby wasn't the end of the world."

His face collapsed with grief. "You were *sixteen!* You had your whole life ahead of you!" He sighed heavily and made an effort to calm down. When he spoke again, his voice was quieter.

"You were my little girl. I had such big dreams for you. You were smart and sassy and beautiful. You had the world at your feet. And then you got pregnant."

She opened her mouth to protest, but he held up his hand. "Cally, just hear me out." His tone brooked no argument and all of a sudden, she felt like a teenager again. As he picked up his coffee cup and took a sip, she threw herself back into her chair and crossed her arms defensively, tamping down her irritation.

"I couldn't bear the thought of you ending up as a single mother, working at the local supermarket. After all my dreams for you... That was all I could think of that night you came to me and told me you were having a baby."

He lifted his arms in defeat and let them fall. "I'm not excusing my behavior, but you have to understand. I'd seen it all before. I'd been a high school principal for many years, remember? There'd been other girls, bright girls with promising futures, who'd thrown it all away over a boy and an unplanned pregnancy. I didn't want that happening to you. I couldn't bear the thought. Not to my little girl. Not to my Cally."

She watched him and tried to remain unmoved. He still hadn't admitted he was wrong. He still hadn't asked for her forgiveness.

As if reading her thoughts, he continued. "I behaved so badly, then and in the years that followed. If I could take back those careless words, I would. I was in shock, Cally. It was the last thing I expected to hear you say. As soon as you walked out of my study, I wanted to call you back. But I didn't. I was angry—devastated even. All I'd planned for you, all my dreams, the future I had mapped out—it crashed down around my ears."

He gave her a sad smile. "I kept hoping you'd phone and ask if you could come back. I was going to let you, of course, after you'd agreed to an abortion."

Her gasp of outrage went unnoticed. He didn't appear to notice. "But you didn't. You didn't call and you kept the baby. The longer things went on like that, the more impossible it became to change it."

He took another sip of coffee. "Your mother would come to me every once in a while and beg me to call you. 'Just pick up the phone and talk to her,' she'd say. 'We have a grandson we've never met,' she'd remind me."

Shaking his head, he placed the cup back on the table. "I wanted to, I really did. But I was concerned by then that *you* wouldn't want to come home; that even if I asked you back, you wouldn't want to come. I couldn't bear the thought of you rejecting me. It was selfish beyond belief, but it was how I was. I'm not proud of it and I've lived to regret it every day since."

Cally stared at him in shock and disbelief at the enormity of his revelation. She could only wonder how things might have been different if he hadn't let pride get in his way. Her shoulders slumped and all at once, she felt weary beyond belief.

"I wasn't throwing away my life, Dad, as you so eloquently put it. I was going to have a *baby*. I had plans, big plans, even with the baby. You could have been a part of them, but you didn't *ask*! You didn't even ask, not *once*, what those plans were."

Unable to sit still, she pushed away from the table and began pacing again. "With Aunt Mary's love and support, I went back and finished high school and graduated from university with a teaching degree. Huh! Fancy that!" She laughed without humor. "I'm a teacher, Dad, just like you."

His gaze dropped to the table. "I never dreamed you'd do so well," he admitted. "I guess that's where I made my mistake. I underestimated you, and I shouldn't have. There's nothing else I can say. I loved you too much."

Her face hardened. "That wasn't *love*, Dad. That was *control* and it bordered on the obsessive. If you'd *really* loved me, you would never have been able to treat me the way you did. And as for Stewart," she shrugged, "we'll never know, will we? He was young too, and scared and in shock—all the things I was. We never gave ourselves a chance. Who knows what might have happened had we been given the love and support from our families when we needed it most?"

"I wouldn't waste time worrying about Brady. He moved on pretty quickly, let me assure you."

Even though she told herself she didn't care, the words tumbled out of her mouth. "What do you mean?"

"Exactly that. It was only a couple of months after he went back to college that we heard he'd gotten another girl pregnant. Tiffany something or other. They met at a frat house party. I heard he actually married her a few months after the baby was born."

Cally reeled back in shock. All the nights she'd cried herself to sleep in Aunt Mary's spare room, praying that Stewart would defy his parents and come and see her, come and declare his love for her, cry over the fact she'd had an abortion and then be elated when he realized she hadn't. And now she discovered he'd already moved on. Long before his son was even born, he'd moved on and fathered another child.

Stupid, stupid, stupid. She couldn't believe how many tears she'd wasted on him. She forced a grim smile, unwilling to let her father see how much his news upset her.

"Well, good for him," she murmured.

"Not really. His wife and child were killed in a car accident about six months ago. He hasn't been quite right ever since. In fact, he's been brought up on serious assault charges. He got into a fight at a gym downtown. Smashed someone over the head with a barbell. The bloke nearly died. The trial started over a month ago, but it was adjourned. Everyone knows he's guilty. Despite his daddy's influence, the talk around town is that he'll do substantial jail time."

Her mouth fell open. A kaleidoscope of memories and images spun crazily through her head. "W-when did you last see him?"

"About a week ago, outside the courthouse. It was just before I got the call from Donaldson to say you wanted to see me."

"I wanted to see *Stewart!* I thought it was *Stewart* who'd gone to Harvey Donaldson. I had no idea it was *you!*"

Hurt flooded her father's face. Gradually, it was replaced with curiosity. "Are you trying to tell me, after all this time, you're still holding a candle for Brady?"

"No!" She grabbed at her hair in frustration. Taking a deep breath, she fought to regain some control. Deciding to leave Andy out of it, she said, "Jack has been asking questions about his father. I thought it was time he met him."

Her father choked on humorless laughter. "Let me get this straight. You never wanted to talk to me at all. It was that no-hoper loser, Stewart Brady, the man who got you pregnant and dumped you and within a couple of months was screwing someone else—it was *this* prime example of manhood you wanted to see again?"

His voice caught on his distress. Cally couldn't help the surge of guilt that went through her at the hurt that had returned to his eyes. She sighed and the fight went out of her. It was possible, over time, she'd come to forgive him and she'd reach out to him for both her sake and her son's, but right at that moment, she couldn't take any more. She'd had enough.

"Think what you will, Dad, but next time you're talking to Stewart, give him my regards. No matter what he may have done to me, no one deserves to lose their family like that."

Her father shook his head in disbelief. "After all these years, I wouldn't have believed it. You still have a soft spot for him."

"I wouldn't call it a soft spot. It's called kindness and

compassion—something you forgot about a long time ago." Heading toward the front door, she opened it and looked back at him, her intentions clear. "I think it's time you left."

"B-but what about us? What about Jack? I thought—"

"Not this time, Dad. I need time to come to terms with what you've told me. I need time to adjust. For ten years, I've lived with the knowledge that you didn't love me enough to be there for me when I needed you most."

She shrugged. "I have my beautiful son and I have a new man in my life. A man who loves me for who I am, warts and all. One day, you might get to meet your grandson. We'll have to wait and see. Right now, I'd like you to leave."

"But—"

"Please, Dad. I want you to go."

"But I love you, Cally. I'm sorry. I'm so sorry. I should never have kicked you out. I should have stood by you and helped you, like any decent father would have. It's all my fault. I should have listened to your mother. She begged me to talk to you. She begged me to ask you to come home." Tears streamed down his wrinkled cheeks and Cally bit her lip against the emotion that threatened to undo her.

She wanted so badly to believe him, to go to him and receive comfort, like she had so many years ago, but at that moment, she simply didn't have the strength.

She stood by the door in silence and tried to suppress the trembling in her limbs. With a last, tortured look in her direction, her father made his way out through the doorway.

She locked the solid wooden door behind him. Moments later, she slid down the wall and crumpled on the floor. With a cry of anguish, she let the hot flood of pain and disillusionment fall.

―――――――――

Cally heard the sound of a key turning in the lock and straightened. She didn't know how long she'd been on the floor, but a quick glance through the side window showed

Andy's shiny silver Audi parked behind her faithful old Toyota in the driveway.

Swiping at the tears on her face, she hoped she didn't look as big a mess as she felt. Her eyes felt puffy and swollen and her nose dripped. So much for the two-hundred-and-fifty-dollar nightdress she'd bought to impress him.

Moving unsteadily into the kitchen, she pulled a handful of tissues out of the box on the shelf near the window and blew her nose vigorously. The back door opened and Andy walked in looking tired but as gorgeous as ever.

His eyes zoomed in on her and his face filled with concern. "Cally! What the hell happened? Are you okay?" He ran to her and took hold of both her arms.

Fresh salty tears welled up in her eyes. She looked up at him, trying to get the words out. "I-it was m-my father." Her words caught on hiccups and half sobs.

He looked confused. "What are you talking about? Your father?"

"M-my father. H-Harvey Don-Donaldson. It was my f-father who hired him." She wanted Andy to understand.

His gaze moved over her, searching her face. "It was your *father* who contacted the investigator? Is that what you're trying to tell me?"

She could only nod, relieved that he finally understood. He was still holding her at arm's length, his eyes intent on her face. "How did you find out?"

She drew in a deep, shuddering breath. "H-he came here."

His eyes widened in shock. "Your father was *here*? In your house?"

She nodded.

"You contacted Donaldson's office, right?"

Cally nodded again, taking comfort from the warmth and strength of his broad chest. Winding her arms about his waist, she breathed deeply of his unique scent and sighed. After a few moments, she spoke again.

"I called his office on Sunday afternoon, after you left for work. I thought about what you said about meeting up with

Stewart—and I knew it was something I had to do—for my sake and for Jack's." Her voice was soft and muffled against the cotton of his shirt.

"So I telephoned Donaldson and left a message. I told him to get his client to contact me." She looked up at him. "Of course, I thought it was Stewart. I never imagined it was my *father*."

Andy stroked her back, while his other arm tightened around her. "I take it the meeting didn't go too well?" he murmured against her hair.

She sniffed and leaned away so she could swipe at the tears in her eyes with the back of her hand. "You could say that." She took a shaky breath. "He came here to apologize and he did, eventually. But it's going to take time for me to forgive him. And I'm never going to feel the same way I did about him again."

She dragged in another breath. "As a parent, I just can't understand it. There's nothing, *nothing* Jack could do that would make me disown him." Her voice hitched and Andy pulled her close, murmuring words of comfort and reassurance against her hair.

"I'm sorry, Cally. Fathers should be forbidden to treat their children so callously. It should be in the book of rules all fathers should be issued when they come to collect their children from the hospital."

She lifted her head and smiled shakily back at him, grateful for his attempt to lighten the moment. For all the heartache she'd experienced in her childhood, it could never compare to what Andy had gone through. And yet, here he was, comforting *her*. She'd never loved him more.

They held each other in silence, each buried in their own thoughts. After a while, she pulled slightly away. "You're a beautiful man, Andy Warwick, inside and out. I'm so glad I found you."

His eyes darkened with emotion. A moment later, his lips found hers. Heat exploded inside her. She kissed him with barely checked passion, pressing herself even closer against him. He moaned against her mouth. His hardness pressed into the softness of her belly.

"I've missed you so much," he rasped. His lips moved lower, biting gently along her neck before his tongue swirled in and around her sensitive earlobe.

Cally twined her arms around his neck and drew his head down.

His hands reached for her blouse and he fumbled with the buttons.

Pulling away, she stood panting before him and tried to regain her breath. Andy stared at her dazedly.

"Cally—"

"*Shh*. I have a surprise for you." Turning away, she stumbled down the hall and into her bedroom. The room was filled with bright mid-morning light. The scent of flowers from the garden wafted through the open window and hung expectantly on the warm air.

The sheer nightdress lay across her bed where she'd set it out earlier. Quickly undoing the rest of her buttons, she tossed her blouse onto the carved wooden rocking chair which sat in the corner of the room. Her bra, shorts and panties followed in quick succession and then she eased the slinky, silky fabric over her head.

Shimmying into the nightdress, she smoothed it over her hips and adjusted the low neckline until her breasts were shown to their best advantage. The smooth, golden skin of her décolletage was in stark contrast to the whiteness of the nightdress and only served to enhance its appeal.

With a final quick glance in the mirror, she summoned a smile. Andy was waiting for her. He loved her. He wanted her. Life didn't get any better.

———

It was a long while afterwards that Andy asked about Brady. Cally lay relaxed and sated beside him after a thoroughly enjoyable session of lovemaking. His index finger drew lazy circles on her naked thigh, the nightgown that had him rock-hard the instant he'd seen her in it had been long since discarded.

The air conditioner hummed quietly in the background, cooling the room from the oppressive summer heat that beat down relentlessly outside the window. He drew in a deep breath, knowing that the subject had to be broached.

"What are you going to do about Brady?"

She turned in his arms and looked up at him. "What do you mean?"

"I mean, you told me you'd already come to the decision you needed to see him and, you know, sort things out. That's why you called Donaldson again, wasn't it?"

"Yes, and my father's made me realize how much I need to close the door on that chapter of my life. Stewart might be Jack's father, but all he did was donate the genetic material necessary to give my son life. He never wanted Jack. He did all he could to make sure I got rid of him. If I had told him the truth, I'm sure he would have badgered me until I'd given in to his demands. I don't need to see him again to give me closure or whatever it is psychiatrists talk about. It's over. It's been over for a long time. I know that now."

Reaching out, she cupped his cheek with her hand. "My father told me a few things about Stewart I didn't know."

He raised his eyebrows and she continued. "Apparently, he was with another girl not long after we broke up and he got her pregnant, too. Dad said they got married after the baby was born."

"Oh, sweetheart!" He pulled her back into his arms and held her close. "He sounds like a right selfish bastard. Be thankful you're not saddled with him."

She smiled softly. "You're right." Reaching up, she tugged his head down to hers and pressed her lips against his. She ended the kiss and pulled away gently. "Dad told me something else about Stewart. His wife and child were killed six months ago. Apparently he's had trouble coming to terms with it."

Andy stared at her. "So, he's single again." He fought to keep his voice even. "How does that make you feel?"

She sighed and settled against him. "I feel for his loss, as I would for anyone who's experienced something like that. But it doesn't change the way I feel about him, or the way I feel about *you*."

Her hand caressed Andy's bare chest with feather-light strokes. "Stewart lost his place in my heart many years ago." Her voice dropped to a whisper. "For a long time, I didn't think anyone would fill the void he'd left. But as the years went by, I found a sort of peace in being independent and raising my son alone. When I met you... Well for the first time in more than ten years, my heart started really smiling again." She looked up at him, her eyes shining with emotion. "You did that to me, Andy. You made my heart smile."

She kissed him again, softly, lovingly and he hugged her hard against him, never wanting to let her go.

CHAPTER 23

Cally glanced at her watch. The week was speeding by. It was already Thursday and was now nearly two. She'd spent most of the day cleaning the cottage and doing laundry. The sound of sheets snapping in the wind on the line outside the kitchen window reminded her they needed to be brought in. Although Andy had never asked her to, she'd started throwing his dirty laundry in with theirs and had made up his bed with fresh sheets.

At the thought of Andy, she sighed. Despite the fact he was on a scheduled day off, two colleagues had called in sick and he'd been forced to go into work. The house seemed quiet and empty without him. Soon it would be time to collect Jack from school and she looked forward to spending another evening with her boys.

Her boys. The thought sent a warm glow coursing through her. She headed toward the laundry to collect the clothes basket. Halfway there, the phone rang. Hurrying back to the living room, she picked up the receiver on the third ring and answered with her customary greeting.

"Cally Savage."

Silence greeted her. She was about to hang up, convinced the caller was a telemarketer, when she heard his voice.

"Cally, it's Stewart...Stewart Brady."

Her heart leaped into her throat and her mouth went dry. *Oh, God. Did he know about Jack?* She tried to breathe over the pounding of her pulse.

"Stewart, what...? Where...? How did you get my number?"

"Your father." He paused. "He-he said you were asking about me."

She almost choked in disbelief. "I-I'm sorry, Stewart. My father's given you the wrong impression. He told me about the death of your wife and child. I expressed my sadness at hearing about it and asked him to pass on my regards. That's all."

"But, I thought... Your father said—"

"Stewart," she interrupted, "I'm not sure what he told you, but I got over you a long time ago." She sighed softly. "It's true, I was in love with you for years after you dumped me, but I worked hard and found a new life and I'm finally happy."

"What about our baby? The baby you told me you aborted."

The sudden ignition of her anger nearly stole her breath. "Our *baby*? You have the hide to question me about our baby? If you'd had your way, there would never have been a baby. I never lied to you. You never asked and you moved on. He's *my* son. *I'm* the one who wanted him—the *only* one who wanted him. Don't go pretending you care, especially now, a decade down the track. Don't you *dare*."

"Cally, I understand you're upset, but surely we can let bygones be bygones?"

Anger pulsed through her veins. All the days and the even longer nights she'd spent crying her heart out over him as a young teen mother flashed through her mind, almost overwhelming her.

"So that's all I was to you? A *bygone*? An unfortunate incident that was best forgotten? *That's* how you remember me?"

Stewart *tut tutted* on the other end of the phone. "Cally, you're getting all emotional about this and there's no need. We had some fun times for a while, then you got pregnant. I was young and stupid. I didn't know anything about being a father. It was the last thing I wanted. But, over the years I've matured. I've learned."

He cleared his throat. "When I discovered I had a son, I was furious that you hadn't told me, but gradually, I came to accept you had valid reasons for keeping it from me. You were only a kid, too. You were probably as scared as I was. I'm beyond embarrassed about my actions back then. I'm sorry I was such an asshole. I'm sorry I wasn't there for you—and for our baby."

Cally shook her head in silent disbelief, her anger dissipating. She bit her lip, wanting to believe he could change, scared that he hadn't.

"I've had a lot of time to think about it, Cally," Stewart continued, his voice low and sincere. "My son needs a father. Every kid needs a father. I-I want to be there for him."

Cally's heart pounded. She pressed her fist against her mouth to hold back a sob—of pain or joy? She didn't know. Where had Stewart been during the long, lonely nights when she'd ached for someone to hold her, someone to help her, someone to love her? As an inexperienced teen, she'd given him her heart, her body and her soul and he'd trampled them into the ground.

"I'll regret for the rest of my life that I wasn't there for you and our son. But I want to be there for both of you *now*. Give me a chance, Cally. Please." His voice was now tinged with desperation. "I need to see him, Cally. I really *need* to."

She weakened. He *had* lost his wife and child. She could understand him wanting to make contact with the child who was still alive.

Besides, when she'd thought it was Stewart who'd contacted the PI, she'd already resolved to meet with him. If it hadn't been for her father's untimely appearance, she would still feel that way.

What she'd told Andy was true. She no longer felt the need to find closure with Stewart. She'd closed that chapter on her life. But Jack deserved to know his father. He had a right to know what he looked like, what he sounded like, to ask him questions. She owed it to her son to make it happen.

Sighing heavily, she heard herself agreeing to meet with

him. "Where are you staying?" she asked after Stewart had babbled his gratitude.

"Um, I'm in a hotel on the Pacific Highway, not far from Chatswood. Your dad told me where you lived."

A spurt of irritation shot through her. *Good old Dad.*

"I'm sorry, Cally. I really thought..." He sounded so contrite.

She sighed again. "Don't worry about it. It's not your fault. That would rest solely with my father." Her voice was as dry as sandpaper.

"When can I see him, Cally? When can I see my son?"

The urgency in his voice momentarily startled her, but she couldn't begin to understand how it felt to lose a spouse and child. All she knew was that she'd be beyond devastated if anything ever happened to Jack and Andy.

"I usually collect him from school at three. There's a park only a few blocks away, at the top of the hill. We could meet you there, if you like."

He sighed with relief. "Thank you, Cally. You don't know how much seeing him means to me."

She gave him directions. "We'll meet you there after school, about three-fifteen."

"Thanks again. I really mean it." His voice broke with emotion and she was reminded once again of all that he'd been through.

"No problem. I'll see you soon."

She returned the phone to its cradle and contemplated their conversation. For years, she hadn't heard a word from her father. Out of the blue, he appeared on her doorstep. For years, she'd worked hard to thrust Stewart from her mind. Now he was apologizing and asking to be part of his son's life. She'd finally gotten her life on track and found love with Andy and now the men who'd been such an integral, albeit negative, part of her past were suddenly back in her life.

It felt a little weird, even a little surreal. She could barely believe that in less than an hour, she'd see Stewart again, face-to-face. Nerves suddenly crowded her stomach. She had to talk to Andy.

The laundry forgotten, she riffled through her handbag and tugged out her cell phone. Absently, she noticed the battery was nearly flat and she made a mental note to put it on the charger as soon as she finished speaking with him.

The phone dialed out. She braced herself for it to go to voicemail. Then, he answered.

"Hey, beautiful, I was just thinking about you."

She heard the smile in his voice and her lips tugged upward in response. Just the sound of his voice made her feel so much better, as if she could handle any of life's hurdles.

"I hope they were nice thoughts."

"I'm not sure I can tell you. Tom's sitting a few feet away from me and boy, does he have good ears."

She blushed and was glad Andy couldn't see. Still, she liked the way his constant teasing made her feel special, as if she was the most desirable woman in the world.

"So, are you calling just to hear the sound of my voice or is there something in particular you wanted to tell me?"

Now the moment was upon her, she was lost for words. It wasn't as if she didn't know he'd be okay about it, but it still felt a little strange telling her fiancé she was shortly going to a park to meet the father of her son.

Her silence must have triggered some concern because his voice turned serious. "Cally? Is everything all right?"

"Of course. I'm sorry, I just… It's been such a weird week with Dad turning up out of nowhere and now…Stewart's telephoned me."

"Stewart? As in your ex-boyfriend?"

"Yes, as in my ex."

"Wow, how did he get your number?"

"That's exactly what I asked him." She grimaced at the reminder. "He got it from my father."

"Your *father*? Why would he do that?"

She sighed. "When Dad told me about Stewart's recent loss, I told him to give Stewart my regards. I told him I felt sad for him. Dad must have misunderstood."

"So he took that to mean you wanted to make contact with him?"

"Yeah, I guess so. He probably thought he was doing the right thing. It's funny, just before he latched onto the idea I was still interested in Stewart, he'd been telling me how unstable Stewart was since the death of his family. Then he goes and gives him my number. Go figure."

"Unstable? What do you mean?" Concern sharpened Andy's voice.

She grimaced. "Oh, I don't know if unstable is the right word. I think the way Dad actually described it was that Stewart hadn't been 'quite right' ever since his wife and child died. Apparently, he got into a pretty nasty fight and is now facing criminal charges. I don't know if it was Dad just being melodramatic. Stewart seemed all right when I spoke to him on the phone."

"What did he want? Did he ask to see you?"

"Yes, he did. Well, he asked to see Jack, actually."

"What did you say?"

She drew in a deep breath. "I told him it was okay. We're going to meet him this afternoon, after school."

Andy didn't respond. As the silence lengthened, anxiety nibbled at the edge of her consciousness.

"Andy? You are okay with it, aren't you? You have nothing to worry about. I'm totally over him. I'll probably take one look at him and wonder what the hell I ever saw in him."

His quiet chuckle sounded strained and she hastened to reassure him again. "I love you, Andy. You're all I ever dreamed of. You're the only man I've ever wanted."

His breath came out on a sigh. "I love you too, Cally. So much, it scares me. I guess a part of me keeps expecting everything to fall apart. My life hasn't exactly been smooth sailing."

"Mine, either." She smiled. "Maybe we're both due for a change. I'm not going anywhere. You're stuck with me, whether you like it or not."

He laughed. "Oh, I like it. I like it a lot."

"I'm glad. When do I get to ravage your body again?"

He chuckled. I should be home by seven, with a bit of

luck. Perhaps Jack might want to go to bed early?"

She grinned. "You never know your luck." Ending the call, she glanced up at the clock. With a surprise, she realized it was time to collect Jack from school. Throwing her cell phone into her handbag, she picked up her car keys and let herself out, locking the door behind her.

―――――――

Stewart threw the roll of duct tape into the black duffel bag and followed it with a length of nylon rope and a wad of paper towel. Lastly, he picked up the Glock semi-automatic pistol he'd purchased in a back alley of Kings Cross a couple of nights earlier.

It had set him back a pretty penny, but he wasn't going to take any chances. There was no guarantee the boy would come peacefully and it was absolutely certain Cally would kick up a fuss. The gun would quiet both of them down. It was insurance, nothing more.

He glanced around the nondescript hotel room to ensure he'd left nothing behind. He'd traveled light, only intending to be in Sydney a couple of days. But it had taken him longer than expected to achieve his goal and time was running out. He was due in court for the resumption of his trial in less than three days.

His mind sheared away from the possibility that if he were found guilty, he'd be heading to the big camp. *It wouldn't happen.* His father would see to it. He was sure of it. Especially when his father realized he had a grandson—a real, live grandson—living down the street.

Satisfied that he'd left no trace of himself behind, Stewart bent down and zipped up the duffel bag. At the last minute, he tore the blanket off one of the beds and rolled it into a tight bundle. It could come in handy. He glanced at his watch and cursed. If he didn't hurry he'd be late.

―――――――

Jack trudged toward Cally, toting his backpack over one shoulder. He looked tired and disheveled. The school week was almost over and from Jack's demeanor, it couldn't come soon enough.

Cally summoned a cheery smile and greeted him through the open car window. "Hi, sweetheart. How was your day?"

He shrugged. "It was all right, I guess." He pulled open the back door and climbed in, tossing his school bag onto the floor and reached for his seatbelt.

Glancing at him through the rearview mirror, she took a deep breath, knowing she couldn't put off telling him where they were going. "Honey, I had an unusual call today. It was from your dad."

"Andy?"

Cally bit her lip, even as part of her silently rejoiced that he'd come to think of Andy that way. "No, not Andy. Your real dad. Stewart Brady."

Jack paled with shock. She prayed that he'd be able to handle what she was going to say. She should have given him more time to adjust to the idea before agreeing to meet, but Stewart had sounded so desperate and she had to teach the next day.

"My *real* dad called you? He actually *called* you?" Disbelief now warred with shock.

"Yes, he did. It was a surprise for me, too. I haven't had contact with him since before you were born." She turned to glance at him over her shoulder. "He wants to meet you."

Jack's eyes were wide as saucers. "He asked to see me? He really wants to *see* me?"

She nodded and kept an eye on the traffic. "Yes, honey. In fact, he couldn't wait. We're going to meet him at the park in about five minutes."

"*Really?*" Excitement shone on his face, obliterating the shock. "Oh, Mom! This is so *cool!* I can't *believe* it! For like *forever*, I had no dads and now I have *two!*"

Cally swallowed hard and blinked away the tears that

welled up in her eyes. She spied the sign for their exit, took the next turn and headed toward the car park that was reserved for the use of park patrons.

Huge, leafy oaks and hundred-year-old fig trees shaded a large area of the park. Swings, slippery-dips, rock-climbing walls and other playground equipment stood in colorful array about fifty yards away.

The mid-afternoon sun was hot and she brushed away a fly that buzzed through her open window. There were no other cars around and it appeared they had the place to themselves.

Jack threw off his seatbelt and opened the door. "Where is he, Mom? Where is he?"

Cally climbed out of the car and looked around. "We're a few minutes early. I'm sure he'll be here soon. Why don't you go and play? I told him we'd meet over there, anyway." With that, Jack tore off toward the flying fox, leaving her to follow behind him at a more leisurely pace.

The butterflies were back in her stomach and her pulse had picked up its pace. She wondered what was keeping Stewart.

Ten minutes passed. Fifteen. Jack kept turning his head toward the parking lot, his face growing more and more disappointed.

Stewart wasn't going to show.

Anger surged through her. *Damn him!* He'd sounded so genuine, so sincere when he'd begged her to let him see their son. Yet here they were, abandoned once again.

At three-thirty, swiping at the perspiration on her lip, Cally collected her handbag off the park bench and slung it over her shoulder. Jack was halfheartedly swinging on the monkey bars. She called out to him softly.

"Hey, honey, how about we go and get some ice cream?"

He looked up at her and shrugged despondently. Hurt and disappointment darkened his eyes. Cally fought back tears of anger. Jack stared at the ground and scuffed at the dirt with his shoe.

"He's not coming, is he?"

Putting her arm around his shoulders, she drew him close. "It doesn't look like it, sweetheart. Maybe he got caught in traffic or something." Hope flashed in his eyes and her heart tightened painfully.

"Yeah, I'll bet that's what happened! I bet there was an accident and he's stuck there, waiting for them to clear the road."

She wracked her mind for a response. Jack's sudden shout interrupted her.

"Hey, Mom! Is that him? Is that my dad?"

She looked in the direction he pointed and her heart leaped into her throat. Stewart Brady strode toward them. He wasn't quite as tall as she remembered and he was thin almost to the point of emaciation, but there was no mistaking the brown eyes, the thick dark hair and the wide white smile, with all its practiced charm.

A duffel bag was slung over one shoulder. As he neared them, he lifted his hands apologetically. "Cally, I'm sorry I'm late. I'm so glad to see you're still here."

Jack hung back and she sensed his sudden shyness. She couldn't blame him. She was a little unsettled too and she'd already met the man.

She shrugged in response. "Jack thought you must have been caught up in an accident...?"

Cally left the thought hanging and watched him closely, hoping he'd explain. Instead, he looked past her, to where Jack was half hidden behind her back.

"So, this is Jack." Stewart's eyes watered.

She gave a slight nod and instinctively put her arm around her son and pulled him in close. "Yes. This is my son."

Jack peeked around her and shook the proffered hand, flicking his gaze up briefly to Stewart's before staring at the ground again. Cally's gaze drifted over Stewart's gaunt face. He looked drawn and haggard and much older than his almost-thirty years. She noticed there was even a sprinkling of gray at his temples. She supposed the tragic loss of his wife and child had aged him, but she couldn't help but wonder what his life had been like since he'd walked away from her. He didn't look like he'd done it easy.

"You look good, Cally."

She looked away, feeling slightly embarrassed that she couldn't say the same for him.

He smiled unsteadily. "I know what you're thinking, but the truth is, I've never felt better." He let out a little laugh. His gaze skittered away and he shifted his weight from one foot to the other.

She couldn't help but feel a little unnerved. There was something so *restless* about him. She didn't quite know what it was, but he couldn't seem to stand still and his gaze roved constantly between her and Jack and the playground equipment.

She looked down at Jack's tousled head. He was still plastered to her side. Stewart thrust his hands into the pockets of his shorts and jiggled his keys.

She frowned. "Would you like to sit down somewhere so we can talk properly? There's a bench over there in the shade. I'm sure there are lots of things Jack would like to ask you."

"What have you told him about me?" Stewart's gaze was suddenly accusatory, trapping her where she stood.

"N-nothing, really." She was flustered and all at once irritated that he seemed to be taking the moral high ground. *He* was the one who'd demanded she have an abortion. That fact alone negated the right to feel put out about the possibility she'd been less than flattering in her description of him to their son.

His gaze drilled into hers. "I hope you didn't turn him away from me. I'd be very unhappy if I discovered you'd done that."

The threat in his eyes was unmistakable. She gasped and took an involuntary step backwards. Outrage ignited inside her. "You're kidding me, right? You're absolutely *kidding* me?" Recalling Jack's presence, she reined in her temper and forced deep breaths in her lungs. With an effort, she calmed her voice until her tone was almost even. "If anyone has the right to be upset about how things turned out, Stewart, it's me. And you darn well know it."

Stewart smiled back at her, his face serene, as if what she'd said was of no more consequence than a discussion about the weather. He looked so...so *removed* from her—from them. She couldn't help but recall her father's words.

She fought against the feeling of uneasiness that had formed in the pit of her stomach. This was Stewart, the man she'd been head over heels in love with. A selfish womanizer he may have been, but dangerous? Not the Stewart she'd known. She was being silly. Just because he was looking at her a little oddly, didn't mean there was anything to be alarmed about.

She owed it to Jack to calm down and try and get their meeting back on friendly terms. She'd simply overreacted. That was all. Plastering a stiff smile on her face, she took a deep breath and tried again.

"Stewart, I'm sorry. I shouldn't have gone on like that." She shrugged in embarrassment and looked away. "I guess I've been storing some of that up for a long time—ten years, at least." She gave a small laugh, hoping to ease the tension, but his gaze remained somber on her face.

"I'd like to spend some time alone with my son."

Her initial instinct was to object and she had to clamp her mouth shut to prevent herself from saying just that. She owed it to Jack to let him get to know his dad, if that's what he wanted.

Moving away slightly, she took Jack by the shoulders and turned him around to face her. "Would you like to have some time alone with Stew...your dad? You could go and sit on the bench over there. I guess you have some questions you'd like to ask...?

She held her breath and awaited his response. Although it would be good for him to talk to Stewart, another part of her wanted to bundle him up and run for their lives. Father or not, Stewart was acting a little too weird for her liking.

"I guess so." Jack's soft reply interrupted her thoughts and she bit down on a sigh. Pulling him in close, she hugged him hard to her side.

"Okay, sweetheart. You can walk over there to that bench. I'll stay right here where you can see me and I'll wait for you. How does that sound?"

He smiled up at her uncertainly. "I guess it sounds all right."

She turned back to Stewart and met his dark, restless gaze.

"So, what's it going to be, Cally? Are you going to let my son spend some time alone with me or have I frightened you off? It's not like I'm going to run away with him or anything." He laughed uproariously and once again she fought off feelings of unease.

Giving him a tight smile, she replied as lightly as she could manage. "Jack's agreed to talk to you alone, as you've asked. He's going to sit on the bench. I'll stay here." She pointed to a bench about forty feet away, well shaded by one of the giant oak trees.

Stewart looked at Jack. "How about it, boy? Wanna get to know your old man?"

Jack glanced up at her. She gave him an encouraging nod while every maternal instinct she possessed screamed not to let him go. She watched as he took hesitant steps toward his father.

"Come on, boy! I'm not going to bite." Stewart laughed again. When Jack was close enough, Stewart slung an arm around his shoulders and pulled him roughly toward the bench.

Cally forced her gaze away from them and made her way back to where she'd been sitting earlier. She still didn't know why Stewart had been late. Was she being overly sensitive, or had he purposefully avoided answering her question about that?

Giving herself a mental shake, she told herself to lighten up. Surely it was normal to be jittery about a meeting such as this? After all, the last time she'd seen Stewart, he'd blithely told her he wasn't ready for a family and that she best get rid of it. It was as if Jack had been no more than an inconvenience that could be cleared up with very little effort.

And as for Jack, she couldn't begin to imagine what *he* must be feeling. He was perched on the edge of the bench. Stewart's head was bent down to his. From this distance, they looked like exactly what they were—a father having some one-on-one time with his son.

She glanced at her watch. A quarter-to-four. She'd give them fifteen minutes. That would be enough. They could always arrange another meeting some other time. A time when Andy was around, she thought—her uneasiness still keeping her belly taut.

Cally maintained her vigil and did her best to sit still. They appeared to be talking and she saw the ghost of a smile cross Jack's face once or twice. At one stage, Stewart moved closer and put his arm around Jack's shoulders and hugged him to his side.

She tensed and then forced herself to relax. A moment later, she glanced at her watch again. Five minutes had passed. It seemed like a lifetime. With a restless sigh, she stood and walked toward the playground equipment, coming within a few feet of where they sat.

Stewart glanced up at her and frowned. She ignored his obvious displeasure at her nearness. She was, after all, under no obligation to even let him see Jack, let alone allow him to spend time alone with her son.

Plunking herself down on one of the swings, she pushed off with her feet, straining to hear their conversation. Stewart had lowered his voice—purposefully she thought—and it annoyed her that he didn't want her to overhear him.

She thought she caught the word "Luke" and glanced over at them. Jack's brow was furrowed in confusion. Stewart's face was animated and he was gesticulating wildly as he explained something to her son.

Another five minutes crawled by. Bringing the swing to a stop, she jumped off it and closed the distance between them. Stewart looked up. Jack made a move as if to get up off the bench.

Stewart's arm snaked around his shoulders and yanked him back against his side. Jack winced and alarm surged through her. She fought to keep her voice calm. "It's nearly four o'clock. I'm afraid we're going to have to go. Jack has homework and—"

"Jack's coming with me." He spoke with cold finality, as if he wouldn't brook any argument. She froze at the icy bleakness in his eyes. Fingers of fear clutched at her belly. Confusion warred in her head.

Stewart's hold on Jack tightened. "D-dad—you're hurting me."

"Shut up," Stewart snapped. "You don't know what hurt feels like." He glared down at him.

Cally forced a deep breath down her dry throat. Ignoring the pounding of her heart, she tried to reason with him. "Stewart, you don't really mean that." A strained smile widened her lips. She moved infinitesimally closer to where they were seated.

Out of the corner of her eye, she caught a glimpse of Jack's fearful face. She clenched her jaw, but ignored him. She had to concentrate all her attention on diffusing the threat Stewart suddenly presented. She forced her lips into a smile and lightened her tone.

"It's been great to see you again, Stewart, but we really need to go. Jack's had a long day at school and we still have a few things to do before we get home. How about we get together again on the weekend? I'm sure we can arrange something." The lie fell easily off her lips and she prayed he'd fall for it.

His gaze narrowed on her. His eyes were even more unstable than they'd been a little earlier. His pupils were dilated and the brown of his irises was almost black. His eyes oscillated over her face.

His lips turned up in a sneer. "Jack tells me you've already replaced me. A copper, no less. It didn't take you long to get over me."

She gulped in outrage. "You have to be kidding! It's been ten years! Ten *years*, Stewart. I waited a hell of a lot longer than you did."

Wild laughter bubbled out of him. His lips twisted into a menacing grimace. "I see someone's been telling tales. It sounds like your old man has a loose tongue."

Anger made her eyes burn. "Considering it was that same loose tongue that helped you find us, I would have thought you'd show it a little more gratitude."

He grinned. "Oh, don't get me wrong. I'm grateful, all right. I'm plenty grateful. If it weren't for that newspaper article with you and Jack on the front page, I'd have never known to even go and ask him." His gaze narrowed accusingly on hers. "As far as I knew, you'd had an abortion."

Guilt and anger warred inside her. Okay, she hadn't told him she didn't go through with the abortion, but she'd known he'd be relentless in his desire to get rid of the problem a baby presented. If she'd told him she'd kept it, he'd have marched her back into the clinic and made sure the deed was done.

"You gave me no choice," she hissed, mindful of Jack close by. She so didn't want to get into this now, but Stewart didn't seem prepared to let it go. His eyes blazed.

"You fucking *stole* him from me. For ten years, I didn't know he *existed*. I admit, when you told me you were pregnant, I was furious. I was nineteen. I didn't want to be shackled with a baby. But things change. People change. You never gave me a chance. For all I know, you were never planning to tell me."

Guilt scorched her cheeks. She dropped her gaze. Stewart pounced again.

"*Fuck!* I knew it! There are *words* for women like you and none of them are pretty."

Cally gasped from the malevolence in his eyes. How had he managed to make it all her fault? *He* was the one who'd discarded her and their baby. He'd never once called her to see if she was okay, or to ask her out. He'd washed his hands of her, just like her family had—and that was the truth of it.

"Not that you deserve any concessions, but for what it's worth, I was going to tell Jack about you. He'd been asking about you and as much as it pained me, I was going to find a way to contact you and tell you about him. But make no mistake, I was doing it for Jack, not for you."

Stewart's gaze narrowed. "You always were a stuck-up little bitch. My father owns that town. You're nothing more than the headmaster's stupid daughter. If it weren't for the fact that you had big tits and were hankering for some cock, I'd have never gone near you."

Cally gasped in outrage. "Stewart, please." She'd heard enough and so had Jack. She stepped forward and grabbed her son by the arm. Stewart hauled Jack back against him.

He grinned, a maniacal gleam in his eyes. "Oh no, you don't. The boy stays with me. I'm taking my son home to Watervale, where he belongs."

Fear held her immobile for a moment before she forced herself out of the fog and shook her head in disbelief. "Stewart, you must be mad if you think I'm going to let you walk away with my son. There's no way in the world I'll let you do that. Now, stop acting so crazy and let's talk about when we can get together again." She took hold of Jack's arm again and tugged him toward her.

Rage purpled Stewart's features. "I don't think you understand me, Cally. Jack's *my* son as much as he is yours. You've spent the last ten years with him. He and I have a lot of catching up to do. He's coming home with *me*."

She scoffed, anger overriding her fear. "You might have donated half the DNA, but that's all he shares with you. In every way that matters you aren't his father." Her gaze burned into his. "You made your decision ten years ago. Don't make the mistake of thinking you can waltz into our lives and become a part of them. It's never, *ever* going to happen."

Stewart laughed uproariously. "Cally, Cally, Cally! You

always did have a spark in you. Stuck-up bitch or not, it's one of the things that used to get me all hot and bothered over you."

Without warning, he jammed his face against hers, his eyes mean and hard. His voice lowered to a cold murmur that sent shivers down her spine. "You're the one making the mistake, bitch. Jack *is* my son and he *will* be coming home with me, whether you like it or not."

Cally's face was inches from his. She returned his icy glare and willed herself not to flinch. "Over my dead body."

He smirked. "That can be arranged."

She froze. Fear snaked a path to her belly. Her mind scrambled frantically for a plan of attack and came up empty. Even if she managed to wrestle Jack free from Stewart's stranglehold, they'd never make it back to the car before he caught up with them. He might have lost a lot of weight, but he was wiry and strong and still a formidable figure and he seemed crazy enough to try anything.

Her thoughts scattered under the icy weight of her fear. Sweat poured down her face and into her eyes. She didn't dare wipe it away. Her focus remained on the man in front of her who held Jack captive. A feral glint crept into Stewart's eyes.

If only Andy were here. He'd know what to do.

Andy. She'd call Andy. He'd bring help.

Slowly and carefully she backed away from Stewart. When she was a few feet away, she forced a shaky smile. "Hey, let's stop being silly. It's been so long since we've seen each other and we parted on...less than friendly terms. Naturally, there are going to be things we've been stewing over."

She smiled again, holding up her hands in mock surrender. "But let's not get into that now. I want to hear more about you, what you've been up to during the last ten years. I'm sure Jack would love to hear about it, too."

Stewart appeared to consider her request. Some of the tension left his face. Cally prayed he'd fall for the distraction.

She smiled again, this time holding his gaze, wanting to reassure him she was genuine.

"How about you take Jack over to the rock climbing wall? He loves climbing to the top of that thing. Maybe you could help him?" she added encouragingly.

Stewart's arm dropped from around Jack's shoulders and he turned his head in the direction she'd indicated. Biting back a sob of relief, she tried to communicate to Jack with her eyes, urging him to go along with her suggestion. He frowned back at her in confusion and her heart clenched in agony, even while she nodded again and smiled at him.

"Jack, why don't you show your dad how far you can climb? I bet he'll be surprised at how high you can go."

Jack continued to look at her, his eyes fearful and uncertain.

"Go on, honey. It's okay." She forced another smile.

Stewart looked back at her. Some of the craziness seemed to have left his face.

"Yeah, sure. Why not?" He gave Jack a nudge. "Come on, boy. I was great at this kind of thing when I was a kid. Let's see what you can do."

Cally held her breath until they headed in the direction of the rock wall. With her gaze glued to their retreating forms, she fumbled blindly in her handbag until her fingers closed around her cell phone. Thank God she'd remembered to bring it.

She pulled it out and her stomach dropped. It was almost out of battery. Praying it would last, she dialed Andy's number. The phone rang out. She was nearly paralyzed with dread when the call went through to voicemail. With their lives depending on it, she stumbled through a message.

"Andy, it's me. I'm at Fullers Park, near Jack's school. I need you urgently. It's Stewart. He's gone mad, or something. I don't know, but he's scaring me. Please hurry, Andy." She ended the call just as Stewart turned back to look at her. Fear clutched at her throat. She didn't know whether he'd seen her on the phone, but she knew she'd have to risk another call. If Andy had been called out on a job, it could be hours before he received the message.

She offered Stewart a friendly wave and another tight smile and prayed he would buy it. He stared back at her with narrowed eyes, his brow furrowed. The menace emanating from him stole her breath.

With a last, lingering look of warning, he turned back toward Jack, who had started to climb the wall. Her legs nearly collapsed underneath her. With shaking fingers, she dialed 000. A disembodied voice came on the line. "What is the nature of your emergency?"

"I-I need the police. Please, get the police. It's my ex-boyfriend, he's—he's threatening me and my son." Her phone beeped. The battery was almost dead.

"What's your location?"

She gave the woman the details. The phone beeped again. Her heart pounded and her throat constricted with fear. Panic nipped at the edges of her control.

"Is your ex-boyfriend armed? Does anyone have a weapon?"

"N-no, at least, I don't think so. I haven't seen one, anyway."

"All right, stay calm. The police are on their—"

The phone went dead in her hand. The battery had died.

Stewart came striding toward her. She almost choked on her fright, but determinably stood her ground. She didn't want him knowing how much he terrified her. While he thought they were merely having a friendly meeting in the park, she might have a chance of getting Jack out of there.

"Who the *fuck* were you talking to?"

She swallowed her trepidation and faced him calmly. "N-no one. I was just checking my messages."

"Bullshit. Give it to me."

"W-what?" She bit her lip against the tremor in her voice.

"Give me the fucking phone!" His face was so close she could see the whites of his eyes. "You think I'm going to fall for that? You could have been calling that copper boyfriend of yours, for all I know."

She pulled the phone out of her bag and handed it to

him, knowing it would be useless without the battery. "Here." Hoping to distract him, she smiled and placed her hand on his arm. "What's all this about, Stewart? You were never this uptight when we were young. You're getting all worked up over nothing."

The madness was back in his eyes and she didn't have a clue whether anything she said was even getting through. He frowned down at her hand where it lay on his arm as though he was trying to work out how it got there.

"Get your fucking hand off me, bitch. Nothing you say or do is going to change my mind. Luke's dead. Tiff's dead. Jack's all I have left."

Throwing her arm off, Stewart strode toward the climbing wall. Jack lay sprawled across it, almost at the top of the twenty-foot wall. Even from a distance, Cally saw the terror in his eyes. She tried to keep the panic from her voice.

"Jack! Don't move! Stay there! Stay right where you are!" Her ears strained for the sound of sirens above the pounding of her heart.

CHAPTER 24

Andy washed his hands at the cracked and stained ceramic sink in the bathroom and made his way back out to the squad room. It was a little after four. Two more hours and his shift would be over. He could make his way home to Cally and Jack: *his family.*

He smiled in anticipation and flung himself into his chair. Swinging his legs up onto his desk, he crossed his ankles and leaned against the faux leather. The noise of the telephones and the hum of conversations faded around him.

It was amazing how things were turning out. Less than a month ago, he'd been riding in the back of a taxi wondering if he'd ever find the love of his life. Now, he had a beautiful woman who loved him as much as he loved her and a boy he couldn't wait to call son.

He had to tell Will. Between meeting Cally and re-connecting with his mother, he hadn't spoken to his best friend for more than a fortnight. Dropping his boots to the floor, he straightened and opened the top drawer of his desk. He pulled out his cell and frowned in disappointment when he noticed a missed call from Cally.

She must have called while he'd been in the bathroom. The screen indicated a new message and his heart lightened at the thought of hearing her voice.

"Tom! Andy! Craig! Get in here!"

Andy's gut clenched at the urgency in his boss' voice. With an inward sigh of regret, he tossed the phone back into the drawer and followed Tom and Craig at a jog toward Redding's office. His boss paced the cluttered space and got straight to the point, his face grave.

"I just took a call from the boys at Chatswood. They have a situation at Fullers Park. Some guy's taken a woman hostage. They don't think he's armed, but details are pretty sketchy. There's a kid involved somewhere, too. I want all of you to get over there right away. See what you can do. There are some uniforms from Chatswood on their way, but they've asked for our help."

The usual mix of fear and adrenaline rushed through Andy's veins. It was the same whenever a call like this came in. His mind was already canvassing strategies. "We're onto it, sir. You ready, fellas?"

Tom and Craig nodded, their faces grim. Without another word, they strode out of the office and into the locker room where they tugged on overalls and began the mental preparation that being involved in a police negotiation always demanded.

Cally knew the exact moment the sound of the police sirens registered with Stewart. He came to an abrupt halt and his whole body stiffened. He spun on his heel and strode toward her, anger in every step.

"The fucking coppers. I *knew* it! You fucking *bitch*! You couldn't leave things well enough alone, could you?" His long strides closed the distance between them, his eyes now as icy as his voice.

For some reason, his coldness terrified her more than his ranting and she shivered uncontrollably. He was mere inches away, his face a picture of dark and menacing fury.

His arm snaked out and grabbed her around the neck, hauling her back against his chest. She cried out in terror. He stumbled backwards, dragging her with him toward the rock wall, where Jack still hung, frozen.

Stewart's hold around her neck tightened and she winced. Her shoe caught on the uneven ground, twisting her ankle and she cried out. Reaching up, she struggled to loosen his hold.

"Mom! Mom! Mom!"

She heard Jack's terrified shouts and prayed desperately that he'd stay where he was. Stewart looked up and she flailed around for a way to distract him. She drew in a breath and pulled hard against him. "Stewart! Stop! You're choking me! Please, let me go."

He sneered down at her. "Not likely, bitch!" He forced her head around and thrust his face into hers. "We could have done this so much easier. You could have handed Jack over without any fuss. After all the shit I've been through lately. Didn't your father tell you about Tiffany and Luke? She hit a fucking tree! It was three o'clock in the afternoon and she was drunk. Who gets drunk by three o'clock and then does the school pick-up?"

His face was almost purple with rage. Cally trembled violently against him, never more terrified in her life.

"My little boy, my little Lukie. Pulverized! Broken in so many places, they couldn't work out what went where. The only thing I recognized was his face. And Tiffany—stone cold dead, but with hardly a mark on her. How's that for fair?"

Spittle from out of his mouth landed on Cally's face. She instinctively pulled back. Stewart tightened his hold and hauled her back hard against him. Her head collided with the solidness of his jaw and she cried out from the impact.

Stewart's lip curled up in a snarl. "Cry your hardest, bitch. I couldn't give a fuck. It's your fault it turned out like this. All I wanted was to find my son and take him home with me. The son you *stole* off me. But, no. You couldn't let me do that, could you, bitch? You've had him all to yourself for more than a decade and you still weren't prepared to hand him over. You had to spoil everything. You had to go and call the fucking coppers."

"*Police!* Let her go!"

Immediately upon Andy's arrival, he recognized Cally's car and he went cold. *Fuck.* He stared at the scene unraveling before him. His heart pounded so hard he could barely hear Tom's shouted command. Stewart Brady had his arm tight around Cally's neck. Her head was twisted halfway over her shoulder. Even from a distance, Andy could see the pain on her face and the tension in her body. All of a sudden, his lottery win, his fancy condo and all the other expensive things he'd surrounded himself with meant nothing: All he wanted was her safe and back in his arms.

He looked around a little frantically for Jack and was filled with relief when he spied the boy clinging to the top of the climbing wall. Terror had him frozen in place. Andy urged him silently to hold on. Right at that moment, it was the safest place in the park.

A handful of uniformed officers surrounded the immediate area. Another half dozen cordoned off the park with police tape and were busy keeping curious onlookers at bay. Stewart's gaze swung from one side to another, taking in the scene.

"Tom!" Andy's voice was low and urgent. Tom glanced at him, a questioning look in his eyes.

"It's Cally. The prick's got Cally."

Surprise and recognition flared in Tom's eyes. His expression turned grim. "I'll take the lead." He murmured the words out of the side of his mouth, his gaze remaining fixed on the couple who continued to struggle in front of him.

Andy nodded. In truth, he was relieved to hand over the responsibility. This was Cally, the love of his life. He could barely think straight at the thought of what might happen to her. He'd never forgive himself if he screwed this up. Besides, Tom had a wealth of experience behind him. There was no one better for the job. Tom was a veteran. He wouldn't let Cally die.

At the shouted command, Cally almost collapsed in relief. *The police were here.* Surely, Stewart would let her go now?

"Come any closer and I'll blow her head off," Stewart yelled back.

Cally stifled a sob. Her neck was twisted at such an angle that all she could see was the sky. She strained as hard as she could to catch a glimpse of Jack. The last time she'd seen him, he was clinging to the wall, terrified.

Stewart dragged her further backwards. Her bare heels skipped over grass and loose stones. She yelped when something sharp dug into her foot. She guessed they were nearly at the climbing wall. Taking a gamble, she drew in as much oxygen as the tight grip on her neck allowed and then she screamed.

"Jack! Stay where you are! Don't move!"

Stewart's hold around her throat threatened to suffocate her. She choked and gasped for breath. Clawing at his hands, her lungs screamed for oxygen. An excruciating white-hot pain stabbed through her chest and she groaned in agony.

Black spots danced before her eyes. Dizziness overwhelmed her. She swallowed convulsively against the surge of nausea that swirled in her belly. Gouging at his hands with her fingernails, she tried desperately to release the pressure from around her neck.

"Hey, Stewart? What are you doing, mate?"

It was the same voice again—the one that had called out the first time. It was a little closer and came from the direction of the car park. Stewart twisted slightly around and his grip on her neck eased slightly. She winced when he shouted near her ear.

"Who the fuck are you?"

"I'm Tom. Tom Munro."

Cally was filled with relief. It was Tom, Andy's partner and a fellow negotiator. *Tom would save them.*

"Who the fuck is Tom Munro and what the fuck do you want?" Stewart's arm tightened across Cally's neck again.

"I only want to talk to you, Stewart. You seem to be in a bit of a spot."

Stewart tensed against her. "I'm not in any fucking *spot*, Tom. If you and your mates take yourselves away quietly, I'll go and collect my son and be off. It's as simple as that."

"What about the lady you have hold of, Stewart?" Tom replied calmly. "How are you going to collect your boy while you have her in your arms?"

"Just leave me the fuck alone!" Fury emanated from Stewart in almost palpable waves. The bag he'd held over his shoulder hit the ground near her feet. A moment later, a cold, solid hardness pressed against Cally's temple. She gasped. Terrified, she realized he had a gun.

"Please, Stewart. Please don't." Tears overflowed and ran down her cheeks. Her shaking intensified and panic threatened to overwhelm her. "Please, Stewart, think of Jack, your son. What will he do without me? What will he think of you if you're the reason I'm not here?"

"He doesn't care about me! He doesn't even *know* me! You turned him against me! I've lost him, just like I lost Luke!"

"No!" Her voice was hoarse. His vice-like grip across her neck didn't budge. She could barely get the words out. "It's not like that, Stewart. You need to give him time, give us both time."

"You don't care about me!" he screamed, spittle once again flying across her face. "You never did! If you'd really cared, you would never have gotten yourself pregnant and screwed up everything we had together."

She gasped. Anger coursed through her. She struggled against him, throwing caution to the wind. "Let *go* of me!"

"*Cally!*"

At the sound of Andy's voice, she went limp. *He was here. He'd come.* She twisted against Stewart, straining to see the man she loved. "Andy? *Andy?*"

"I'm here, Cally. Stay calm, sweetheart. I'm here."

Stewart tensed behind her. "Andy? That's his name? The

man you replaced me with? The man I've been watching you fuck like the little slut you are? You didn't even bother to draw the blinds."

Clamping her mouth shut against the shock of Stewart's revelation, Cally bit down hard on her lip to stifle the sob that threatened to escape. Andy had told her to stay calm. She had to do what Andy said. He'd come to save them. She sucked in tiny breaths when she could and tried to keep her panic at bay.

She thought she was doing a pretty good job of it until Stewart shouted again. "Which one of you is Andy?"

Cally cried out. Terror pulsed through her. Her breath came fast and her heart beat overtime. Try as she might, she couldn't stop the panic that liquefied her limbs.

"I'm Andy."

His voice was strong and firm and much too near. Cally moaned in agony. *What was he doing?* Didn't he know how close Stewart was to snapping?

Stewart turned slightly in the direction from where Andy's voice had come. "Yeah, I see the resemblance now. I barely recognized you with your pants on."

"Why don't you put that gun down so we can talk?" Andy's tone was composed and unhurried. He sounded even nearer. Stewart's arm tightened painfully around her neck.

"Stop right there!" he yelled. "Don't come any closer or I'll put a bullet through her brain."

Cally panted and did her best to focus on her breathing. *She had to stay calm.* Andy wanted her to stay calm. He told her to stay calm.

Stewart's breaths were ragged. The erratic pounding of his heart thudded beneath her ear. He was on the brink of losing control. Silent, frantic, desperate prayers fell from her motionless lips. Despite her best efforts, her terror was beginning to overwhelm her. Her teeth chattered. Her neck burned under the cold, menacing, metallic presence pressed hard against the side of her head. She had no doubt his gun was loaded.

Andy watched Cally and saw she was close to her breaking point. Her face had lost all color. She was limp against the man who still held her captive. Tom shot him a questioning look, but he resolutely ignored it. He'd complicated matters by getting involved, but there was no choice now but to see it through to the end.

He thrust aside the anger that burned like ice in his belly and tried again. "Put the gun down, Stewart. You're not going to achieve anything by holding a gun to the lady's head. Just lay it on the ground and we can talk properly."

"Do you think I'm fucking *stupid?* The minute I drop this gun, you're going to blow my fucking head off. I bet you have some of those sniper blokes with their guns trained on me right now."

"No guns, mate," Andy replied. "Just you and me. I promise." He eased closer, his gaze never wavering from the two people in front of him.

The unmistakable sound of a gun being cocked sent terror rushing through him. The deadly metallic click echoed in his ears. Memories of the standoff with his father flashed before him. He blinked and pushed them away.

Cally stirred and tried to pull away from the madman who held her in a viselike grip. Stewart lifted his arm and struck her across the head with the barrel. She screamed and Andy clenched his fists, forcing himself to remain calm and stand his ground. Despite his best efforts, panic edged his consciousness.

"Put it down, Stewart. Don't do it, mate," he murmured, hating the fear and urgency that had crept into his voice.

"What do I have to lose? I've already buried my family. Lukie, my little Lukie." Stewart hunched forward and his shoulders began to shake. His hold on Cally loosened the slightest bit.

Andy saw his chance. "Now, Cally! *Now!*"

She wrenched back with her elbows, catching Stewart by surprise with a hefty jab to the ribs. His arms fell away and she hit the ground hard. She yelped with pain.

Andy drew his gun, pleased he hadn't had time to hand it over to one of the other officers. He aimed it with deadly accuracy at Stewart's head. The gun in Stewart's hand swung wildly from Andy to Tom and finally settled on Andy. As if in slow motion, he saw Brady depress the trigger. A second later, there was a roar of gunfire from Andy's sidearm. Stewart crumpled to the ground, only inches away from Cally.

Andy gasped. Relief that it was over surged through him. He raced to close the distance between him and Cally. Moments later, his arms were around her, lifting her, carrying her, kissing her. He stumbled away from the scene of carnage.

"Jack?" she whispered hoarsely. "Where's Jack?"

Andy looked down at her, still weak with relief. "He's fine. He's still on the climbing wall. Tom's gone to get him."

Relief and delayed shock sent uncontrollable tremors through her body. She collapsed against him, gasping for breath. He eased her onto a bench near the car park which now overflowed with police cars and other emergency vehicles. She lifted her head off his shoulder and stared into his eyes, hers wide with shock and disbelief.

"Is it really over?" Her voice sounded raw from the recent trauma. Andy saw her swallow against the pain.

"*Shh*, sweetheart, don't talk. It's over. It's all over. You're safe. You're both safe. I promise."

Her eyes darkened with emotion. "Thank you," she whispered.

Andy's chest tightened. "I came so close to losing you." Pulling her close, he pressed desperate kisses against her hair, her cheeks, her lips. His arms tightened around her as if he'd never let her go.

CHAPTER 25

ally poured coffee into the cups set out on the table that stood on the balcony of Andy's beachside condominium. A cool Fall breeze blew off the ocean and lifted tendrils of her hair. She smiled at Jack who stood at the far end of the balcony, thoroughly immersed in watching the ships and other floating objects that were scattered across the blue sea. It had taken awhile for Jack to come out of his shell and after the traumatic events he'd witnessed a little over a month earlier, Cally only marveled at his resilience.

"The coffee's ready. I just made a fresh pot."

Andy smiled up at her from where he sat in a deck chair. "That sounds great, sweetheart." He folded the newspaper closed and dropped it near his feet. "I just read the police out at Campbelltown cracked the gang of thieves who were burglarizing the houses along your street. The boys found a stash of stolen goods in an abandoned warehouse near Camden. You might even get your stuff back."

Cally smiled. "Wow, that's great news. Not that Jack would ever want those old things back, but it's good to know the people responsible have been caught."

Andy nodded and glanced over toward his son. "Jack, are you going to have something to drink?"

Jack grinned at him. "How about a Coke, Dad?"

Andy shook his head and grinned back at him. "Cheeky,

boy. You know you're too young to drink Coke. What about a Sprite instead?"

"Yeah, that sounds good."

"I'll get it for him," Cally offered and opened the sliding glass door that led inside. She reached the refrigerator and pulled the door open. Bending over, she tugged out a can of Sprite. Andy came up behind her and put his arms around her, filling his hands with her breasts. She came upright with a gasp.

"What are you doing, you naughty man?" she smiled.

"Just checking your reflexes, sweetheart. I don't want you going stale." Taking the can from her hand, he set it on the counter and pulled her into his arms.

"Jack's right outside. Don't you think you'd better wait—"

Andy nuzzled her neck and shook his head. "I've been waiting all day to get you alone. It seems like every time I turn around, there's someone watching."

His hand stole under her T-shirt and gently fondled her breast. When his fingers flicked over her nipple, she groaned. Desire kindled low in her belly, but she fought its tempting pull. It was broad daylight. Her son was a mere twenty feet away, separated only by a thin wall of glass. She and Andy might still be newlyweds, but some propriety had to be maintained.

She tried to pull away, but Andy's arms only tightened around her. He ground his hips into hers and his erection pressed against her belly, leaving her in no doubt about his intentions. He lifted her T-shirt and released the clasp on her bra. She gasped when his mouth found her nipple.

"Andy, stop it! We can't do this here! Jack might see!"

"That can be fixed." With one swift movement, he bent and lifted her into his arms. His lips claimed hers once again, silencing any further protests. He strode out of the kitchen and down the hall, kicking the door to their bedroom closed behind him and turning the lock. He lay her down on the bed and made short work of removing their clothing.

"What about Jack?"

"He won't miss us for a few minutes."

Pressing her naked body against his, he sighed a deep sigh of contentment. "I love the way you feel in my arms. I'll never get tired of this."

She cupped her face in his hands and kissed him on the mouth. Andy's lips moved under hers and before long, he'd deepened the kiss until both of them were left gasping. Releasing her, he leaned down and sucked one of her nipples into his mouth, swirling his tongue over the hard nub.

She closed her eyes and gave into the sensations that stirred once again inside her. "You're very good at that," she murmured.

He moved his attention to her other breast. "I'm good at lots of things."

A smile tugged at her lips. "Is that so?"

"Oh, yeah." His hand slid down her flat belly and tangled in her curls. His fingers delved into her moistness. She moaned. He flicked her clit with the tip of his finger and then slid lower to tease at her entrance. Her legs fell open and she pressed against his hand, still amazed at her forwardness. They'd spent a week at the Whitsundays on the Great Barrier Reef—their hastily arranged honeymoon—and had done little but explore each other in bed and in the shower and in the...

Andy's tongue slid inside her and lapped at her soft folds. She gasped from the ecstasy of it and made a grab for his hair. Holding him still against her, she luxuriated in the sensations he created. Need burned deep inside her. She squirmed and whimpered and moaned, climbing toward her release. The relentless pressure of his tongue continued until she couldn't stand it a second more.

She cried out in relief from the sweet torture. Her orgasm crashed around her in waves of delight and release. Andy lifted his head and grinned at her. "I told you I was good at a lot of things."

With her body still shaky from her orgasm, she spread her legs wide in invitation. Andy's eyes grew dark with desire and his cock sprang thick and hard from his groin. He positioned himself between her legs and plunged into her wet center. Hard and fast and furious, he pumped his hips in a frenzy of need until at last he groaned his release. He collapsed on top of her, panting hard.

"That's something else I'll never get tired of," he mumbled against her hair.

"You and me, both," she whispered and meant every word she said.

EPILOGUE

Eight months later

Cally groaned when another contraction seized her, twisting her belly in fiery torture. She held onto the side of the bed with a death grip.

"Come on, Cally; you can do it," the nurse urged. "Take a big breath now and *push*!"

Cally put her head down on her chest and pushed as hard as she could. The pain was excruciating.

"That's it, Cally. Good girl! You're doing great!" The young midwife with the glossy curtain of brown hair leaned over her, smiling encouragingly. "Not long now. Another push like that one and we should be able to see the head."

The contraction eased. Cally looked up at Andy and offered him a weak smile. His face was pale and there were beads of perspiration on his forehead. He swiped at them with the back of his hand.

"You're doing great, sweetheart. Just great," he murmured, sounding as though he was trying to convince himself as much as her.

Much too soon, another contraction seized her. She reached for his hand and squeezed it while she tried to breathe through the pain.

"Keep going, Cally. That's it. You're nearly there. Come around here, Dad. In a few minutes, you're going to meet your baby."

At the nurse's urging, Andy moved to stand at the foot of the bed. He gazed down upon her and his eyes widened in shock and delight.

Groaning again, she clung to the edge of the bed and leaned forward while yet another contraction tortured her belly. A sharp stinging sensation burned between her legs.

"That's it, Cally. Push! Push! *Push!* Here it comes, here it comes. Good *girl!* The head's out now, Cally. It's nearly over."

Cally gasped and pushed with all her might, determined to get it over with. A last ditch effort, and it was finally over. Her body surrendered. The baby slid from her body and Cally cried out in relief.

"It's a girl!" The midwife laid the squalling red mass of humanity on Cally's chest. and she cuddled the tiny body against her.

"Hello, little Grace Mary," she whispered. "Welcome to the world." She pressed a kiss against her daughter's tiny cheek and looked up at Andy with a love that almost overwhelmed her.

"Come and meet your daughter, Daddy.

Cally watched Jack carefully lift his little sister out of the pram, his face a picture of concentration. The baby gurgled and waved her arms, already taking note of her surroundings. She wasn't even a fortnight old. Andy told everyone he came in contact with how advanced she was for her age.

Jack took a seat on the couch beside Cally and cuddled Gracie close. "She's so cute, Mom and so tiny. She looks just like one of Jimmy's sister's dolls. I'm so glad to have a sister, like Jimmy does. I'm going to be the best big brother, *ever.*"

The earnestness on his young face filled Cally's heart to overflowing. This was what being a family was about. This was what she'd been missing. Her thoughts drifted to her father and she gave a little sigh. He'd sent the biggest pink teddy bear she'd ever seen. It took up one corner of Gracie's bedroom. She'd call him soon and thank him and maybe, she'd invite him over to meet his new granddaughter.

Her husband strode in from the kitchen, a skillet in one hand and a plate of bacon in the other. "Would you like me to whip up some breakfast? I went down to the shops early with Gracie. We bought bacon and eggs and warm crusty bread and if that doesn't suit, we also have pancakes."

"Yay! Pancakes," Jack cheered and then laughed when the baby in his lap waved her arms.

"I guess pancakes it is," Andy smiled and moved over closer to Cally. Mindful of the things in his hands, he leaned down and pressed a kiss on her cheek. "*Mm*, you smell good," he murmured, "but then again, you always do."

She turned her head until her lips met his in another lingering kiss. "Have I told you this morning how much I love you?"

"Yes, but feel free to say it again. I'll never get tired of hearing it."

NOTE TO READERS

I do hope you have enjoyed reading Andy and Cally's story. Please feel free to leave a review for The Negotiator. Every review is appreciated and really helps a new author like me.

The Christmas Vigil—a Munro Family Series novella is the next book in the Munro Family Series and is Duncan and Marguerite's story. Duncan and Marguerite are the parents of the Munro children. You will catch up with all the siblings you've met already and some that you haven't.

Here's a sneak peek:

When former New South Wales District Court judge, **Duncan Munro***, is found lying unconscious in a hotel room surrounded by evidence incriminating him in an affair, his close knit family are rocked to their core.*

Marguerite Munro *is unwilling to believe her husband of forty years has been cheating on her, but the evidence doesn't lie. Roses, champagne, massage oils, lingerie...it's obvious he was expecting a woman and she knows darn well it wasn't her.*

When the distress call goes around the family, they gather together in shock and disbelief. No one wants to believe their father is an adulterer, but the Munro siblings have law enforcement running through their veins. They've learned to look at the facts and draw logical conclusions and all of the evidence is pointing toward their father's guilt...

Will Duncan regain consciousness and provide the explanation they're praying for, or will this be the end of Marguerite's marriage and the Munro family as we know it...?

The Christmas Vigil will be released on 1 December, 2014 and is available now for pre-order from your favorite retailer.

If you would like to subscribe to my newsletter to receive news on upcoming Munro Family stories, release dates, book launches and other snippets, please go to my website at www.christaylorauthor.com.au and follow the link. I love to hear from my readers. Please feel free to contact me at christaylor@antmail.com.au Let me know who your favorite Munro family member is.

About The Author

Chris Taylor grew up on a farm in north-west New South Wales, Australia. She always had a thirst for stories and recalls writing her first book at the ripe old age of eight. Always a lover of romance and happily-ever-afters, a career in criminal law sparked her interest in intrigue and suspense. For Chris to be able to combine romance with suspense in her books is a dream come true.

Chris is married to Linden and is the mother of five children. If not behind her computer, you can find her doing the school run, taxiing children to swimming lessons, football, ballet and cricket. In her spare time, Chris loves to read her favorite authors who include Richard North Patterson, Sandra Brown, Kathleen E Woodiwiss and Jude Devereaux.

You can find out more about Chris and sign up for her newsletter at her website:

http://www.christaylorauthor.com.au